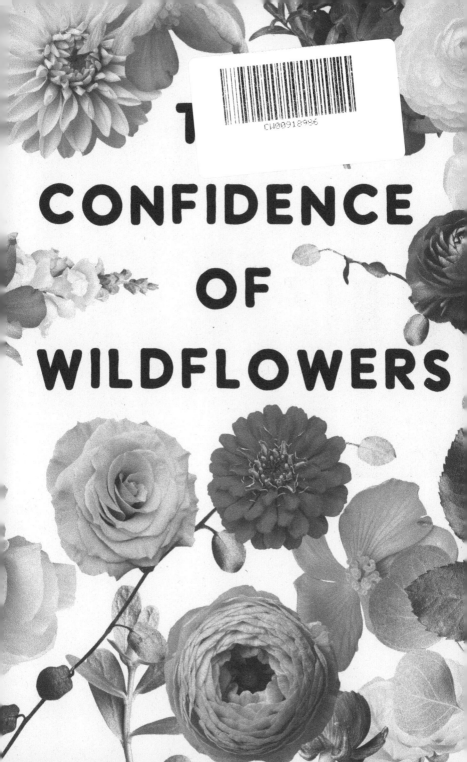

THE
CONFIDENCE
OF
WILDFLOWERS

THE CONFIDENCE OF WILDFLOWERS

For everyone who's had to fight for something they love.
Whatever that might be.

TRIGGER WARNING

"Love is like wildflowers;
It's often found in the most unlikely places."

—*Ralph Waldo Emerson*

PROLOGUE

Five Years Ago

I didn't cry when my dad died.

As the cancer consumed his body, eating away at his muscle, tissue, every little bit of him—I didn't cry.

When his body was hauled out of the house in a black bag on a stretcher, I didn't cry.

Staring at his once emaciated form in the casket puffed up with fillers and whatever magic the mortician worked, I didn't cry.

On the drive to the cemetery, I didn't cry.

I didn't cry as the preacher spoke of life and death, the inevitability of it all despite a life well lived.

I didn't cry.

My sister didn't cry either.

1

Karma's a b*tch but she's always fair

Neither did my mother.

Abusers don't deserve tears.

When the last flower was placed on the casket, and it was all over, I didn't cry.

I smiled.

ONE

a little too relatable if you ask me.

You're supposed to have your whole life figured out at eighteen.

No one says that, not explicitly, but it's implied in the way you're expected to have a college picked out, an entire career path already in mind. A plan on where you want to be and who you want to be.

My older sister knew she wanted to go to college to be a nurse. From there she wanted to move to a big city and do big things and be this big person.

But now she's back home in our small town of Hawthorne Mills, Massachusetts.

Plans don't always work, but people push them on others anyway, like if you have the path set before you everything will be okay.

What a fucking lie.

3

I don't have a plan and I don't want one.

Two weeks ago, I crossed the stage and became a high school graduate with no plans to go to college. My boyfriend is going, and he still doesn't understand why I don't want to follow him to his school.

I'm not a dog on a leash.

Following someone else's desires sounds like a one-way ticket to my version of hell—I've already been there and I'm not going back.

A light wind ruffles the hair around my shoulders, and I pull it back, securing it with an elastic. Drawing my knees up to my chest, I wrap my arms around my legs. There's a bruise on my knee that I have no idea how I got.

My mom's car turns onto the street, and I scurry back through my window before she can spot me on the eave of the roof outside my bedroom. She hates it when I sit out there, convinced I'm going to fall off, despite the fact I've never even slipped. I've explained numerous times that roof tiles are textured, but she doesn't listen. But I guess she's just doing her motherly duty looking out for me.

Closing the window shut behind me, I let out a sigh and smile at my black cat with glowing green eyes curled up on my bed. He peeks at me with a look that says, *"You're going to be in trouble if she spotted you."*

I nod back. *I know.* HOCUS POCUS. I need to watch it.

I found Binx, named after the cat in my favorite movie, as a kitten —he was dumped in the alley behind the antique shop my mom owns. I couldn't leave him there. At the time, I only had a learner's permit and was riding my bike. I wrapped him up in my jacket and took him home, begging and pleading with my mom to let me keep him. I didn't think she would say yes, but by some miracle she did. I think he stole her heart too.

The front door opens and a moment later my mom calls out, "Salem?"

Yep, I'm named after a fictional cat too.

Actually, I'm named after the city I was conceived in—or so I've been told. Talk about gross.

"Yeah?" I venture out of my room and stand at the top of the steps.

The Victorian home my mom has slowly been remodeling boasts

4

a grand sweeping staircase, the kind you see in old movies where the debutant comes gliding down with her hand elegantly perched upon the railing.

Unfortunately, I'm no debutant and there's nothing elegant about me.

Not if my ripped jean shorts, dirty sneakers, and tank top have anything to say about it.

"Do you have plans this afternoon?" She blows her bangs out of her eyes, her hands full of paper grocery bags. I head down the stairs, taking some from her.

"Not at the moment."

"After I put these away," she heads toward the kitchen and I follow her, "I thought maybe you might want to help me bake some cupcakes. Thelma is going to host a bake sale and I want to try out some different recipes."

Thelma Parkington, otherwise known as the town busybody. She's well into her seventies, always wears oversized glasses and colorful, weirdly patterned dresses. She's a big gossip and knows everything there is to know about everyone in this small town.

I shrug, pulling out a box of cereal from one of the bags and setting it on the counter. "Sounds fun."

"Good." She smiles, a box of crackers clasped in her hands. "I love it when you help me in the kitchen."

I smile back. Things weren't always this simple and easy, not while my dad was alive. He was an abusive, controlling asshole behind closed doors, while in public he portrayed something entirely different. Life was hell. My mom, sister, and I lived in a constant state of holding our breath, waiting to see what would upset him next. It could be something as small as a light left on or not cleaning up the kitchen as fast as he thought we should.

Now, we can make cupcakes together and leave the kitchen a mess for days if we want.

We won't, but it's the fact that we *can*.

We get all the groceries put away before my mom pulls out one of her many aprons, this one brightly colored with pie slices on it, and passes me one of her others with a floral design.

"What flavors do you want to try out?" I tie the apron around my waist, securing it tightly so I won't dirty my clothes. Knowing me, it won't matter, and I'll get flour or frosting somewhere on my body.

"I was thinking my honey and lavender recipe, chocolate since it's tried and true, maybe lemon and mint." She bites her lip. "It was too minty last time, so I'll have to tweak the recipe."

"What about your cookie dough cupcake? That's always a crowd pleaser."

She chuckles, her eyes following me as I reach for her personal recipe book in case she makes adjustments to anything.

"You only want that one because it's your favorite."

I turn to her, laying the book on the island. "Guilty."

She shakes her head, her lips twisted with amusement, but she doesn't deny my request, so I smile with glee. We work companionably, pulling out ingredients, mixing bowls, and everything else we'll need.

I'm not as good of a baker as my mom, but I'm decent and it's something I enjoy doing with her.

It's already a bit hot in the house—the joys of living in an old house and not having central air—so I turn on the ceiling fan as well as the floor fan to help keep the kitchen cool. Once the oven starts preheating it'll get miserable.

My mom puts some music on while we work, both of us singing and dancing along. Our laughter fills the space and I remember a time when that sound was entirely absent in our old home.

I try not to think too often about *before*—our life when my dad was still alive—but some days it's hard to ignore those thoughts.

Taking the batter, I put even amounts into the lined pans while my mom starts making the three different frostings. The kitchen is the most updated part of the house, and my mom insisted on having double ovens since she loves baking so much. At times like this with multiple batches of cupcakes, it certainly comes in handy.

Popping them in, I set the timer—even though it's useless.

My mom always has this sixth sense about these types of things. It's strange how she can tell when things are ready, but the skill has never failed her yet.

She glances at her phone, wrinkling her nose. "What is it?" I wash my hands free of batter that splattered on me.

"Your sister."

I roll my eyes. I have a decent relationship with my older sister, but it doesn't mean I'm blind to her faults—of which there are many.

"What did she do now?" Drying my hands on a dish rag, I start gathering up dirty bowls and spatulas.

"She won't be home for dinner. She's going out with Michael."

I try to hide my reaction. Michael has been Georgia's on-again off-again boyfriend for *years* now. He's not the worst person, but the two of them together are a lethal combination. Wild, spontaneous, an absolute disaster waiting to happen.

Georgia swore when they ended things the last time that she'd never see him again.

What a little liar.

Don't get me wrong, it's her life to do what she pleases with, but I want to see her find someone who treats her like a queen and not a second thought, who, despite *years* spent together, runs at the mention of marriage. I might only be eighteen, but I'm not stupid. A couple should be on the same page about things they want, and those two are all over the place.

"I thought they were done?" I scrub at the stainless-steel mixing bowl harder than necessary.

"You know Georgia. She loves him and thinks things will be different every time."

"Maybe they will this time." I try to instill some false hope into my voice, but we both laugh, knowing that's not likely to happen.

I finish washing everything up and help her finish up the frostings.

"The cupcakes are done." Her head jerks up quickly and she rushes to the oven, slipping a mitt onto her hand. She sets the trays out to let them cool. "Would you mind seeing if the mail has been delivered?"

"No problem."

Opening the side door, I take two steps down and my feet land on the driveway. It's recently paved—my grandparents paid for it to be done—and I miss being able to kick at the gravel.

I glance at the house next door. It sold a while ago, no one's moved in yet, but today a truck is parked outside. I squint my eyes as

I walk further toward the street, trying to make out the writing on the truck.

Holmes Landscaping.

Huh. Maybe whoever bought it hired a landscaper to come in and clear out all the over-growth. It certainly needs some TLC, the yard and the house, but like ours it's beautiful with so much potential. When my mom purchased this house, at first, I thought she was crazy for not getting a new build, but then I understood. There's so much more character in an older home. All you have to do is show it a little love.

Opening the mailbox, I grab the letters and turn to head back inside when I hear a grunt of pain come from over the side of the fence separating our yard from the one beside it.

"Hello?" I call out.

There's no response, but it sounds like someone's struggling.

Hesitantly, I step into the yard and find the gate open to the backyard. I glance back at the truck parked on the street.

Salem, this is how people get murdered.

But that thought doesn't stop me from going into the backyard.

"Hello?" My voice rings out in the afternoon heat. "Is someone there?"

Huffing and puffing, like someone is about to blow a house down, is the only response I get.

I round the side of the house and find a man furiously weeding overgrown flowers and brush. On his hands and knees, it's impossible not to notice how muscular his arms and legs are. Not to mention his ass.

Stop staring at the stranger's ass!

He's deeply tanned, the kind of tan you only get with hours spent in the sun.

Which, I guess, makes sense if the landscaping truck belongs to him. His hair is a chocolate brown, with natural streaks of blond in it.

He throws everything behind him, a lot of it landing in the dirty pool that's sat unused for way too long.

"Hey. Can I help you?"

He freezes at my voice and turns, around. Chestnut brown eyes

8

narrow upon me. He looks me up and down. Dirty shoes, the mail clasped in my hands, up my body, back down again.

"You're trespassing," he grunts, sitting back on his legs. There are freckles sprinkled across his nose, and even though I'd guess this man to be in his early thirties, they somehow make him look younger, boyish. The heavy scruff on angular cheekbones counteracts the boyishness of it.

"You should be wearing sunglasses." I have no idea why that's the first thing to come out of my mouth.

"Huh?" He pushes shaggy hair out of his eyes, squinting up at me. Apparently, he agrees that it was a stupid thing to say. Even if he *should* be wearing them.

"Sorry." I shake my head. "I live next door." I toss my thumb over my shoulder at the house. "I heard you over here, and it sounded like you were struggling, so I thought I better check on you."

"I'm fine." His voice is deep, rich, with a timbre to it that sends a shiver down my spine. "You can go now."

I narrow my eyes on him. "Are you supposed to be here?"

His lips twitch with the tiniest hint of amusement. "This is my house, so yes. Are *you* supposed to be here?"

We both know the answer to that.

"Oh." I take a step back. "I ... no ... I suppose not." I blunder over my foolishness. "I'm sorry."

He ignores me, already turning back to his laborious task. Based on the state of the yard, it's going to take a long ass time for him to clear everything out on his own, but maybe he plans on getting help later, but right now needs to exact his frustrations on the yard himself.

"I didn't mean to intrude," I ramble, backing up toward the open gate in the corner. "I was concerned." He ignores me, tossing more greenery behind him. "Anyway, if you need anything, feel free to knock on our door."

I realize he's not going to say anything at all, so I rush back through the gate and cross onto our driveway.

The side door opens, and my mom pokes her head out. "I was just coming to check on you. I was worried."

Shaking my head, I scurry up the steps into the house. "Sorry, I just met our new neighbor."

"Oh." Surprise colors her tone and she peeks around like she might spot someone. "I didn't know they'd moved in already."

"He doesn't seem very friendly."

She frowns, locking the door. She's already removed the cupcakes from the pans and lined them on the counter. "That's unfortunate."

"Mhmm," I hum.

"He could be in a bad mood. Moving can be stressful."

I shrug indifferently, but my eyes drift to the window above the breakfast nook that overlooks his yard. I can't see him, but I imagine him over there in his crouched position.

"Maybe."

Somehow, I doubt it, and even with his less than kind behavior, I can't help but be curious about our new neighbor.

TWO

(handwritten note: whys she so vexed about not knowing his name?)

The new neighbor—it's been three days and I still don't know his name—works methodically on tending to the yard. He's made decent progress and yesterday he was aided by a few others. *(handwritten note: a bit creepy ngl.)*

He hasn't noticed me sitting on the roof watching him.

My mom would call it spying if she caught me, but I don't like that term.

I've always liked to watch other people—not in a Peeping Tom sort of way—and think about their lives, who they might love, what they might be worried about. So many people, so many intersecting lives, and yet we all pass by without a thought for each other.

Watching him work in the yard, aggressively tearing at weeds, wiping sweat from his brows, I find myself wondering what demons haunt him. It seems like he has a lot of pent-up anger and I wonder what put it there.

But I can't ask him.

So, I watch instead.

Watch, and wonder.

The curiosity is eating at me. Climbing back through my window, I shut and latch it before giving Binx a scratch on his head and bounding down the stairs.

No one else is home at the moment, so I have no one stopping me as I pull out one of each of the cupcakes we made the other day, as well as a glass of my mom's fresh lemonade.

Carrying everything next door, I say a silent prayer that he's in a better mood than he was the other day, but after watching him work for the last hour something tells me not to get my hopes up.

"Hi," I call out in a chipper tone.

The man stops digging up a bush, his eyes narrowing upon me.

He's not wearing a shirt today, and up close I can see the sweat clinging to his muscular chest. His shoulders are wide, with his waist tapered in. Based on the muscles this guy is sporting, he has to spend a lot of time in the gym when he's not working.

He wears a baseball cap today, shielding his eyes from the sun. My lips twitch with amusement when I think about my sunglasses blunder. It must've had *some* impact on him.

His eyes drop to the tray in my hands, and he flips his cap around backwards.

"Trespassing, again?"

I roll my eyes. "I'm being neighborly. Cupcakes and lemonade." I hold the tray out triumphantly. His tongue slides out the tiniest bit, wetting his lips. He makes no move to take it. "It's not poisoned," I cajole. "The cupcakes are cookie dough, lavender and honey, and lemon with mint frosting. My personal favorite is the cookie dough."

"You talk a lot."

I shrug, unbothered by his observation. "I've been told."

Hawthorne Mills, Massachusetts has a majority of chilly days in the year, but the summers can be sweltering. Today's definitely one of those days. Just in the short time of trekking across our two yards and standing in front of him, I can already feel sweat dripping down my back. I eye the pool to my right, wondering if he plans to clean it out and open it up before the end of the summer.

With a sigh, he wipes his fingers on his shorts. "Which one is the cookie dough?"

I nod at the one in the middle and long tanned fingers reach out to take it. "You don't want the others?"

He shakes his head. "No." He starts to turn back to his work.

"What about the lemonade?"

He hesitates and takes it, setting it down on a flat piece of ground.

I wait, hoping he'll say something, like you know, maybe a *thank you*. But he picks up the shovel, ready to dig again.

"Is there something else you need?" He switches his cap back, so the brim is low, hiding his brown eyes.

"No. That was it."

Defeated, I turn to head back to my house. When I get to the gate, I yell back, "You're welcome!"

The faintest chuckle echoes behind me.

WALKING INTO THE ANTIQUE SHOP LOCATED ON MAIN STREET of our small town, the bell chimes happily, signaling my arrival.

A Checkered Past Antiques is my mom's pride and joy. While she loves baking at home, she never had dreams of owning a bakery. No, this is what she always wanted. A cute little shop filled with pieces she's chosen herself. Some she's done nothing to, others she, or I, have given a bit of a facelift in the garage behind the back of the building.

"Hey, Mom," I call out, heading toward the back. I set down my bag behind the counter.

"Hi, sweetie." She looks up from a display she's rearranging for the fourth time this week.

Some people might hate working for their mom, but I love it. Chatting with customers, sprucing things up, watching people fall in love with old things ... all of it is so magical.

It's also nice that my mom lets me sell the candles I make. It started as a small hobby, a suggestion made by my therapist to help me channel my anger and depression into something productive. Well, candles weren't her specific suggestion. She said things like painting, or photography, sports, but somehow, I landed on candles. Now, they've become popular in our small town, and I even sell them online. I need to start making the fall scents, so they'll be ready come the autumn season.

"Do you need help?" I approach the table.

She shakes her head, adding one of my candles with the Salem & Binx logo—a small black cat with S&B—to the display. "Almost done here and then I'll head out."

I'll man the shop on my own for the afternoon before I close up and head home for dinner in the evening.

My mom doesn't stay long after my arrival and heads out after giving me a hug.

A few people stop in, some local, some tourists, and I'm not surprised when I've been there about an hour and my boyfriend, Caleb, stops in.

"Hey," he greets, holding up a bag of food from a local diner. "I hope you're hungry."

"Starved." My stomach rumbles in agreement.

Caleb Thorne is the quintessential All-American boy. Descendent of our town's founder, star of our high school football team, and blessed with wavy blond hair, icy blue eyes, and cheekbones you only see on models.

And he's all mine.

He sets the food down on the counter, leaning over to kiss me. "Missed you." He gives me the grin he reserves only for me.

"I missed you, too." He's been in Boston the past few days, getting a feel for the city since he'll be moving there to attend Harvard in the fall.

"Anything exciting happen while I was gone?" He starts unpacking the bag while I reach beneath the counter and pull out drinks from the mini fridge my mom keeps there.

I think about my mercurial new neighbor but decide to skim over that. "Nah. I sat on the roof and people watched. Brainstormed some new scents for my candles." Holding up my arm marred with scratches, I add, "And I gave Binx a bath because he snuck outside and smelled like ass when I found him."

"Ouch." He inspects my arm carefully. "It looks like you went to war."

"I practically did."

He chuckles, releasing me before leaning in to steal another kiss. "I'm happy you survived." He pops open one of the Styrofoam containers and passes the turkey club inside to me.

"How was Boston?" I pop the tab on the Diet Coke.

"Fucking amazing." He can't help but smile, a wistful expression on his face. Caleb has been dreaming of attending Harvard since we started dating our sophomore year. He was convinced he wouldn't get in, but I knew better. "You'd love it there."

I frown. This is an issue we've been facing as of late. Caleb thinks it makes perfect sense for me to move with him and live off-campus. While I think that's silly. I don't even like the city all that much and Caleb's going to be busy with school. What would I do? Sit in an apartment and twiddle my thumbs? I mean, logically I'd get a job somewhere, but I have one here—one I love—and I can continue to build my candle business.

"I'm sure I will when I visit you."

He sighs, shaking his head. Picking up a fry, he spins it around in his fingers. "You really won't go, will you?"

"Caleb," I sigh, exasperated, "I wouldn't be happy there."

"Babe, you don't know that."

I pick up my sandwich, taking a bite. I'm too hungry for even this topic of conversation to steal my appetite. "And you don't know that I would." My tone is firm but not argumentative. "I need to stay here. Figure out what *my* next step is."

His shoulders sag. "I know, I just..." He glides his fingers through his hair. "I'm going to miss you, that's all."

"I know, and I'll miss you, too. But Boston isn't that far. I can still visit you and vice versa." Boston is only a three-hour train ride from our little town. He acts like it's a world away, but it's really not.

"You're right."

By some miracle, no customers come in while we eat and catch up. When the food is gone, Caleb gathers everything up and gives me a kiss goodbye with plans set for us to see a movie this weekend.

The rest of my shift goes smoothly, and I head home after locking up behind me, surprised to find the neighbor's truck still parked in the driveway. Normally he's gone before five, but it's pushing six o'clock.

With a shake of my head, I start up the driveway to the side door, pausing when I see something on the steps.

It's the glass for the lemonade and beneath it is a ripped piece of paper with something scrawled across it. I squint, trying to make out the handwriting.

It's one word, but I can't help but give a small laugh and shake of my head.

Thanks.

THREE

There are nights where no matter what I do, I can't sleep. It doesn't happen as often as it used to, but when it does, I've learned not to fight it. It's a little after five in the morning when I slip from my bed. Binx cracks one large green eye open and glares at me for disturbing his slumber before closing it and going back to sleep.

Changing out of my pajamas into my running gear, I quietly tiptoe down the stairs, so I don't disturb my mom or sister. Scribbling a note to let them know I've left for a run, I step outside and inhale the early morning air. Dew coats the blades of grass as I stretch my legs for a few minutes before I take off in a light jog.

I never listen to music when I run, partly for safety reasons, but also because I don't like the distraction. Emptying my mind, steadying my breaths, and reconnecting myself with the world around me is what I *need* when my insomnia hits.

My breaths are even as I enter the small downtown area, running around the gazebo in the center of town—this time of year it has ivy and crawling flowers growing up the sides—past the antique store, and back toward home. It's a three and a half mile loop by the time I make it back to my street.

The gray pickup truck turns down the street from the opposite end as I slow to a walk. It stops in front of the house and our new neighbor hops out. He pauses on the sidewalk, hands on his hips as he stares at the house like it's some mighty obstacle he needs to overcome.

It's not a stretch. The siding needs to be painted, the roof replaced, and several of the shutters are hanging on by a thread. But with only a few days work, the yard is starting to look like—well, an actual yard and not a jungle.

He turns his head at the sound of my footsteps, those shrewd eyes narrowing upon me.

"You're up early." His voice is gruff as he turns back to his truck, opening the passenger door. He procures a travel coffee cup and is closing the door when I reach him.

"I'm up early a lot."

He sips his coffee. "You're young. You need to be careful out there."

I snort, the unflattering noise lingering in the air between us. "Don't worry about me. I'll be fine."

I don't tell him, but everyone worries so much about monsters lingering outside they forget about the ones that can haunt you behind closed doors.

"You went for a run." He finally notices my attire. I guess he thought I hung around outside early in the morning for funsies.

It's not a question but I answer like it is anyway. "Yes. When I can't sleep, I go for a run. It clears my head."

He gives me a funny look. "You don't sleep?"

"Sometimes." I shrug, noting that the back of his truck is filled with fresh mulch. "Insomnia is a bitch."

He cracks a tiny smile. "I better get to work."

"Right, of course." I start to walk away, but turn back around. "You're my new neighbor, but I still don't know your name."

He raises a brow. "Thayer."

I dip my head. "Nice to meet you, Thayer. I'm Salem."

He doesn't say anything, so I start walking again. I've made it a few feet onto our driveway when he says, "Do you have any more of those cookie dough cupcakes?"

I glance back with a smile and nod.

WE DIDN'T HAVE ANY CUPCAKES LEFT, BUT FOR SOME REASON I hadn't been able to tell Thayer.

Thayer.

I've never heard such a name before, but it perfectly suits the rugged man next door.

My mom and sister have both left for work, so that's how I find myself in the kitchen whipping up cupcakes. I know my mom will be curious about why I made them, so I'll have to come up with some other excuse than giving them to the grumpy neighbor. Something tells me she wouldn't understand.

The house is quiet as I bake, but I don't mind it. I like being alone, crave it. When I'm alone I don't have to fake anything, paste a smile on my face if I don't feel like it or participate in conversation when I'd rather be silent.

Binx circles through my legs and I smile down at the cat. He really is my best friend—not that I'd tell Lauren that. She'd be greatly offended if I told her I ranked a cat above her.

As if conjured by my thoughts alone, my phone starts ringing with a FaceTime from her. With a sigh, I wipe my fingers on the apron I tied around me and prop my phone up before answering her call.

"Hellooooo!" She yells a little too loudly when I answer.

"Hey," I reply back, adding frosting to a bag.

Her nose wrinkles, her red painted lips pouting with contemplation. "Are you baking?"

"Yes." I twist the bag shut.

"Huh." She hums, swishing her long dark brown hair over her shoulder. "Anyway, I was calling because Oscar is throwing a pool party this weekend and we're going."

"We are?"

She rolls her eyes at me. "Of course, we are. This is like our last summer to goof off. Parties, too much alcohol, sex, it's all happening."

I shake my head at her. "You're insane."

"But you love me."

She's right, I do. Lauren can be a bit over the top at times, but she's the best kind of friend you could ask for. Fiercely loyal and protective.

"I need a new swimsuit," I admit, thinking about the rough shape mine is in after the last few years of use.

"Perfect." She claps her hands eagerly. "We can go shopping this afternoon."

"I work." I turn the light on in the oven to check the progress on the cupcakes before clicking it back off.

"Tomorrow, then?"

"Tomorrow."

"I'll pick you up at eleven? We can get donuts and coffee before we hit the mall."

"Sounds great."

"All right, see you then."

She ends the call without a goodbye. That's Lauren. Always in a hurry.

An hour later, I'm walking over a batch of freshly frosted cookie dough cupcakes. I kept six and I'm giving Thayer the other six.

When I reach his yard, he's crouched in the front, knees in the dirt as he installs some sort of plastic thing in a swooping shape. I notice half of the mulch is already gone.

"I come bearing cupcakes," I say by way to announce my appearance.

He glances over his shoulder before rising to a standing position and yanking off his gloves. "I've been dreaming about these."

He seems to be in a better mood today than the previous times I've encountered him. I wonder what's changed—or more importantly, what put him in such a foul mood.

20

"They're pretty dreamy."

He takes the container and pops it open, he sniffs them, then pulls out one before putting the top back on. He unwraps the cupcake and takes a massive bite, eating about half in one go.

"Delicious." Some crumbs go flying out of his mouth and he gives a boyish laugh, swallowing the bite. "Sorry about that."

Unbothered, I shrug. "I'm glad someone else likes them." Before I can stop myself, I blurt out, "You're in a better mood today."

His nose crinkles. "You noticed that, huh?" He finishes the rest of his cupcake.

"Kind of hard not to when you've been a bit of an asshole."

He flinches, and a part of me wishes I could take back my words, but another part is glad I said them. I think people need to get called on their bullshit more. "Sorry about that." He glides his long fingers through the waves of his hair. "Just a lot of shit going on." He glances over his shoulder at the house and I'm sure that's *some* of this so-called 'shit' but definitely not all of it. I'm not one to pry, though, so I dip my head.

"Enjoy the rest of the cupcakes."

He nods back and I turn to walk away.

"Thank you, Salem."

I pause at the sound of his voice, my name on his tongue sending a shiver down my spine I don't understand.

One foot in front of the other, I keep walking.

FOUR

"These are all hideous." Lauren plucks my swimsuit choices out of the dressing room. "You wait here, I'm going to pull a few."

"Nothing too scandalous."

She throws up her hand in an *I know* gesture.

Sitting on the bench in the dressing room, I wait for her to return. The walls are covered in bright tropical wallpaper and the store boasts loads of neon signage with loud pop music blasting through the speakers.

Lauren returns a few minutes later and holds up three options. I pick the plain black one with a bikini top and high waisted bottoms that fully cover the butt.

Lauren laughs. "I knew you'd choose that one."

"The other two are..." Well, they leave little to the imagination. I don't care how other girls choose to dress, but I like to have more of my body covered. It's just personal preference.

"I know, I know." She pushes me into the dressing room with the black choice. "You change into this and I'm going to see what else they have."

"I only need one," I argue, already hopeful this will work just fine.

"Blah, blah, blah," she cajoles in a playful tone.

I change into the bikini and look at myself in the mirror. Thick blonde hair hangs down well past my breasts, but thanks to the horrendous lighting in the dressing room it looks more like an awful shade of pink. I've already formed a light tan this summer, freckles sprinkled across my chest despite lathering myself in sunscreen.

The curtain swishes open. "God, you're hot," Lauren compliments, making my cheeks turn red.

"I could've been naked!"

She rolls her eyes. "I've seen you naked."

"We're in public!"

"Stop being dramatic. All your bits are covered." She looks me up and down. "Only you could make a bikini that plain look so good. I found it in this color too." She holds up a pink one.

"Fine. I'll get both." I swipe it from her. "Now get out of here so I can change."

"So dramatic," she jokes, leaving me be.

I check out with my swimsuits while Lauren continues to browse the store.

"I'm having so much fun." She loops her arm through mine as we head out of the store into the mall. "Are you?"

"Absolutely," I fib, not wanting to rain on her parade. Malls and shopping aren't really my thing.

She throws her head back and laughs. "You're such a little liar, but I'll let it pass." She tugs me toward another store. "Let's see you *absolutely*," she mocks, "enjoy this store too."

Great.

CALEB'S HAND IS ENTWINED WITH MINE AS WE TREK TOWARD the backyard of Oscar's house. Lauren skips ahead of us, a tote bag large enough to fit a small child on her shoulder. She glances over her shoulder at us, a tiny pair of sunglasses perched on the end of her dainty nose. Those are way too small to actually protect her eyes.

"Hurry up, you slow pokes."

Caleb chuckles, squeezing my hand. "She's never going to change, is she?"

"You mean, stop bossing people around?" I crack a smile. "No, never."

I know Lauren can be a bit much for some people. She can be bossy and abrasive, though I never think she purposefully means to be that way, because the girl has a heart of gold. A lot of people aren't blessed enough to see that side of her, but I am, so I consider myself lucky.

Oscar's family owns a massive new build and when we round into the back, my breath is stolen at the beautiful, luxurious space. You can tell that it's been professionally landscaped. The pool is a curving work of art, complete with not one, but *two*, slides.

This is nothing like the rubber ducky plastic swimming pool I had growing up.

Caleb seems to be just as in awe as I am. His house is an old historic mansion, it's beautiful, but it's not *this*.

The only high school parties I've ever attended were field parties after games and the occasional basement one. Those looked nothing like this one.

"There are literal waiters," Caleb mutters lowly so I'm the only one who can hear.

"Is that—?"

"Yep. Pretty sure that's champagne."

"Wow. I didn't know Oscar had ... well, this." I sweep my hand at the palace in front of us.

"Me either. I don't hang out with the guy much."

While Caleb might be a golden boy, he doesn't relish in the lime-light and usually avoids these kinds of things unless he's with close friends or me. In which case, I suckered him into coming with me today.

There are a good amount of people here, which makes my anxiety spike. I don't particularly like big crowds and small talk.

Caleb knows this, and bless him, he makes a beeline for a lone chaise lounge off in the distance that no one has occupied. It's in a less populated area of the backyard since most of the guests are either in the pool or hanging out by the food and drink table.

I set down my bag, looking around for Lauren and spot her by the table speaking with Melanie, a girl from our class. I raise my hand in a wave when Melanie looks over. She waves back, her smile forced as she eyes Caleb at my side.

That happens a lot. Girls were jealous that he chose me, acting as if I stole him or performed witchcraft to get him to fall in love with me.

I duck my head in embarrassment and turn back to the chaise. Caleb is oblivious to the exchange. "I'm thirsty, you want anything?"

"Diet Coke if they have it."

He nods. "Be right back."

I pull a towel out of my bag—much smaller than Lauren's—spreading it out onto the chaise. Kicking off my flip-flops I reach for the hem of my oversized shirt, the Coca-Cola label on it. Caleb got it for me as a gag gift since I like the Diet kind so much. Rolling up the shirt I stuff it inside my bag. I reach for the button on my shorts and hesitate a moment before I take them off.

Caleb returns just as I'm putting my shorts away and sits down on the chaise, setting our drinks on the ground beside him. He motions for me to take the spot between his legs. I do, resting my back against his chest. I let out a sigh as he rubs his hands over my arms. "Did you put on sunscreen?"

"Ugh, no." I groan, reaching for the bottle in my bag. I spray it onto myself and pass it to him.

Once we're both fully protected from the sun, I lean against him and close my eyes.

His lips brush against the top of my head and I can't help but smile. "I feel like I've hardly seen you since graduation."

"We're busy," I sigh sadly. Between my job, Caleb's job, and him preparing to go off to college in a few short months—*weeks*, really—

25

there hasn't been a lot of 'us' time like there normally is. "Are we still on to see a movie tomorrow?"

He winces. "Fuck, I forgot to tell you. My mom needs me to clear out the garage. I think since I'm going to be moving out, she's finding every job she can that requires my help."

I laugh, picturing Mrs. Thorne scouring her house for things that need to be fixed that she knows Caleb will be better help with than her husband. Sure, she could hire someone, but where's the fun in that?

"I'm sorry," Caleb says, bringing my attention back to him.

"It's okay." I'm not bothered. I understand that things are changing. Soon, I won't see him at all unless I go to Boston, or he comes home for a weekend. My chest pangs. He's been a constant in my life the past three years. It'll be strange for him to be gone, but I think, maybe, good for me. It'll force me to focus on myself. My wants and needs. Hopes and dreams for the future. Whether that's college or something else.

"It's not." His lips touch tenderly to the exposed skin of my shoulder, already warmed by the sun. "I want to spend time with you."

"We'll do something else. Maybe you can come over for dinner," I suggest.

He frowns, thinking. "We'll see."

I don't feel like talking about this anymore. Looking around at the party, it seems as if everyone from our graduating class is here, even some underclassmen. It's not like we have a lot of kids at our school anyway. The town is small, the population even smaller.

"You want to get in?" Caleb points to the pool.

I shake my head. "You can if you want."

"Nah." His arms tighten around me. "I'm fine right here."

I smile, but he doesn't see it since he's behind me, and sink further against his body.

"Bleh," Lauren fake-gags, as she walks by, setting her stuff up on the pavers beside us. "You too are so sickeningly sweet you make me sick. Sick, I tell you."

"You need to get a boyfriend," Caleb tells her, to which she pulls a disgusted face.

"No thanks. I'm okay not tying myself down right now."

"Suit yourself." He wraps a strand of my blonde hair around his finger. "Don't forget your drink."

"Oh, right." I lean over and pick up the glass, taking a sip and letting the bubbles hit my stomach. I know I should stop drinking soda, regular or diet. It's awful for you, but I haven't been able to curb the habit.

"You two losers can keep hanging out here—" Lauren adjusts her bikini bottoms. "—but I'm going for a dip in the pool. Keep an eye on my shit for me." She doesn't wait for a response, heading straight for the pool. I expect her to take the stairs and walk daintily down into it, but instead she shouts, "Cannonball!" and plunges inside. When she surfaces, she glances around frantically. "Where'd my top go?"

FIVE

The purple, orange glow of sunrise filters in through my blinds as I tie my shoelaces, securing my running shoes onto my feet.

Binx watches me through slitted eyes from the bottom of my bed, irritated at me for leaving early again.

"I'm sorry, Binx."

I swear he huffs before his eyes shut completely. Cats. Can't live with them, can't live without them.

Pulling my hair into a ponytail, I glance in the mirror above my dresser smoothing out any bumps. Satisfied my hair won't fall out mid-run, I swipe Chapstick on my lips, give Binx a scratch behind his ears, and quietly head down the stairs. I have to take my time since the old stairway creaks like an achy back.

Scribbling down a note, I slip out the door. I take a moment to stretch and fill my lungs with the crisp early morning air before it heats up in just a few short hours.

Walking to the end of the driveway, I stifle a groan when I see Thayer at the back of his truck, the bed lowered and filled with all kinds of plants and shrubbery.

He sets the flowers on the sidewalk, his gaze catching my shoes. He looks up quickly.

"Another early run?"

"Yes," I drawl.

His eyes narrow. "Don't you own a treadmill or something?"

"No. Even if I did, I prefer running outside."

"Do you carry pepper spray with you?"

"No."

He shakes his head, settling his hands on his hips. "It's not safe."

"I'm not asking you for permission to run in my own town. I've been doing this long before you graced us with your presence." I nod my head at his house.

"Sorry for being concerned about your safety."

"I can look out for myself."

"Are you sure about that? You seem young."

"I'm eighteen." Admittedly, when I say it out loud it does sound, in fact, *young* and does nothing to prove my point. Trying to change the subject, I point to one of the plants. "You're planting jasmine?"

"You know plants?"

"Some." I swish my hand back and forth.

"Hmm," he hums, looking mildly impressed. "Since I can't stop you, you better get started."

I shake my head. This man is baffling.

"See you later, Thayer."

"Have a good run, Salem," he replies, already turning back to his truck to continue unloading.

My run goes a long way to help clear my head and when I reach our street, another truck has arrived and a whole crew is working at Thayer's house now.

Interesting.

I ignore the men, some who stare blatantly at me as I walk past.

"Stop staring and work!" I hear Thayer yell at them in a disgruntled tone.

Shaking my head, I check the mail and walk up my driveway, my eyes narrowing upon something left on the steps. Bending, I pick up the object with a shake of my head.

"Pepper spray," I say aloud, in disbelief, turning the black cylindrical tube over in my hands. There's a price sticker on the back from the convenience store down the road.

"If you're going to go on runs so early, you need to carry some with you."

I look over at Thayer who stands right behind me. For someone so large and with heavy boots attached to their feet, he moves quietly.

"Look who's trespassing now."

His lips twitch the tiniest bit. "You caught me."

"Thanks for this." I hold up the can like he doesn't know what *this* is.

"You're welcome."

We stare at each other, silence hanging between us, but neither of us makes a move to change it. Not for a full minute at least.

Then, he shoves his hands in the pockets of his cargo shorts, glancing over the fence that separates our two houses. "You don't by any chance need a job do you? It wouldn't be full-time or anything … just twice a week, maybe a few hours some weekends."

I hesitate, curious. "What kind of job? I'm not sure I'm cut out for landscaping. My plant knowledge is mediocre at best."

He chuckles, shaking his head. "No, not that. I need a babysitter, nanny, something, whatever, for my son. Once I get this place fixed up, he'll be staying here with me some."

"Oh." I wasn't expecting that. "You have a kid?"

He laughs. "Yeah, Forrest. He's six."

"That's cute." I smile. I love kids. They're fun, so openly curious about anything and everything. Sometimes, I envy them for that, because my childhood was ripped so cruelly away by a monster. "I have a job already," I admit, his face turning immediately crestfallen. "But I do work for my mom—she owns an antique shop in town—so I might be able to work something out." It's the best I can offer him.

"All right." He nods, running his fingers through his hair. "Okay.

I'm hoping to have this place ... livable in the next few weeks. Not that it's worthy of being condemned, but some things have needed to be rewired, the plumbing," he rambles. With a shake of his head, he chuckles. "Sorry. We'll revisit this conversation soon."

"Sure," I agree. "We can talk whenever."

He doesn't say anything else, just turns and walks back to his house.

Head down, I open the side door and kick off my sneakers. Peeling off my socks I stuff them inside. I need to shower, I'm sweaty and smelly, but I can't help taking a moment to inhale the scent of pancakes.

"Mmm, Mom, those smell delicious."

She smiles gratefully, flipping over a pancake on the griddle. "Thanks. Are you hungry?"

"Starving," I admit. "But I should really shower first."

She rolls her eyes, adding pancakes to the already growing stack on a flowered patterned plate to her left. "Your stench hasn't sent me running for the hills yet," she jokes. "I think I'll survive."

"Mom," I laugh.

"Just eat." She points to the kitchen table. "Your shower can wait a few minutes."

Georgia's feet sound on the stairs, and she enters a moment later. Her long blonde hair is pulled back into a ponytail, her makeup expertly applied. Her scrubs are a navy blue color and somehow they hug her curves.

"I've gotta go. I'm running late." She swipes a pancake from the plate, shoving half in her mouth while turning to the coffee pot. "Morning, sis." She turns to me with a smile while pouring coffee into her travel mug and then dumping in a heaping spoonful of sugar and creamer.

"Hey."

"Love you, guys." She plasters a kiss on my mom's cheek and gives me a quick hug before swiping another pancake and dashing out the door.

That's Georgia for you. Always late. Always in a hurry.

But somehow, she manages to be perfectly on time to everything. It's baffling.

Her car rumbles in the driveway, tires screeching as she peals out of the driveway.

My mom shakes her head, smiling with amusement. "That girl."

I'm sure she says those same two words to Georgia about me at times.

After stuffing my face with pancakes, I head upstairs to shower, the ancient pipes creaking and groaning. My shower ends up being colder rather than hot, but it's okay, I need the cool down anyway. Thank God it's not winter though, or I'd be halfway to sick.

Brushing my hair out after my shower, I change into a pair of shorts and a tank top before slipping out my window. I lay down on the roof, closing my eyes and letting the heat warm my skin. The noises next door soothe me, and I find myself dozing off.

Only a short time passes before I crack my eyes open. Sitting up, I rub my tired eyes. I glance at my phone, cursing under my breath at the time, and hurry back inside.

I'm supposed to meet Caleb at the mall for lunch at one of our favorite places before going to work, so I change my clothes and put away laundry. By the time that is done, I need to make the thirty-minute drive to the mall.

When I arrive, Caleb is already there. Somehow, he makes a basic pair of khaki shorts and a white shirt look good and I plant a kiss on his lips when I reach him, having to stretch on my tiptoes. He wraps his arms around me, smiling into the kiss.

"What was that for?"

"I missed you, that's all." I settle back on my feet. "I'm also starving. Feed me."

The two pancakes I had this morning weren't enough.

He chuckles, wrapping an arm around me. "Your wish is my command."

He steers me into the restaurant, and we're quickly seated at a table. We catch up on little things that we haven't talked about over text the past few days and when our food arrives, we both dive in like we haven't eaten all day. I know Caleb is spending a lot of his free time at the gym or on the field working with his old coach to prepare for college, but I miss him, so it's nice to get to spend this time together.

Taking my hand as we leave the restaurant, I browse some stores as we venture back to the parking lot. "Ooh, hold on." I tug him toward a sunglass kiosk.

"You need new sunglasses?" He questions, brows furrowed.

"Uh ... yeah," I lie. I don't know what makes me lie about it and not tell him that I'm looking at them for my new neighbor, but I try not to think about the reasons why that might be.

I pick up a pair of men's and look them over before putting them back and grabbing another.

"Those are for men," he points out.

"I know. I want them for when I run so I want something more sporty."

Another lie.

In the span of less than a minute I've lied to my boyfriend twice. I'm a horrible girlfriend.

But I know if I explain, he'll read into it and think it's something it's not.

I purchase a pair and we say our goodbyes in the parking lot.

As I drive back to town to the antique shop, I keep glancing at the bag from the sunglass kiosk. I couldn't resist, not after Thayer got me the pepper spray. I'm not sure he'll find it as amusing as I do, but I don't dwell on that. *I* think it's funny and that's all that matters.

Parking, I head inside the store to find my mom chatting with Thelma about the bake sale. Thelma glances my way, lighting up and I try to hide my cringe.

"Oh, good, there she is. Just the girl I was looking for." *Oh no.* "I volunteered you to work one of the game booths at the bake sale."

There are game booths too?

"You did?"

"I knew you'd say yes so I didn't see the big deal."

Over Thelma's shoulder my mom stifles a laugh, shaking her head. She knows I would've never said yes. Thelma knows it too.

"Of course," I agree, no point in arguing. "Can't wait."

Thelma gives a self-satisfied nod. "Good girl."

Why do I feel like I just got a verbal pat on the head?

My mom gives a soft laugh and says something to return Thelma's attention to her. Bless her. I scurry to the back storeroom and set down my bag. I linger a few minutes before poking my head out.

"She's gone."

"Oh, thank God."

She gives a soft laugh, picking up her purse and tossing it over her shoulder. "Marcy Hill is coming by to pick up that serving buffet in the front when her husband gets home with his truck. Other than that, just man the store."

"Okay." I go over to the floor to ceiling shelving unit that houses most of my candles, straightening them.

"I'll see you for dinner."

"See you later," I call after her.

I haven't mentioned Thayer asking me to nanny some. I'm not even sure why I haven't told her.

In fact, I'm not quite sure she's even met our new neighbor.

SIX

"Isn't this fun?" Lauren leads me to her basement, Caleb trailing behind me.

"I didn't know the fun had started yet."

Lauren gives me a playful swat as we round the corner to the theater like set-up in her finished basement. There's a screen that pulls down with a projector, a drawer full of snacks and candy, and even a working popcorn machine.

"The fun always starts as soon as you see me," she quips, flipping her hair dramatically over her shoulder for extra flare.

"Hey, man." Caleb fist bumps Dawson, Lauren's flavor of the week.

She doesn't have boyfriends. She has dates.

Long-term isn't for everyone, especially at our age, and that's fine.

"What movie are we watching?" I follow Lauren over to the massive stack of DVDs that belong to her dad.

"I was torn between these." She holds up three different choices.

"That one." I point at 'The Hitman's Bodyguard' there's action for the guys and Ryan Reynolds for us."

She snaps her fingers. "I like the way you think."

She puts the movie in and pops some popcorn.

The four of us settle on the giant bean bag like chairs in the middle of the room, two of us in each one.

Caleb wraps his arm around me, picking up a handful of popcorn.

"Are you okay?" He whispers in my ear. "You seem a little tense."

I press my lips together, trying to think of an excuse. I'm happy he's here, but I'm not happy he told me he lied to his mom to be able to come. He shouldn't have to lie to her to see me. That's ... not right. I've always thought she liked me fine, but now it seems like she's trying to fill his time with everything else, so he doesn't have any left for me. I don't like that it leaves me feeling needy.

"I'm fine," I lie instead, not wanting to bring up my insecurities. "Just happy you're here." At least that part isn't a lie.

"Shush, you lovebirds," Lauren hushes from our right.

Caleb chuckles, burying his face into the crook of my neck. He presses a kiss there and I relax against him, doing my best to let the tension leave my body. I want to enjoy whatever time we have left before summer ends. I know time will fly by.

Snuggling my body further into Caleb, I focus on the movie, but my eyes grow heavy—perhaps sleep senses that I feel safe for the moment—and I drift off.

I JOSTLE AWAKE TO CALEB CARRYING ME OUT OF LAUREN'S house and to his waiting car outside.

"I can walk," I mutter sleepily.

His chest rumbles with a laugh against my ear. "I've got you, babe. You're not even heavy."

"I'll get the car door for you." Lauren's voice is near and I hear the cheery beep of Caleb's SUV getting unlocked. The vehicle is brand new, a gift from his parents for graduating.

He sets me in the passenger seat and secures the seatbelt across my body.

"Sorry I fell asleep."

Caleb starts up the car. "Babe, it's fine. You must've needed the sleep."

He has no idea just how much. It becomes even more evident when I fall asleep again on the way home. Caleb jostles me awake when he gently pulls me from the car and back into his arms.

"I'm the worst girlfriend ever," I groan into his neck.

He gives a soft laugh. "No, you're not."

"No, I am."

"Hey!" A sharp voice sounds from nearby. "What the fuck is going on here?"

Oh no. I know that voice.

"Uh ... who are you?" Caleb asks.

"Neighbor," Thayer replies. "What's wrong with her? You didn't drug her, did you? I'll fucking beat your ass."

"What?" Caleb gasps offended. "Are you kidding me? No!"

"It's a legitimate question. She's passed out in your arms."

"Thayer," I groan. "I'm just sleepy. That's all."

"You know this prick?" Caleb looks down at me in his arms.

"Neighbor, remember?" Thayer interjects.

"I wasn't talking to you." Caleb sounds angrier than I've ever heard him, though I'm sure I'd feel very much the same way if I'd been accused of drugging someone.

"Are you okay?"

It takes me a moment to realize Thayer is talking to me. "Yeah. Just tired. You don't need to worry. Caleb is my boyfriend."

"Even more reason to worry." He glowers at Caleb while I struggle to keep my eyes open.

"Thayer," I groan.

"Fine." He finally lets us pass, me still carefully cradled in Caleb's arms.

"Your new neighbor is a fucking psycho."

I don't agree or disagree. Thayer is ... well, *Thayer*. Or so I'm learning.

My mom lets us inside and Caleb finally sets me down, kissing me goodnight before departing. I trudge up the stairs, take a quick shower, and dive into bed.

But the sleep that was so easy with Caleb becomes non-existent.

I'm NOT SURPRISED WHEN I LEAVE FOR MY RUN AND THAYER'S outside. I should be pissed at him, and I am a little peeved, but I know he was genuinely concerned when he saw what appeared to be my unconscious body being unloaded from a teenage boy's car.

The sunglasses case is clasped in my hand as I walk over. He sits on the steps of his front porch eating a sausage McMuffin and sipping a coffee. He looks up at the sound of my approaching feet.

"Good night of sleep?"

"No," I snort.

"Hmm," he hums, chomping into his sandwich.

I take it we're not going to acknowledge last night. Whatever. Suits me fine. I'm not one for confrontation.

"I got you something."

He arches a dark brow. "That so?"

Thayer is a man of few words.

"Yes." I hold out the case, trying not to smile in amusement.

He wipes his hands on a napkin before taking the case. His lips curl with amusement before he even lifts the hinged lid.

Pulling out the sunglasses, he fits them on his nose tilting his head up at me. "How do I look?"

Hot.

Ice runs down my spine at the unbidden thought.

"Great ... you ... they look great."

He chuckles, slipping them off. It's still dark out and not necessary to wear them yet.

"Thanks. You didn't have to do that."

"You didn't have to get me pepper spray, either." I point to the can clipped to my shorts.

"That's for your protection," he argues, going back to his breakfast.

"So are those."

He fights a smile—I don't understand why he battles against them instead of letting one shine through. What does he have against smiling? "You have a point."

"Of course I do."

He shakes his head. "Enjoy your run, Salem."

"I will." I start to walk away, already warmed up and ready to go. "Oh, and Thayer?" I look over my shoulder at the man that's too handsome for his own good.

"Yes?"

"Don't threaten my boyfriend."

SEVEN

July comes in with a blast of heat that our small town hasn't seen in recent years, and everything seems to be happening at once.

A moving truck is parked on the street, unloading furniture into Thayer's house. Sitting on my roof with my knees drawn up to my chest, I watch them carry in everything from a couch to a child's bed. I need to broach the topic of nannying again for him, because I do actually have the time to spare and wouldn't mind the extra money.

The bake sale is this weekend, but unfortunately, I won't make any extra cash manning the booth Thelma volunteered me for.

Thayer's made great progress on the house, at least on the outside. I can't speak for the inside since it's not like he's invited me in. Why would he?

But the pool is a crystal clear shiny blue, the bushes and flowers are carefully manicured, and the once patchy grass is now lush and full.

Thayer has a green thumb, that much is obvious.

His little boy runs around with unleashed excitement. It's the first time his son has ever made an appearance here. Thayer's never mentioned his ex or the situation with his son, but I'm not stupid. It's obvious it's complicated.

I know I should crawl back into my room and stop 'spying', but I can't help it. Curiosity gets the best of me so I stay out as long as I can until I grow too hot. Besides, my mom will be home soon, and I can't have her catching me on the roof. She's never said it, but I'm pretty sure she's afraid I sit out here and contemplate jumping. I'm not suicidal, and even if I was, the fall wouldn't be enough to kill me. Break some bones? Sure. Death? Not likely.

When my mom arrives home that afternoon, we get to work on the cupcakes, so we'll have enough for this weekend. The store was closed today, and she spent her time hanging up flyers and talking to locals about the bake sale—as if they probably haven't already heard about it from busybody Thelma.

"Thank you so much for your help," my mom says when I pull the last batch of cupcakes from the oven. We ended up adding a few more popular flavors on top of the more unusual ones. Cookies n' cream, vanilla, and red velvet.

"It's no problem, Mom."

"Still, I appreciate it. I'm sure you'd rather be with Caleb or Lauren."

"I like baking with you."

She smiles at that, pulling me into a hug. "I love you."

The side door into the kitchen opens then and Georgia walks in. "Aw, am I missing out on the love fest?" Mom laughs, opening up her arm to beckon Georgia into our embrace. "Well, how can I resist that?" Georgia sets her tote bag down and joins us. My nose wrinkles at the scent of antiseptic clinging to her hair and skin.

"Go shower," my mom tells her, "and we'll start on dinner."

Georgia narrows her eyes. "Is that your way of telling me politely that I stink?"

41

My mom shrugs, her lips twitching with amusement. "You smell like a hospital."

Georgia sighs, bending to scoop up her bag. "What are you guys making?"

We exchange a look. "Haven't figured it out yet," I reply.

Georgia gives a small laugh. "All right, you two figure it out and I'll ... try not to stink when I return." Her footsteps creak up the stairs a moment later.

While my mom prepares the cupcakes to be frozen so we can frost them later, I scour the refrigerator for something to prepare for dinner. I end up settling on a salad and baked lemon chicken. Simple and easy—you can never go wrong with that.

When Georgia rejoins us, her hair is wet from the shower and she's wearing a pair of cotton shorts and a big holey shirt I know belongs to Michael.

"This smells amazing. Need help with anything?" She gathers her hair up, securing it with an elastic at the nape of her neck.

"Can you pop the garlic bread in the oven?" I point to where I have it ready to go in.

With the table set, we sit down a few minutes later to eat.

Sometimes, in moments like this, where I'm enjoying a peaceful moment with my mom and sister, I can't help but think about when there were never times like this. When we walked on eggshells, lived in fear of an outburst, or worse.

We don't have to worry about that anymore, but the scars are still there. They always will be. They cut too deep to ever go away fully.

We made it to the other side thanks to a simple twist of fate.

Others who are in our situation aren't as lucky, and that's something I never let myself forget.

EIGHT

My tank top sticks to my chest, my body already covered in perspiration. Despite the cover of a tent, the shade and the small portable fan set up on my table are doing nothing to help. Instead of a game booth, Thelma decided to have me do face painting.

Me? Face painting?

I don't know what Thelma was drinking that possessed her to think this was the perfect fit for me. I don't have an artistic bone in my body.

"What am I?" The little girl looks in the hand mirror I hold out for her.

"I ... um ..." *Isn't it obvious?* "A butterfly."

"Oh. That's cool." She flounces off, her dress swishing around her legs. Her mom sticks some dollar bills in the donation jar before running after her.

I motion the next kid forward, a boy with a mop of red hair and freckles on his nose.

"I want to be a lion," he declares proudly, pointing to his chest.

Turning to the paints, I sigh. "I'll do my best, kid."

I'd so much rather be with my mom selling cupcakes, but *no*, Georgia got the job of helping her. I swear Thelma has some sort of weird old lady vendetta against me.

Swirling the brush in the paint, I set about doing my best to make this kid look like a lion. All while making small talk and keeping a smile plastered on my face. The kids are great, really, they're nice and here to have fun. I just get annoyed getting dragged into things instead of someone extending the courtesy of *asking*. I would've said yes if Thelma had, but she just went ahead anyway and I find that to be extremely rude.

On and on it goes.

One kid wants to be a snake, another a unicorn, one wants to be Spiderman, the next a planet. Despite my lack of artistic capabilities, I do my best to meet each and every request.

A little boy jumps up to me, bouncing like a little kangaroo. "Hi." His voice is high-pitched and chipper. "I'm Forrest, like—"

"The forest?"

"Yeah." He nods enthusiastically. "Can you paint a dinosaur on my face?"

"I thought you said you wanted a car," a familiar voice speaks up, a big, tanned hand falling on the boy's shoulder.

"Dad," Forrest drawls, "I changed my mind. I'm allowed to do that."

Thayer cracks a smile at his son. "All right. Dinosaur it is. How are you, Salem?"

"Your name is Salem?" The kid asks, eyes wide. "Like the place where all the witches burned?"

I try not to laugh. "The very one."

"Wait," he pauses, nose crinkling with thought. "How do you know her, Dad?" He glances up at Thayer, willing him to fill in the blanks.

44

"She's my new neighbor."

"Oh, that's cool." Forrest seems appeased by this answer. "So can I have a pink dinosaur?"

"Sure thing." I dip my brush into the pink paint and set to work.

"You stick your tongue out when you do that."

"Huh?" I look up at the sound of Thayer's voice. "Shoot." I left a streak of pink paint on Forrest's cheek. I grab my damp cloth and wipe it away while Thayer explains.

"When you're concentrating. Your tongue. You stick it out."

"I didn't know."

He looks like he wants to say more but chooses not to. I finish the dinosaur—honestly it looks like a giant pink blob and nothing at all dinosaur shaped about it—but when I give Forrest the mirror he smiles with glee.

"Awesome! Thanks, Salem!"

Thayer shakes his head, a full-blown smile on his face. His teeth are white and mostly straight, but one of his canine teeth is chipped. It's sort of endearing.

He slips a twenty into the jar and I smile gratefully. "Be sure to stop by mom's booth. There are cupcakes."

His brown eyes light up. "I do love cupcakes. Have a good day, Salem."

"You too."

I watch him walk away, speaking with his son, and that's when I spot Caleb heading toward me. I wasn't sure he'd be able to get away from his family's booth selling pies and a few other things. He carries two cans of sodas and I sigh in relief at the sight of them. Caleb, however, is watching Thayer with a shrewd gaze.

"What's your neighbor doing here?" There's a sneer to his voice, not that I can really blame him since Thayer accused him of drugging me.

He passes me a can of Diet Coke and pulls out the plastic folding chair on the other side of the table while I motion the next child forward.

"Well, this is a bake sale in the center of town open to everyone..." I trail off, letting him fill in the blanks. When he doesn't say anything, I add, "And he has a son, who wanted face painting."

He takes a swig of his regular Coke. When he sees I'm too busy to open the top on my can, he reaches over and pops it for me, the soda fizzing excitedly inside.

"Thanks."

"Something about that guy rubs me the wrong way," Caleb continues while I start on another unicorn request. He wears a funny expression, a cross between confused and disgusted. "He's just ... odd."

"I don't know about odd. Grumpy, though? Definitely that."

"That too."

"How's it going at your mom's booth?"

"Almost sold out."

I'm not surprised. His mom makes the best pies around. "Did you snag a peanut butter pie for me?"

He chuckles. "Yeah, babe. Put it away first thing."

"Thank you. I would kiss you if I wasn't otherwise occupied at the moment." I wiggle my paint brush in the air. "Have you seen Lauren?"

"Yeah, she's working a ring toss booth. I thought this was a bake sale, so what's with all these random booths?"

I give him a look. "Since when does anything Thelma does make any logical sense?"

"Good point." He runs his fingers through his hair. It's gotten even lighter from all the sun he's getting this summer, his skin a deep tan.

We're down to *weeks* now before he leaves for Harvard and a full week of that he'll be gone on vacation with his family. My heart aches. Even though I don't want to go to college, or move to Boston, it doesn't mean I'm not going to miss him.

Time is a precious treasure, limited in quantity, and it can be squandered so, *so* easily.

I do a few more kids before the line, thankfully, begins to dwindle.

"I'm starving. Do you mind grabbing me something to eat? I have cash in my wallet." I nod to my bag hanging over the back of the chair he sits in.

"I don't need your money, babe. I got it." He finishes his soda and gets up. "I'll be right back."

He's only been gone a minute when I feel a presence behind me. Thinking he's come into the tent from behind me, I turn around, already saying, "Wow, that was fast."

But it's not Caleb behind me. It's Thayer. His son is at his side holding a paper bag filled with my mom's cupcakes—I know because, I spent a good hour last night putting stickers on them for the antique shop. *"Free advertising,"* my mom said.

"What are you doing back?" I inspect Forrest's face to see if the horrible dinosaur painting smeared or something, but it's still the same weird shape it was before.

"Brought you something." Thayer reaches into the bag and pulls out one of the boxes that contains a single cupcake.

"You said your favorite is cookie dough too, right?"

I can't believe he remembered that.

"Yeah." I take the offered box.

"Thought you might need a snack."

"Thank you." I mean it. It's a thoughtful thing for him to have done.

He dips his head in acknowledgment and leads Forrest back out of the tent.

Caleb returns a few minutes later with a box of treats. His eyes narrow on the cupcake I haven't eaten yet.

"Where did that come from?"

"My mom." The fib comes to my lips before I even make the conscience decision to lie about the origin. "She thought I might be getting hungry."

Does he notice the shake in my voice? Why am I even nervous?

He glances around, his eyes falling back to the box. He swallows before his eyes meet mine.

He doesn't believe me.

"Okay." He sets the box down on the table. "I have to go help my mom."

"Caleb," I call after him, but he ignores me, disappearing into the crowd.

Shit.

NINE

On the roof again, watching the sunset, I notice an unfamiliar car turn onto the street and park in front of Thayer's house. My eyes are pulled from the beauty of the sun going down for the evening to the woman who climbs from the SUV. A girlfriend? His ex?

From this distance, all I can tell is that she's thin—the kind of thin that's almost willowy in a way—and has dark brown hair. She walks toward the front door, but before she even reaches the porch steps the door opens and Forrest runs out with arms wide open.

"Mommy!"

Well, that answers that.

She squats down, opening her arms for the boy. He hugs her fiercely and lets go, running back into the house calling for his dad. I watch as she hesitates outside, and Thayer appears a few moments later, barefoot in a pair of shorts and a plain cotton t-shirt. He sets a small bag on the ground by his feet and crosses his arms over his chest. His lips move rapidly as he speaks to his ex and then Forrest reappears, a teddy bear clasped under his arm. It's a chestnut color with a red ribbon around the neck.

The two of them speak for a few minutes and I can tell from their body language that it's a bit heated. Finally, she takes Forrest's hand and leads him to her car parked on the curb. Thayer follows with the bag and puts it in the trunk. Crouching down, he hugs a teary-eyed Forrest goodbye and helps him into the car. He closes the door and turns to his ex. They say something more and he walks back up the front pathway, pausing to turn around and wave at Forrest as they leave.

"Bye, Dad!" Forrest calls out the window, his little hand waving. "Love you."

"Love you, bud!" Thayer calls back, watching the car disappear. When it's no longer in sight his shoulders sag with sadness. He turns to head back inside but he pauses, his head jerking up. His eyes lock with mine and my heart gives a jolt at being caught. He squints up at me before turning back around and walking through his front gate and into our yard.

"What are you doing up there, Salem?" His hands slide into his pockets and he rocks back on his bare heels.

"I was watching the sunset."

"Was," he repeats. "And what distracted you?"

"My neighbor." He glances to his left where his house is, lips thinning. "You were fighting."

His mouth twitches. "Why do you think we got divorced?"

I shrug, wrapping my arms around my legs and resting my chin on my knees. "Couldn't agree on the best cupcake flavor?"

A full smile cracks his lips and I feel like I've won some sort of victory. "Yes. That's typically what makes or breaks a marriage. Disagreeing on a cupcake flavor."

"You never know."

"Hmm," he hums, cocking his head to the side. "You hang out up there a lot?"

"Yes."

"Why?" The question is a low drawl.

"Because I like it."

"And your mom lets you?"

I resist the urge to roll my eyes. I know the immature move wouldn't help my argument. "I'm eighteen."

"And you live with your mother," he points out.

"She doesn't like it," I admit, figuring he won't let it drop until I give him more. "But I ... out here I'm free."

God, it sounds so dumb coming out of my mouth, but that's how I feel.

"Free. Like a bird? Do I need to worry about you trying to fly off the roof?"

"No."

"That's good." He glances at his house, taking a step backwards. "You're welcome to use the pool any time you want. Your sister, too."

"You've met my sister?"

He pauses in his retreat, his face scrunching. "Yes."

"You said that funny," I accuse.

He rubs a hand over his stubbled jaw. "She yelled over the fence at me when I was weeding."

Oh, God. There's no telling what Georgia said.

"What did she say?"

"Well, after she said *'nice ass'* she asked if I was single."

"Sounds like Georgia," I try not to laugh. "She has a boyfriend."

He arches a brow. "Trying to warn me off?"

I pale, realizing I *am*, because the idea of Thayer and my sister? I don't like it. Not one bit.

"No," I say, but there's no confidence in the word.

Suddenly I'm flushed, frazzled, downright *confused.*

Thayer's eyes drop to our driveway, staring at his bare toes. "About nannying—"

"Yeah?" I latch onto the change in subject, wanting to get my mind off why I'd possibly be bothered by my sister flirting with Thayer.

"Are you interested?"

"As long as it doesn't interfere with my job at A Checkered Past."

He nods, like he expected this. "We'll make it work."

He doesn't wait for me to respond with anything else. He gives his back to me and returns to his house, not looking back at me once.

TEN

I swing my tote bag over my shoulder—filled with snacks, water
bottles, Diet Coke, a swimsuit, and other odds and ends—and
set off to make the short trek next door for my first day
watching Forrest. When I told my mom Thayer had asked if I could
babysit some, she thought it was a great idea. It's a new experience
and extra money for me to stow away for whatever comes next
for me.

The porch is freshly painted, the white is bright, almost blindingly
so. Tilting my head back, I notice he's painted the ceiling of the porch
a light blue color. Interesting.

Pressing the doorbell, I wait. I hear fast-paced steps running
toward the door and the rumble of voices.

It swings open, revealing Thayer with his hand on his son's shoulder, holding the boy in place who hops up and down excitedly.

"Hi, Forrest." I smile down at the child. He has something dried around his lips, syrup from his breakfast maybe.

"Thank you for doing this." Thayer looks ready to dash out the door. "I have a big project and I..." He glances down at his son. "Taking him with me isn't easy."

"My dad owns a landscaping company. Right, Dad?" He looks up at his father for confirmation.

"That's right."

"Oh." I look over at his truck, now parked in the driveway instead of the street, taking in the name. "Holmes Landscaping," I read aloud. "Is that your last name?"

"Thayer Landscaping has a nice ring to it," he quips easily, rubbing his jaw. I give him a look and he chuckles. "Yes, Holmes is my last name."

"Interesting," I muse, rocking back on my heels. Arching a brow, I point past him. "Are you going to invite me inside?"

"Oh." He shakes his head rapidly. "Sorry, yeah." He steps aside, pulling Forrest gently alongside him.

I step into the foyer, the smell of fresh paint clinging to the walls that are painted a muted gray color. The floor looks newly redone and there's a beige runner on the stairs. That's about it. No photos. No personality. Just a blank slate. But I guess this house is a work in progress for him. There's time to add more to it later.

"I'll only be gone a few hours, three tops," Thayer says, guiding me past what I assume will be the dining room on my left but currently looks like a makeshift storage area, and straight back to the kitchen.

"Wow." It's not a good 'wow' either. The appliances are missing, the cabinets, the counters, *everything*. There's a table set up against one wall with a microwave and a toaster oven.

"My dad's...what was the word you used, Dad?" Forrest looks up at his father for clarification.

"Renovating," he supplies, glancing at me. "I couldn't put off moving in any longer, my lease agreement was up on my apartment, but a lot of the things I ordered are on backorder. Like..." He waves his hand at the empty kitchen.

"The cabinets?" My lips quirk.

"Those, and the appliances, and all of it pretty much. At least it gives me a chance to redo the floors."

I notice several tiles laid out on the floor, like he's deciding between them.

"You could carry the wood through?" I suggest.

"Mmm, maybe," he hums in thought. "Anyway, I've gotta go. You have my number, contact me if you need to. And you're welcome to swim, just keep an eye on him."

"Absolutely. Don't worry, I have things covered here."

His gaze flits over me and then his son. With a resigned sigh, he nods. "I'll see you in a few hours." He crouches down, opening his arms for a hug. Forrest gladly dives into his arms. "Love you, bud."

"I love you, too, Daddy."

I think my heart just melted.

Thayer leaves, the front door clicking quietly closed behind him.

"Well," I look down at Forrest, "what do you want to do?"

THE POOL IS SURPRISINGLY WARM, AND I WONDER IF THAYER has it heated. Forrest climbs out for the umpteenth time and cannonballs right beside me. I think he loves soaking me.

"What was the score on that one?" His little head bobs up, goggles slipping off his nose. He takes them off, their imprint left behind around his eyes and bridge of his nose. Cleaning them off he slips them back on and gets ready to go again.

"Eleven out of ten."

His nose scrunches. "You can't get an eleven out of ten. That's not possible. It's out of *ten* so the most you can get is that."

"Ah, you caught me." I've learned pretty quickly that Forrest is smart—or maybe I haven't been around enough six-year-olds and they're all like this. "Ten outta ten then." I hold up all my fingers and wiggle them accordingly.

He dips his head in a nod. "That's better."

He goes to jump and stumbles, nearly belly-flopping into the water, but I catch him in time.

"Whoa," I set him down gently in the water, "careful."

"Sorry." He says sheepishly, kicking his legs. "My dad says I have no fear."

"I'm thinking I agree with him."

Forrest beams like this is something to be very proud of. "If your name is Salem what's your middle name?"

"Grace."

"Grace," he repeats with a laugh. "That's way different than Salem."

"It is," I agree, swimming backwards. "What's yours?"

"Xavier."

I wasn't expecting that. "That's a cool name."

"It sounds like a superhero, so I think so too." He floats on his back, looking up at the sky. A laugh shakes his chest. "That cloud looks like a cat licking his butt."

I glance up, but I don't see what he sees. "Totally." Lowering my head before I get dizzy, I add, "I have a cat."

"You do?" He brightens, swimming over to me. "What kind?"

"He's a black cat. His name is Binx."

"Can I meet him sometime? I want a dog, but my mom says they're dirty and my dad always says maybe one day. I think that's just parent talk for never."

I'm immensely amused by this kid. "Who knows. We can't predict the future. And sure, you can meet him any time."

"How'd you get him?"

I pause, thinking about how I discovered Binx in that alley. "He sorta found me, I guess." I can tell this explanation doesn't suffice for him. "Someone left him in the alley behind my mom's store."

"Whoa." His eyes get wide. "Your mom owns a store? That's so cool."

"I guess."

"What kind of store?" He dunks his head under the water and comes back up, pushing his hair out of his face.

"It's an antique store."

"Antique?" He fumbles over the word.

"Yeah, old furniture and stuff."

"Oh, that's not as fun as I thought."

I can't help but laugh. "What kind of store did you think she had?"

He shrugs his small shoulders. "I don't know. A toy store."

"That would be cool."

"Maybe I can have a toy store when I'm all grown up."

I smile, charmed by this kid. "You can do whatever you want."

"That's true. Maybe I'll be a firefighter, or fly a plane. Ooh or a dinosaur wrangler."

"The possibilities are endless," I assure him.

That's the beauty of childhood. You have the ability to dream up anything and have the belief that you can do it. And then you grow up and the world around you likes to crush those dreams and bring you back to reality.

Granted, dinosaur wrangler doesn't actually exist.

"I'm hungry," Forrest announces, swimming for the stairs that lead out of the pool. "Can you fix me lunch?"

"Sure." I have no idea what kind of food Thayer has, there wasn't anything I could see in the kitchen when we passed through and there's no fridge so...

We wrap up in towels, and Forrest leads me inside to a small freezer plugged in a random side room. He tries to lift the lid, but it's too heavy for his bony arms. I grab it and push it up before he can hurt himself.

It's filled with microwave and oven-ready meals. Makes sense.

Forrest grabs some kind of kid's meal with dinosaur shaped chicken nuggets. "This please." He shoves it at me, and runs off.

I haven't explored Thayer's house yet—I'm nosey, but not *that* nosey—and since it's mostly still a work in progress I'm not sure if I could deduce anything profound about him anyway.

Back in the kitchen I pop Forrest's meal in the microwave, tightening my damp towel around my body, but it doesn't do much to protect me from the chill of the AC with my wet hair dripping down my back.

"Forrest?" I call, wondering where he ran off to. "Forrest?" Panic seizes me and I run out of the kitchen straight outside, nearly tripping on my towel in the process. "Forrest," I scream when I see him face down in the pool.

He pops up, giving me a funny look. "What?"

My heart beats a mile a minute, panic freezing me to the spot I stand. "You can't get in the pool without supervision," I practically shriek. "And definitely not without telling me." I press a hand over my heart, waiting for the organ to slow down but I'm not sure that's going to happen any time soon.

"I'm sorry," he frowns, looking ready to cry.

It's on the tip of my tongue to tell him it's okay, but I bite back the words. It's not. It's not okay at all and I want him to understand that.

"Come eat your lunch and we can swim after."

"Okay." His voice is small, chin quivering. He eats his lunch at a folding plastic table and chair set, avoiding looking at me for as long as possible. I munch on an apple I brought with me and sip at my Diet Coke, waiting for him to make the first move. He dips his chicken nugget in ketchup, munching on the end. "Do we have to tell my dad about this?"

I try not to crack a smile. "Yes, we have to tell him."

He hangs his head. "He's gonna be real mad. He told me not to, but I didn't think it was a big deal." He perks up, eyes round. His nose is reddened from the sun and I make a mental note to apply more sunscreen on him before we go out again. "I'm a strong swimmer. Real good."

Softening my gaze and my voice, I say, "It doesn't matter how strong of a swimmer you are, something bad can happen to anyone."

"Even you?"

"Even me."

"What about my dad?" He thinks he's stumped me with this one.

"Him too."

"Hmm," he hums. "So, he's not invisible like he says?"

"Invincible," I correct, not missing a beat. "And I don't know your dad well enough to attest to that. He could be entirely indestructible for all I know."

Thayer does have this larger than life, untouchable, persona about him.

Forrest nods at this. "He does have really hard muscles."

I throw my head back and laugh. I think I love this kid.

57

ELEVEN

I awake with a cold sweat sticking to my skin. Binx opens one green eye, deduces that I'm not dying and promptly goes back to sleep. My heart races in my chest from the nightmare.

The door creaks open.

Hands on my body.

Hands that should protect me, shelter me, only destroy instead.

The tears pour steadily down my cheek. Not a nightmare—reality, my past, always circulating back to haunt me.

My shaky feet hit the hardwood floor and it groans in protest like I've woken it up too.

I push my hair out of my eyes, it's damp.

Choking from lack of oxygen I stumble to my window and open it. I know in my current state I shouldn't get on the roof, but I need to feel the air on my face. I crawl out the window on all fours.

Normally the dreams—nightmares, memories, whatever you want to call them—don't affect me *this* badly. I saw my therapist yesterday for the first time in three months and it stirred a lot of shit up, and apparently, in my vulnerable state of sleep, my brain decided to attack me.

Gulping in lungsful of air, I try to slow my heartbeats back to a normal speed, but I'm not sure it's going to happen any time soon.

It's too early even for me to go on a run—when I opened my eyes and glanced at the clock the numbers flashed two a.m.

But I can't imagine going back to sleep. Something stirs in the night, and my head whips to the side, spotting the small glowing ember of a cigarette. Fear spikes inside me at the realization that someone else is awake at this hour and might spot me, but then I realize—

"Thayer," I gasp.

The cigarette disappears and it's too dark for me to see anything. I keep telling my mom we need to install motion lights, but she hasn't listened.

Thayer suddenly appears in our front yard, looking up at me with fear in his eyes. I know I look crazy up here on my hands and knees, my hair matted to my forehead and eyes crazed.

"What the fuck are you doing?" His arms fumble through the air like he thinks he's going to have to catch me.

"Nightmare," I explain.

"And that made you think, "hmm, let me climb on the roof in the middle of the night?'"

"I wasn't thinking clearly." My fingers dig into the shingles.

"Obviously," he snaps, still looking mildly panicked.

"Do you want me to climb down?" I start to crawl forward.

"No!" He cries out, arms flying in the air again. "Go back to your room."

"I don't want to," I confess. "I won't be able to go back to sleep."

He runs his fingers through his hair. "Well, you're not climbing down from the roof." He looks dismayed that I'd even think of trying.

"I've done it before." His eyes widen in horror. *Whoops, wrong thing to say then.* "Why aren't you asleep?" I ask, trying to distract myself and him.

"A lot on my mind."

"So much that you needed to smoke?" I inquire. I've never seen him smoke before, so I don't think it's a regular habit.

He sighs, rubbing a hand over his jaw. "Sometimes I need one when I'm more stressed than normal. It calms me down."

"Interesting." My hand slips from my sweaty palm and Thayer makes a noise below. "I'm okay." I steady myself.

"Get down from there right now. You're stressing me the fuck out and I'm already anxious enough as it is."

"Threats don't work on me."

"How about a deal then?"

"What kind?" I probe, cocking my head to the side.

He shrugs. "I can't sleep, apparently you can't sleep either, so climb back in your room and come down here and we can just talk or whatever. Just please get off the roof."

I press my lips together, thinking over his offer. "Deal."

"Thank God." He exhales a gust of air.

"But you wait right there." I wiggle a finger at him in warning.

He raises his hand. "I'll be in this spot."

Crawling on all fours, I turn myself around and quietly climb back through the window. I close and lock it before stuffing my feet into a pair of sneakers.

Sneaking down the stairs, I slip out the side door and run around to the front of the house where Thayer waits in the same spot he was in, just as he promised.

"I'm glad you didn't die climbing back in your window," he quips. He tips his head toward his house for me to follow.

I roll my eyes, falling into step beside him. "You're being dramatic, I was fine."

"You looked like you were having a panic attack."

I wince. I *was*.

"I had it under control."

He arches a brow, opening the gate that leads to his backyard. "Do you want something to drink?"

I mock-gasp. "Are you offering an underage girl alcohol, Thayer? How scandalous of you."

He lets out a gruff laugh. "I said a *drink*—that includes water and soda."

"You have Diet Coke?" I perk up.

"Yes."

"I'll have that then." I sit down on the back step, looking out at the pool. The water glimmers with the reflection of the nearly full moon.

He arches a brow. "You don't want to come in?"

I shake my head. "No, I need the fresh air."

"Ah, yes, hence you climbing out of your bedroom window at—" He checks his watch. "—two in the morning."

He waits for me to say something but when he sees that I'm not going to he just heads inside to get the soda. He returns less than a minute later, sitting down on the stair beside me. His leg brushes mine, sending a shiver up my spine.

"Here," he says gruffly, extending the bottle my way. "That stuff will rot your teeth, you know."

"Then why do you have it?" I retort, unscrewing the top. The soda fizzles and I take a sip.

"I keep a stock of all kinds of drinks and sodas for my team."

"Ah, your team. You're a football coach too?" I arch a brow, kidding around with him.

"My landscaping team."

"That's nice of you."

"A lot of the guys forget to hydrate, so I started taking a full cooler with me on jobs. I learned pretty quick most of them refuse to drink the right stuff." He wags a water bottle between us.

"This quenches my thirst plenty," I joke, tapping my bottle against his in an awkward cheers.

He shakes his head in amusement. "So, are you going to tell me what that nightmare was that sent you crawling out of a second story window at such an early hour?"

I drop my head, my blonde hair swinging forward to shield my face. It's stringy from the sweat I broke out into in my sleep. "No." My voice is small. Frail. Cracked.

"You don't want to talk about it?" He doesn't wait for me to answer. "Fair enough."

"Are you going to smoke another cigarette?" I'm not sure what makes me ask the question.

"No," he sighs, rubbing his fingers over his lips. "I shouldn't have had one in the first place. My ex..." He pauses, flinching, like he didn't mean to let that slip. "Let's just say she knows how to push my buttons like no other."

"That bad, huh?"

He rubs a hand over his jaw. "I don't want to bad mouth her. We had good times, we made an amazing kid together, but sometimes people just grow apart and sometimes you start to see what you thought you had was all a very beautiful lie."

My eyes narrow in confusion. "What does that mean?"

He shakes his head. "Just manipulative bullshit I finally clued into, and when I started really looking at my life, I realized I was just ... not happy and life's too short for that. I never pictured myself divorced, and I was conflicted because of my son, but I decided he was better off growing up with parents who are separate and happy than together and miserable."

"Makes sense." I nod along. "That's what scares me—not being happy," I elaborate. "Settling. Being complacent."

"It happens all too easily." He drinks his water, his Adam's apple bobbing. "Be smarter than me." He winces. "Fuck, that sounds terrible. To be honest, I wouldn't take any of it back. Like I said, we did have good times, and got an amazing kid out of it." He runs his fingers through his hair. "I'm just digging a hole for myself."

I laugh, bumping his arm lightly with my elbow. "Don't feel bad. I understand what you're saying."

Silence settles between us, only filled by the music of summer's insects.

He knocks his knee against mine. "Does that happen often?"

I jolt from my runaway thoughts. "Huh?"

"The nightmares?"

I give a shaky nod. "It's why I don't sleep a lot and go for a run."

His lips press to a thin line, probably wondering what could've possibly happened to an eighteen-year-old to make her like this. But he doesn't press further.

Instead, he changes the topic of conversation altogether. "I'm

THE CONFIDENCE OF WILDFLOWERS

going to install one of those fences around the pool itself. Hopefully that'll keep anything from happening again like the other day." I wince at the memory of discovering Forrest had snuck back into the pool. "I'm sorry he scared you. I had a long talk with him about it. I mean, we'd already had one so who knows how good it did a second time, but I'm trying. He's only six, but he thinks he's eighteen and can do whatever he wants."

I laugh at that. "Well, he's a great kid."

"He is." He nods. "I can't thank you enough for babysitting some. I like to spend as much time with him as I can, but sometimes—"

I bump his knee with mine. "You're a parent but you still have other obligations. It doesn't mean you love him any less."

He knocks his knee back into mine. "You better try to get back to bed."

"I know," I sigh heavily. "But I won't sleep." He gives me a sympathetic look. "It's okay," I wave away his concern, "I'm used to it."

"Do you ever take sleeping pills?"

I look into the distance, beyond the fence surrounding his entire yard. Behind it is a field of wildflowers that extends for an acre or so before it butts up against a forest. It's protected historical land which is why it was never developed—probably thoroughly haunted land if you ask me—but it is beautiful to look at.

"In the past I have," I admit begrudgingly, "but I hate how they make me feel. So much so that I'd rather go without sleep." Sympathy coats his face. "It's okay," I say by reflex.

His eyes narrow. "No," he shakes his head roughly, brows furrowed, "it's not."

Setting my half-drank Diet Coke beside me, I rub my hands on my legs before standing. "You're right. I better go back home."

"You know," he says before I move, "this doesn't help you with your sleeping problem?" He gives the bottle a light shake.

"Caffeine doesn't hype me up."

He doesn't stop me as I leave, but I feel his eyes follow me as I go.

TWELVE

didn't fall back asleep after I returned home. Instead, I tidied up my room the best I could while everyone else was still sleeping, then went for a run. I don't know if Thayer saw me leave on my run, but he was getting in his truck for work when I returned, his eyes watching me shrewdly. I can tell he's worried I don't sleep enough. It's something I worry about too, but I hate sleeping pills and I can't force my body to sleep when it doesn't want to.

Out of my shower, I dress for the day in a cute summer dress with a floral pattern. I'll be working at the store all day today while my mom works in the back, preparing things for our big summer blow out coming in a few weeks for the end of summer.

Downstairs I find Georgia sitting at the kitchen table with a bowl of her favorite vanilla crunch cereal while our mom pours coffee into a mug.

"Morning," my mom smiles when she spots me, "did you sleep good?"

"Yeah," I lie, tucking a piece of hair behind my ear so she can't see any tells on my face. She'll be upset if she knows it's getting worse. I go to the fridge and pour a glass of orange juice. Popping a piece of bread in the toaster, I turn around as my mom slides into the chair across from Georgia.

Georgia's hazel eyes meet mine. "I was telling mom she should have you introduce her to the new neighbor since you're babysitting for him."

I give her a funny look. "Why?"

She mirrors my expression. "Because mom is a beautiful, single woman who deserves her second chance at love."

My mom blushes, staring into her cup of coffee. She confessed to me once that she feels undeserving of falling in love, not after how awful my father was, and she couldn't protect us. I told her she was being crazy. She's a victim too.

But Thayer?

"He's too young for me," my mom says my next thought, but she doesn't know that one I had right behind it.

That I can't stand the idea of her with Thayer, because *I* like him, and not in a platonic he's kinda-sorta my boss way.

Holy shit.

I have a crush on our neighbor who has to be in his early thirties.

I have a crush, a big one, and I have a boyfriend.

My stomach roils and when my toast pops up, I suddenly don't feel hungry, but I know after my run I have to force something in me.

Grabbing the butter from the fridge, I apply the thinnest layer possible, wrinkling my nose with distaste at the toast in my hand. My mom catches the gesture and frowns.

"Are you feeling sick, honey?"

"I'm fine." I force myself to take a bite. I don't want her making me stay home today.

Georgia finishes her cereal, drinking the last of the milk out of the bowl and rinsing it. "I've gotta get to the hospital." She grabs me and places a loud, dramatic kiss on top of my head. "Love you, guys." She kisses Mom's cheek.

Scooping up her bag and car keys, she's out the door and gone.

Mom shakes her head. "That girl has always been a hurricane."

It's a good way to describe Georgia. Wild, unpredictable, a tad dramatic.

Sometimes I wish I could take a page out of her book and let go more. I know I can be too uptight at times.

"Are you sure you're okay?"

"Huh?" I jolt back to reality.

"You seem really out of it," she explains. "Are you okay?"

"Y-Yeah. Just a lot on my mind," I stutter, finishing my toast and brushing crumbs off my dress. My mom eyes the mess now on the ground and I give a small laugh. Grabbing the vacuum from the pantry I sweep them up.

"Is it about Caleb?" she questions when the vacuum cuts off.

I almost blurt out *no*, but I realize she's just given me an excellent out for my behavior. "It is," I lie, easily, too easily, "it just sucks that he's leaving so soon."

She doesn't remind me that I could've gone with him, or headed off to a college of my choice, we both know I've already turned down those options. She's never asked me why and I'm glad for that, because frankly, I don't know. I just know that I'm a little lost right now and I'm not going to find myself that way.

Her lips downturn sympathetically as I stick the vacuum back where it belongs. "I know it sucks, honey."

"I'll get over it," I mumble, hoping we can move on from this topic of conversation. It's not that I won't miss Caleb, I *will*, but I don't know that I'm going to miss him as much as I should.

She moves Georgia's bowl from the sink to the drying rack. "If you don't mind, go on over to the store and open up. I'll be there in another hour or so." Her shoulders fall tiredly.

I narrow my eyes at the gesture. "Is everything okay?"

She sighs, rubbing a hand over her face. "Yes."

I don't believe her, but I'm lying as well, so I'll let her keep her secrets too.

ICED COFFEE IN HAND, I CROSS THE STREET TO A CHECKERED Past Antiques and unlock the door, switching the sign on the door to OPEN.

I flick lights on as I go, setting my bag down behind the counter.

Luckily, my vanilla iced coffee tastes way better than my toast did.

Settling behind the counter, I flip through a magazine left there by my mom. You can never predict days at the store. Sometimes it's constant traffic in and out and other times it's dead to the world. I know my mom's been lucky that the store is popular enough that people from the city make the trek all the way here to seek out unique pieces for their homes.

My phone vibrates with a text, and I grab it in case it's my mom asking me to do something.

It's Lauren. A smiling selfie stares back at me as she holds up peace fingers, her eyes shielded by a tiny pair of sunglasses. The ocean reflects behind her. She's gone for the week on vacation, soon that'll be Caleb too. My mom mentioned maybe taking a short trip somewhere, I think she felt bad since all my friends are getting vacations, but I told her not to worry about it. Money is tight and I don't want her spending unnecessary dollars on a frivolous trip. She dropped it and didn't bring it up again.

Me: I hope you have so much fun!

Lauren: I wish you were here!

Me: Me too.

I'm sure a beach trip would be fun, but secretly, I'm glad to be here.

Home is where I want to be.

Where I need to be.

Besides, no matter where I go or what I do, the nightmares will always find me.

THIRTEEN

"**G**o Fish," Forrest says, and I grab another card off the coffee table, eyeing the massive amount of cards in my hands. Either I suck at Go Fish, Forrest forgot the rules, or the little devil is cheating.

From his coy grin my vote is on cheating.

Keys rattle in the front door and Forrest tosses down his cards, the much smaller amount than mine scattering everywhere. "Dad!" His feet pound on the floor as he runs for the foyer. I pick up his cards and stack them along with mine, putting everything back in the box.

"Hey, buddy, did you miss me?" I hear Thayer say in reply.

"Yeah! Did you bring me a pizza?"

"That's what's in my hands."

"You're the best dad ever."

Forrest runs past the archway of the living room, heading toward the kitchen, with a Pizza Hut personal pizza clasped in his hands.

I pick up a throw blanket from the floor and fold it, returning it to the back of the couch. Thayer clears his throat, leaning against the archway. Brown hair tumbles over his forehead messily, and not in the purposeful way like so many of the boys I went to school with tried to achieve. This is just pure mess and I love it.

Pressing a hand to my chest, I mock gasp. "And where is *my* pizza?"

He chuckles softly, rubbing the back of his hand. "Stolen by a pigeon."

"Damn carrier pigeons," I cluck my tongue, "can't trust them."

"It's true," he shrugs, easily playing along. "They work for the government."

I throw my hands up in pretend frustration. "I hope the pigeon enjoys my pizza."

"I'll ask him if I see him again."

"Him?" I arch my brow. "How do you know it wasn't a girl pigeon?"

"Could've been," he concedes, stepping into the room. He drops his crossed arms to his sides. "Thanks for watching him."

I wave away his thanks. "No problem." He pulls out his wallet and grabs some cash, passing it to me. "Thanks."

He dips his head in acknowledgment.

"Salem," Forrest calls from the kitchen, "do you have to go home?"

I glance at Thayer. "I can stay a while longer," I whisper in case Thayer wants me to go. I totally understand if he wants time with his kid.

He shrugs. "You can stay if you want."

"All right," I say louder so Forrest will hear me, "I'll stay for a little while longer."

An hour later I find myself curling up on Thayer's couch with a bowl of popcorn. Forrest sits on one side of me, leaning his small body against mine, Thayer on the other careful to keep six inches of space between us.

On the TV, *The Santa Clause* plays. Apparently, those movies are Forrest's favorite, and it doesn't matter that it's July, he wants to watch them anyway.

"Daddy," he asks, crunching popcorn between his teeth, "do you think I'm on the naughty or nice list?"

"Definitely nice," Thayer nods at this, "but that can always change. That's why you have to always be on your best behavior. Santa is always watching."

"This is true," I agree.

Forrest looks up at me with wide eyes while on the TV screen Tim Allen climbs up a ladder in his boxers. "Have you ever been on the naughty list? Does he really give you coal?"

I love that Forrest doesn't wait for me to answer the first question before adding the second, like he automatically assumes I've been on the naughty list at some point.

I shake my head. "Nope, always the nice list for me."

He frowns, dejected at not having a proper answer to his naughty list question. "Do you know anyone who was on the naughtly list?" He tries again.

"Nope, sorry."

"What about—"

"I thought you wanted to watch a movie?" Thayer butts in.

"I do," Forrest replies enthusiastically.

"Then why aren't you watching it?"

"Oh, right." He fixes his gaze back on the TV screen.

The living room is in much better shape than the kitchen. The floors are finished, the walls painted, and the comfy sectional is obviously brand new. Thayer's even mounted the TV above the fireplace.

Thayer reaches over for popcorn, his fingers grazing mine in the process. Our eyes meet. I'm the first to look away, dropping my stare to the kernels. He puts another couple of inches between us. Almost a whole foot.

Interesting.

I force myself to focus on the movie and not the man beside me.

As the evening progresses, the popcorn moves to the coffee table and Forrest's head drops to my lap. Despite his soft snores, neither Thayer nor I make a move to stop the movie and get up. When the end credits roll, Forrest is still passed out. My fingers glide idly through his hair.

Thayer stands up with a groan, stretching his arms above his head and exposing smooth, muscular abdominals, deeply tanned from all his time in the sun.

Stop staring! He's practically your boss!

And much older than me. But I'm not sure exactly how much.

"How old are you?" I blurt.

Thayer gives me a funny look. "Thirty. I'll be thirty-one next month. Why?"

"No reason," my voice squeaks.

Thirteen years—almost fourteen. That's more than an entire decade.

My face heats at my thoughts, but if he notices he doesn't say anything. He bends down, scooping Forrest into his arms. He brushes my arm, glancing at me and muttering, "Sorry."

I hope he doesn't notice the shiver that rushes down my spine.

"It's okay." I tuck a piece of hair behind my ear and stand, grabbing the popcorn bowl.

Thayer heads upstairs, carrying Forrest. I dump the last of the popcorn in the trash and rinse the bowl in the downstairs bathroom sink since there's currently not one in the kitchen.

I'm headed for the door to let myself out when Thayer comes down. He runs his fingers through his hair, looking tired.

"You're headed out?" I nod in reply. "Have a good night." I press my lips together at that, thinking about how I rarely have a good night of rest. He notices my expression and adds, "Maybe you'll sleep."

"Maybe," I echo. There's always a chance.

FOURTEEN

A shrill scream wakes me up at eight in the morning. I didn't have any nightmares, but that's only because I didn't go to sleep until four in the morning. My eyes barely want to open, but I force them to.

"God, you're such a pain in my ass!" The yelling starts up again.

Yawning, I slide out of my bed. Binx is in the corner on his cat tree, craning his neck to peer out the window.

"I'm so glad I divorced you!" The same voice screams.

I open my window, poking my head out to find the woman I saw before who's clearly Thayer's ex, standing on his front porch poking him repeatedly in the chest. She's short, having to stretch her neck nearly all the way back in order to see him.

Thayer's voice isn't as loud, but it is still raised, and our houses

72

are close enough together for me to hear him. "I asked for the divorce."

She throws her hands up. "You infuriating—"

"You're making a scene," he remarks, nodding his head across the street to where our elderly neighbor, Cynthia, has stepped outside on her front porch, sweeping the already immaculate stoop.

She looks over her shoulder briefly before focusing back on him. "I don't care. Let them hear. Let them all hear!" She throws her arms out wide.

Thayer merely shakes his head. He's in a pair of sleep pants and a cotton shirt, his hair messy like he hasn't been awake long. "You're making a fuss, Forrest asked for five minutes to get his stuff and I said to take all the time he needed."

"Exactly!" She cries like he's just proven the point of her entire meltdown. "You're trying to steal him from me! Manipulate him like—"

"Krista." His voice is a biting reprimand. "Do you hear yourself? He's a child. He's finishing packing his things."

She bites her cheek, glancing to her right where she spots me hanging out the window eavesdropping.

Shit, I've been caught.

I pop back into my room and close the window. Listening time is over.

"Well, Binx," I eye my curious cat, "that sure was interesting."

I take a hasty shower and put on a minimal amount of makeup. Caleb is supposed to pick me up for breakfast at nine, so it's not like I could've slept much longer anyway.

He doesn't know about my insomnia, the nightmares, restless sleep. It's not something I've wanted to burden him with. Caleb has enough on his plate.

I hastily dry my hair—well, half dry it—and pull it into a bun. I glance at the clock and I have less than ten minutes until he's due to show up. I swipe some mascara on my lashes and dot gloss on my lips.

My phone vibrates by the sink with a text.

Caleb: Be there in 5.

I head downstairs, sitting on the front porch. My shoelace has come untied on my right foot, so I bend down and retie it. A shadow falls over me and I look up, expecting to see Caleb, my smile ready for him. But it's Thayer. He's changed clothes—a pair of athletic shorts and a shirt with the sleeves cutoff. I try not to check out his biceps but fail immediately.

"Hi," I squeak at the man that towers above me.

His dirty tennis shoes toe the ground. "I'm sorry about this morning. What you overheard."

I arch a brow. "Are you going door to door apologizing to everyone on the street?"

"No," he admits. "Just you."

I place a hand over my heart. "Aw, I'm special."

He doesn't say anything, but his eyes say *you are*. I try not to read into that, in case it's my imagination playing tricks on me.

He looks away, shoving his hands in his pockets. He does that a lot when he's uncomfortable or nervous.

I draw a circle around a bruise on my knee. "I don't really understand why you're apologizing for someone else's behavior, though?"

He winces. "You're right, I shouldn't, but—"

"She's an adult. Her actions only reflect on herself. If she hasn't figured that out yet, that's on her."

Staring off into space, he nods woodenly.

Caleb pulls his car into the driveway, and Thayer narrows his eyes on the small vehicle.

"We're going to breakfast," I explain, even though I don't owe him an explanation.

"Well," he steps back, "enjoy your breakfast."

He throws his hand up in a wave at Caleb, though his expression is anything but friendly. Caleb raises his hand in response, also glowering. Men are so weird.

Hopping into the car, I lean over and kiss Caleb. "Hi," I say brightly. "Morning."

"Morning." His voice is still thick with sleep.

"You sound tired."

"A little," he admits. "Dad's running me ragged."

I frown. I hate that Caleb is so busy this summer, working, preparing for college ball, and not getting any break at all.

"I'm sorry."

He reaches over and entwines our fingers together on his leg. "At least we can have breakfast this morning."

"That's true," I brighten. His hand is warm in mine, rough from lifting weights and practice.

"You want the windows down or up?"

"Down." I bounce in my seat a little, eager to feel the air on my face.

He chuckles, accommodating me even though I know he hates having them down. Wisps of hair that escape my bun smack against my face. I ignore it, breathing in the fresh summer air.

A few minutes later he parks outside our favorite breakfast diner filled with greasy, artery clogging food. AKA the good stuff.

Maybe not good for your body, but delicious for your taste buds.

Caleb hops out and I follow him inside. The place is busy, like usual, but we find a table in a back corner and sit down. I swipe a menu from the napkin holder, perusing the items.

Caleb watches me with an amused tilt of his lips.

"What?" I look at him over top of the plastic menu.

"We come here all the time and you always look at the menu."

I shrug, flipping it over to scan the back. "You never know, I might change my mind and order something different one of these times. Plus, what if they add something new to the menu or get rid of—"

"If it isn't my two favorite people." Darla, our usual waitress, smiles down on us, tapping her BIC pen against her notepad. "The usual? Veggie omelet and Diet Coke for you," she points at me, "sausage, egg, and cheese biscuit with hash browns and water for you?" Her pointed finger moves to Caleb.

"Yes and yes," he tells her.

"You got it."

She heads over, already hollering our order out to the cook.

"What does your mom have on your agenda today?" I ask him.

He winces. It's subtle but I don't miss it. I didn't mean to make a dig at his mom, but it's a legitimate question.

"We're heading to the mall later. There are some things she wants to get before we go to the beach, and she's got this whole big ass list of things she says I need for school. I told her I don't think I'm allowed to have a toaster in my room, but she won't listen."

Darla drops our drinks off and I mouth *thank you*, already ripping off the paper from my straw. I take a sip. Sweet sustenance. Some people rely on coffee—and don't get me wrong I like that too—but Diet Coke is my drug of choice. Okay, probably a bad way to phrase that.

I ball up the paper wrapper. "I wish I knew why your mom hates me."

"She doesn't hate you." I give him a look and he lowers his head. "Maybe a little, but it's nothing personal. I think she's scared that you're going to take me away from her, but she'd feel that way with any girl I dated."

"Any girl, huh?" I joke. "Are you saying I'm not special?"

He chuckles. "That's not what I'm saying at all."

"Good." I toss the wrapper at him playfully. He peels it off his shirt and slides it back across the table to me. He knows I play with my wrappers through every meal.

"Have you thought any more about what you're going to do?" He pulls the sugar dish closer to him, reorganizing the multicolored packets.

"What do you mean?" I look up from the balled-up piece of paper in my hands.

He raises a brow. "Salem, you can't work at your mom's shop forever."

His words sting. I love working there. What's so wrong with that? "No, I don't know, and that's the whole point of not going to college. I need time to think."

"And what if you still don't know then?"

"Why are you giving me the third degree?" I demand, feeling defensive. He's my boyfriend. He's supposed to be on my side, right?

His shoulders sag. "I'm not trying to be a hard ass. I just want you to find something that makes you happy."

"I *am* happy. I love making my candles and working for my mom. It's nice babysitting Thayer's son, too."

Caleb frowns at the mention of Thayer. I'm not sure he'll ever like my neighbor after their horrific first encounter. "I just wish you knew what you wanted to do."

He's known since practically forever that he wanted to play football and go to law school. He can't fathom someone not knowing what they want to do with their life. Just like I can't relate to someone being so certain. I'm not the same person I was a year ago, I can't imagine settling into a plan and trusting it to work, not when future me is a stranger. I'm trying to get to know her, so I know she'll be happy. That's all.

Darla sets our plates down, refills of our drinks as well. "Enjoy, guys."

I dig in immediately, not having realized how hungry I was until the food was placed in front of me.

"Hungry?" Caleb smiles in amusement.

"Starving. I'm pretty sure this is the best thing I've eaten all week." I point my fork at the omelet.

"So, you're saying I need to be a better boyfriend and feed you more often?" He jokes playfully.

"Definitely. Food is the way to my heart."

"Man, I wish I would've known that before I got these." My brows raise at his segue. He slides his hand into his pocket and pulls out two rectangular pieces of paper. He slides them across the table to me and I pick them up, squinting at the tiny print.

My mouth drops. "Concert tickets? For Willow Creek? Are you kidding me?" I gape at the tickets, shocked. They're one of the biggest bands in the *world* right now. Selling out whole stadiums. I tried to get tickets and got kicked off the website for some stupid reason. "How did you even get these?"

He grins, pleased by my reaction. "I have my ways."

"If we weren't in the middle of a restaurant, I'd kiss you right now."

He chuckles. "Kiss me anyway." He leans across the table, and I do the same, our lips meeting halfway. His hand cups the back of my head, holding me there a little longer before releasing me.

"This is," I stare at the tickets in my hand, "amazing. Wow." His grin says everything. "Thank you."

"You don't have to thank me, babe."

I look at the date on the tickets. It's a few days before Caleb moves to Boston. It's a bittersweet feeling knowing we'll get to go together but that he'll be leaving so shortly after.

But that's life.

It's fluid, always moving, always changing. You either flow with it or you drown.

FIFTEEN

"**M**ichael! What are you doing here?" My sister's shrill shriek, not a happy one, echoes through the house. I glance at Binx who sits on the desk in my room while I flip through a magazine.

"Babe," I hear Michael's pleading voice on the other side, "I'm sorry. I'm really sorry."

"That's the problem," my sister volleys, "you're always sorry for something. How about you don't do something to be sorry about in the first place?"

The door slams and then Michael immediately hits the doorbell.

I should be used to the fact that these two constantly fight and break up then make up a week later, but it's exhausting. I wish they'd either break up for good or stay together. It can't be that difficult.

"Ugh, what?" Georgia must swing the door open again.

79

"I got you flowers."

I ease out of my desk chair, poking my head out the door to try to peep down the stairs. Michael stands there with a bouquet of white daisies—Georgia's favorite—clasped in his hands. It's a big bundle too, not one of those cheap bouquets from the grocery store.

"They're beautiful." Her voice begins to go all lovey dovey.

"I swear I wasn't looking at that chick's ass."

I snort and both turn to look up the stairs, but I think I manage to pull my head back inside fast enough. Not that they won't know it was me anyway.

"Let's talk outside," Georgia says to him, the door closing behind her.

Alas, my entertainment has disappeared.

I return to my desk and magazine. My notebook rests beside it with candle scent ideas as well as possible names. I turned my attention to the magazine when my brain started to get tired.

Scratching Binx behind his ear, I tell my beloved cat, "I'm so happy Caleb and I aren't like those two."

He purrs in agreement. I tug my notebook closer to me, pop my earbuds in, and get back to brainstorming.

"YOU MADE DINNER?" MY MOM GASPS, SETTING HER BAG down by the door. "I was going to suggest we order pizza."

I shrug. "We had stuff we needed to use up in the fridge." I slide the casserole out of the oven, tucking the mitts under my arm. I grab the rolls I heated up and start plating.

My mom grabs the plates and puts them on the table. Glancing at me over her shoulder, she suggests, "Why don't you ask the neighbor if he wants to come over for dinner? He got in at the same time as me. I'm sure he's hungry and this is already made. Besides, Georgia is with Michael tonight."

"Thayer?" I ask stupidly.

"Yes," she says slowly, giving me a funny look.

I almost ask *why*, but I realize she's only trying to be nice. "Um, okay," I hesitate, my fingers curling against the counter. "I'll go ask him."

She's already making an extra plate, like it's a given that he'll be joining us as I head next door. Head down, I shuffle hurriedly down our driveway and over to Thayer's house, bounding up the front porch and knocking, since I know the doorbell is disabled at the moment since he's replacing it.

I don't have to wait long before I hear heavy boots thudding against the floor. The door swings open and—

Oh my God.

The plaid shirt he wears is unbuttoned revealing a tanned, well-muscled chest speckled with chest hair. I'm staring, God am I staring, but I can't look away. Thayer is the perfect specimen of man. I have to force my hands to stay at my sides, so I don't poke him to test if he's real or not.

"Hey," he says, sounding tired.

"Hi." My voice sounds smaller than normal, an octave higher.

"Did you need something?" He prompts when I stand there stupidly.

"Oh, yeah, my mom wanted to invite you over for dinner. I made a casserole. There's plenty, so it's no trouble."

He cocks his head to the side, thinking over my proposal. "All right."

For some reason I didn't expect him to agree so easily. He starts rebuttoning his shirt and I try to hide my frown at the disappearance of his perfect chest.

You shouldn't be staring at him. I silently scold myself. *You have a boyfriend.*

Tucking a piece of hair behind my ear, I take a few steps back as Thayer shuts the door behind him.

"Casserole, huh?" He seems amused by my meal choice.

"There were a lot of random things in the fridge, so casserole seemed like a safe bet."

"Do you like to cook?"

I nod. "Yeah, I do actually." I open the side door and wave him inside first, but he insists on waiting for me.

"Oh, good!" My mom claps her hands together. "I hoped you'd agree to dinner."

Thayer dips his head. "I appreciate the offer. I've been living off McDonald's and frozen meals."

My mom frowns. "That's awful. Well, it's no trouble at all. You're welcome to have dinner with us anytime or Salem can run leftovers over to you so you don't have to eat with us."

"You don't have to do that."

"It's no trouble at all. Plates are on the table. What would you like to drink? We have," she opens the fridge, "water, Sprite, Diet Coke, there's some beer too."

"I'll just take a water. I don't need the caffeine this late or I'll be up all night."

She laughs, filling a glass of water for him. "Man, I wish Salem was like that, but this girl can drink copious amounts of caffeine and be perfectly fine."

"What can I say?" I shrug, grabbing a Diet Coke. "I'm blessed."

Thayer watches me, amusement sparkling in his brown eyes. He follows me to the table and for some reason I'm surprised when he pulls out the chair beside mine and sits down. I expected him to take the one on the end.

My mom pours a glass of wine, a rarity for her, before joining us at the table. I study her appearance, noting the dark circles beneath her eyes. I wonder if, like me, she's not getting much sleep.

"Thank you for having me over," Thayer says before we all dig in, "it's really nice to have a homecooked meal."

My mom waves her hand away. "It's no trouble at all and we always have plenty."

This is true. I always seem to make an abundance of food. Especially pasta—I can't seem to get the serving size down and just keep adding more noodles to the water.

We eat our first couple of bites in silence before my mom asks him a question. "Where are you originally from, Thayer? Do you have family nearby?"

He shakes his head. "My folks are in Florida, they moved there after they retired, and I have a brother out in Colorado. If you count my ex-wife, she's just a few towns over."

82

"You have a brother?" I blurt.

It's not like Thayer and I sit around and paint each other's nails, having lengthy conversations about our lives, but this serves as a reminder of how little I truly know about him.

"Mhmm." He nods, taking another bite of food.

"Is he older than you?" I find myself curious about this brother I've never heard of. He doesn't have any personal photos in his home, either, at least not yet, so I haven't been able to get an idea of his family life other than his ex and son.

"No," he chuckles, like the idea of his brother being older than him is preposterous. "Laith is twenty-six."

"Do you see your family often?" I'm thankful for my mom taking over the conversation. I drop my eyes to my plate of food, pushing it around with my fork.

"When I can. I try to take a trip down to Florida every winter to stay with my parents for a bit."

"That's nice," my mom smiles, "I'm sure they're always happy to see you."

He jerks his head in a nod. "They come up here some too. Usually in the fall. They make a road trip out of it because my dad hates to fly." He gives a sudden laugh. "He'll tell you it's my mom that hates flying, but nah, that's all him."

"Men love to blame their wives for their fallacies." My mom pales, realizing her blunder. "Not *all* men, of course, but some—"

Thayer cracks a smile. "I understand what you're saying."

Her cheeks color. "My husband—he's passed—but he was..." She flounders, searching for the right words to say in front of a relative stranger.

"Not the best," I finish for her.

Thayer's eyes ping-pong between us. I'm sure he's taking in that a lot is being left unsaid. "I'd say I'm sorry for your loss, but I'm not sure that's the right thing to say here."

My lips thin, trying not to laugh.

"Oh, uh, it's all right. Sorry is fine, or not sorry, either or." It's rare for my mom to get so flustered. "I'm going to see if we have any dessert." She shoves her chair back and scurries over to the refrigerator.

I feel Thayer's eyes on me, but he won't dare ask something, not with my mom present. I'm sure he's formulating plenty for another time. I push my food back and forth some more and then his big warm hand settles atop mine.

"If I have to watch you push your food around for another minute, I'm going to force feed you." My jaw drops at his statement. "Good, you're halfway there already." He tries to take my fork from me to, no doubt, shove food in my mouth.

"Okay, okay," I say, getting his point. "I'll eat." I heap casserole onto my fork and put enough in my mouth that it's overfull.

My mom returns to the table with a defeated expression. "We don't have any dessert. I haven't made any lately and—"

"Mom," I quiet her, "it's fine."

She gives me a grateful look and takes her seat once more. She finishes eating at the same time we all do and goes to gather the plates.

"No, let me." Thayer stands, taking her plate from her and stacking his and then mine on top.

"Oh, you don't need to do that," she insists. "You're our guest."

"It's no trouble." He's already walking toward the sink.

"I'll help. You can go on up to bed," I tell her, worried about those dark circles beneath her eyes.

She doesn't argue so it's only further confirmation that she's truly tired.

Thayer carries everything over to the sink, thanking her again for the dinner invite. We wait to speak until her footsteps disappear upstairs.

"Dinner was delicious," he says, running water in the sink.

"Thanks. My mom's not kidding, we always have plenty, so feel free to pop over anytime."

"Are you worried I'm not eating enough?" He arches a brow as if to say *he's* the one worried about *me*.

"We always have extra, that's all." I shrug off the real question he's asking.

He cleans the plates and passes them to me to dry. My mom would love a dishwasher, but every time she finally thinks she's getting one something invariably happens that she has to use the money for instead.

"Your dad," he prompts, and I immediately begin shaking my head, not wanting to delve down that path. "There's more there, I know it."

"There is," I confirm, "but I don't want to talk about it."

"Salem—"

My fingers curl against the counter, knuckles turning white. "I don't want to talk about it," I bite out. "He's dead, gone, and that's all that matters."

Thayer studies me through narrowed eyes. I can see the words on the tip of his tongue, how he wants to ask what happened, to demand answers from me. Instead, he ducks his head and utters one word. "Okay."

He lets the water out from the sink, turns his back on me, and walks right out the door.

SIXTEEN

"You look thirsty." I hold out a bottle of water to Thayer. Sweat clings to his tanned skin, dampening his hair. The extended plastic bottle is a peace offering. We haven't spoken in days. I don't like it one bit. Somewhere, along the way, Thayer has become my friend. It feels weird not speaking.

He hesitates, eyeing the bottle and my hand, refusing to meet my eyes. I almost think he's going to reject my offer and ignore me all together. The rejection stings and I start to pull the bottle back toward me, but he reaches out with quick reflexes and swipes it.

A gruff, "Thanks," leaves his lips.

I toe my worn shoe against the deck. "What are you doing?" I eye the wooden pieces scattered around him. I can deduce what he's building on my own, but I want to make him talk to me. Something more than one word.

"A swing."

Well, at least it was two words.

"Why?"

He doesn't look at me, searching the deck for a specific piece. "Because I want a porch swing."

I lean against the column. I'm not going to allow his dismissive tone to force me to leave. "What are you going to do with this porch swing?"

Yes, I'm pushing. For more words, more anything.

He pauses, screwdriver in hand. "Swing on it."

I sigh, crossing my arms over my side. "Are you mad at me?" I cringe as soon as the question leaves my mouth. It sounds so juvenile.

He arches a brow, settling his hands on the top of his thighs. "What gave you that idea?"

"You're in a bad mood," I state, but I make no move to leave.

He lets out a gruff laugh. "I'm usually in a bad mood." He's quiet for a moment, searching for a piece on the ground. "It's nothing to do with you."

"Do you want to talk about it?"

He glares at me. "Do you?"

Translation: If I'm not sharing, he's not either.

"I never want to talk about my dad," I supply, looking away.

"And I," he groans, stretching to reach something else, "don't like talking about my ex. I guess we're even."

"I guess so." I bend down and pass him the piece I think he's looking for. His glare settles on my hand, and he swipes it from me without a thank you. I don't let his grumpy attitude ruffle my feathers. "Do you want any help?"

He opens his mouth, I'm sure to say no, but he sighs and runs a hand through his hair. "You want to help?" He sounds entirely doubtful.

"Sure."

"All right." I think it takes a lot for him to concede.

I make myself comfortable—well, as comfortable as I can get—on the porch, settling in to help him.

We don't speak except for when he asks me to pass him something. I'm fine with that. I don't need conversation. It's nice to exist with someone without the need to fill every silence. It's taken me a long time to become comfortable with my own thoughts.

Thayer finishes putting the swing together faster than I'd think possible.

He already has metal hooks drilled into the ceiling and he lets me help balance the swing as he attaches some sort of thick rope to the hooks.

When it's all done, he steps back to assess his handiwork, hands on his hips.

"It looks good."

He jerks his head down once, the nod the only acknowledgment he gives of his handiwork. He turns toward his front door, and I expect him to go inside without saying anything more to me, but he pauses, waiting.

"You coming?" I smile, following him inside. He leads me to the kitchen and opens the mini fridge. He pulls out deli meat, mayonnaise, and lettuce. "Do you want a sandwich?"

"Sure," I reply, taking in the base cabinets that have been installed. They're missing the doors, but at least it's progress.

"What do you want?"

I shrug, pulling a chair out at the card table. "You can make it the same as yours. I'm not picky."

He makes the sandwiches in silence and plops a plate down in front of me without ceremony, pulling the chair out across the table.

"Thanks."

"Mhmm."

I eye him before taking a bite of my sandwich. "You're a man of few words, aren't you?" He gives me a funny look. Brows furrowed, nose scrunched. "That must've driven your ex-wife crazy."

His sighs running his fingers through his hair. "I don't want to talk about her. And need I remind you, that not everybody is perfect."

I wipe a crumb from my mouth. And think about what I'm going to say next. "Nobody is perfect," I agree, nodding at my own words. "But that doesn't mean that we shouldn't be aware of our flaws. If we're not mindful of them, then we can't improve on them."

Thayer grunts an unintelligible response. "You're wiser than me."

I don't know about that. I look away. "Some days I feel so much older than I am, and some I feel so much younger than I am." I don't think that he realizes how big of a confession this is for me. It took a lot for me to admit that.

He studies me with narrowed brown eyes. I think he sees more than I want him to see. Maybe even knows more than I've said or thought or confessed. I wonder idly if perhaps I could share the darker parts of myself with him. But it's terrifying to think about letting somebody in like that. Not even Caleb, who I've been with for years, knows everything. Lauren does, but she's my best friend. You can't not tell your best friend all the pieces of you. I know I should tell Caleb. He deserves the truth. But for some reason I can't bring myself to. It makes me sick to think that I might share those parts of myself with Thayer and not him. Maybe it's because Thayer is older that I feel like he could handle it better. I guess that's a backwards way of thinking, since Lauren is the same age as Caleb. But I can't help but feel that Caleb just couldn't handle it. The last thing I want is for my boyfriend to look at me differently. To see someone who's not whole. I just want to be Salem to him. That's who I want to be to everybody. I know, though, that this truth can always change how people think of me and how they see me. I'm lucky to have a friend like Lauren because she never, not once saw me as broken or less than anyone else.

"Where did you go?" He asks softly.

"Just lost in my thoughts." I force a smile, but I know there's a shadow in my eyes. And from the way he looks at me, I know he sees it too.

Maybe one day, I think to myself. *I'll tell him.*

Someone else in this world should hear my truth.

SEVENTEEN

"Cat!" Forrest screams, running out of his dad's truck.

Ever since I told him about the cat in *Sabrina the Teenage Witch* named Salem, he's taken to calling me Cat. I think it's cute and I like that we have a thing that's just ours. Thayer shakes his head at his kid.

Forrest barrels into me, hitting me full force in the legs with his body weight. I rock back, steadying myself. "Whoa, bud."

"Hi." He tilts his chin back, taking me in. "Are you coming over today?"

I glance at Thayer, unloading Forrest's bag from his truck. "I don't think your dad needs me today."

"Dad!" The little boy shrieks. "Can Salem come over? I want her to swim with me."

Thayer's eyes meet mine, trying to silently communicate with me if I'm okay with that or if I want him to tell Forrest I'm busy. I don't have anything better to do. Caleb's at the gym and then going out with his friends. Lauren is with her boyfriend of the week.

I shrug. "I don't mind."

Thayer nods. "Head over when you feel like it."

Forrest tosses his hands in the air, letting out a whoop of joy. "Let's go swimming, Cat!" He grabs my hand, trying to yank me forward.

"Hold up," I tell him, taking my hand back. "I have to put my swimsuit on."

"Oh." His face falls.

I tweak his nose. "I'll be right over after I change."

"Wait!" He brightens again. I've already taken two steps away from him. "Can I meet your cat? Binx, right?"

I look to Thayer. "I don't mind," I say.

"If you're okay with it. I'm going to unload the groceries."

"My dad got me more Kid's Cuisines," Forrest whispers conspiratorially. "He told me I'm going to turn into a dinosaur chicken nugget if I keep eating so many, but I don't think that's possible."

"There are worse things you could be than a dinosaur chicken nugget."

"True," Forrest follows me in through the side door, "I could be a murderer."

I glance back at the child. "Should I be afraid of you?"

"I don't know." He stares at me with large round eyes. Then he lifts his hands in a clawing gesture. "Rawr!"

I pretend to be terrified. "Come on, this way." I curl my finger for him to follow me upstairs to my room. Binx sits perched on his cat tree, watching us with careful green eyes. "I brought you a friend, Binx. Say hi."

"*Meow.*"

"See, he said hi," I tell Forrest.

"Hi, Binx." Forrest waves. "Can I pet him?"

"Sure." I step away and let Forrest take my place. He reaches up, letting Binx smell his hand before he scratches him behind the ear. My cat immediately starts to purr. "Aw, he likes you."

"He does?"

"Yep." I open my dresser drawer, pulling out my bathing suit. "You hang here with Binx, and I'm going to change in the bathroom."

"Okay." He's too taken up with Binx to care much about anything else.

After I've changed, I return to find Forrest sitting on my bedroom floor with Binx curled up in his lap.

"I wish my dad would let me get a cat," he says, patting Binx's side.

"Maybe one day. You never know." I pull my hair back into a ponytail and yank on some shorts over my swimsuit.

"True. I'll keep asking."

"Are you ready to head back to your house?"

He frowns down at Binx. "I guess so."

Hands on my hips, I say, "Well, jeez, don't sound so excited to go swimming with me."

He brightens. "Oh, right! Swimming!"

I lift Binx off his lap and put him back on his tree. "Come on, Forrest," I hold my hand out to the child, "let's go swimming."

THIRTY MINUTES INTO SWIMMING AND THE BACK DOOR opens. Thayer steps out in only a pair of swim trunks hanging low on his hips, revealing every perfectly sculped muscle in his chest and abdomen. He even has that V-shape so many guys work hard to achieve dipping beneath the band of the board shorts.

My thighs clench together.

Stop staring at your boss like that! He's thirteen years older than you!

The reminders do nothing to quench the desire pulsing through my body.

He slips a pair of sunglasses onto his face and joins us at the pool edge.

"Having fun?"

"So much fun!" Forrest replies, splashing water when he lifts his arms in the air. "We've been playing Marco Polo."

"I wanted to play mermaids," I explain.

"That's for girls," Forrest repeats the argument he gave me from the start.

"And I am a girl," I retort, trying not to laugh.

Thayer shakes his head, but I can see his amusement in the slight uptick of his lips. "Mind if I join?"

I shrug, swimming backwards. "It's your pool."

Translation: I'm not going to stop you.

Thayer steps into the pool and I watch the water ripple against his waist when he reaches the five-foot section. My eyes trail up his toned stomach, the smattering of hair on his chest and around his naval. Then, to my horror, my boss splashes water at me and says, "Eyes up here, Salem."

I flush all over at being called out. He's smiling though, amused. At least he's not pissed, but I mean, talk about embarrassing. I want to hide my face behind my hands, but I make no move to do so because I feel like that would only please him more.

"Come on, Dad," Forrest tries to climb on his dad's back, "let's play."

Thayer scoops Forrest up easily, practically holding him upside down. His laughter fills the air and Thayer dunks his hair in the water.

There's a newly installed pool fence around the perimeter now, but when I came out here with Forrest it did little to stop him. He flipped the lock and dove right in. The kid is fearless, and I think that's both a good thing and a bad thing.

Thayer lets Forrest go and the boy swims over to me, smacking a wet hand against my arm. "Tag, you're it."

"Oh," I laugh, already swimming after the little guppy, "we're playing tag now, huh?"

His laughter fills the air as I chase him, Thayer shaking his head as he watches us. I never imagined this was how I would be spending my summer, but honestly this is so much better.

An hour or so later, we climb out of the pool—a tired Forrest complaining that he's most definitely not tired at all—and Thayer towels off his chest, passing me one to dry with.

"Thanks." I take it gratefully and wrap it around my body.

"I'll grab you some cash."

My brows scrunch. "Why?"

He hesitates, giving me an equally confused look. "For hanging out with Forrest."

I shake my head. "No, no. This was just for fun. You didn't ask me to watch him."

"But—"

"No," I insist. "Seriously, Thayer."

He still looks hesitant, but he nods. "Okay."

"Forrest," I call out, since the little boy has already run inside.

"Yes?" He pokes his head out the door, Poptart in hand.

"I'm heading home, so I wanted to say bye. I had fun."

He takes a bite and says, "Bye," around a mouthful.

I turn to Thayer and a moment I don't quite understand passes between us.

The way he looks at me feels like *more* and that both intrigues and terrifies me.

"I'll see you," I say to Thayer, already walking away.

His voice is soft behind me. "See you."

EIGHTEEN

aleb's leg rests against mine, my head on his shoulder. We watch the sun go down on the roof outside my bedroom. It's something we do a lot, but our days together are dwindling. He leaves for vacation tomorrow, and then, we only have one week left together when he gets back.

Before school ended, we did talk about the possibility of breaking up, or at least taking a break once summer ends and he leaves, but we decided against it—wanting to try to make it work. I don't tell him, but some days I wonder if we're being silly thinking we can do this. We're so young. It's not right, not fair to him, to think that our end is inevitable, but—

"I'm going to miss this." He draws random shapes on my bare knee. "Sitting on your roof, watching the sunset, just ... existing with you."

"Me too."

And I will. Despite my fears and reservations of our longevity, I will miss Caleb so much. He has a piece of my heart I know I'll never ever get back.

"Do you have to leave tomorrow?"

He rubs his jaw. "Unfortunately. But I'll be back at the end of the week."

"And then we only have *days* together," I remind him.

He nods, Adam's apple bobbing. I know he's affected by this—maybe even more than me. Change is hard. "At least we have the concert."

I brighten. "I'm so excited about that."

I've wanted to see my favorite band in concert since I was in middle school, but tickets always sell out insanely fast or cost an arm and a leg. It was just never possible. This means even more to me because Caleb knew it would make me happy.

Guilt plagues me for only minutes prior thinking maybe we should break up.

It's all so complicated.

"We leave early in the morning. I'll text you every day, I promise."

"Don't worry about me." I want him to enjoy his vacation. He deserves this break before his big move to Boston. "I'll be fine. I have work and lots of things to keep me busy."

At my words his gaze drifts next door.

"Hey," I touch my finger to his jaw, bringing his gaze back to me. "Don't worry about him."

He frowns and I worry that maybe I've accidentally told a lie.

The way Thayer looks at me...

The way I look at him...

It's more than it should be.

But nothing can happen, I silently remind myself.

Caleb jerks his head in a nod. "Sure."

He doesn't sound convinced. I loop my arms through his. "I love you."

And I do. Caleb has been my rock the past few years, the boy who healed the heart of a broken girl. I'll *always* love him, no matter where the future takes us.

He cups my cheek, leaning in to press a tender kiss to my lips. "I love you, too."

He looks at me like I'm something, precious, fragile, a treasure that's all his.

I cuddle closer to his side and close my eyes.

I don't want to break your heart.

NINETEEN

The sound of a lawn mower stirs me from a restless sleep. I got up and went for a run at five-thirty this morning, running until my limbs couldn't move one step further, exhausting myself to the point that I got back to my room and crashed on my bed with my shoes still on.

"Ugh," I groan, wiping drool from my mouth. "Gross."

Sitting up, I kick my shoes off the rest of the way and roll over onto my back. My body feels spent. I went too hard, pushed myself too far, but sometimes it feels like the only way to escape.

Get yourself moving, Salem, I silently scold. With a groan I pry myself off my bed. My running shirt lies on the floor in a heap. At least I managed to get one thing off.

Stifling a yawn, I glance at the clock and see that it's a little after ten. That means I got around three hours of sleep once I got back. It's better than nothing and at least it was a solid few hours, compared to all the tossing and turning I did before that.

Opening my window, I slip out onto the roof, searching for the source of the noise, not at all surprised when I see that Thayer is out mowing. What is a surprise is that he's across the street mowing Cynthia's grass. She watches him from her front porch, sipping a cup of coffee, and appreciating the view. And by view, I mean a shirtless Thayer, his chest damp with sweat, looking like a rugged sports magazine model—too good looking for our small little town.

Cynthia notices me and raises her mug in a cheers. My cheeks flush at being caught, but I make no move to crawl back inside.

Drawing my knees up to my chest, I wrap my arms around them. Thayer's been working on building a greenhouse in his backyard so I haven't seen him around as much and he didn't ask me to watch Forrest this weekend. It's been a bummer, because with Caleb gone, I could've used the distraction. Yesterday, I went with Lauren to the mall and bought an outfit for the concert. Even though shopping isn't really my thing, I had fun.

Thayer looks up, no doubt having noticed Cynthia's gesture, and lifts his hand in a wave. I wave back with a smile. He fights a tiny grin, shaking his head but he continues to mow.

I watch for a little while longer before my grumbling stomach demands I put something in it.

Binx swishes his tail lazily, watching me from the floor as I climb back inside.

"You know," I say to him, "you could've extended a paw in help, but no, you just watch."

He blinks his owlish green eyes at me, completely unbothered. Cats.

Kicking my shoes out of the way, I head downstairs. The house is empty—my mom's at the store, and I'll take over in a few hours—and Georgia is at work too. I pour myself a bowl of cereal and sit down at the kitchen table.

My phone buzzes with a text.

Caleb: Miss you. Can't wait to get back and see you.

I stare at the text, feeling a heavy weight in my chest and tears prick my eyes. Everything is changing already, I feel it, can't he?

I finish my cereal, rinsing the bowl out in the sink. There's a knock on the side door and my nose scrunches, wondering who it could be. Possibly Lauren, but...

I open the door and the smile that overtakes me when I see Thayer standing there is downright criminal.

Good, eighteen-year-old girls, *do not* smile at their thirty-one year old divorced neighbor like that.

"Hey," I say, the word breathy.

"I thought I'd see if you wanted me to mow for you guys while I'm out." He pulls a bandana from the pocket of his shorts, using it to wipe the sweat from his brow.

"Oh." I look around at the overgrown grass. We've all been too busy to mow like we usually would. "Um ... maybe, if you don't mind, that is?"

It's a big yard and he's already done Cynthia's.

"I don't mind." He tucks the bandana back and grabs a baseball cap from his back pocket, slipping it over his head. His eyes are shadowed from me, but I still feel their intensity.

"What can I do for you?" I cringe as soon as I ask the question. Maybe it's just my brain slipping into dangerous territory, but I thought it sounded dirty. "What I mean is, can I make you some cupcakes or something?"

"Or something," he repeats, his tongue sliding out and over his lips. He gives a soft laugh. "Cupcakes would be amazing."

I nod shakily.

Why does he make me so jittery?

He tosses his thumb over his shoulder. "I'll see you when I'm done."

"Mhmm." I close the door and face the kitchen. I need to get to work on those cupcakes.

But first, I text Caleb back.

I'M IN THE MIDDLE OF WASHING UP EVERYTHING IN THE SINK, the cupcakes cooling on a rack, when Thayer knocks on the door.

"Come on in," I call out, up to my elbows in sudsy water. He opens the door and pokes his head inside. "Your cupcakes are almost done. I just have to put icing on them when they're done cooling." I look over my shoulder at him, watching as he takes a seat at the table. He's even sweatier than he was before. "Do you want something to drink? You can grab anything from the fridge."

He nods gratefully, and gets up and grabs a bottle of water. He doesn't return to the table, instead sidling up beside me.

"I appreciate the cupcakes, but I would've mowed without them."

"I know." I dry off the mixing bowl. "But I was happy to make them."

He walks over and picks one up, sniffing it. "They smell delicious."

"You can never go wrong with cookie dough." He starts to unwrap one and I squawk in fear. "You have to wait until they're frosted. It's sacrilege to eat a cupcake without one. A cupcake without icing is a muffin!"

He holds it above my head. "Just a little taste."

I jump up and down, not caring how ridiculous I look. I still haven't showered yet and since it was hot in the kitchen while I was baking, I didn't bother to put a shirt on so I'm still in my jog bra. Thayer's eyes drift down, like he's realizing this too.

My stomach clenches at the heat in his eyes.

I'm stepping into dangerous territory, but I don't know how to back pedal from this.

I stumble, Thayer's hand quickly landing on the small of my back to steady me.

Our eyes meet, his gaze heated with desire. I'm young, but I'm not stupid. He wants me.

I think I hold my breath as he stares at me.

Kiss me, the thought pounds through my brain unbidden. *I want you to kiss me.*

Like he can hear my thoughts, he lowers his arm that was holding the cupcake high, holding me with both arms now, and his head starts to lower.

Kiss me, kiss me, kiss me!

The timer goes off, the one I set to remind me to see if the cupcakes were cooled enough, and I curse silently.

Thayer pulls away from me, clearing his throat. He sets the stolen cupcake on the counter. "You're right. These need icing."

"Y-Yeah," my voice shakes, "I'll get them ready."

He scoops up his water bottle, heading for the door without looking at me. "I'm going to go shower. I'll come back for the cupcakes."

"Okay." My voice is small, shaky, but he doesn't notice because he's already gone.

TWENTY

step out of my car, shrieking into my phone, "What do you mean you can't go?" Tears prick my eyes. I just got home to get ready for the concert and Caleb's telling me *now* that he can't go? We're supposed to leave for Boston in two hours! "Caleb?" I practically beg into the line, willing him to take back what he said.

"Fuck, I'm sorry, okay? I didn't know my mom—"

"You didn't know, but *she* knew we had plans," I hiss, my keys shaking in my hands. I haven't been able to move from my spot beside the car. I'm frozen, from anger, sadness, just a whole wave of emotions.

"Salem," he says remorsefully. "I can't say no to this."

I pinch my eyes shut, a tear leaking out the corner of my right eye. His mom got him invited to some sort of dinner with alumni from Harvard. I know, *I know* this is an amazing opportunity for him, but it doesn't lessen my pain, the sting of disappointment.

"You can still go," he insists over my silence, "Lauren can go with you. Or Georgia. Even your mom."

"Lauren's in New York," I remind him. She went with her two sisters for three days. "And Georgia's out with Michael."

"Your mom, then?" He insists.

"My mom…" I hesitate. "She's been really tired lately. It's strange. But I won't drag her out all night to a concert, Caleb, and I'm not going all the way to Boston by myself."

"Salem," he says my name remorsefully.

"I'm mad," I tell him. There's no point in sugarcoating it. He can hear my pain in my words. "This was supposed to be a night for us."

We even have hotel reservations.

"I know, babe. I'm so sorry. I'll be in Boston anyway, you can go with us and just go to the concert by yourself."

"Do you hear yourself?" I argue. "I want to go, believe me, but I wanted to go with *you*." My tears are coming forcefully now. I hiccup, wiping at my wet face. "Don't worry about it. I'll be fine."

"Salem—"

I hang up and when he immediately calls back, I silence my phone, stuffing it into my pocket. I don't even feel sorry for it.

Covering my face with both hands, my keys fall to the ground. I feel like throwing up, and I'm made even more upset by the fact that I hate that I'm being so dramatic. But I was looking forward to this so much. Caleb and I haven't had much alone time this summer, and it's left me feeling confused and lost. I thought tonight would help me reconnect with him, to feel surer of where we stand with him leaving in just a few days.

And now…

"Are you okay?"

Are you kidding me? The last person I want seeing me breakdown like this stands at the front of my car.

"Ugh." I wipe my snotty nose. "I'm *fine*," I bite, more harshly than I normally would, but with Caleb's news, plus the fact that things have been awkward with Thayer since the day in my kitchen, I just don't have it in me to deal with this.

"What happened?" His eyes narrow upon me, voice gruff. "Did someone hurt you? I swear to God if it was your preppy pretty-boy boyfriend I'll—"

"He hurt me, but not like you think," I confirm, walking away from him.

"What did he do?" He growls behind me.

"It's none of your business, Thayer."

"You're sobbing on the public street, so that makes it my business."

I give a short, humorless laugh. "No, it doesn't."

"Hey." He grabs my arm, his hold gentle enough for me to pull out of, but I don't bother.

"What?" I look up at him, chin lifted defiantly.

"Tell me what's wrong."

"Give me one good reason why," I argue. I know my face has to be red and splotchy from crying, but I make no move to hide myself.

"Because I care about you."

Dammit, I told him to give me a good reason and he did.

"I was supposed to go to a concert tonight with my boyfriend and he canceled. That's it. I'm being stupid." I drop my gaze, shrugging my shoulders like it's no big deal.

"You're allowed to be upset, Salem." His voice is soft, more gentle than usual. "You're allowed to *feel*. Don't let anyone ever let you think otherwise."

I wipe away fresh tears. "It sucks," I explain. "I was really excited. It's my favorite band, and we were going to spend the night in the city."

He looks me over, his jaw ticking. "I'll take you."

Stunned, I blink at him. "What did you say?"

"I'll take you," he repeats.

It's not possible I heard him right. "I ... you're going to take me to a concert? In Boston?"

"Sure," he shrugs, his shirt pulling taut over his muscular arms and chest, "I don't have anything else going on."

"You have work," I remind him.

"And I own the company, so I call the shots. I can take off tomorrow. We can spend the rest of the day in Boston and come home in the evening. I'll drive us."

"You're serious."

It's a statement, but he answers anyway. "Yes. Do you have both tickets?"

I nod. "Yeah, he gave both to me."

"Good." He releases my arm and takes a couple of steps back. "When do we need to leave?"

"Two hours."

He nods to himself at this timeline. "Okay. Be at my truck then."

"This is seriously happening?"

I can't believe Thayer is swooping in like some knight in shining armor to save the day. It feels too good to be true.

"Seriously," he responds. "You're not missing out on this."

Tears spring to my eyes once more, not like they'd really dried up to begin with. "Thank you."

"You don't have to thank me for this."

"Believe me," I say, getting a little choked up, "I do."

He nods, backing further away. "I'll see you in two hours."

TWENTY-ONE

'm riding in Thayer's truck.

On our way to Boston.

Together.

I pinch my arm, and sure enough, this is real.

The AC blasts cold air in my face, but I don't mind, and a rock station plays on the radio. The leather interior is a chestnut color, warm and rugged just like Thayer. He drives with one hand on the wheel, his eyes shielded by the pair of sunglasses I bought which makes me smile every time I look at him.

We've been on the road an hour already. My phone continues to blow up with text messages from Caleb.

"Your boyfriend?" Thayer asks, not bothering to take his eyes off the road.

"Yes." I silence my phone, looking out the passenger window.

"You're ignoring him?"

I sigh. "It's petty, I know, but I need to cool off and I can't do that if I talk to him right now, so it's better if I just ignore him. Besides, it's not like we can say anything that hasn't already been said."

Thayer nods, rubbing his jaw with his free hand. "Relationships can be complicated, but I want you to know it's okay to be hurt and upset. Feel what you need to feel."

"I know." I pull the mirror down, checking my makeup. I'll touch it up when we get to the hotel and change into the outfit I got for the concert. Originally, Caleb and I planned to be ready when we left Hawthorne Mills, but we were taking the train which adds time onto the trip. With Thayer driving we'll have time to change at the hotel. Well, *I'm* changing. Who knows with him. Right now, he's in his usual attire of cargo pants and a t-shirt. If he doesn't change it's no big deal. I mean, he didn't have to do any of this at all. I could be missing out on the concert all together.

"Thank you," I say for what feels like the millionth time since I climbed in his truck.

He grunts. I think it's either another *you're welcome* or *stop thanking me*. I'm not versed in caveman speak.

He turns the volume up on the radio, and I think that's code for he's done talking. That's fine with me. I watch out the window as we approach the city. It's so vastly different than our small town. A whole world apart.

Thayer glances at me every so often as we drive through the bustling streets toward the hotel that's only a few blocks from the concert venue.

"What are you thinking?" he asks, curiosity in his voice.

I crack a small smile. "Probably not what you think I am."

"Enlighten me."

I pick up my bottle of water and take a sip, carefully screwing the cap back on. "I was thinking about how unappealing I find all of this." I wave my fingers at the horde of traffic congestion. "I much prefer our small town."

He rubs his fingers over his lips, trying to hide his smile. "I would think most kids your age would idolize the big city life."

"I'm not a kid." I don't say it defensively, just matter of fact. "And I'm not like most people."

"That you're not."

"**WHERE THE FUCK IS THE OTHER BED?**" THAYER CURSES, following me inside the hotel room. He sets our bags down. "I'm going to go talk to the concierge."

I grab his arm. "Calm down. I was staying here with Caleb, remember? And they're all booked, I called before we even left home. I'll sleep on the couch."

"You're not sleeping on the couch," he grumbles.

"Well, you're not either," I argue back, flicking on the light in the bathroom. "You're doing me a favor, so you can get the bed."

"I can't believe we're arguing about this." He pinches the bridge of his nose like I'm giving him a headache.

"We can share the bed," I volley back, and before he retorts, I add, "It's a king size bed, Thayer. I can keep to my side, can you?"

"Yes," he growls, eyes darting to the bed. "You got one bed with your boyfriend?"

"Yes." I open my overnight bag on the floor. "He's my boyfriend." His eyes narrow upon me and I roll mine back. "Yes, Thayer, I planned on fucking my boyfriend tonight, but he bailed."

His face reddens. "Don't ... don't say that again."

I laugh, shaking my head. "Men are so weird. Obsessed with sex, but God forbid a woman be open about it."

He wets his lips. "That's not ... just ... *fuck*." He puts his hands on his hips. "Just get ready." He waves me toward the bathroom.

"Are you shooing me away, Thayer?"

"Yes," he huffs.

I shake my head. Flustering Thayer might be my new favorite thing. "You'd think I was talking about murder, not sex. Don't be such a baby."

"Salem." My name is a warning, a threat on his sharp tongue.

I look over my shoulder at him, getting way too much enjoyment out of torturing him. "You didn't think I was a virgin, did you?"

He looks up at the ceiling and I'm pretty sure he says a prayer.

I decide to give the big guy a break and take my clothes to the bathroom. I change out of my jean shorts and tank top into a pair of fake black leather skinny jeans and a black bustier top. The outfit is out of my comfort zone, but I wanted to wear something different tonight. There's also the fact I thought Caleb would be the one taking it off of me at the end of the night.

I fluff my hair up, giving the strands more body, and touch up my makeup. Opening the door, I keep my head down as I hurry into the room and grab my heeled boots. I look up before slipping them on and my breath catches.

Thayer watches me with heated brown eyes, desire evident in the way he looks at me. He scans me from head to toe and my stomach rolls over.

Caleb has never looked at me like this.

Like I'm something precious, a treasure meant to be worshipped. With him staring so unabashedly at me, I stare back. While I was in the bathroom, he changed into a nice pair of jeans and a white v-neck that, like most of his shirts, clings to him like a second skin. It looks like he's even brushed his hair. I wish I could turn my attraction for him off like a switch, but I can't. It's a curse. But I know this isn't one-sided, not with the way he's looking at me right now.

He clears his throat. "You look nice." He looks away hastily, rifling through his bag like he's just realized he was looking at me for too long.

"So do you." I sit down on the edge of the bed and yank my shoes on. "I'm not used to wearing shoes like this." I wiggle my foot before I zip the shoe. "You might have to hold me steady tonight."

"Whatever you need."

Unbidden, one word comes to mind.

You. I need *you*.

Thayer grabs his wallet from his shorts and stuffs it in the pocket of his jeans. Glancing over his shoulder, he asks, "When should we head over to the venue?"

I check my phone, ignoring the string of text messages from Caleb. I'll reply back to him soon, just not right now. "We can go now. It'll give me a chance to get any merch I want to grab."

"Are you hungry?"

I shake my head. "I'm too excited."

He chuckles. "That means you'll be starving later."

"Exactly." I grab the crossbody bag I packed, stuff some cash, my ID, and phone inside. "Okay, I'm ready now."

He opens the room door, nodding for me to head out first. "Let's go."

TWENTY-TWO

The line is long, snaking around the arena. We stopped and got a bite to eat on the walk over, Thayer insisting, "You might not be hungry, but I am." I ate anyway, because what he said before we left the hotel was true, I might not have been hungry then, but I would've been.

Thayer looks around, hands in his pockets at the gathered crowd of girls ranging in age from about fourteen to late twenties.

"This band ... it's really popular, huh?"

I beam, nodding eagerly. "Yeah. They're amazing."

"I've probably heard some of their stuff, right?" He scratches the back of his head.

"On the radio, I'm sure."

"They're a boyband?"

A girl behind us gasps. "Willow Creek is *not* a boy band. They're a *band*."

"Band ... that consists of *boys*, correct?" Thayer argues. I'd be irritated if he didn't look so genuinely confused.

The girl behind me sighs. "A boyband usually just sings. Willow Creek is a band—with a lead singer, guitarist, bassist, and drummer."

"I got it," he says, but I think he's just placating her. She seems satisfied enough, nodding her head like a job well done.

Thayer runs his fingers through his hair, the line moving forward at a more rapid pace now.

When we near the entrance, I open my bag and search for the tickets.

I pale.

ID, phone, cash ... no fucking tickets.

"Oh my God," I turn to Thayer with horror-filled eyes, "I left the tickets in the room."

"No, you didn't," he insists with a shake of his head. "Salem," he growls my name.

Tears pinch my eyes. This is the *worst* day ever. "We have to go back to the hotel." My chin quivers with the threat of tears. "We have time."

Not much, not since we stopped to eat, but we can make it work. I'll miss the opening artist, possibly even Willow Creek's first few songs, but I won't miss the whole concert and that counts for something.

Thayer shakes his head and grabs my hand, pulling me out of line and over to the ticket booth. "Wait here," he instructs in a growly tone, walking up to the window where SOLD OUT blazes.

"Thayer," I beg. "We're wasting time. Let me get an Uber."

He ignores me, tapping on the window forcefully.

I cover my face with embarrassment while he speaks to the person. He's wasting precious time. His name is on the tip of my tongue, to beg and plead for him to hurry up so I have some sort of chance of seeing the show. I watch him nod and take something before returning to my side. "We're good to go."

"Huh?"

A door suddenly opens and the person he was speaking to at the ticket booth waves us hurriedly inside.

"What's going on?" I hiss at Thayer, letting security look through my bag.

He pulls two tickets out of his pocket.

"Thayer," I practically whine his name, "I had tickets, what did you do? Buy two more? It said they were sold out. How did you even...?" I trail off my eyes zeroing in on the tickets. "Those are pit," I state.

The tickets Caleb purchased were *good* tickets, nothing to complain about, but these are amazing—what dreams are made of.

"I know." He says it so calmly, so assuredly.

"They had to cost a lot of money."

The man beside me shrugs. *Shrugs*. Like, "No biggie."

"Thayer," I continue, "this had to cost thousands."

"It doesn't matter what it cost. I want you to be happy." His forehead creases at this admission, like he didn't mean to say it out loud.

"We could've gone back to the hotel," I point out, looking through the glass doors we came through.

"And you would've missed part of it."

"It wouldn't have been the end of the world."

"Salem?"

"Yes?" I arch a brow, curious.

"Just say thank you."

I smile up at him, at this man who I realize has become my friend. "Thank you."

He dips his chin. "You're welcome."

His warm hand settles on the small of my back, steering me toward where we need to go. I'm glad one of is paying attention.

We pass the merch booth and I study the items, trying to figure out what I like so I can grab something during intermission. "I love that shirt." I point to one hanging up at the top. It's navy blue with the band's logo of a Willow Tree with a tire swing all in white with neon blue outlining it.

Thayer grunts out a response.

As we search for a good viewing spot in pit, girls run around screaming, shrieking with excitement. I don't join in their theatrics. I'm sure I will later, but right now I'm too stunned.

"Wow." I try to take it all in, letting Thayer tug me along. With his big body he moves much easier through the crowd of people. Some people give dirty looks, but I ignore it.

I'm at a Willow Creek concert—something I've dreamed of for years.

Sure, I was supposed to be here with Caleb, but...

Guilt settles inside me when I realize I'm *happy* I'm here with Thayer.

I eye the man at my side, wondering why I have to be so taken with him. Why can't I look at him like everyone else? Why does he, of all people, have to stir something inside me? It's not fair.

Thayer finally reaches a spot he must deem good enough because we stop walking and he looks down at me. "Stay *right* here. I'll be back."

"I—" He's already gone before I can say another word.

Pulling my phone from my pocket, I turn it back on and read through the string of texts. I had let my mom know I made it to Boston, so I text her again to tell her I'm at the concert and will let her know when I'm back at the hotel. It'll be late, but I know it'll make her feel better to have me check in, even if it wakes her up. I told her Thayer was bringing me and when she asked why he would do something like that; I lied. I said he had business he needed to handle in Boston, so it wasn't out of his way.

Now, not only have I dragged this man to the city and to a hotel overnight, but he's had to buy new tickets. *Pit* tickets at that. I know they weren't cheap, not for a band of this caliber. My stomach roils. I'll never be able to pay him back for this—literally or figuratively.

Scrolling through Caleb's texts, mostly 'I'm sorrys' and 'I'll make this up to you', I figure out what to say.

Me: School is important to you. Football too. I get that. Don't worry about me. Enjoy the dinner and make connections.

As soon as I send the text, reply dots appear, but I shut my phone off. I want to enjoy tonight, and Caleb needs to focus on his.

The lights begin to dim, the opening act getting ready to take the stage. I worry Thayer won't be able to find me, but I promised I wouldn't move, so I don't.

The band starts up and I lose myself in the music. It's a small indie band, and I love that Willow Creek is giving their platform to a smaller artist to help them build their own career.

They're on their third song when I feel a hand on my elbow. I look up into brown eyes, glowing blue, then pink, then green from the neon lights.

"For you," he says in that rough tone he uses a lot.

"What?" I blink at him.

He holds out a bag and a bottle of water. He keeps the other bottle for himself. "For you," he repeats.

I open the bag hesitantly, like something might jump out at me. I can't make out any of the lyrics of the song being played because I'm too zeroed in on what's in the bag.

"Thayer," I say his name softly, I doubt he hears it, tears rushing to my eyes. Inside is the shirt I pointed out along with a tote bag and beanie. "You didn't need to do that," I tell him, speaking loud enough for him to hear me. "But thank you." I don't want him to think I'm not grateful, because I am. Extremely so. "This is ... way more than I ever expected. Thank you."

"You're welcome." He's nodding along to the music, not paying attention to me, and I'm not sure if that's because to him it's really no big deal or because he's trying to give me a moment to rein in my emotions. I wish now I had brought a bigger bag, and as if he senses my thoughts, he scoops the plain black bag out of my hands. "I'll hold onto this."

I flash him a grateful smile.

The opening band plays three more songs before they exit the stage. Excitement pulses in the air, the energy electric.

"It's happening!" I clap my hands excitedly, grinning up at my broody companion. The lights go dark and then one spotlight comes on. From somewhere an electric guitar starts playing. "Oh my God!" I put my hands around Thayer's muscular arm and give it a shake. Then Joshua Hayes comes into view in the spotlight. It's like the crowd isn't even there as he completely tears it up on the guitar. "That's Hayes," I scream, pointing like Thayer can't see him.

116

The guitar cuts off and he fades into the darkness when the light goes out.

Then the drums start, and I jump up and down, screaming like the girl beside me. She starts crying. "Maddox! Oh my God, I love you!" When the spotlight reveals him behind his drum set, I worry she might faint.

Like with Hayes, the light cuts out the sound of the drums ceasing.

Next is the sound of the bass and the light cuts to Ezra strumming lazily at the instrument, his curly black hair flopping over his forehead.

The lights cut out again and a hush falls over the arena.

My hand is still clutched around his arm, but he makes no move to shake me off.

It feels like we're all collectively holding our breath, then the music starts up again, all the lights exploding at once and revealing the entire band.

Matthias Wade—the lead singer and twin brother of the drummer—croons into the mic and I think I swoon a bit. The brooding, intense singer is my favorite. I steal a look at Thayer. Maybe I have a type.

He bends down to my ear, his lips brushing my sensitive skin when he speaks. "This is pretty good."

"I told you!" At least, I think I told him. I start dancing and Thayer smiles—a big, blinding, too good for this world smile. "This is the best night of my life!" I give him this truth and he takes it, pleased to have given this to me.

Thayer Holmes might not realize how special he is, but I know.

TWENTY-THREE

'm on a high as we walk into the hotel room.

I spin in a circle, my arms outstretched as I sing one of my favorite Willow Creek songs in a very out of tune voice. But I don't care. Tonight, was amazing. Out of this world.

"Out of this world, huh?" Thayer asks, locking the door up behind us.

"Did I say that out loud?" My cheeks are flushed.

"Yeah." His eyes sparkle with amusement.

"Well, it's true." I collapse on the bed. "Can you help me get these off?" I lift one leg, wiggling my foot.

He shakes his head but doesn't argue. He takes ahold of my foot and unzips my boot. "Damn, that's really on there." He wiggles it back and forth and finally my foot is free. He sets my boot down on the ground and grabs my other foot. That one comes off easier.

I already texted my mom when we got back to the hotel, and she replied right away that she was glad I was safe and had fun.

There was one text from Caleb.

Caleb: You're important to me too. I love you.

Guilt settled inside me, and I texted back that I loved him too.

"My feet hurt," I whine, sitting up and rubbing the heel of my right foot. "I'm never wearing shoes like that ever again."

He chuckles. "I don't blame you. These never fail me." He points at his work boots.

Standing up, I grab my pajamas from my bag. "I'm going to shower, if that's okay."

"Take your time." He sits down, removing his own shoes.

"Need any help with those?" I joke.

He gives me a half-smile. "I've got it."

"If you're sure." I wink and shut myself in the bathroom.

Oh my God! Salem! Why did you wink at him?

Ugh. I hate myself.

I turn the shower on and while it warms, I remove my makeup. Despite my lack of skill, it managed to hold up decently through the night. My mascara did smear beneath my eyes a bit, but it could've been worse.

Hopping in the shower, I use the shower gel the hotel provided to lather up my body. It smells strongly of orange and vanilla. When I feel like all the sweat has been washed off my body, I turn off the shower and step out on the small towel, drying my body and slipping into my pair of sleep shorts and an oversized t-shirt.

"Your turn," I tell Thayer, exiting the bathroom with a trail of steamy air following me.

He stifles a yawn. "Thanks."

He's already turned the bed back and clearly picked a side, so I take the other. A soft sound leaves my lips when my body sinks into the comfy mattress. Tonight, was amazing, but I'm exhausted. I stifle a yawn, waiting for Thayer to come to bed before I crash.

When the shower turns on, I try not to think about Thayer being in there naked, but it only makes me think about it *more*.

I cover my face with my hands, groaning. "Hormones," I mutter, the sound muffled. "This has to be out of control hormones."

It's the only thing that makes sense.

Scooting down into the bed, I grab my phone and check my social media. I don't post a lot on my personal account, but I've been trying to build the one I have for my candles in case one day I decide to turn that into something bigger. Five new followers and I haven't even posted this week. Not bad. I've only been working on building the page for a year and it's already nearing two-thousand followers. It's nothing compared to other accounts, but I'm pretty proud of my little venture.

The bathroom door opens, and Thayer asks, "Do you want me to leave the bathroom light on?"

"It doesn't matter to me."

He decides to leave it on and closes the door so only a thin stream of light leaks into the bedroom.

His bare feet pad across the floor and he removes his watch from his wrist, laying it on the table and then plugging his phone in to charge.

I stifle a yawn, trying not to ogle Thayer in the pair of sweatpants he wears. It's practically indecent the way the fabric hugs his...

"See something you like?" His tone is surprisingly flirty and a flush heats my cheeks.

"No." I lie, sinking beneath the covers and pulling them up to my chin.

"Sure," he grunts, eyes narrowing upon me. "Are you going to jump me if I sleep without a shirt?"

"No shirt I can handle."

Fuck. I want to facepalm myself. I just implied that if he removed his pants I would jump him. Ugh.

He yanks off his t-shirt and settles onto the bed. Since it's a king size there's plenty of space between us, enough for a whole other body, maybe two.

"Thank you for tonight," I tell him for the millionth time. "You have no idea what it meant to me."

"You don't have to keep thanking me."

"I know, but—"

"But nothing," he responds. "I was happy to do it."

My voice is practically a squeak when I ask, "Why?"

Why would he do this for me? A man that's over a decade older than me. He's my neighbor. My boss. He owes me nothing.

He's quiet for a moment. I can sense him struggling with something. Finally, he hands over his answer like he's giving me something precious to cherish. "Because I wanted to." His eyes flicker over me. "I don't do things I don't want to, Salem. I'm a selfish man."

Man. He lays that word between us like a grenade, reminding me gently that while we might be lying in the same bed, he's thirty-one and I'm eighteen.

He doesn't wait for me to reply. He turns the light out on his side of the bed. "Night, Salem."

I whisper back, "Goodnight."

TWENTY-FOUR

"N-No! No! NO!" I thrash my arms and legs, fighting off an adversary that feels so very real.

"Salem," a familiar voice speaks past the terror crawling through my body. "*Salem.* I have you. You're safe. *Wake up, dammit!*"

I feel warm hands on my face, the weight of something against me.

"Don't touch me!" I scream. "Stop," I beg the body pressing against me. I throw my arms around, nails ready to claw. "Get off of me! I'm your daughter," I sob, begging and pleading though I know it'll do no good, it never does, "stop, I'm your daughter."

A gasp penetrates my nightmare, and the weight vanishes. "Wake up," the same voice begs. "*Please*, wake up."

My eyes fly open, my body drenched in sweat. I cry, tears wetting my face.

"Hey," Thayer says, his hand hovers above me and then he gently, hesitantly, brushes my sweaty hair off my face. "You're okay. You're safe with me."

He doesn't just say that I'm safe, he makes sure to emphasize that I'm safe with *him*.

My whole body shakes and I can't stop crying.

"Is this okay?" He continues to stroke my face, his body above mine. One of his knees rests between my legs. I nod, my bottom lip trembling. "Your nightmare..." He pauses, closing his eyes. A pained look punctures his face. "It was real, wasn't it? A memory?"

I nod brokenly. It seems to be the only thing I can do in the moment.

"Fuck," he growls. "Salem."

I shake my head back and forth roughly. I don't want him to say it. I don't want to talk about it. Therapy has helped me *so* much, but there are those residual things that haven't gone away—like my nightmares. Some scars don't heal as quickly as others.

"What can I do?"

"Nothing," I gasp brokenly.

He can't fix this. No one can. I just have to deal with it.

Thayer stares down at me, a haunted look in his eyes as he sees the demons swirling in mine.

"I'm sorry," he says, his fingers still stroking my face gently, with so much reverence. "I'm so sorry, Salem. That should've never happened to you." He clears his throat and tears swim in his eyes. "Fuck, I'm just so sorry."

It's on the tip of my tongue, to say those words that we all say to try to make things okay, but if I say "I'm all right" it would be a lie and we'd both know it.

"Can you hold me?" My voice sounds so small, so incredibly broken.

Beneath the window, to my right, the AC kicks on and I jump.

Thayer nods, swallowing thickly. "I'll hold you as long as you want me to."

He rolls back onto the bed, gathering me into his arms. My leg wraps around him. His warmth seeps into me and I soak in every ounce of comfort. My hand splays on his bare skin, my fingers rubbing against the chest hair smattered across his pectoral muscles. He has one of his hands curled around my arm and rubs his thumb in small circles, around and around. With his other hand, he cups the back of my head, gently massaging. I try my best to get my breath under control. If I keep hyperventilating it won't end well.

"Breathe," he murmurs, as if sensing this.

I squish my eyes closed. "I'm trying." I rub my damp face against his bare chest.

I'm *cuddling* Thayer. Holy hell. It's like I've stepped into some sort of alternate universe. Granted, I'm not all up in his business for any sort of fun reason, but it doesn't matter. I'm in his arms. He's holding me.

"I'm right here," he soothes, his fingers stroking through my hair. "I'm not leaving you. You're not alone." The reminder that I'm not alone sends relief coursing through my veins. "I've got you." I jolt at the gentle press of his lips against my forehead. I'm not sure he even realizes he's done it. He's too busy trying to calm me down and comfort me.

"I'm so sorry," I hiccup.

"For what?" I can feel him tilt his head down my way, and I reluctantly open my eyes.

"Waking you up."

"Salem," he growls, his chest rumbling with the two syllables of my name. "Don't be fucking sorry. I can't fucking take you being sorry for *this*."

I don't think it sunk in before now that I was talking in my sleep. That means he *knows*.

Oh, God. I stiffen in his arms, and he senses this, trying to pull away because he thinks I don't want to be touched. I quickly latch back onto him like a koala bear. I don't want his warmth, his comfort, going anywhere.

"Please, don't look at me differently after this. *Please*."

He holds me tighter. "Never."

Somehow, some way, in the sanctuary of his arms, I drift back to sleep.

"OH MY GOD!" I WAKE UP, CRYING OUT WITH PLEASURE, MY hips undulating against something hard. My orgasm hits me so forcefully that flashes of light shimmer across my eyes, blocking everything else out. I moan, coming down from the high, but my hips continue to rock and rock and—

"Oh my God," I gasp for an entirely different reason, everything coming into focus around me.

The hotel room.

My nightmare.

Thayer holding me.

Mortification reddens my face as I take in the situation. My crotch pressed against his muscled thigh, hands splayed on his chest, and his brown eyes watching me in awe.

Panic surges in my veins.

I can't believe that happened. I know I was still half-asleep, but that doesn't change the fact that I just got myself off on his leg. I cover my mouth with my hand.

"I didn't mean to," I mumble around my fingers.

"It's—"

Yanking myself from his body, the blankets, from the bed itself, I tumble to the floor and grab my bag, secluding myself in the bathroom where he can't see me, but I can't escape my embarrassment.

I grip the edges of the granite counter in my hands, leaning forward. I'm out of breath, cheeks flushed, hair a mess. I look exactly like I just had a good fuck which is apparently what I was attempting to do in my sleep.

And if that wasn't bad enough, I had a nightmare he had to comfort me from. I brought one of my sleeping pills with me, intending to take it so I'd be knocked out and that wouldn't happen. Since I normally don't take them it slipped my mind.

Grabbing my toothbrush, I wet it under the water and slather on a ridiculous amount of toothpaste in my haste. I'm a mess.

After braiding my hair to the side, I change out of my pajamas into the fresh pair of shorts I packed and cropped t-shirt that says All Love on it.

I keep expecting Thayer to knock on the door and ask if I'm okay, or to demand I talk about what happened, but I realize that's not really his style.

Smoothing stray hairs away from my face, I take a deep breath, burying my embarrassment down deep.

I open the door and step out to find Thayer already changed, snapping his watch into place on his wrist.

God, he has nice hands.

SALEM! You just orgasmed on the man's leg, now is not the time to be thinking about his hands! Get a grip!

There's a tray on the table with coffee, orange juice, water, and various breakfast items ranging from a muffin to a bagel with cream cheese and a few cereal options.

"I went downstairs," he says by way of explanation. "Wasn't sure what you might want so I grabbed a bit of everything."

I take the blueberry muffin that has some sort of streusel concoction on top. "Thank you."

Don't think about what happened, I chant to myself, or else I'll lock myself in the bathroom again.

Carrying the muffin and orange juice over to the chair in the corner, I sit down to eat.

"After you eat, we'll head out." Thayer's already scanning the room, even getting down to peer under the bed to make sure nothing has dropped there. As if we've been here for a whole week and made a mess of the place.

"Okay." I brush crumbs off the arm of the chair to the floor. I feel his eyes on me, watching and appraising my behavior.

The adult thing would be to talk about what happened, but in this moment, I feel very much eighteen. Young and stupid. Finishing my muffin, I down the rest of the orange juice and grab my bag.

"All right, I'm ready." He effortlessly slides the bag down my arm, throwing it over his own shoulder. "You don't need to do that."

"It's fine, Salem." His eyes are soft, no hint of walls being put up after what happened this morning and last night. In fact, he seems more open than usual.

I dip my head. "Okay."

Thayer loads the car and I check us out since the room is in my name. When I exit the lobby, his truck is parked at the front, and he messes with the radio.

When I open the door and climb inside, a song from Willow Creek is playing. I can't help it, I grin. He notices, because Thayer misses nothing.

"What?" He asks innocently. "They're not so bad."

I shake my head, still smiling, and strap the seatbelt across my body.

TWENTY-FIVE

I jolt awake when the engine to Thayer's truck cuts off. "We're
home," he announces unnecessarily.

"When did I fall asleep?" I rub my eyes, stifling a yawn.

We ended up heading straight home instead of hanging around
Boston for the day.

He looks at the clock on the dashboard. "About thirty minutes
ago."

Not too long then.

I open the door to get out, and he follows suit. "I'll take your bag
to the door."

"I've got it." I brush a strand of blonde hair behind my ear. "It's
not heavy."

"I'm carrying your bag, Salem." His tone brooks no room for argument. I walk side by side with him down the driveway, pausing at the

side door. He waits for me to slide the key in the lock before he sets my bag down.

"I owe you all the cupcakes for this." I open the door wide, standing on the top step.

He watches me carefully and I wish I knew what he was thinking. "You don't owe me anything."

With that, he turns and walks away, leaving me alone with my thoughts.

THE DOORBELL RINGS SOMETIME AFTER TWO AND I'M NOT surprised to come downstairs to find Caleb on the front porch.

Opening the door, I give him a small timid smile. "Hi."

"Hey." He clasps his hands in front of him, his smile as thin as mine. His shoulders sag and he runs his hand through his hair. "Fuck, Salem, I'm so sorry. I'm an ass." He drops his head. "You have every right to hate me."

"I don't hate you. I was hurt—*am* hurt," I amend. "But I don't hate you."

He rubs a hand over the side of his nose, a nervous gesture. "My mom knew we had the concert. I don't know why she signed me up for the dinner. I—"

I hold up a hand silencing him. "It was an opportunity you couldn't pass up. I understand."

As I've had time to cool down, I know it was too good for him to say no to. Does that make it hurt any less? Not really, but I won't stand in the way of Caleb's dream. It would be selfish of me, and I won't be that girl. Besides, I orgasmed on my neighbor's leg so it's not like I'm a saint in this situation either.

He nods, but it seems wooden, like he's not sure. "Are you going to come in?" I ask him and he gives me a genuine smile.

"I thought maybe I wasn't allowed."

I roll my eyes playfully. Grabbing him by the shirt I yank him inside. "Get in here."

"Do you want to stay for dinner?" I watch Caleb pull his shirt back on, covering his chest from my eager eyes. I search the floor for my bra and slip it on. He spins his finger, motioning for me to turn around. He clasps my bra back into place. His lips press a tender kiss to the back of my neck.

"Do you want me to?"

I laugh, scooping up my tank top. "I wouldn't ask if I didn't want you to."

"All right." He buttons his jeans. "Are you cooking it? I can help."

I nod. "I'd love that."

Both fully dressed, we make our way downstairs and I dig through the fridge searching for something I can throw together to make a meal. I set a pack of chicken breast out from the freezer and then find a frozen bag of veggies. Caleb grabs the chicken and pops it in the microwave to defrost.

I set out some seasoning for the chicken, turning to find Caleb leaning against the counter watching me.

"What?" I ask, tying my hair back in a ponytail.

He smiles, his eyes lighting up. "I can't watch my hot as fuck girlfriend?"

"Caleb," I laugh, shaking my head in embarrassment. Turning to the sink, I wash my hands. I realize we really do need to talk. In hindsight, I shouldn't have pulled him straight up to my room for sex, but I still felt out of sorts after what happened this morning with Thayer.

I needed to erase the memories of getting myself off on Thayer's thigh from my brain.

Only now I'm thinking about it again.

Ugh.

Rubbing a hand over my face, I blow out a breath. "I want to move past this," I start off with, and Caleb cocks his head to the side listening, "I'm not the best at talking things out, but I know we do need to talk."

"Okay," he hedges.

"I said I accepted your apology and I mean it," I insist, opening the bag of veggies and spreading them on a pan, adding some olive oil, salt, and pepper. "But I need to be honest, that it did hurt me. It *does* hurt me, when you do this." He opens his mouth to speak, but I hold up a hand, begging him to let me finish what I have to say. "You're leaving," I remind him. "In just a few days you'll be gone and I just … wanted to spend as much time with you as I could." Treacherous tears sting my eyes. "It feels like everything is changing. *We're* changing. And it scares me."

"Salem," he murmurs, reaching for my arms and tugging me into his body. He's leaner than Thayer, a little bit shorter, but his body is warm and full of comfort. "I love you. This isn't going to change us."

I squish my eyes closed, holding on tighter like I can make sure he doesn't disappear.

But something tells me that no matter how snug I hold on, things are going to change anyway.

TWENTY-SIX

L auren and I swing our legs back and forth, soaring into the air on the swing set at our local park. There are no kids around, so it's not like we're hogging them from the children. In fact, as it nears sunset, it's eerily quiet. There's an older couple walking their golden retriever and us. That's it. It's like everyone's gone ... just like Caleb. He left for Boston yesterday. He FaceTimed me last night, showing me his dorm, and despite feeling sad at his absence I couldn't help but be genuinely happy for him. This is what he's always wanted.

"How are you feeling?" Lauren asks, interrupting the quiet between us.

I know she means about Caleb. "I'm okay," I assure her. "Sad, of course, but I knew this was going to happen."

She bites her lip, twisting the swing around. "I've been thinking."

"That's dangerous," I joke.

"Ha." She leans over, pushing my shoulder. "I know it's crazy, but I need a change of scenery. An adventure."

"Okay?" I hedge, urging her to go on when she doesn't elaborate.

"I want to move to New York. *City*," she adds. "I ... I don't know. When I was there with my sister I felt like that's where I'm meant to be."

"Wow." Her confession is unexpected. She hasn't mentioned this at all.

"I know, I know," she chants, shaking her head. "This wasn't my plan at all. I'm supposed to start community college next week." Her voice squeaks on the end. "But ... I won't be happy, Salem. I know I won't. I want bigger things. I already talked to my advisor, and I can take my classes online, I don't want to give up on college completely, but this way I don't have to stay here."

"You've given this a lot of thought, haven't you?" She nods, pumping her legs to gain more height as she swings.

"I hate leaving you like this. It's why I want you to come with me." She brightens, slowing to a stop. "We can be roommates. Get jobs waitressing and be discovered by some awesome talent scout."

"And what are our talents exactly?" I joke.

She wiggles her nose. "I haven't figured that part out yet."

"I'm excited for you. If this is what you want, I won't stop you. But I ... I'm staying here, Lo."

She ducks her head, dark hair shielding her face. "I understand."

"Are you looking at apartments?"

Her gaze drops. "I already put a deposit on one. It's small, of course, but it's going to be mine and that's all that matters."

"I don't want you to go." She already knows this, goodbyes suck. "But I'm so happy for you. You deserve to do whatever your heart wants and if it's moving to New York, *do it*. I'll always be your cheerleader."

She smiles. "You've always believed in me."

I roll my eyes, fighting a smile. "It's not a big deal. I know you'll succeed at whatever you set your mind to." I pause, rubbing my lips together in thought. "When do you leave?"

Her smile falls. "Next Wednesday."

I drop my head. "I thought it might've been even sooner."

"The offer will always stand for you to move in with me. Like I said, it's small, but there's a loft for an extra bed."

"You never know, I might take you up on it."

She reaches over, squeezing my hand. "I hope you'll go shopping with me. I want to buy a few things for the apartment before I go. New bedding, some dishes, stuff like that."

I squeeze her hand back. "Of course."

Leaning back, I start swinging again, letting the last of the sun's summer rays warm my face.

Everybody kept telling me this summer would be different from all the previous ones. I didn't quite believe them, but they were right. It's been full of change. It's scary, exhilarating, but I realize this has been the first step into our adult lives, of course change was inevitable.

Caleb's in Boston, Lauren is moving to New York City, and me?

I don't know what's in store for me, but for the first time in a long time, I'm excited to find out.

TWENTY-
SEVEN

I pause in surprise at the end of my driveway. It's a little after five in the morning, so I guess it's no surprise really that I'm up for a run. What *is* a surprise is Thayer leaning against the lamp post in a pair of long jogging shorts and an old t-shirt with his company's logo faded on top.

"What are you doing?" I bend down, tightening the laces on my right shoe.

"What? I can't hang out against the street light at five in the morning? Isn't this normal?" His lips lift into a smile.

"Is that a joke?" I know it is. I stand up straight, hands on my hips. "Are you making jokes with me now, Thayer?"

He shrugs. "Sure, why not?" He moves away from the light, stretching his arms above his head and gracing me with a sliver of his stomach. My core clenches at the sight. "I thought I'd join you on your run."

"Am I that predictable?"

He frowns, a dark look stealing over his face. "Yes."

Stretching my legs, I look up at him skeptically. "You've never run with me before, so why now?"

He looks away, jaw taut. "It'll be good for my health."

"Sure." I don't believe him one bit, but I also have no reason to suspect him of lying.

I arch a brow. "And you think you can keep up with me?"

He grins. "I think I can."

"YOU DO THAT EVERY MORNING?" THAYER HUFFS, TRYING TO catch his breath. We're stopped outside his house stretching.

"Pretty much. Except when it gets too cold, then I use my membership for the twenty-four-hour gym over by the grocery store."

His brows furrow deeply. "You're too young to be going to a gym like that at any hour."

"When I need to run I don't have much choice," I argue, stretching my calves.

He shakes his head. "I don't want you going there so early on your own."

I give him the stink eye. "I've been doing it for years."

He makes a sound like he tried to swallow his own tongue. "Worrying about you is going to be the end of me."

"All right, Dad."

He glares. "Do not *ever* call me that."

I pale. "Sorry, it was a joke." Color quickly returns to my cheeks when I remember that I *humped* his leg.

He shakes his head. "I didn't mean to sound so harsh."

"It's okay." I walk away from him, toward my house.

"Wait," he calls, his hand wrapping around my arm.

I look over my shoulder at him, biting my bottom lip. "Come inside. Please?"

I can't resist his warm brown eyes. I'm a complete sucker for this man. "Why?"

I want him to give me a good reason—a reason to say yes, even though I should most definitely say no.

"Because I want you to."

Damn him.

I give a tiny nod. It's barely a shake of my head, but with the way he's staring at me, he doesn't miss it. Tipping his head at his house for me to follow, I fall into step beside him. His arm brushes mine, sending my heart tripping over itself.

Unlocking the front door, he lets me in first. "I'm going to make breakfast. You want any?"

"Sure."

In the kitchen he grabs a carton of eggs from the mini-fridge and some bread for toast. He's added a portable stovetop to his smorgasbord of temporary appliances.

"When are the appliances due in?" I take the bread from him to pop some in the toaster.

"They're telling me this week." He grabs a cup to crack the eggs into. I watch his movements, the way his biceps work, and unbidden my eyes drop to his athletic shorts and the way they cling to the shape of him.

"You sound doubtful." I push the button down, watching the bread disappear and forcing myself not to look at Thayer's dick. At the thought of his dick my stupid, treacherous eyes dart back to his crotch.

He clears his throat and I redden at being caught. I look away hastily.

He scrambles the eggs together. "They said the same last week, so I'm not trusting their understanding of how long a week is. I think they're just trying to appease me."

"It's looking beautiful, though." The cabinets are a sage green color and he picked white counters with streaks of gold running through it. I find the combination to be unique and beautiful.

"Thanks." He pours the eggs into the hot skillet. I keep my eyes on his hands which is *almost* as bad. He has nice hands.

"Seriously, you're doing a great job with the place."

He gives a half-smile. "I knew it would take a while to get it where I want it, but it'll be worth it in the end."

"The best things take patience and time."

He chuckles. "I guess that's why I love puzzles so much."

I take this morsel of information he's handed to me, cradling it into my palm gently, holding onto it like a treasure.

"You like puzzles?"

"Mhmm," he hums, using a spatula to move the eggs around. The toast pops up and I grab plates and butter.

"Like puzzles you buy in a box, in a bunch of little pieces, put them on a table, kind of puzzle?"

He laughs—truly *laughs*. I think it might be my new favorite sound in the world. "Yeah, I'm working on one right now." He motions to the card table. "I can only do small ones at the moment, which isn't as enjoyable for me, but it's a nice decompressor in the evenings."

With the toast slathered in butter, I walk over to see the puzzle he's working on. It's a field of lavender. "It's beautiful."

"I know that's a lavender field, but it reminded me of all the wild-flowers behind our houses."

The wildflowers are one of my favorite things about living here. Before Thayer moved in I used to wish my room overlooked them, but Georgia got that space. "I love the wildflowers," I murmur, picking up a piece of the puzzle and eyeing the shape of it.

"You do?"

I look at him over my shoulder and give him a nod. "Yeah, why would I lie about that?"

He shrugs, adding the eggs to the plate. "It's just … I guess I would think a girl your age would find them ugly, a nuisance. In the way, I suppose."

"No." I put the piece back with the others. "Wildflowers are strong. Resilient. They can grow under most conditions. I want to be like that." I let my hair down, his eyes watching my movements. "I want to have the confidence of wildflowers—to never give up, to flourish, and thrive."

He rubs his stubbled jaw. "I've never thought about it like that. I like your way of thinking." He sets our plates down on the table. "Orange juice?"

"Yes, please." He pours two glasses, and we sit down to eat. "Thanks for running with me this morning."

He waves away my thanks. "It was nice to run again."

"I expected you to be huffing and puffing."

He narrows those chocolate-colored eyes on me. "Are you implying I'm out of shape?"

I look over his muscular build. "Well, no. Certainly not that. But a lot of people are in shape and can't run. Cardio is hardio."

His lips twitch like he wants to laugh but doesn't want to give in to the temptation. *"Hardio,"* he mouths with a shake of his head like he can't believe such a stupid made up word came out of my mouth.

"It's the truth." I take a bite of eggs. "Wow, these are really good."

"I add cheese."

"Really? I didn't notice."

Another twitch of his lips. "You were too busy staring at my..." He pauses, the bastard. "Puzzle."

Now it's my turn. "It's a very nice ... puzzle."

"You like puzzles, huh?"

The fact that puzzle has suddenly turned into a euphemism for *package* doesn't escape me. Or at least I *think* that's what's happening here.

"Some of them."

He rubs his fingers over his lips. There's been a line between us, a blurry one, but it's been there. I feel like the night in the hotel blurred it even more, and now we're more willing to toe past it. I've never been attracted to guys much older than me. With my trauma, that was never something I could stomach, but I'm attracted to Thayer for so many different reasons and his age isn't one of them.

"Eat your food," he says in a gruff voice, and I swear there's pink in his cheeks.

I let him take another bite of food before I ask, "Are we not going to talk about the fact that I orgasmed on your leg?"

He chokes, pieces of egg flying out of his mouth. "Fuck, Salem. Warn a guy before you say something like that."

"Why?" I smile brightly. "This was way more fun."

He wipes up the mess with a napkin. "You are a menace." Recovering from my surprise attack, he asks, "Do you want to talk about it?"

I shrug. "Not really, but I thought the mature thing to do would be to talk about it."

His eyes narrow. "If you want me to forget it ever happened, I will. After ... *fuck*, Salem, after your nightmare, what I learned, I didn't want to bring it up and frighten you or something, okay? I wasn't trying to brush it under the rug."

I tuck a piece of hair behind my ear. The shorter strands never stay in my ponytail when I'm running. "It's okay, I was just joking around. It was embarrassing." Normally I wouldn't be bold enough to bring it up, but I haven't been able to get the incident off my mind.

"Hey." The tip of his finger lifts my chin. "Don't hide from me. Ever. I see you. I want to see you. All of you." I bite my lip, tears stinging my eyes. "I know I can be a dick, but I would never push you to talk about anything you don't want to."

"I know." And I do know it. Thayer isn't the pushy type. Quiet and broody? Yes. But not pushy. Changing the subject, I ask around a bite of toast, "Are you running every morning now?"

Today was the first time I've had a nightmare since we got back from Boston, so I can't be sure when he started.

He shrugs. "Just when I feel like it."

"Hmm," I hum. Searching for the coffee pot, I ask, "Did you make any coffee this morning?"

He shakes his head, cringing. "I'm out."

I mock gasp. "Out of coffee? That's a crime."

He arches a brow. "We can go get some."

I wave away his words with a flick of my hand. "It's no biggie. I'll get some later."

"I have some Diet Coke if you want that?"

I perk up. "I'll never say no to that." With a shake of his head, he gets up from the table and returns with a bottle. I take it gratefully. "Thank you." Popping the top, I take a generous sip. "This is better than coffee."

He groans. "I don't know about that."

"Well, *I* think it is."

Finishing my breakfast, I wash my plate up in the kitchen sink—yes, there's *finally* a sink. Thayer is moving on up in the world.

He steps up beside me, his body heat radiating against me. My eyes close and I bite my lip so I don't moan. Everything about this man draws me in.

Caleb, I chant. *You have Caleb. You love him. You can't hurt him.*

Even though this summer wasn't ideal with Caleb, I do love him. I care about him so much. Being attracted to Thayer? I can't be. I need to stop.

Stepping away from him, I force a smile. "Thanks for running with me."

"Salem," he calls after me, but I don't stop.

I close the front door behind me and inhale a breath.

Get a grip, Salem.

TWENTY-EIGHT

Binx meows from the corner of the workshop behind A Checkered Past Antiques. "I know, buddy," I croon from across the room, pouring wax into the glass jars I use for my candles. "We'll go home soon. I'm almost done."

I'm working overtime to keep my fall scents out in the store. It's only mid-September but several have already sold out. I'm happy people love my candles because making them is a good decompressor for me.

I bring Binx with me from time to time. I think he appreciates getting out of the house and in a new environment for a while.

My phone rings, startling me and I curse when some of the hot wax hits my fingers. I finish pouring and swipe to accept the call.

"Hey, babe," Caleb's voice comes over the line.

My chest aches with missing him. "Hey. How are things?"

I can't believe he's already been gone a month. Lauren left two weeks ago. She's insistent that I come visit soon.

"It's school," he says like that's the only explanation needed. "I wish I could see your face."

"You could FaceTime me?" I laugh. "I look like shit, though."

When I make candles, I toss my hair up in a messy bun and wear old clothes so it doesn't matter if I ruin them.

"You're always beautiful." He switches the call to a FaceTime and I swipe to accept it.

"I warned you." I blow a piece of hair from my eyes.

He grins, his eyes sparkling. His dorm room sits behind him. I can tell he's at his desk, his bed behind him. "Nah, you look hot." I roll my eyes. "You do," he insists. "It's getting kind of late. When are you going home?"

I shrug, pouring more wax. "Soon." He looks doubtful. He knows I tend to get in the zone and overwork myself. "Promise."

He shakes his head, not believing me one bit. With the last of the wax poured, I carry my phone with me over to another one of my stations where wax has already hardened in the jars so I can start adding the sticker labels.

"Make sure you're taking care of yourself."

"I am, please don't worry about me. You have enough on your plate. I don't want to be a burden."

He blows out a breath. "You're not a burden. You never could be."

I drop my eyes, pretending to be focused on the stickers. I wonder what he'd think if he knew the truth about me. About what my father did to me. To my sister. He knows he was physically abusive to my mom, but he doesn't know the worst of it.

"You need to focus on school," I remind him.

"Hey." His voice is tight. "Something's wrong. Talk to me."

"Nothing's wrong." I force a bright smile. And really, there isn't. Not anything he can concern himself with, that is. Sometimes I just get in these ruts.

"I love you," he says softly. "You can talk to me."

I don't think he'd like me very much if I told him about my very complicated feelings for my neighbor. Caleb is perfect—well, as close to it as you can get. He's a *good* guy. A great guy, even. Our relationship is easy. He makes me happy.

But something has to be off for my thoughts to constantly stray to Thayer, right?

Or maybe there's something off with *me*.

"I know I can," I finally say. "It's just hard. Missing you. Lauren." This feels like a good enough excuse to get him off my back.

"I miss you, too, babe. Maybe you can come down for a weekend soon."

"I might."

I won't.

I can feel his stare through the camera. "Did I do something wrong?"

"No!" I rush to say. I don't want him thinking he did anything, because he hasn't. This is all my fault—the way I'm feeling. "God, no." I shake my head roughly. "I'm just distracted." I hold up a smore's scented candle.

"All right." He doesn't sound quite believing. "I love you. I'll talk to you later."

"Love you."

I hang up first.

And then I cry.

I don't break down often. It's been a while since the last time it happened, a good six months or so, but the emotions flood over me. I think about my therapist, things she has said about coping with trauma, and I let myself feel. Let myself mourn for the little girl who had to be so strong when she should've only had to be a kid.

IT'S RAINING AND I'M DRENCHED AS I STAND ON THAYER'S front porch with Binx in my arms, meowing angrily over being wet.

I knock on his door, then ring the doorbell over and over.

I don't know what possessed me to walk up to his door instead of my house, but I'm here now and I can't make myself leave.

The door swings open and reveals Thayer standing there in nothing but a pair of sweatpants. No shirt. Just his package front and center—and we've already established how much my eyes like it, so of course they zero in right on it.

"What the fuck?" He takes me in from head to toe, soaked from my walk from my car to here. It wasn't far at all, I mean I live right beside him. That's just how bad it's raining. "What the *fuck?*" He repeats, his eyes landing on the angry black cat in my arms.

"Binx doesn't like the rain."

"Then why is he in it?"

"I needed to talk to you."

"So, you brought your cat?"

I roll my eyes. "He was with me in my workshop. I was making candles."

He gives me a quizzical look. "You make candles?"

"Yeah, but that's not why I'm here." He seems to just then take in my state beyond being rain drenched. His eyes linger on my red-rimmed ones.

He tips his head toward the inside. "Come in." He closes the door behind me. "So, why *are* you here?" Shaking his head he curses under his breath. "Let me get you a shirt or something. I don't want you getting sick."

"I'm fine." And just to contradict me, my treacherous body shivers.

He chuckles. "Wait here." He jogs up the stairs.

Binx squirms angrily in my arms. With a sigh, I let him down, hoping Thayer won't mind the cat hair.

He returns less than a minute later with a gray t-shirt scrunched up in his hands. "This should work." He holds it out and I take it, tucking it between my legs. Without thinking, I take my shirt off. A choked gasp comes from Thayer. I quickly tug his shirt on and down over my body.

"It's just a bra, Thayer," I try to kid. "You've seen me in my bathing suit." Granted, I always choose one that covers a lot of skin, but still, it's not like he saw anything indecent.

He clears his throat, his eyes narrow and dark. "What did you want to talk about?"

"Do we have to do it right here?" I look around this foyer. This doesn't exactly feel like the kind of conversation you have with someone by the front door.

"We can go to the living room." He starts walking, expecting me to follow. He pauses, glancing back at me. "Where did your cat go?"

"Oh—"

Sighing, he waves a hand. "Never mind. Maybe he'll find some mice and kill them. Might as well make himself useful while he's here."

Thayer takes a seat on the couch, motioning for me to sit wherever I'd like. I pick the end of the same couch, tucking my legs under me. I pull my damp hair away from my face, securing it with an elastic. Now that I'm here, I'm not as confident as I was before.

"Do you need a drink or something?"

I nod eagerly at the momentary reprieve. He doesn't ask what I want when he gets up, returning all too quickly with a Diet Coke. Wrapping my fingers around the bottle, I unscrew the top and take a fortifying sip.

"Not many people know the truth about my dad," I begin, and his eyes widen in surprise. He didn't expect the conversation to go in this direction. "My mom and sister. They both lived it. Lauren, because I told her. My therapist. And now you."

"Your boyfriend?"

I shake my head. "He knows my dad was abusive but not the other stuff." I can't bring myself to say it. I might never be able to properly say those words, but my therapist said that's okay. I'm not avoiding what happened. "It's not something I share with others. I don't want them to look at me differently. My sister is the same way. I didn't know I talked in my sleep."

"Salem—"

"Let me get this out," I beg, fighting tears. "Call me crazy, but I'm kind of glad you know, that there's someone else out there in the world who knows the truth."

His face has darkened. "When you said what you did in your sleep..." He rubs his jaw. "Fuck, if he wasn't already dead, I would've killed him myself."

I give a weak laugh. "He wouldn't be worth going to jail."

Those warm brown eyes stare me down, looking, searching. I don't know what for, but finally he says, "But you are."

"Huh?"

"You're worth it, Salem."

"Oh." I duck my head. "I ... anyway ... I'm not saying I want to go into details or that I'll ever bring it up again but I'm glad you know the truth. That's ... that's all I wanted to say."

"There's something I've wondered," he muses softly. "If it's okay to ask?"

"I don't have to answer." It's the only go ahead I'll give him.

"Why didn't your mom leave him?"

I eye him, feeling more than a tad annoyed. "You know, it always amazes me that that's the first question people ask." I inhale a breath. "As if the blame lies on my mom and not on the man responsible. The man who beat his wife, snuck into his daughters' rooms at night," I rant, feeling my blood pressure rise. "It's *never*, 'Wow, what an awful human being he was. Your poor mom must have been terrified.'" I let him absorb this before I continue. "The blame always gets put on the victim or victims. Why is that?" I can tell I've stumped him. "It's because," I gather everything I have inside me so I can say this last bit, "society never wants to accept that monsters are real—just weak women."

His lips are parted, and he blinks, taking in what I've said. "Fuck, Salem. I never thought about it like that."

"Well, now you can." I play with the hem of his shirt that dwarfs my much smaller body. "She was scared to leave him. I've heard the threats. Ones where he said he'd hunt us to the end of the world or kill us and himself if she even tried. Sometimes I used to lie in bed and wish he would—that death would be better than *that*."

"I can't imagine what you went through and I'm a selfish fucking prick because I also can't imagine a world without you in it."

"I just wanted you to know. I mean, since you kind of already did. I felt like you deserved to know more."

His jaw ticks. "I would've never asked you to share more."

"I know." And I do. "But you deserved to understand."

"I want you to know," he begins, sounding a bit choked up, "no one, no child, should've ever had to endure what you and your sister

147

did. As a parent, I can't ... well, I don't know what kind of sick fuck you have to be to do that."

Wiping a tear that's escaped, I whisper hoarsely, "Thank you." Binx hops up onto the couch and into my lap. He curls up and lays down, knowing I need the comfort. I pet his head, feeling calm fill me. "I don't dwell much on the past anymore," I say softly, staring down at the cat in my lap. It's easier to look at him than Thayer. "But sometimes it creeps up on me and tonight was one of those times."

His warm hand curls around the top of mine. Tipping my head up, I meet his eyes. There's no judgment. In fact, he doesn't look at me one bit differently. I'm still Salem.

And that's all I ever want to be.

Me.

I hear my therapist in my head again, reminding me that my father can't take my identity if I don't let him.

TWENTY-NINE

'm more than a little surprised when the bell chimes over the door in the antique store and Thayer strides in, moving his sunglasses to rest on his baseball cap.

"Hi," I say warmly, trying not to smile like a fool. "What brings you in here?" He clears his throat, looking around at the chandelier section.

"My parents are going to come up for Thanksgiving and I know it's a month away, but I want to get them a gift. I thought I might find something for my mom here."

"Sure." I slide off the stool. "What does your mom like?"

"Flowers." He smiles sheepishly. "I guess she's where I got my love for plants and nature."

"We have some unique vases she might like." I lead him around through the maze of odds and ends. "What about this?" I hold up a classic blue and white design.

"She hates blue."

"That's out then." I put it away quickly. "What about this one?" I pull out a crystal one.

"Too stuffy for her taste."

"Hmm." I bite my lip. "Hold on." He follows after me as I go over to the display where my candles are. There's a vase there with fresh flowers inside. "What about this?" I hold it up so he can see the cream vase with tiny hand painted flowers.

"That," he takes it from me, spinning it around so he can see it from every angle, "is perfect."

"Good." I smile, pleased I could find something so easily for his mother. I set the vase behind the checkout counter, returning to where he still stands at the candle display. "What about your dad?"

He shakes his head. "Antiques aren't his thing."

I laugh, taking the vase back from him. "I'm not surprised."

He picks up one of the candles, reading the details on it before unscrewing the lid and taking a sniff. "These are yours."

It's a statement, not a question, but I answer anyway. "Yes."

He picks up another and sniffs. "I'll get one for my mom. Which is your favorite?"

I beam. "All of them." He chuckles at my response. "I put a lot of love into each of them, but this is my favorite." I pick it up and hand it to him.

He reads the label, a smile threatening to lift his lips. "Cookie dough? Why am I not surprised?" I shrug, clasping my hands behind my back. "I'll take one."

"Just one?" I kid. "Don't get cheap on me now, Thayer."

This time he gives me a full-blown smile. "All right." He grabs up two more of the cookie dough scent. "Does this suffice?"

I smile back at him. "It'll do."

"I HAVE BIG NEWS. HUGE. ABSOLUTELY OUT OF THIS WORLD." Georgia breezes into the house from her date with Michael—the sound of his motorcycle driving off echoing in the distance.

I look up from the cupcakes I'm making for Thayer—he didn't ask for them, but after he came into the store today, I figured we both could use some. My mom sits at the kitchen table, eyeing the mess I'm making but not saying a word. It's late so it has surprised me she hasn't asked why I decided to make cupcakes now.

"What is it, dear?" My mom turns in her chair to face Georgia. Her eyes look tired, bags bigger than normal beneath them. She looks pale, too. I need to make sure she's eating every meal and drinking enough water.

Georgia looks radiant, glowing and happy. Maybe Michael is finally getting his shit together and treating her the way she deserves. He's not a bad guy, not really anyway, just a little misguided.

Smoothing her blonde hair down and straightening her top, she meets each of our gazes. Before she speaks, she meets my eyes and taps her nose.

"Huh?"

"You have flour on your nose."

"Oh!" I wipe it away with the back of my arm.

"Anyway," she claps her hands together, "Michael asked me to move in with him."

"Wow," my mom blurts, surprise evident in her tone. "That's ... wow."

"I know! It's so exciting! I think we'll be engaged by Christmas!"

If that's what she wants, if *he's* who she wants, then I hope for the best. "That's amazing, Georgia." I smile at my sister. Michael might not be my favorite person in the world, but my sister is, and I want her to be happy.

"I don't have much to move into his apartment, so I think I'll be out by the end of the week."

Mom's eyes widen. "Really? That's so soon."

"I know, but it doesn't make any sense to wait."

Either that or she's afraid if she waits too long, he'll change his mind.

"I'm happy for you," I tell her, hoping to distract her from our mom's obvious worry.

"Thank you, sis." She moves behind the island counter and hugs me—well, half hugs me since she doesn't want to dirty her dress.

Mom stands up, adjusting the apron she wears. This one has multi-colored fall leaves on it. I love her collection of aprons, the fact she has one for every season, holiday, and pretty much everything you can think of.

"My little girl is growing up." There are tears in her eyes as she hugs Georgia. She looks at me over my sister's shoulder. "Both of you."

"Are you okay with this, Mom?" Georgia holds her hands between hers.

"Of course, I am. I'm going to miss you, but this is the natural progression of things. I knew you girls would fly the nest one day."

"I love you," Georgia says, and I think my normally in control sister might cry too. She hugs our mom again. "I'm so excited. It'll be nice to girl up Michael's bachelor pad." She sashays away, singing softly as she goes.

My mom snickers. "Poor Michael, he doesn't know what he's in for."

"Oh yeah," I agree, sliding cupcakes into the oven. "Georgia's going to feminize his man cave, and he's going to lose his shit." Her laughter is soft as she returns to the table. She winces a bit as she sits, a sigh leaving her throat. "Are you okay?"

She waves away my concern. "Fine. I'm fine."

I hesitate, biting my lip. I don't believe her, but I don't push it.

THIRTY

The next day, I keep an eye out for Thayer's truck to return home. When it does, I wait about an hour before I gather up the plate of cupcakes and head next door. The chilly weather is coming in now that we're in the middle of October. My jeans hug my legs and hips and I chose a fitted top. I wanted to look cute, but not like I'm trying to seduce him.

Which I'm not.

That would be bad.

A good kind of bad, but bad nonetheless.

The door opens and Thayer grins, eyes crinkling at the corners. I think he smiles before he means to, because he clears his throat and quickly sobers. Eyes dropping to the dish of cupcakes, there's another hint of a smile.

"Cookie dough?"

"There's no better kind."

He steps aside, his hair damp from the shower and curling at his nape. "Come on in." I step inside and he closes the door. "You want a drink?"

"Sure."

I follow him to the kitchen, and he pulls out a beer for himself and a Diet Coke for me. I trade the plate of cupcakes for the Diet Coke. He sits them down, removing the top and plucking one out.

"If you keep feeding me these, I'm going to gain fifty pounds."

I take in his trim, muscular build. I don't purposely mean to check him out, that's just what happens.

"I think you'll be fine." Clearing my throat, I step away from him.

His woodsy scent fills my nose, making me feel lightheaded. Or maybe it's just him that makes me feel that way. I make a mental note to try to replicate his scent for a candle.

"You want one?" He asks around a bite, pointing at the plate.

"No, it's okay. I saved some for myself."

"Do you need to go somewhere or...?" He waits for me to fill in the blanks.

"I don't have anywhere I need to be." With Lauren and Caleb gone, all I have is work and my candles.

"You want me to put a movie on or something?"

"That would be nice." I move closer to the doors that open to the back deck. "The greenhouse is coming along."

"It's a slow project since I only work on it when I have spare time, but it'll be worth it when it's done."

"What about Forrest's treehouse?"

He winces. "That kid doesn't stop talking about it, even though I told him from the get-go that I wouldn't be able to build it until next spring and summer."

"He's just excited." I take a sip of the soda.

"I know." He finishes the cupcake and grabs his beer. "Come on." I follow him into the living room and plop on the couch while he grabs the remote. "Is there anything in particular you want to watch?"

"Are you offering me the choice, Thayer? That's a dangerous game."

"Don't make me regret this decision," he mutters, but he doesn't sound mad.

"What if we watch your favorite movie and then watch mine?"

He thinks it over. "All right."

"What is it?"

He turns the TV on. "What is, what?"

I roll my eyes playfully, tugging a pillow onto my lap. "Your favorite movie?"

I swear his cheeks turn the tiniest bit pink. "The Lord of The Rings trilogy, we'll only watch the first one, though."

Mock gasping, I ask, "Thayer, are you a closet nerd?"

He arches a brow. "I own a landscaping business and know a hell of a lot about plants and you're assuming I'm in the closet about my nerdoms? No, Salem. I'm very open about the fact that I'm a nerdy individual."

I laugh, curling my legs under me. "Tell me more."

"About what?"

"Your hobbies. Anything." I shrug. I sound so desperate, and I guess I am. I want to know everything there is to know about Thayer Holmes.

He opens an app on the TV and scrolls through for the movie. "Um, well I love camping. Does that count?"

"That's definitely a hobby," I concur, twisting the soda lid back and forth.

"And you know about the puzzles."

"I love the puzzles." I blush when the words come out as a sultry purr.

He chuckles, shaking his head. "You know all the dirt on me. I'm losing all my cool street cred."

"I highly doubt I know all there is to know."

"More than most." He hits play on the movie and takes a seat, purposely putting a cushion's worth of space between us. I suddenly hate that particular cushion.

We watch the movie in silence, and I'm surprised to find that I actually enjoy it. When it's over, he stands up and stretches. If he hears my moan at the sight of the sliver of skin above the waistband of his jeans he says nothing.

"I'm starving," he says, picking up his empty beer. "Do you mind if I order dinner before we start another movie?"

"Not at all." I don't know why he's even asking me. It's his house.

"Pizza or Chinese?"

"Either is fine."

"Salem," he says in a warning tone.

I laugh. "Pizza then. Pepperoni," I add before he can ask.

"I'll go order. Use the bathroom if you need to." He scoops up his phone in his other hand, heading out of the room.

My bladder is screaming, so I head to the powder room. Washing my hands, I open the door and hear him on the phone.

"Miss you too, buddy. I'll see you Friday after school." There's a pause. "Mhmm, I'll pick you up from school." Another stretch of quiet as I walk into the kitchen. Thayer's eyes meet mine as he says, "I'm sure Salem misses you too and will be happy to see you." I smile at that. Forrest is a good kid and I like hanging out with him. I never know what's going to come out of his mouth. "All right. I love you, buddy. Sleep tight. Don't let the bed bugs bite."

He hangs up, looking at me with a sad smile.

"I'm sorry," I say, because I don't know what else to say.

He runs his fingers through his hair, grabbing another beer from the mini-fridge. "About what?"

"That you can't be with him."

"It is what it is." He pops the top and takes a swig of the liquid.

I slide onto a barstool across from him. "How'd you meet Krista?"

He rubs his jaw. "You really want to talk about this?"

I shrug, picking up the notepad on the countertop. It's a grocery list. "Why not? We have time to kill before the pizza gets here and we start my movie."

"All right." He leans against the counter. "We met in high school. She was a freshman, and I was a sophomore. We were only friends at first. We started dating the next year."

"So," I draw random designs on the granite with my pointer finger, "you were high school sweethearts, then?" My thoughts stray to Caleb.

"Yeah." He nods, a glum set to his shoulders.

It seems like he's not going to say anything more. "When did you get married?"

He rubs his stubbled jaw. "During college."

I shake my head, fighting a smile. "You're a man of few words."

He sighs, seeming to fortify himself. "We were young and in love. Marriage seemed like the next logical step. We got married my senior year." He sips at his beer. "I guess, in a way, it seemed easiest. She was all I knew, and I was content. Things didn't seem so bad. My parents loved her, and I did too. Then we had Forrest and it seemed like everything should be perfect now, but as the years went on, I think we both realized we had settled. I wasn't the right fit for her and vice versa." He runs his fingers through his hair. "Growing apart, that breeds resentment. I think we both stayed in the relationship longer than we should have because of Forrest. But in the end, we realized he was better off having happy parents that are apart than miserable ones together." A haunted look overtakes him, and I wish I could wipe it away.

"I think that's admirable. I can't imagine it's easy with a kid involved." Biting my lip, I ask, "Do you think Caleb and I are doomed then? That if you fall in love young it's only destined to end in heartbreak?" I hold my breath, waiting for his response.

He slides his beer to the side, having only taken a few sips and grabs a water bottle.

"I'm cynical about a lot of things, love being one of them." He exhales a weighted breath. "I'm not saying you're doomed or anything. Plenty of others make it. But it has to be worth fighting for."

"And your love with Krista wasn't?"

He meets my eyes. "No."

He says it so sure that I almost feel sorry for her. "Why?" I cringe as soon as I ask that. "You don't have to answer."

"She became someone I didn't recognize. Vindictive, spiteful, angry. All the parts that I fell in love with had disappeared. The manipulative games she played were the worst, and I was done."

"What do you think changed her?"

"Honestly, I think she always had a lot of that in her." He picks at the label on the water bottle. "I can't prove it, and I wouldn't change anything because I love my son, but I'm pretty sure she got pregnant on purpose. We'd only been married around two years at that point and were going through a rough patch. I think she thought a baby would fix things. I suppose it did for a while, but you can't fix a broken house with lies."

The doorbell rings then and he heads to get the pizza.

"I'll pay you back for this," I say, following after him. "I don't have any cash on me, but I'll give you some the next time I see you."

He pauses, hand on the doorknob. "Don't worry about it, Salem. I mean it."

There must be something wrong with me because that bossy tone of his makes my core clench with pleasure. I'm seriously fucked up.

He pays the delivery driver and closes the door. He carries the boxes into the living room and sets them on the coffee table.

"I'll get our drinks." I head back to the kitchen for them. I grab another Diet Coke from the fridge and turn to get his, but nearly smack into his chest. "Jesus Christ!" My hand flies to my chest. "Don't sneak up on me like that." He makes no move to back up. "Thayer?" His brown eyes stare at me intently. "W-What are you doing?" His tongue wets his lips and I realize he's staring at my mouth. "Are you going to kiss me?" I blurt my thoughts out loud.

He towers above me, lowering his head so I'm cocooned with the mini-fridge behind my legs and his body blocking everything else. I know if I wanted to move, he'd let me pass, that's the kind of man he is. But the fact is, I don't want to.

His voice is deeper than normal when he asks, "Do you want me to?"

I swallow. *Do I?*

"Yes."

He doesn't hesitate.

His hand cups the back of my neck, his other at my waist. I'm pulled against his body. We're fitted together so tightly that you couldn't stick a piece of paper between us if you tried. His mouth meets mine, his lips warm and firm but somehow gentle at the same time. He begs my lips to part with the tip of his tongue, and I answer with a gasp, letting his tongue delve into my mouth.

Oh my God, I'm kissing Thayer!

It'd be a lie if I said I hadn't thought about this moment. What it would be like to kiss him. What his mouth would feel like. Would he be hard? Soft? Eager?

He's everything and more.

My ass bumps into the top of the fridge and he lifts me up, sitting me on top with him between my legs. He angles my head back, deepening the kiss. My hands are fisted in his hair. I don't want him to stop. If he suddenly changes his mind I'll be devastated.

He keeps one hand cupped to the back of my neck, but his other moves to my cheek. His thumb rubs my skin in slow, soothing circles.

He pulls away slowly, our noses touching. Long dark lashes touch the tops of his cheeks every time he blinks.

"Hi," I say stupidly.

"Hi."

"You kissed me." I bite my lip to hide my giddy smile.

"I did."

"Did you like it?"

He tries not to smile. "I did. Did you?"

"Mhmm." I nod eagerly, perhaps too eager. "I think we should do it again."

His eyes narrow on my swollen lips. "I shouldn't have done it."

I frown, panic surging in my veins. "But you said you liked it."

"And I did," he assures, leaning close enough that his lips brush over mine. "But it doesn't change the facts."

"What facts?" I'm pretty sure his kiss killed ninety percent of my brain cells.

"You're eighteen, Salem."

I duck my head, gripping onto his t-shirt. "Please, don't ... don't use that as an excuse. Not when this feels ... like *this*."

"I don't want to take advantage of you."

"You're not!" I rush to say. "God, Thayer." I shake my head roughly. "You would never."

"You're young." I flinch, hating that he's so focused on my age. I know, believe me, *I know* what it looks like with him so much older, but this attraction has to be worth battling what others might think. "Hey." He tips my head up with his finger. "I'm not saying that to be mean. It's just a fact. You're at a different part of your life than I am mine."

"So, what?" I retort. "That automatically means I don't know what I want?"

He shakes his head, his hair tickling my forehead. "Fuck, that's not what I meant." He presses his lips into a thin line, thinking. "It's just ... you have a life to live and—"

"What? When you turn thirty suddenly, you're old and don't have a life to live?"

He presses a hand over my mouth. "Don't sass me."

My gaze thins. "What are you going to do about it? Spank me?" I challenge.

His eyes flare with lust. "You're playing a dangerous game."

"So. Are. You."

He growls low in his throat, and I gasp when his mouth is on mine again. He's rough, like he's trying to scare me away, but it only awakens something inside me. I claw at him, trying to get his shirt off. He obliges, quickly tearing it over his head before he's kissing me again.

"Salem," he murmurs my name between kisses.

I wind my legs around his waist, gasping when I feel the hardness of his erection.

We are chaos. Unrestrained passion igniting with a single spark.

I moan, grinding myself against him.

Thayer. Thayer. Thayer.

His name is a chant in my mind. He fills all my senses. My thoughts, too. He's everywhere and I don't want him to ever leave. His warm, calloused hands skate beneath my shirt, and I shiver at the feel of them against my bare skin.

"Are you cold?"

"No," I pant. I don't tell him, but I feel like I'm on fire.

I'm hot. Achy. Fucking needy.

"We should stop," he says, but he keeps kissing me.

"No." I take my shirt off since it's bunched under my bra.

His eyes take me in, filled with lust and desire and something more, something infinitely tender.

"I'm not sure I can," he murmurs before he dives back in.

160

We're a clash of lips, teeth, and roaming hands. I moan when he cups my breasts, rubbing my hardened nipples through my bra. I curse myself for putting on one of my plainer ones instead of one of the sexier lace ones I own, but it wasn't like I expected this to happen when I came over here tonight.

Thayer picks me up and I wrap my arms and legs around him. He carries me to the living room, sitting down with me on his lap. His hardness presses against my core, eliciting a moan from me. My fingers tangle in his hair, yanking his head back away from my mouth so I can look at him.

His brown eyes are heavy with lust, but concern begins to fill them. "Salem—"

I silence him with a kiss. Whatever is happening right now, I don't want it to stop.

Grinding against him, his fingers dig into my hips. My fingers go to his leather belt, his hand shooting out to grab mine. I look at him questioningly. "Are you going to let me take your pants off?"

His tongue wets his lips. He counters with, "Are we doing this right now?"

I grin wickedly, running my hand over his length, hard and ready for me. "It feels like you want to."

He drops his head back against the couch cushion. "I won't take advantage of you."

"You're not." I press a kiss to his neck. God, I want this. Want *him*.

"Your age—"

I press my hand over his mouth, shutting him up. I don't want to rehash the conversation we had in the kitchen before mauling each other.

"I'm young, I know, but that doesn't mean I don't know what I want." I know I have more growing up to do. More maturing. But right now, I know myself. I know how I feel about Thayer. I know I want this. And I know I won't regret it. "I want you," I tell him. "Right now, that's what I want. I'm not asking you to put a ring on my finger. Just to fuck me."

With a growl I find myself flat on my back on the couch with him fitted between my legs. He wraps his hands around my wrists, trapping them above my head.

"You want me to fuck you, Sunshine?"

Sunshine. He's never called me that before. It's officially the best nickname I've ever heard.

"Y-Yes." Normally I would be embarrassed over how breathless and needy I sound, but I can't bring myself to care.

He holds my hands in just one of his, using his free one to gently glide his fingers over my cheek. "I shouldn't want you." His chocolate-colored eyes move to mine. "But I do."

"I shouldn't want you," I echo, biting my lip so I won't move my hips. "But I do."

With those words, his resolve crumbles. He kisses over the swells of my breasts, his hand sliding around to undo the clasp of my bra. The sound of it unsnapping seems so loud in the otherwise quiet living room. Suddenly feeling shy, I squeeze my arms against my sides so he can't pull it off.

"I want to see you," he begs. "All of you."

Loosening my arms, I allow him to pull the bra away from my skin. His eyes take me in, my small but perky breasts, round pink nipples. He looks at me like I'm the most stunning thing he's ever laid his eyes on.

"I have a confession to make," he murmurs, dipping his head to suck on the skin of my neck.

"W-What?" I ask, desperate to hear what he has to say but also not wanting his mouth to part from my skin.

"That morning," he begins, moving his lips over my collarbone, "in the hotel. After you, got off on my leg..."

I *hate* that he's bringing this up right now, but luckily the way he's kissing my skin is easing my embarrassment. "I remember," I say breathily when it becomes obvious he wants me to say something.

He raises up, pecking a kiss on my lips. "I went to the bathroom and had to jack off." He kisses me again. "You have no idea how hot that was." I feel a blush flush my entire body. "You're fucking gorgeous." He squeezes my breast. "And right now," he swirls his tongue around one of my nipples, eyes never straying from mine, "you're mine."

162

"Yours," I echo on a whimper.

He presses tender kisses down my stomach, swirling his tongue around my naval. His eyes never leave mine, his breath hot against my bare skin when he pops the button on my jeans. I wiggle impatiently, my pussy clenching relentlessly, desperate to be filled by him.

"Patience," he murmurs, unzipping and then wiggling the material past my hips.

My heart beats so fast that I fear I might pass out. My fingers tangle in his hair, yanking at the strands. "I need you."

"Tell me where you need me." He places a soft, barely there kiss on my pubic bone above the band of my panties.

"Your mouth," I pant, my hips rising up on their own. "I want it on my pussy."

His eyes flash hot and molten. "Fuck, say it again."

"I want," I enunciate each word, "your mouth," I lick my lips, "on my pussy."

His chest rumbles with pleasure at my declaration. He moves my panties to the side, exposing the most intimate part of me that's aching with want for him.

"Is this okay?" he asks.

"Yes," I cry out, ready to beg him to touch me.

His fingers skim lightly over my skin. "You're soaked," he groans.

I wiggle, worried he's going to delay this even longer, but then he lowers his head, tasting me with one long sweep of his tongue. I cry out, my hips rising off the couch and my hands splaying out to grab something, anything.

He licks and sucks at me like he's starving and I'm his last meal. He's an expert with his tongue. It's never felt this good before.

I whimper and cry as he works me to an orgasm and when I fall over the edge, faster than I ever have before, I scream his name over and over like a prayer.

He rises over my body and kisses me. I taste myself on his tongue, but surprisingly I don't mind it. His erection presses against me and I reach down, cupping him over his jeans.

"Need to be in you." He sounds like he's aching with the same need I am.

He shoves his jeans down and his boxer-briefs with them.

Thayer Holmes is naked in front of me.

I don't look away.

I take in every inch of him.

Every. Long. Perfect. Inch.

A part of me wonders how he'll fit. He's the most well-endowed man I've ever seen, but I know it'll be fine. My body is ready, desperate to be filled by him.

I touch the smattering of chest hair on his pectoral muscles that grows heavier beneath his belly button, framing his thick cock.

I wrap my hand around him and he bucks his hips forward, eyes falling closed. "Fuck, Salem. You're going to make me come too fast like a teenage boy."

I lick my lips, rubbing my thumb around the head of his cock and wiping the bead of precum into his tip.

"I like that."

"What?" He pants, clearly struggling for control. "That I can't control myself?"

"No." I shake my head, biting my lip. His eyes zero in on my breasts, watching the way they move when I do. "That you want me so bad."

"I've wanted you for way longer than I should've."

"Since when?"

"Since you brought the asshole next door cupcakes and tried to be his friend. You were all long tan legs and blonde hair and gorgeous green eyes. I couldn't get enough but I knew it was wrong."

"And now we're here." I continue to stroke him, his hips rocking forward to meet my hand.

"So we are." He curses and it's not the good kind of curse. "I don't have condoms."

"I'm on birth control and ... and Caleb always wears a condom."

His eyes darken at the mention of my boyfriend.

God, I'm an awful person. Thoughts of my boyfriend should make me stop, to cover myself and flee, but I do no such thing. My need for Thayer is so acute that I'm afraid stopping might kill me.

"I'm clean," he promises me. "I got tested after my divorce. Are you sure about this?"

"God, *yes*. Please, just get inside me, Thayer." I grab his ass, my fingers digging into his skin and pulling him forward.

He doesn't hesitate. Grabbing the base of his cock, he plunges into me. I cry out, my back arching. He's so big and I'm so full.

"Fucking hell, Salem," he curses, exhaling heavily.

"Am I too tight?" I squeak, because my God, he's stretching me.

He shakes his head, brown hair falling over his forehead. I reach up, brushing it away so I can see his eyes. I need to see them. He can't hide from me that way.

"No," he rocks slowly out and back in, "it's just…" His fingers tighten around my hips, angling me up to meet his thrusts. "You feel like mine."

I press my hand to his stubbled cheek. I don't say it, not with words, but it's felt between the movement of our bodies.

Because I am.

We've never said that one special word to each other.

Love.

But that's what he does.

He doesn't fuck me like I asked.

Thayer makes love to me.

Mind.

Body.

Soul.

I'm filled with him in more ways than one.

And I know, in this moment, in this space between us, I've been irrevocably changed.

I am his. He is mine.

Nothing, not time, distance, nor the complete obliteration of our world can change that.

THIRTY-ONE

Post sex pizza and Hocus Pocus playing on the TV might officially be one of my favorite things ever. I'm only wearing Thayer's t-shirt, completely naked beneath it. Every so often he lifts it to knead my breasts, suck my nipples, or simply to smack my ass.

Post sex Thayer is also now one of my favorite things. He's in a good mood, a weight that's normally on his shoulders gone for the moment. He smiles, laughing and joking with me. He seems younger somehow.

"I can't believe this is your favorite movie." He points a slice of pizza at the TV. He had to heat it back up in the oven but neither of us complained.

"This is amazing," I scoff. "I watch it all the time."

"Does this mean Halloween is your favorite holiday?"

"Yes, of course. It should be everyone's favorite."

He tries not to smile. "And why is that?"

"Because it's *awesome*." I bite into my pepperoni pizza.

"Has anyone ever told you that's a weak argument?"

I point to my face. "Do I look like I care?"

"No." This time he does smile. "But come on, you really think it's better than Christmas?"

"Yes, abso-fucking-lutely. I take it that's *your* favorite?"

"Yeah." He nods, reaching for another slice. "My mom would go all out for my brother and me growing up. I'm talking going as far as to make it look like reindeer had been in the yard. It was..." He pauses, searching for the right word. "Magical. I've tried to keep that alive for Forrest. Kids deserve to believe in the unthinkable. Reality can be a slap in the face. Let them dream with their eyes open while they have the chance."

I take in his words, nodding. "That's a really beautiful way to look at things." With a shrug, I add, "I just like the spooky stuff."

He chuckles. "Do you carve pumpkins?"

"You know it." I tuck a piece of hair behind my ear, feeling suddenly shy with his gaze on me. "The town always puts on a pumpkin carving contest every year. There's a snowman building one too."

"That's kind of..."

"Over the top?"

"No. I think it's neat that this town is so tightknit."

"It's a community, not just a town, that's for sure."

He reaches over, wrapping his big hand around my thigh. "What are you—"

He pulls me against his side and presses a kiss to my lips. "I wanted you closer." He skims his nose along my cheek to the shell of my ear. "I'm not finished with you yet."

A shiver runs down my spine at the thought of more delicious pleasure at Thayer's capable hands. "Well, you might not be finished with me, but I'm not finished with this pizza. Someone made me burn a lot of calories."

He chuckles. "Have your fill."

"And then?"

"And then I'll have my fill of you."

IT'S LATE WHEN I WALK BACK NEXT DOOR TO MY HOUSE. WE finished Hocus Pocus and then he made love to me again, on the floor this time. It was sexy, intense, everything I didn't know sex could be.

The door creaks open when I step inside, and I silently curse the old house for being so loud. It's not that I'm worried about sneaking in. I don't have a curfew and my mom trusts me, but if she's asleep I don't want to wake her.

She's in the living room and sits up from the couch at the sound of the door.

"Sorry, Mom." I lock the door behind me. "I didn't mean to wake you."

"Where were you?" She yawns, stretching her arms. "I didn't mean to doze off down here."

HGTV plays softly on the screen, the only light in the room.

"I was with a friend."

"Oh." She looks a tad puzzled, probably because she knows other than Caleb and Lauren I don't talk to anyone else.

Caleb.

God, what am I going to do?

The guilt begins to settle into a pit in my stomach and I worry I'm going to be sick. This isn't like me—doing something like this.

She starts to rise from the couch, but sways. A hand shoots to her forehead as she sits back down.

"Mom." I rush to her side. "Are you okay?"

Her eyes are squeezed shut and she looks like she's in pain. "Fine. It's okay. Just dizzy. Lack of sleep, I think," she rambles.

I frown, concerned. I know she can have restless nights like I do, but this seems different and I can't help but be worried.

"Mom," I probe, gripping her hand to help her up. "What aren't you telling me?"

She pales. "Nothing." Once she's standing, she heads for the stairs, her hand shaking.

"I know when you're lying," I tell her retreating figure.

She pauses, her hand on the railing. She doesn't look at me when she says, "And you think I don't know the same about you? We all have our secrets, Salem, and we're allowed to keep them."

With those parting words, she disappears upstairs for bed, but I'm suddenly frozen.

Ice all over.

I look out the window at Thayer's house and then back upstairs.

There's no way she knows.

I have to believe that.

THIRTY-TWO

'm solemn on the train ride to Boston. It's an unexpected trip but a necessary one. I'm revolted over my betrayal of Caleb. It's not right what I did, even if it felt so good, and I can't let this continue.

When the train arrives, I hop off and head toward the campus and the address for his dorm that he gave me.

I'm nervous.

I love Caleb. He's my friend, my lover. He's been a rock in my life, a constant I could rely on, and I'm about to sever that. I know when I end things more than likely I'll never hear from him again. It sucks, because I don't want to lose him, I really don't, but I have to.

It's rainy and chilly, the sky a murky gray color. I tug the hood of my jacket over my head, tucking my hands into my pockets as I walk down the street.

I'm not good at this. I've never had to break someone's heart before, and it makes it even worse because I love Caleb. But what I feel for Thayer is all consuming, intense. It's a magnetism I can't deny.

Before Thayer came along, I thought what I have with Caleb was normal, how relationships are, how love feels. But I couldn't have been more wrong. Caleb has never made my heart race the way Thayer does. I should've ended things sooner with him, but I was confused over my feelings and didn't understand.

Now, I do, and I have to do the right thing.

I shoot Caleb a text and he gives me the information to come straight to his room.

I was hoping he'd meet me outside.

But I follow his instructions and suddenly I'm outside a door with a white board hanging on it. I knock on the door and there's some shuffling inside.

Then Caleb is there, opening the door with a beaming grin and yanking me into his arms.

He squeezes me tight, burying his face into my neck, and despite myself I sigh in relief at the contact. I *have* missed him.

I wrap my arms around him.

Are you really going to break his heart?

I already did. The moment things started swaying from platonic with Thayer, I hurt him even if he doesn't know it.

He sets me down and turns to someone in his room. "Matt, this is Salem."

Matt inclines on a raised bed playing some handheld gaming device. He has dark, almost black curly hair. "'Sup."

"Let's go." Caleb takes my hand. "Let me show you the campus."

He's so excited, his eyes lit up with happiness, so I can't say no.

We head out of the room holding hands. By the time we leave the building I've managed to extricate my hand from his. The guilt ... I just can't hold his hand right now.

Caleb leads me around the Harvard campus, pointing out various buildings and giving me information about when they were built and who paid for them and a bunch of other details that go right over my head.

After walking around for an hour, we grab coffee from a stand and find a bench to sit on. He wipes it dry with the sleeve of his jacket.

"It's beautiful here," I say, letting the pumpkin spice latte hit my tongue. "I can see why you like it."

"I wish you were here."

"I could never get into Harvard."

"I'm sure you could, babe. But there are other schools or you could live and work in Boston. Next year we could get an apartment together—"

"Caleb," I cut him off. *Don't cry. Don't cry.* "There's something we need to talk about."

"Sure, what's up? Is it my mom? Look, I know she was a hard ass this summer, but—"

"It's not your mom." *I. Will. Not. Cry.*

His brows knit together. "Then what is it?"

I wrap my fingers tightly around the coffee cup. "Caleb, be honest, can you say that things have been good with us since we graduated?"

"I ... Salem, it's normal for couples to go through rough patches from time to time. We've had some growing pains with me going to college, but it's nothing serious." He gives a rough laugh. When I don't join him, he sobers, his voice dropping. "Right?"

"Caleb," I choke on his name.

I don't want to break, but it feels inevitable.

"You're breaking up with me, aren't you?" He sounds shocked. Hurt. Broken-hearted.

I nod, chin wobbling. "This isn't working."

"Not for you, apparently. I ... I thought it was." He rubs a hand over his jaw. Normally it's clean shaven, but there's the barest hint of blond stubble.

"We're growing apart—"

"Really? Are we? Because I hadn't noticed."

I hadn't expected him to seem so blindsided. Is it possible I'm the only one who's felt the distance between us?

"Yes," I say softly. I don't want to turn this into an all-out screaming fight. "You spent most of the summer playing football and at the gym or doing whatever it was your mom wanted. You didn't even go to the concert with me—"

"I said I was sorry for that," he points out, eyes sad.

"And I forgave you, and I meant it. But you're here now," I gesture to the campus, "and this is where *you* belong. Not me. I think we need to break up. We need to grow and we can't do that together."

"Wow." He exhales heavily, rubbing a hand on his jean clad thigh. "You're really doing this, huh?"

I nod. "You're amazing, Caleb, but I need this. I need to see who I am on my own."

He shakes his head, looking up at the dreary sky. "It's not you, it's me? That's what this is?"

"I don't want to hurt you."

"Then why are you?" My face contorts with pain, tears burning my eyes. "It's someone else, isn't it? You have feelings for another guy."

"No!" I say too quickly. "Yes," I admit begrudgingly.

He laughs humorlessly. "Who is he?"

"It's not important."

Hurt flashes in his eyes. "Fine, don't tell me." He stands. "I hope you're happy with him, Salem. I know that sounds sarcastic right now, and maybe it is, but I really do just want you to be happy."

He walks away, head ducked low. I wait five minutes, letting myself have a moment before I get up and walk back to the train station.

When I get home, I climb in bed and cry.

THIRTY-THREE

"What about this one?" Forrest runs ahead of us in the field, picking up a pumpkin, tiny muscles straining as he tries to give it a shake. He gives it a knock on the side. "No, this one is a bad nut." He runs to the next.

Thayer gives me a speculative look at the bad nut comment. "We watched *Charlie and the Chocolate Factory* last week."

He shakes his head, trying not to smile. I wonder why he holds his smiles so close. He doesn't let them loose often. "Don't you mean *Willy Wonka and the Chocolate Factory?*"

"No." I scoop up a pumpkin, but find the bottom rotted. I frown. It was the perfect shape for carving. We're supposed to be picking out pumpkins to carve with my mom tonight. "I hate the first one. It gave me nightmares as a kid." I shudder. "Nope. Never again."

He throws his head back and laughs. God, I love that sound. "You're an interesting woman, Salem."

Woman. Not girl. I love that.

Up ahead Forrest groans, trying to pick up a massive pumpkin that not even Thayer could lift.

"Forrest," he scolds, jogging over to his son and squatting down. He's dressed today in a pair of khaki colored work pants, a plaid button-down shirt, and a vest. I didn't know vests could be so hot, but mountain man Thayer has changed my mind.

"I want this one, Daddy. It's huuuuge." Forrest spreads his arms as wide as they'll go.

"It's not ideal for carving," Thayer tells him.

"Don't care."

Thayer sighs but chooses not to argue. "Here, help me out."

And then Thayer picks up the huge pumpkin with Forrest attempting to help. Huh. Here I thought he couldn't do it and he proved me wrong.

I pull the cart behind me, and Thayer deposits the pumpkin onto it with a wink. "We'll conveniently lose that before we leave." Forrest is already oblivious, running ahead through all the pumpkins. "He'll be exhausted by the time we finish with this and a hayride."

"Don't forget the maze," I point out.

"And the maze," he adds. Arching a brow, he says, "Are you trying to get lost with me in a field of corn, Matthews?"

"Maybe, Holmes."

He walks beside me and picks good pumpkins for all of us, then ditches the massive no good one when Forrest is distracted by the goats.

"I'll tell him they wanted to keep that one but thanked him for picking such a good one."

"Good idea."

He nods, his smile a little broken. I know he's sad he won't be spending Halloween with his son this year. Apparently, Krista didn't even offer for him to tagalong with them and I know without a doubt Thayer would've extended an invite to her if he was supposed to have him. It makes me sad for Thayer. He just wants to be there for his son, but it's harder for dads.

"Dad," Forrest runs up to us as we're heading to the booth they have set up on the farm to purchase goods, "can I feed the goats? They said there are babies you can give bottles to!"

"Sure, bud. I gotta pay for it first." He points to the line we're in. "Go play and I'll get everything taken care of."

There's a huge area with well-built wooden play equipment off to the right.

"Okay." Forrest takes off running.

Thayer pays for the bottle for the goats and all the pumpkins, despite my protests to let me buy the ones for my mom and myself. I should know by now that arguing with Thayer is pointless. He's stubborn to a fault.

Thayer loads up the pumpkins while I grab Forrest and take him to feed the goats. Thayer joins us, watching the way I interact with his son.

It's funny. I never grew up with that innate desire to be a mom. I didn't dislike kids but didn't particularly think about what it would be like to be a mother. Perhaps it's my childhood that stole that from me. Regardless, kids have always liked me, and I find them to be pretty cool, fascinating little creatures. They say whatever is on their minds and their love is pure. But interacting with Forrest, hanging around him, it makes me think about the future. One where maybe I am a mother. I could see myself with a couple of kids, maybe more than a couple if I'm being completely honest with myself.

The goats empty the bottle Forrest was given and he begs for another. Thayer obliges once more before the three of us make the trek over to the corn maze.

"You know," Thayer starts, Forrest running out ahead of us, "it makes me fucking sad that I didn't appreciate these moments with him as much before." I wait, letting him say more if he wants. "When I was married it was all just *right there* and even though things weren't great, I guess I took for granted the idea that it would always be there. But it's not. And now I don't see him every day, sometimes not even every week, and so now every moment is that much more special."

"You're a good dad, Thayer." I feel like he needs to hear that.

"Thanks." I let out a small squeak when his hand snakes down to take mine. I love the feel of his large, rough hand encasing mine.

I look down at them and back up at him. "Is this okay?"

"Is it okay with you?"

I nod.

"Then it's okay."

We follow Forrest, who I'm pretty sure is oblivious to our hand holding because he's too busy running around trying to locate the exit and running into dead ends.

A squeal pulls from my throat when Thayer yanks me into one of the dead ends Forrest just darted out of. His eyes are heated and my pussy clenches at that look.

"Wha—"

He cuts off my question, pressing me into the corner of the maze, the dried corn stalks rough against my back, and then he kisses me. It's a rough, searing, soul-stealing sort of kiss.

Thayer Holmes has branded himself on me.

And I know, without a doubt, that whatever this is, whatever we become, if we grow and flourish like the wildflowers behind our houses, or crash and burn, it won't matter because when I'm old and gray, lying in bed thinking about my life, he'll be the best part.

"WHAT ARE YOU CARVING, SALEM?" FORREST ASKS, TRYING TO figure out what I'm making. He's drawing on his pumpkin so Thayer can carve it.

"A cat," I answer him, swiveling the pumpkin so he can see it better.

"You really like cats," he giggles, the sound light and sweet. In the background, *The Nightmare Before Christmas* plays on TV. My mom had Thayer bring in one of her folding yard sale tables and set it up in the living room on top of a sheet to collect the mess. Normally she would've done that herself, but she looks extra tired. I'm worried about her. I know I need to push her, because I have a feeling she's hiding something.

"I do. Cats are the best." Beneath us, Binx swirls between my legs and then Forrest's.

"Dad, am I old enough for a cat yet?"

"No," Thayer answers. He's extremely focused on his pumpkin. A dark curl of hair falls into his eyes and he flicks it away with a toss of his head. His tongue sticks out slightly between his lips, eyes zeroed in on his creation.

"When are you going to build my treehouse?"

"When I have time," he replies, not missing a beat. "But the weather is getting cold so it'll have to be spring."

"Fine," Forrest grumbles. He brightens almost immediately. "What about Christmas? Can I have a cat then? A puppy? What about a turtle?"

Thayer sighs. "You're not letting this go, are you?"

"No. Never."

My mom laughs at the little boy. I can tell having him here has lifted her spirits.

"In the meantime," I tell Forrest, searching for a way to appease him, "you can visit Binx anytime you want."

"Really?"

"Really, really."

Thayer chuckles, his eyes finally leaving his pumpkin to look across at me. "You're going to regret that."

I shrug. "I've extended the invite before. I think I'll be fine." I wink at Forrest.

The small boy tries to mimic the gesture but ends up blinking both eyes open and shut rapidly.

"Did I do it?"

"Not quite. We'll work on it." I pat his hand.

Beaming, he says, "I'm a quick learner."

"You sure are." I ruffle his hair.

Quiet settles between the four of us as we work diligently on our pumpkins. When mine is done I'm fairly pleased with my cat. It's not perfect, and pretty basic, but I like it and that's all that matters.

"You get a gold star sticker," Forrest tells me with a thumb's up. "That's what my teacher gives us when we do a good job."

"Thank you, Forrest," I tell him. "I'm going to check on dinner."

We have a pot roast simmering in the crock pot since Thayer and Forrest are joining us.

In the kitchen, it looks like everything is coming along nicely. I grab a can of Diet Coke from the fridge and pop the top, listening to it fizz.

A hand presses against my lower waist and I gasp, spinning around to face Thayer.

"Sorry, I needed a drink." He acts innocent as his hand sweeps over my ass before opening the fridge. "You prefer the cans," he notes, nodding at the one clutched in my hand.

"Yeah, I think it tastes better."

"You should've said something. I would've bought those instead of bottles."

I lift my shoulders. "It's not that big of a deal."

"Still, I want to get you what you like." He pulls out one of the beers my mom keeps stashed in the back. She offered him one earlier and he turned her down. "Dinner smells amazing." He lowers his head, burying his face into my neck. "But *you* smell heavenly."

Cold hits my skin when he sweeps away and out of the kitchen like a figment of my imagination.

I take a moment, letting my heartrate settle before I return to the living room.

"What do you think?" My mom asks, turning her pumpkin my way and showing me the witchy face she carved into it.

"Whoa!" Forrest says before I can say anything. "That's so good, Mrs. Matthews."

"You can call me, Allie, sweetie."

Thayer's working on carving Forrest's. "What did you do?" I ask him.

"Hmm?" He's intent on his project.

"Your pumpkin. What is it?"

"Oh." He sets down the carving knife and leans over to pick up his pumpkin.

Stop staring at his biceps!

But I can't help it, not with the way they flex and strain beneath his shirt.

He turns the pumpkin around to show me the Sanderson Sisters and I know he only did this for me. I can't help but think of that night. In his arms. Him above me. Moving inside me.

God, I crave it again.

"I didn't know you were such an artist," I say, hoping the lust doesn't show too plainly on my face, not with my mom in the room. I told her I broke up with Caleb. She was confused but said she understood and even expected it with him leaving for college.

He shrugs. "I'm really not."

"That," my mom points at the pumpkin, "takes talent. *Hocus Pocus* is Salem's favorite movie. Is it one of yours too?"

He shrugs. "I saw it for the first time recently and enjoyed it. Seemed fitting."

"We'll put it on next." She points at the TV. "Play it while we have dinner."

"Yeah, I wanna watch it!" Forrest bounces in his seat.

"Careful," Thayer admonishes quietly when Forrest nearly bonks his head into his dad's elbow.

"Sorry." He stills, climbing off his chair. He goes over to where Binx sits in the window and pets his head.

"Do you want to set ours on the front porch?" My mom asks, indicating our finished pumpkins.

"Sure." I take mine out and then hers, not wanting to risk dropping one by taking both.

I set them both on the chairs on the stairs, making sure they're angled properly toward the street. When I head back inside, Thayer is laughing at something my mom said. It's so incredibly silly, but I flash back to what Georgia said over the summer, about our mom maybe going out with Thayer. I know she's not interested in him, but that doesn't stop this fierce feeling of *he's mine* from overtaking me.

I scurry into the kitchen before I do something stupid, like go sit in his lap as if I'm marking my territory. The roast is done, so I start cutting up the meat. Everything else is already made—mashed potatoes, peas, and rolls.

I feel his warm, calming presence before he steps up behind me.

I find myself sinking into him, feeling grounded in his presence.

How is it possible that one person, someone I've only known a few months, can make me feel this way?

"What's wrong?" He murmurs, ducking his head into my neck. He presses his lips to the skin there, his hands wrapped around my waist.

"Nothing."

"Are you sure?"

"Just being irrational. I'm fine."

"Irrational, huh?" He lets me go, taking over with cutting the meat.

"Yeah. I felt jealous."

His movements halt. "Of what?"

"My mom was talking to you and it reminded me that my sister said at one point she thought my mom should date you."

He wets his lips with a swipe of his tongue. "That so?"

"Mhmm."

He resumes slicing. "Lucky for you, there's only one Matthews woman on my mind."

"That so?" I echo his words.

"Mhmm."

I smile. I love this game we play sometimes, where we spin things around and say each other's words back.

He glances over his shoulder, making sure we're still alone, and then presses a quick kiss to my lips. "You have nothing to worry about. I'm all yours."

I love the sound of that—that Thayer Holmes is one-hundred percent mine.

THIRTY-FOUR

The grump next door is handing out candy. For some reason, I didn't expect him to. I mean, he has a kid so it makes sense that he'd partake in the tradition, but I figured with Forrest being with his mom tonight that Thayer wouldn't feel like giving candy.

But I was wrong.

I ring the doorbell, bucket clasped in my hand. It's past the appropriate hour for trick or treaters, I did that on purpose. My mom's out with her friends tonight—a much needed night out for her if you ask me—and I haven't seen much of Georgia since she moved in with Michael. That meant it was only me passing out candy at our house, and once that was done I couldn't resist coming over to Thayer's.

The door swings open, candy bowl in his hand.

He's not dressed up—why would he when he already has the wardrobe of a lumberjack?

His lips part, taking me in. I'm in a black, bodycon dress with slits up the sides. I don't usually wear a lot of makeup, but for tonight I did a smoky gray eye and red lip.

I flash him a sharp-toothed smile.

"Trick or treat?"

"Trick," he answers, eyes heating with lust.

I pout. "That's not how this works. You're supposed to give me treats." I hold up my empty pumpkin shaped bucket.

"I'll give you treats." He nods for me to come inside. "What are you two?" He points at Binx in my arms. "A vampire and...?"

"He's my bat." I flick his little bat wings. "See? Every vampire needs a pet bat."

He shakes his head, shutting the door. "Only you would dress up your cat for Halloween."

"He likes it," I argue, setting my cat down.

When I straighten back up, Thayer wraps a hand around my waist, yanking me into his body. My hands land on his solid, hard chest.

"This dress," his chest rumbles, hands roaming over my body and ending up on my ass, "is something."

"You like?"

He rubs his lips together. "Very much."

"I put it on for you," I admit, running a finger down his chest. "I thought you'd like it."

"Mmm," he hums, stepping back to rake his eyes over me again. "I really, really do."

Standing on my tiptoes, I whisper in his ear, "I think it'll look even better on your floor."

Those words break the last of his self-control. With a low growl, he picks me up and pins me against the wall in his foyer. The dress bunches around my hips with my legs around his waist. He kisses me passionately; in a way I never knew existed before.

I worried, after that night on his couch, that he'd back away and regret what we did. It was a fear that kept me up at night. It was terrifying to think that it might've meant more to me than him.

But instead, that night unlocked a part of Thayer I'm not sure even he knew existed.

His hips push into mine and I gasp at the feel of him hard and ready.

"Thayer," I pant.

He wraps a hand around my neck. I moan, surprised at how much I like his hand there. "Do you want me to fuck you against the wall, Salem?"

God, yes.

"Yes."

"Good."

Reaching between us, I undo his belt and make quick work of the button and zipper. He uses his legs and body weight to hold me against the wall, wiggling his jeans and boxer-briefs down enough to free his cock. I stare down at it. I can't help it. I stroke him as best I can with him holding me, but he shakes his head.

I give him a puzzled look, worried maybe I did something wrong, but he shakes his head.

"Need to be in you."

He shoves my thong to the side. Normally I'm a boy shorts kind of girl, but this dress wouldn't allow that.

And then he's inside me, both of us sighing in relief.

I've been dreaming of this moment since our first time.

He stares into my eyes, his hands gripping my hips as he lifts me up and down onto his cock.

"Fuck." The veins in his neck strain, holding himself back. "You have no idea how good you feel."

"I know how good *you* feel." My head falls back against the wall, his fingers finding my clit. "Thayer," I pant, breathless, "right there. Don't stop."

I fall over the edge, my orgasm rattling me to the bone.

His lips press open-mouthed kisses to my neck. He pumps his hips harder, faster into me, and impossibly I feel my body building toward another high.

"Thayer!" I scream his name, my orgasm rippling through me.

He groans through his own release. Without pulling out of me, he carries me up the stairs and to his bedroom. I've never been in here

184

before. The only part of the upstairs I've seen is a hall bath and Forrest's room. It's dark inside, so it's hard for me take much in when he sets me on the bed.

"Hang tight," he tells me, flicking on the light in his attached bathroom.

It gives me enough glow to look around his room.

Black furniture, gray walls. A picture of him and Forrest on the dresser. Blinds, no curtains.

It's very basic, but somehow so perfectly Thayer. It smells like him too. I let my body sink into the mattress.

He returns with a washcloth and gently guides my legs apart, cleaning me up. I shiver when he places tender kisses on my inner thighs. "I didn't hurt you, did I?"

I shake my head. "No. I'd tell you."

He nods, rising up from the bed. He tosses the washcloth into a laundry basket in the corner. Turning to me with hands on his hips, he says, "I should've talked to you about this before, but..."

I sit up, a bit worried where he's going with this. "But?"

"Look, with your past, I don't know your triggers or anything like that, so you have to be open with me if I do something you don't like or if there's a position that bothers you or just fucking anything, Salem."

I nod. "Of course. I would tell you. I..." I look away, not meeting his gaze. "Therapy helped me a lot. I still go sometimes when I feel like I need it. Yeah, I get nightmares, but I've come a long way. You don't know how bad it was. I'm in a good place now."

"Okay." He nods, his Adam's apple bobbing with a swallow. "I just always want you to be honest with me. I never—"

I sit up and grab his wrist. His skin is warm, the hair on his arm rough against my palm. "You wouldn't hurt me, Thayer. Please, stop worrying."

He stares into my eyes, searching for any hint that I'm lying. "Okay," he finally agrees.

Undoing the buttons on his shirt, I look up at him. "Stop worrying and make love to me."

He cups my face in his hands, kissing me deeply. "That I can do."

THIRTY-FIVE

t's been too cold for a while now to run outside so I've been going to the gym with Thayer joining me. He's a grump, more than usual anyway, of the mornings but I think he doesn't like the idea of me going to the gym that early on my own, so he insists on tagging along.

Therefore, I'm not surprised when I trudge out into the cold—wind whipping my hair around my shoulders—to find him leaning against my car.

"How long have you been out here?" I ask, like always.

He shrugs, like always. "Not long. We're not going to the gym, though."

"We're not?"

He shakes his head. "Nope."

I narrow my eyes. "Listen, sex is great and all, but that's not the workout I'm looking for right now."

He huffs, his breath fogging the chilly air. "I should fuck you just for using that sassy tone with me, but sex wasn't what I was referring to, smart ass."

"If we're not going to the gym then what are we doing?"

I thought he understood how much I need to run when I'm like this, but maybe not?

"Come on, this way." He motions for me to follow him over to his house.

I narrow my eyes but fall into step beside him. "What are you up to?"

"You'll see soon enough."

He leads me inside, and down the basement stairs, flicking on another light to illuminate the area.

My hand flies up to my mouth. *"Thayer."*

The whole basement has been outfitted as a gym. The floor is an extra cushy mat-like material, and there's a treadmill, elliptical, rower, and weight machine. There's a TV mounted on the light blue walls as well as mirrors all along the back wall.

I spin around, taking it all in. There's a yoga mat rolled up in the corner with hand weights that I missed before.

"You did all this for—"

I almost say *for me*, but that's silly. This is his house. He wouldn't put in a home gym for me.

"For you."

My mouth falls open. "What?"

"I did this for you. I know you prefer running outside, but the gym has to do when the weather is bad, but I figured this was better than going to a real gym and it's free." He shoves his hands in the pockets of his athletic shorts, shoulders hunched like this is no big deal.

But Thayer Holmes put in a home gym in his basement *for me*.

I think I'm going to cry.

He notices the tears gathering in my eyes and gently tugs me into his body, wrapping his arms around me. "Baby, please don't cry. I didn't mean to make you sad."

187

"I'm not sad." I rest my chin on his chest, tilting my head back to look at him. He places his hands on my cheeks, their large size nearly swallowing my face whole. "These are happy tears, because you are the kindest, most thoughtful human being."

He kisses the tip of my nose and it's so surprisingly sweet and gentle coming from my lumberjack.

"I want you to be happy, Salem."

I wet my lips with a slide of my tongue. "You make me happy."

He rubs his thumbs in gentle circles around my cheeks. "You make me happy too." The words are a quiet confession on his lips, one that I savor.

Who would've thought that the grumpy neighbor who was so rude to me when I first came over would now look at me like this?

Like I'm the entire universe grasped gently between his palms.

"I don't know if anyone's ever told you this," I whisper up at him, "but you have one of the most beautiful souls."

He laughs. "I thought you were going to say cock."

I grin. "That too."

Pushing up on my tiptoes, I kiss him. He deepens it, sliding his tongue past the seam of my lips. He groans when I pull away, eyes heavy-lidded with lust.

I give his chest a pat. "Time for me to go run." I eye the brand-new treadmill. It's a beast, and I know from the brand name it's expensive too.

"I'll just be over here." He tosses his thumb at the weight machine. "Pretending not to check out your ass."

"You can if you want." I do a little booty pop. "I won't mind." He growls looking ready to pounce on me. I wiggle a finger. "Nuh-uh. I need my run."

Maybe it's because I use the word need, but he sobers and nods. "Take your time."

Pulling my earphones and phone out of my pocket, I pop them in and start my music with my favorite playlist to get me through a workout. I don't always listen to music, but sometimes it helps. It takes me a minute to get the treadmill started up, I almost ask Thayer for help, but I figure it out on my own and he's left in the corner on the weight machine.

I can see him in the mirror as I run, but it doesn't take me long to fall into a rhythm and forget all about him. I just run and run, leaving all my problems behind me.

I'M SWEATY AND GROSS BY THE TIME I FINISH MY RUN AND even spend a little bit of time checking out everything else. But Thayer doesn't let it stop him from pulling me into a searing kiss. I could kiss this man for the rest of my life and never get tired of it. I might be young, but I know this truth; his lips were made for mine.

"Come on," he gives my ass a light smack, "let me make you breakfast."

I press my lips together, trying not to show my smile. I love playful Thayer a little too much.

Love.

That word suddenly invades my thoughts as I follow him upstairs.

Do I love Thayer?

I think I do. No, I *know* I do. But I'm scared to tell him that. For now, I keep those words bottled up close to my heart. I'll tell him eventually, but today isn't that day.

In his now fully completed kitchen Thayer starts setting out ingredients for breakfast.

"What are you making me?"

"My famous breakfast sandwich."

I pick up a bag of arugula. "I'm intrigued."

He arches a brow, setting out orange juice. "You should be." I go to pick up the orange juice to pour a glass, but he snaps his fingers together. "Water first."

Sighing, I grab a clean glass and fill it with ice and water from the refrigerator. "Happy now?" I take a big sip.

He watches me down the entire glass through narrowed eyes and then gives a gruff nod of approval when it's drained. "Thrilled."

I refill the glass, leaning a hip against the counter while he cracks eggs into a mug. "Is there anything I can do to help?"

"Rinse off the arugula."

"You got it, Captain."

"Captain," he mutters.

"Aye, aye."

He shakes his head. "You're in a good mood."

"Don't you know exercise releases endorphins?"

Those brown eyes stare at me, and I know what he's thinking before he says it. "You know what else releases endorphins?" He pours a little bit of Club Soda into the mug, then grabs a fork to scramble the eggs together. "Sex. And sex is way more fucking fun than a workout."

"I disagree." I open the fridge and grab the bowl of grapes, popping one in my mouth before bending to search for a strainer for the arugula. "I think both can be equally invigorating."

"Hmm," he hums. "Maybe I just need to fuck you better."

"Thayer!" I nearly hit my head on the side of the counter on my way back up. I give him a light swat on his arm, my cheeks twin flames.

"What?" He plays Mister Innocent.

"You know what."

His eyes heat, raking over me. My hair is a damp mess, falling half out of my ponytail. My shirt over-sized and baggy, falling halfway down my thighs over my black running leggings. There's nothing sexy about what I have going on right now, but you wouldn't know that by the look in his eyes, and dammit if that doesn't make me feel like the hottest woman on the planet.

He pours the eggs into the hot pan, adding some sort of seasoning to them, and then drops two English muffins into the toaster while I make sure the arugula is thoroughly rinsed. I do an extra good job with it, because after getting food poisoning one time I'm never letting that happen again. I spent hours puking my guts up.

Opening the fridge, he grabs two slices of cheddar cheese and spicy mayo.

We work together seamlessly, and when the muffins pop up, I plop them onto plates and slather some mayo on.

"This smells amazing," I say when Thayer adds the eggs onto each of our muffins, cheddar cheese melting on top.

"Hopefully it tastes amazing too." He puts some arugula on top of each and then I top them with the other half of English muffin.

We sit down at the breakfast table—a real handmade wooden table one of his friends crafted—and he waits for me to take the first bite.

"Oh my God, Thayer this is amazing." I didn't know a simple egg sandwich could taste so good.

He chuckles, clearly pleased. "I'm glad you like it."

I go in for another bite, saying around a mouthful, "Like it? I love it." I put a hand over my mouth while I chew my too big bite.

His smile is amused. "You're saying I should cook for you more often?"

"Duh. I do bake you cupcakes."

"We should do something today."

His statement surprises me. "Do something? Like what?"

He shrugs. "I don't know. Just go out together. To the store or something."

I run my tongue over my lips. "Okay. That sounds fun. I have to work at the store this morning but I'm off at two."

"All right. I'll pick you up."

"You're going to pick me up?"

He shrugs. "Why wouldn't I?"

"I..." I lower my head. "Okay."

"You don't want me to pick you up." He frames it as a statement.

"No, it's not that." I tuck a loose blonde hair behind my ear. "I assumed you wouldn't want people to see that. It's a small town. People talk."

He finishes his sandwich. "I'm not in the habit of giving a fuck what other people think."

I crack a smile. "Good."

THIRTY-SIX

Sure enough, Thayer's truck is waiting outside A Checkered Past Antiques. I told my mom he wanted my help getting things to decorate Forrest's room. A total lie since the little boy's room was done before probably anything else. But I had to give her some sort of reason as to why our neighbor was picking me up from work.

Sliding into his truck, the leather warm on my jean-clad bottom, I smile at him. He's too handsome in a navy sweatshirt, jeans, and baseball cap. It's really not fair to my heart for him to be so hot.

"How was work?" He pulls out of the spot he was parallel parked in.

"It was good. It always is."

"Is that what you want to do? Continue running the store?"

"I don't know," I muse, looking out the window. "Maybe. I'm not sure. I'm not sure about a lot of things."

"Hey," he says softly, like he's worried he's offended me, "it's okay to not know everything and have it all figured out. You'll get there."

I bite my lip. "You think?"

"Sometimes paths aren't always clear, but as time goes by and you experience life, things start to make more sense."

I nod along. His words mean a lot to me, because it seems like most people expect me to have it figured out by now.

Thayer drives out of town, relaxing as he does. He rests his hand on my leg, his fingers wrapped around my thigh. I try not to let on that it makes me ache in all the right places.

"Where are we going?"

"I need to run to the nursery for some plants I need for a project."

"That's fine."

"You don't mind?" He looks at me skeptically.

I just want to be with you. I don't say that out loud though.

"Nope."

"All right."

We ride mostly in silence, but it's comfortable. I never realized how important that is, to find comfort in silence with someone else's presence. It's nice.

It takes us about thirty minutes to get to the nursery and when we do I follow him out of the truck and inside the greenhouse.

Upon entering he grins when he runs into a guy he knows.

"Hey, Marcus." He claps hands with him and gives him a half-hug. "How have you been?"

"Good, I've got what you need pulled to the side so you can checkout and load up."

"Thanks, I appreciate it." Thayer looks over his shoulder at me lingering behind him. "Salem, come here." He reaches for my hand, tugging me forward to his side. "Matt, meet Salem. She's my new neighbor. Salem, meet Matt, a good friend of mine."

"Hi," I smile, extending a hand, "it's nice to meet you."

He takes my hand, giving Thayer an amused look. "It's nice to meet you, too."

With introductions over, Thayer says, "I'm going to take a look around and see if there's anything else I should grab before we go."

"Take your time," Matt says, already turning away. "I'll be around. Just yell when you need me."

Thayer and I walk down the rows and rows of plants.

"This nursery is huge," I tell him, noticing how it goes on for as far as I can see.

"Matt's family is a big supplier to a lot of places. They even ship plants around the states."

"Wow." I tug a flower near my nose and give it a sniff. "And I guess you know what most of these are?"

He points to the flower I just smelled. "Gladiolus italicus." I arch a brow. "Better known as just Gladiolus or Sword Lily."

"Interesting," I muse. I move to a shrub of peonies. "My favorite."

"Peonies? I wouldn't have guessed that."

I nod. "I love the pink shade and how intricate and delicate they look." I bend, giving it a sniff too. "If you wouldn't have chosen a peony, what did you think my favorite would be?"

"Sunflowers," he answers without hesitation. "I guess that's because you remind me of them. You're so bright and happy most of the time."

"I didn't used to be," I admit mournfully.

His finger is warm beneath my chin, lifting my head to look at him. "Who we used to be doesn't matter, it's who we are now, what's in our hearts that matters most. You're sunshine, Salem, but even the sun doesn't always shine." His hand moves to cup my cheek. A sigh passes through my lips as I lean into his touch. "I'm not bright like you, but I promise, when your days are dark, I'll be your light."

Tears prick my eyes. It's the most beautiful thing anyone has ever said to me.

"Thank you."

He rubs his thumb over my cheek. He does that a lot. I wonder if it's as much to comfort me as it is him. "You don't have to thank me, baby."

Standing on my tiptoes, I wrap my arms around his neck and kiss him. His hands go to my waist, and I know he wants to touch my skin, but it's not possible with my coat.

Stepping back down, I can't help but look at him and wonder how it's possible to feel this much for someone. Especially someone I haven't realistically known that long. Perhaps sometimes it's not about how much you know someone's personal details and more about how you feel about them. There has to be some sort of faith put into gut instinct, right?

"WHERE ARE WE GOING NEXT?" I CLIMB INTO THE TRUCK, THE bed loaded up with shrubbery and small evergreens.

"I'm going to drop these off at the job site."

I look at him in surprise. "You're going to take me to your job site?"

"Yeah." He cranks up the truck, turning the heat up. "You don't want to go?"

"No, I do, but—"

"But nothing," he cuts me off, backing out. "No one's going to say anything if that's what you're worried about."

I take in the strong set of his jaw. His wide shoulders. "Okay, then."

"I'm going to swing by and pick up some donuts for the guys first," he says, turning onto the road and heading south.

"What job are these for?" I toss my thumb over my shoulder like he doesn't already know what I'm talking about.

"A new bank that's going in over in Huntsburg." It's a town about twenty minutes from ours.

"That's cool. I bet things slow down a lot this time of year."

"Yeah," he sighs. "It's why I have some trucks for snow plowing. That brings in good money once it gets too cold and the ground freezes."

"Oh. I didn't even think about something like that. If you weren't doing this, what do you think you'd do?"

His eyes drift briefly over to me. "Are you interviewing me?"

I shrug. "Just curious."

I'm curious about all things Thayer Holmes. I want to know every detail about him.

"I'd probably be a carpenter. Make furniture, cabinets. Something like that. I do some of it now, just for myself, but I'm not that good."

"What have you made in your house?" He makes a noncommittal noise. I poke his side and he twitches like it tickles. "Tell me."

"I did the crown molding and the stair banister."

"You did?" I don't know why I ask this, since obviously the answer is yes.

"Yeah." He gives a gruff laugh. "I like to work with my hands."

My eyes zero in on his hands gripping the steering wheel—thinking about how those strong, capable hands feel on my body.

Thayer pulls into the drive-thru line of Dunkin' and asks me if I want anything. "Ooh," I bounce a little in my seat, "a strawberry sprinkle donut *and*—" I draw out the word, tapping my lip as I think. "—a caramel latte."

He places the order, tacking on a hot chocolate for himself. "Their hot chocolate isn't as good as what I make, but I want something hot."

"You make hot chocolate?"

"Mhmm," he hums, sitting up to pull his wallet from his back jeans pocket. I don't know why that's so sexy, seeing his arm flex as he takes out the folded leather wallet, but it is. He passes a credit card over to the drive-thru worker when we reach the window. "Hold onto those." He hands me the two boxes of donuts for his crew, a small bag with my donut and his on top. He takes his card back and tucks it away, returning his wallet to his pocket. Our drinks get handed out and then he's driving away.

"Do you want your donut now?" I ask, already reaching in the bag for mine.

"Yeah."

I pass him the apple streusel donut and then take out mine. "I think I'm a sugar addict."

"Think?" He flashes an amused smile.

I roll my eyes. "Okay, I totally am. But I do drink Diet Coke."

"And it has enough artificial sweetener in it that you'd be better off with sugar."

I frown. "I know but ... it tastes better."

THE CONFIDENCE OF WILDFLOWERS

He looks at me like I'm insane. "People who love Diet Coke are crazy."

I stare blankly at him, mouth agape. "Take that back."

He shakes his head vehemently. "It's true."

"You keep it in your house!" I argue.

He comes to a stoplight and slows for the red, flicking on the blinker. He gives me a slow, lingering look. "Yeah, for you."

I mean, I knew this. Or I guess I assumed, but hearing him confirm it sends this weird bubbly feeling through me. "You like me," I say slowly with a smile.

He shakes his head, fingers over his mouth to hide a growing smile. "I put a gym in my house for you and it takes stocking Diet Coke for you to realize I like you?"

I press my lips together. "But do you like me? Like really like me, Thayer?" I reach over, rubbing his scruffy chin between my fingers.

The light changes and he turns left. "Yeah, Sunshine, I like *really* like you."

My heart swells. Being liked by Thayer Holmes is a rare thing, that much is obvious. But he likes *me*. The girl who trespassed on his property—by accident of course—who brought him cupcakes and practically pestered him into being my friend.

But I wonder if that like has the potential to turn into something deeper, more meaningful, or if maybe after his divorce he's not ready to love again. Maybe he'll *never* be ready to love again.

Thayer pulls into the freshly paved parking lot of the new bank and parks his truck.

I hop out with the boxes in my hands, following him over to the crew of about ten guys.

"Paul, can you unload the truck?" He delegates to one of the men. "We brought donuts too."

The guy who must be Paul, older probably in his forties and wrinkled from time in the sun, passes us for the truck.

A few of the others stop what they're doing and give me a once over. One's eyes linger longer than necessary on me and Thayer snaps his fingers.

"Donovan, watch where you're looking."

The guy, younger than the others, smirks. "Boss, you can't expect to bring a hot piece of ass like that around and me not to take a look."

I want to shove the boxes of donuts at the jerk. How fucking rude. I'm standing *right here*.

Thayer's eyes thin to slits and he takes the boxes from me, like he knows what I want to do with them and doesn't want me to ruin the treat for the other guys. "Watch your mouth."

"What?" Donovan's smile grows and he leans against the metal rake he's using. He's probably in his early twenties, and he'd be good looking if he wasn't running his mouth. "Maybe you'll be more tolerable now that you're getting laid again."

The other men still, the silence louder than anything. Thayer passes the boxes to one of the men, his hands going to his hips while his jaw works back and forth. "Drop the rake, grab your shit, and leave."

"What?" Donovan's smile falters. "I'm just joking boss. You know me, I—" His eyes dart from me to Thayer, as if only just now realizing what kind of hole he's dug for himself.

"Do I need to spell it out for you?" The other men back away from Donovan, grabbing their donuts and pretending not to pay attention to what's going down. "You're fired, Donovan. Get off my site."

"Boss," Donovan's face falls this time, "I was just kidding around. She knows I was joking. I—"

Thayer holds up a hand. "She has a name. You didn't bother to ask, did you? Take your misogynistic ass to your car and *leave*. I mean it."

Donovan must know better than to argue. Head hanging, he sets the rake down gently despite the anger obviously radiating off of him. He walks away and gets into an old Ford Ranger.

Another of the men clears his throat. "Boss, we—uh—you're gonna need him. We can't afford to lose someone with Terry and Brooks leaving."

Thayer hangs his head, rubbing his jaw. "I know ... it doesn't matter. We'll be fine. I'll find replacements soon." Nodding at the guys, he tells them things that need to be done and then leads me back to his truck, the bed now empty. "I'm so fucking sorry about that."

"It's okay."

"Don't say that. Don't fucking say that. It's *never* okay for a man to talk about a woman like that, let alone when she's standing right there."

"They said you needed him—" Guilt settles inside me over the fact this guy got fired because of me. If Thayer had come without me, or I stayed in the car, he'd still have a job.

He shakes his head roughly. "Don't you feel fucking sorry for him or bad for me. He made his bed."

"He was just being a guy." I don't really believe that and from the look on his face he doesn't either.

"I'm raising a son," he says firmly, "and if I ever heard him say that shit about a woman, I would know I failed him. Just being a guy. Boys will be boys, it's a bullshit excuse, Salem. Don't ever let some loser make you think otherwise."

"Okay," I say quietly, staring at my lap.

"I'm not mad at you." He feels the need to say.

Looking out the truck window, I reply, "I know."

He reaches over, taking my hand so our fingers are wrapped tightly together. It's hard to tell where his hand begins and mine ends.

"You're my girl," he says it so surely, like it's a fact already known, "and *no one* talks about my girl like that."

THIRTY-SEVEN

Thanksgiving approaches, and with it, comes a pile of snow. We've steadily been getting snow for weeks now, but this was the worst one yet. Thayer was worried his parents wouldn't be able to make it for the holiday after all, but I watch as an older couple gets out of a car and Thayer comes out to help with their bags. I'm not spying—not on purpose anyway. With the turkey cooking in the oven, and the sides ready, I'm watching for Georgia and Michael to arrive. My mom wanted me to alert her—saying she needed a moment to fix her face before they come in. And by fix her face she doesn't mean makeup or anything of the sort. No, she has to remove the perturbed look on her face because they just got engaged and she knows Georgia is going to be excited. Mom, bless her, doesn't want to rain on her parade despite her dislike of Michael.

I'm not the guy's biggest fan either, he's kind of ditzy, but honestly in a lot of ways he's a good fit for Georgia and at least it *seems* like he's maturing.

Thayer greets his parents with hugs and a kiss on the cheek for his mom.

His brother arrived yesterday, but I didn't see him when he got there and haven't met him yet. I'm sure I will at some point. Especially since Thayer told me that he let him know I might be coming over to use the gym some. He added that he'd leave the outside basement door unlocked. He knew the last thing I'd want to do is disturb his family so he made sure I knew I could still use it without that happening.

I didn't ask him specifically, but I don't think he's told his brother or his parents about us. Not that there's really an "us" to tell them about. We're just ... fooling around, I guess? That feels like the wrong label for it. I know it's more than that, but we're not dating.

My phone buzzes in my pocket, and I pull it out expecting a text from Georgia or maybe even Thayer. But it's from Caleb.

Caleb: I just wanted to say happy Thanksgiving. We were friends before we were a couple. I miss that. I miss you.

I frown down at the message, my chest heavy with remorse for hurting him. I know I should've handled the whole thing better, but I didn't know how, and I hate that Caleb got caught in the crossfire of my actions.

Me: Happy Thanksgiving. Miss you too. Have a good holiday.

He replies right back.

Caleb: Thanks. You too.

When I put my phone away, I spot Georgia and Michael arriving.

"Mom!" I yell out. "They're here."

She pokes her head into the living room. Pointing to her face, she mimes a happy smile. "Does this look genuine? I need this to scream that I'm so thrilled my oldest daughter is engaged."

"It doesn't quite reach your eyes," I tell her honestly, moving away from my creeper perch by the window. Binx's green eyes watch me steadily from his spot on the back of the couch, black tail flicking lazily.

"How about now?" She tries again

I stifle a cringe. "You keep practicing in there," I wave her to the kitchen, "and I'll stall."

"Great. Good idea." She smooths her hands down her apron that's decorated with turkeys.

Opening the door, I let Georgia and Michael inside. They remove their coats, much too heavy to be wearing in the warm interior.

Georgia hugs me first, squeezing me tight. I won't lie, I've missed having her around even though I didn't see her much with her shifts at the hospital. Michael grabs me into a hug next, lifting me off the floor.

"Oh," I say in surprise. "Hi, Michael."

He sets me down, grinning from ear to ear. His brown hair is slicked back and his cheeks are freshly shaved. The clothes he wears, fitted jeans and preppy sweater, screams rich prick elitist. Which he's not. He just has expensive taste in clothes.

Beside him, my sister is wearing a light blue sweater dress that compliments the dark blue of his top. I bet she coordinated that.

"Let me see the ring," I tell my sister, shoving as much elation as I can into those five words. I *am* happy for her, this is what she wants, but sometimes I lack the enthusiasm I know she wants.

She extends her hand, showing off clean nails and the shiny diamond ring on her finger. It's pretty and feminine, exactly what I would picture for my sister. It's not what I would want at all. I prefer something more unique, an antique with character and history. Georgia and I are polar opposites, but I wouldn't ask for a different sister. She's the best.

"It's beautiful," I say sincerely, cradling her hand in mine.

"Isn't it?" She grins at Michael. "He did so good."

He lowers his head, giving her a kiss. "Thanks, babe."

"Where's Mom?" She fluffs her perfectly curled hair. "I want to show her my ring."

"The kitchen."

She flounces off that way, leaving me alone with Michael. He's been around long enough that I can't help but rib him. "Break her heart and I'll gut you like a fish."

He chuckles, rolling up his sleeves. "You've always been something, Salem."

I narrow my eyes on him. "Fear me."

He ruffles my hair, making me wrinkle my nose. I'm not five. I smooth it back down. "You're too funny."

We meet the others in the kitchen, and I find my mom doing a much better job at acting happy for Georgia. It can be hard to see someone you love, love someone who you know isn't good for them. But after a while you can only say so much before you have to sit back and let whatever happens happen.

The food's almost ready so Michael and I get tasked with setting the table—which means I do most of the setting while he drones on and on about his job as an *assistant* to a realtor.

I'd rather watch paint dry, but I do a good job of slathering on a syrupy sweet smile and nodding in all the right places.

We never eat in the dining room except for holidays and birthday celebrations. Sometimes it feels like this completely separate part of the house that only exists on these days.

With the table set, it's time to bring the food in which all four of us take part in.

My mom lets Michael carve the turkey and he does a surprisingly good job at it. I find my mind drifting to next door. Does Thayer carve the turkey or his dad? Maybe his brother?

I'm snapped from my thoughts when we start passing food around the four of us. No one sits at the head. It's Georgia and Michael on one side and my mom and I on the other.

All in all, the meal is delicious, and the conversation never dulls.

We send Georgia and Michael home with leftovers, stuffing the rest into the refrigerator. We're going to be eating turkey for a week.

I don't mind, though.

When everything is stuffed away, my mom turns to me. There's a sadness in her eyes that I can't pinpoint. She looks around, almost like she's trying to take everything in. Savor the memories.

"Is everything okay?" I ask her.

She nods, eyes shimmery. "Of course, Salem. Everything is fine."

But when she excuses herself from the room, head down like she doesn't want me to see her face, I know she's lying.

Whatever it is, it'll come out eventually.

The truth always does.

THIRTY-EIGHT

I couldn't sleep, and not because I had a nightmare. No matter what I tried, I couldn't stop thinking about my mom. She's keeping a secret.

It's five in the morning when I finally trek over to Thayer's, letting myself into the backyard through the gate, then down a set of three concrete stairs, in through the door.

And there he is, almost like he was waiting for me.

I shuck off my long coat—meant to help keep your legs warm too —and drape it over the back of a chair.

He sits on a workout bench, dressed in athletic shorts and a long sleeve shirt that clings to his muscular form.

"Were you waiting for me?"

It seems strange, that he'd get up early just to wait in case I'd show up. But I think about those days when we first got back from the trip to Boston. Every time I had a nightmare and got up early to run, he was outside waiting. Then when I started going to the gym, he was there too.

"No."

I walk over to him, sitting on the bench beside him. I retie my shoes, making sure they're tight enough. His thigh is plastered against the side of mine. "Are you lying to me? You've been waiting for me every time since Boston."

He sucks his cheeks together, blowing out a breath. "You shouldn't run alone," is his only response.

"I was fine and safe before you came along. Don't feel obligated—"

"It's not about safety. Okay, that's some of it," he acquiesces, picking up his water bottle. "Mostly, I just don't like the idea of you by yourself after a nightmare like that. You deserve to know you're not alone, that someone's beside you to fight your battles with you."

I think I might cry.

"Thayer..."

"You don't have to say anything. That's why I didn't tell you what I was doing before." He shrugs, setting his water down and standing. He stretches his arms, and I know it's because he's nervous. Thayer is the kind of person who does good things just because they're the right things. He doesn't seek out praise. That's not the kind of person he is. "Do you want to talk about it? Your nightmare?"

"I ... no nightmare tonight. I just couldn't sleep."

His eyes are warm with concern. "Why not?"

Moving from the bench to the floor, I stretch my legs. "I can tell my mom's keeping a secret and I have this gut feeling it's bad."

He hesitates, cocking his head to the side. "Like what?"

"I don't know, that's the problem. I can tell she's not sleeping much, and she's not eating a lot either. She seems stressed and ... scared," I tack on the last part. "I've tried asking her about it, but she gets cagey and I just ... hate waiting for the shoe to drop, you know?"

"I know what you mean. I can't guess what she has going on, but I'm sure she'll share it when she can."

I lower my head, staring at my purple leggings. "I hope so." Wanting to change the topic, I ask, "How was your Thanksgiving?"

"It was good. Would've burned the house down if my mom wasn't here to cook."

"Liar." I know he can cook.

He smirks, grabbing some weights. "How was yours?

"It was good. Lowkey. Just my mom, me, Georgia, and her fiancé."

"Sounds nice."

"It was." I walk over to the treadmill, pausing before I step on. "You really don't have to do this." I want him to know I don't expect him to get up at the crack of dawn every morning in case I have a nightmare.

"I know," he says, reaching for the dumbbells. "But I want to. It's what you do when you care about someone."

"What exactly?"

Chocolate brown eyes flicker over my body. "You find a way to let them know they aren't alone."

His answer chokes me up, and I don't say anything more. Turning the treadmill on, I run.

But for the first time in ... maybe, ever, I'm not running away from something. I'm running toward it.

THIRTY-NINE

I t's a few days after Thanksgiving when my mom asks my sister and I to meet her for lunch. It's Georgia's day off and I can tell she's a bit disgruntled over the request in the group text, probably because she wants to be wedding planning, but maybe like me she senses that this is important and accepts the invitation.

I asked about the store, but my mom said it would be okay to close it for an hour.

In the middle of the day.

During holiday season.

I've never seen a brighter, more glaring red flag in all my life.

Bundled up against the cold—and to think it'll only get colder in the coming months—I shuffle my way outside and to my car.

My car, my trusty reliable car, chooses today not to start.

"No, no, no," I chant, trying again but the engine never turns over.

"You have to be kidding me." I bang my hand against the steering wheel. "Don't fail me now, baby." Maybe if I sweet talk it, it'll work. "Come on, come on." I'm completely aware I'm begging with an inanimate object, but I don't have it in me to care.

The car isn't listening to my pleas.

A knock on my window nearly has a scream flying out of my throat. My hand goes to my chest, and I look over at Thayer, bent down at my car window with furrowed brows.

Opening my car door, I tell him, "My car won't start and I need to meet my mom and sister for lunch."

"I can take a look. You might need a new battery, but I'm about to head into town with my brother." My shoulders fall. "We can give you a ride."

"I don't want to inconvenience you."

He opens my door further. "Get in the truck, Salem."

Stifling a smile, I get out and lock my car. Not that anyone would want to steal the hunk of junk anyway.

Thayer's truck is already running in the driveway, the exhaust pluming in the air.

"You'll have to ride in the backseat," he tells me, walking up behind me, "Laith isn't enough of a gentleman to offer you the front."

"That's fine. I didn't expect for you to give me a ride."

His fingers gently stroke mine as he passes me, reaching for the back door to open it.

"Your car isn't starting. I'm not enough of an asshole to leave you stranded here."

"I'm hardly stranded," I argue, climbing in the seat. "My car is parked outside my house."

"Doesn't matter," is his response, closing the door on me.

Up front, his brother turns around with a wry grin. "Hey," he says in a smooth, deep voice. It's buttery and smooth. A purr where Thayer's is gruff and abrasive. "I'm Laith." He extends a hand to me while Thayer joins us in the truck.

"Salem." I fit my hand in his. It's softer than his brother's.

"Nice to meet you." His smile grows and he's not shy about looking me over.

Thayer smacks the back of his head. "Stop checking her out. She's eighteen and too young for you."

Too young for you.

I know his brother is younger than him by a few years. If I'm too young for him, then does Thayer really think the same about us?

Buckling the seatbelt, I cross my arms over my chest as he backs out of the driveway.

I don't want to overthink his words. He's probably trying to keep his brother from hitting on me, but dammit if it doesn't sting.

Thayer glances at me in the rearview mirror. "Where is it you need me to drop you off?"

I rattle off the name of the restaurant. Laith swivels around to face me in the back. "So, what's it like being this asshole's neighbor?" He gives Thayer a good-natured rough pat on the shoulder.

"Um…" I rub my lips together. "It's … uh…"

"Don't grill her," Thayer growls, "and turn your ass around."

Laith sighs, spinning back around. "Always gotta be the big brother."

"One of us has to be the responsible one."

Thayer turns his truck onto Main Street, pulling up outside the restaurant. "Thank you so much for the ride," I tell him sincerely.

"It's no problem, Salem."

I feel his eyes on me as I climb out of the car, heading inside. The door is starting to close behind me when I hear the truck pull away.

I spot my mom and sister. Georgia waving at me madly so I can't miss them. Weaving through the tables, I join them and find a stack of bridal magazines at Georgia's side. Sometimes I feel so un-girly because I've never given thought to a wedding while my sister has been planning hers in her head since she was probably in diapers.

Giving each of them a half-hug I settle into a seat beside Georgia since my mom has her bag on the one at her side. "Have you all ordered yet?"

Georgia brushes blonde hair over her shoulders. "Just drinks."

I peruse the menu and set it aside. We've eaten here a lot, so it never takes me long to decide.

"It's so nice having just you two girls together." My mom smiles across at us, something wistful and thoughtful in her gaze. "We don't spend enough time together anymore."

"Life's busy," Georgia reasons, sipping at her glass of wine.

Wine. At lunch time. Huh.

Maybe it's because I've never been one much for alcohol that I can't imagine wine at lunch.

The waitress swings by the table and we place our orders and I tack on my drink.

Diet Coke, of course.

The waitress has barely left our table when Georgia starts in. "I'm thinking a summer wedding, so that means I need to start pining down the location soon. Photographer and caterer too," she rambles, ticking them off on her fingers. "And I need to start dress shopping. The sooner the better. You know how picky I can be. Oh, and Salem, I was going to do this more formally, but will you be my Maid of Honor?"

"Oh." I'm taken off guard. We're plenty close, but I figured she'd reserve that spot for one of her friends. "Of course, Georgia. I'd be honored."

Her smile is beaming. She wraps her arms around me in a hug the best she can with us sitting side by side. "I'm so excited! And Mom," she lets me go, facing our mother, "I was hoping you'd walk me down the aisle?" She bites her lip nervously like she's afraid she might say no.

"Here's your soda," the waitress interrupts the moment, setting my glass down and breezing away.

"Georgia." My mom clasps her hands beneath her chin, tears swimming in her eyes. "I would be honored."

Chat revolves around the wedding as we eat our food. My plate is almost empty when my mom sighs, pushing her half-eaten one away from her like she can't stomach another bite let alone continue to look at the plate.

"There's a reason I asked you girls to meet me for lunch."

"Insisted," Georgia points at her with her fork. "You insisted we be here, Mom."

She inhales a shaky breath. "There's no right way to say this—"

"Are you dating someone?" Georgia interjects and I could kick her for interrupting. It's so rude.

"No." She shakes her head, a humorless laugh bubbling out of her throat. "I ... no, it's not that."

"Mom?" Somehow, already, just from the crushing agony on her face I know this is going to be bad.

"I ... uh..." She sits up straighter, taking her napkin off her lap and setting it on the table. Steeling her shoulders, she drops the bomb.

"I have cancer and ... it doesn't look promising."

You don't just feel your heart break.

You hear it.

It's in the echo of words battering around in your skull like a pinball in a machine.

I have cancer.

I have cancer.

I have cancer.

"Salem!" My mom yells after me.

I didn't even realize I'd gotten up from the table. I stumble outside, throwing up what I'd just eaten in a nearby frozen bush. Someone on the sidewalk curses and runs like I have the plague.

Cancer.

My mom has cancer.

I don't even know what kind.

Does it even matter?

She said it doesn't look promising.

I ... I might lose her.

I inhale a ragged breath, struggling to get enough oxygen into my lungs. It's so cold and the air burns my lungs. Staggering down the street, I wrap my arms around myself. I fled the restaurant without even grabbing my coat. At least I have on a heavy turtleneck sweater.

Reaching the end of the street, I have enough presence of mind to wait for the crosswalk to let me across.

I'm almost to the other side when I hear my name.

But it isn't my mom calling after me.

Not Georgia.

Or even Thayer.

FORTY

"**S**alem!" He yells my name from across the street, exiting the Chinese restaurant with a to-go bag in hand. I can tell from the way he says my name this isn't him trying to get my attention in a friendly way. He sounds worried, sensing my obvious distress. He's the last person I want to see me having this breakdown. Caleb throws his hand up at a car that waits for him and he runs across to meet me where I crossed on the other side. His eyes are filled with nothing but concern and worry for me.

Me.

The girl who broke his heart.

"You're crying," he says, his gaze roaming over me. "What's wrong?"

I wipe hastily at the tears. They're cold on my cheeks. "N-Nothing," I stutter, rubbing beneath my nose. *Ew.* "It's nothing, Caleb." I look down at the ground, away from his penetrating stare.

His finger gently tips my chin up. "I know you better than that."

"It's cold," I say, hoping that'll be enough to get him to leave.

"Is your car around?" He spins in a circle, searching for it.

I shake my head. "No, it died this morning."

Died.

Like my mom might.

My face crumbles and I start crying all over again. "Salem," Caleb says softly, pulling me into the protective cushion of his body. "What's going on? I know you're not like this about your car."

"I..." I can't choke out the words between my tears.

"It's freezing and you're not wearing a coat. My car is down the block. I can drive you home." He sets the to-go bag down and starts taking his coat off. "Here, put this on."

"No," I sniffle, wiping beneath my nose. "I can't take your coat."

"You can and you will," he insists, giving it a shake for emphasis. "Come on now, babe, put it on." He winces at the endearment that slid so naturally off his tongue.

"T-Thank you," I stutter around my tears, slipping my arms inside. It's warm from his body heat.

He reaches for my hand but catches himself, nodding for me to follow him instead. Down the street sits his car and he unlocks it, opening the passenger door for me. Once I'm inside, he closes the door, puts the food in the back and climbs in himself, cranking up the engine. The heat is turned all the way up and it doesn't take long for the car to warm up.

"Do you want to go home or somewhere else?"

He's already driving toward my house, but I find myself saying, "Would you mind driving around for a little bit? I need to calm down."

He gives me a speculative look but doesn't ask. "Okay."

We've been riding around in silence, save for the soft sound of the radio in the background, for around twenty minutes when I find the strength to tell him.

"My mom asked Georgia and me to lunch." I look down at my lap, spreading my fingers wide and flexing them. Stalling. "She has

213

cancer." My chin wobbles. Fuck, I don't want to keep crying, but all I can see in my mind is another funeral, but this time different. So different. There are no feelings of relief. Just crippling fear at how I'd go forward without my mom.

"Fuck," he blurts with an exhale. "God. Fuck. I'm so fucking sorry. Did … do you know what kind?"

"I don't know." I wipe at my damp face and Caleb reaches over, opening the glove compartment and revealing the stash of napkins there. I forgot that he always keeps the thing stuffed full or I would've grabbed one myself. He passes it to me, letting me get control of myself. "I ran out before she could say. She just said that it doesn't look promising, and I freaked out."

When my dad got diagnosed with cancer, I thanked the universe and then pleaded with it to take him out of this world.

But not my mom.

Not her.

Please, don't take her from me. I'm not ready. I might be an adult now but I still need my mom.

"Salem, I want you to know that no matter what I'm always here for you. You always have me. We might not be together," he swallows thickly like it still hurts him to say that, "but I'm not going anywhere."

"She's too young," I croak. "It's not fair."

People like to argue that life isn't fair, and I think that's a stupid way to brush off things like they're no big deal. I don't want to ever overlook things or not acknowledge my own feelings on something because of that mentality.

"Your mom is strong," Caleb says assuredly. "She's a fighter."

"She is," I agree, sniffling, "but it doesn't matter how strong someone is, there are some fights you can't win."

Pity fills his face and I hate that. I don't want him or anyone else to pity me.

"It is what it is," I say, steeling my shoulders. "We'll get through this."

"You will, Salem. And so will she. I believe it."

I press my lips together, holding back more tears. "Thank you."

He nods, tightening his hold on the steering wheel.

Caleb takes me home then and before I slip out of the car, I curse. "Oh, fuck, Caleb I forgot about your food. It's going to be cold now. I'm so sorry."

He smiles that same blinding boyish smile that first made my stomach explode with butterflies years ago. "It's no biggie. That's what microwaves are for."

"Well, thank you."

For the ride.

For driving me around.

For listening.

For just being there.

He gives me a sad, longing look. "Always."

Inside, I find my mom waiting for me at the kitchen table. Her fingers are wrapped around a hot cup of coffee and there are cupcakes baking in the oven.

Cookie dough.

A pink apron with purple polka dots is wrapped around her torso.

"Sit." She tips her head at the chair across from her.

I walk forward, my feet heavy, and slump into the chair. The tears come immediately when I look across at my mom.

My beautiful, vibrant, resilient, mother who has faced so much and deserves her happy ending. Not ... this. Not a battle she might not win the fight of.

"Hi," she says, like that's the simplest, easiest greeting.

"Hi," I echo back, the word flat and choked sounding.

Her lips turn down in a frown as she reaches across the table, gripping my hand. Hers is cold, slightly clammy. "I'm so sorry."

"You're sorry?" I parrot. "Mom," I shake my head back and forth, trying my hardest to hold it together, "you have nothing to be sorry for. It's not like you asked for this to happen to you. It just did."

"I know, honey." She gives me hand a slight squeeze. "But that doesn't mean I'm not sorry that you have to go through this."

"Please," I beg brokenly, "stop apologizing for something you can't control. What kind is it?"

"Breast," she replies. "They said for me to have a fighting chance a double mastectomy is the way to go." She clears her throat, obviously struggling for composure. "I hate that you girls have to see me go through this."

"Mom," I beg, tightening my hold on hers. "Don't say things like that. We're here for you. *I'm* here for you. Whatever you need." Her eyes pool with tears. "We're going to get through this. I promise."

Getting up from the table, I go around to hug her. We cry together, and I hope with everything I have in me that it's a promise I can keep.

FORTY-ONE

I wake up to an unfamiliar sound and glance at the clock. It's eight in the morning. That means I slept through the whole night. That rarely happens. Even without the nightmares I usually have trouble going to sleep. But apparently crying your eyes out exhausts the body. Who knew.

Remembering the noise, I climb out of bed, straightening my too-big shirt that's twisted around my torso.

Reaching the window, I peer outside to see the hood of my car up with Thayer bent under it.

He's ... what is he doing?

Throwing on a sweatshirt, stuffing my feet in boots, and then grabbing my coat on my way out the door I stomp my way up the snowy drive, arms bunched under my chest like as if he could even tell I'm not wearing a bra with all the layers.

"What do you think you're doing?"

He looks over his shoulder at me. A worn brown beanie sits on top of his head, sandy brown curls poking from beneath. The scruff on his cheeks is heavier than normal and a plaid flannel collar pokes out haphazardly from beneath his coat.

"Working on your car," he says in a 'duh' tone.

"But *why*?"

His eyes shift from under the hood to me. "Because your car wouldn't start. I'm trying to figure out if it's the battery, or the ignition, or—"

I hold up a hand. "Car speak is a foreign language to me. Speak English."

He turns around, crossing his arms to face me fully. "I know a little about cars. I figured I might be able to save you some money."

"You ... I ... okay." I take a step back. "Wait," I pause, "didn't you have to get into my car to pop the hood?"

"Yeah, you really need to start locking your car. Anyone can get in it."

"Thayer." I can't help but start laughing. "All right. I'll leave you to it, then."

"Don't worry, I'm on my way to help." Laith saunters over to us, grinning crookedly with a thermos grasped in his hand. He claps Thayer on the shoulder. "Can't let big bro have all the fun. Goddamn, though, maybe I should. It's colder than a witch's tit out here."

Thayer shakes his head. "I don't need your help."

"Aw, bro, see—that's your problem. You never need anyone's help. That's why you're divorced and I'm not."

I have to admit it's fun seeing Thayer get ribbed by his younger brother.

Thayer snorts, shoving his brother. "Shut up, you've never even been married."

Laith snaps his fingers. "Exactly! That's why I'm the smart one."

Rolling his eyes, Thayer turns his attention back to underneath the hood of the car. "Trust me, that's not how it works."

With a laugh, I walk away from the brothers, kicking the snow off my boots before walking into the kitchen. I'll make Thayer some cupcakes today for taking the time to look at my car.

My mom has already left to open the store for the day, which means it's only Binx and me. Speaking of my beloved cat, he saunters into the kitchen and meows loudly, demanding me to fill up his bowl.

It's already full but I make a show of adding a few crunchies on top. He sniffs, and satisfied he digs in.

So picky that one.

Grabbing a bowl, I pour some cereal and add milk. Eating as I go, I look out the front window. Thayer is still hunched beneath my hood, Laith off to the side talking a mile a minute and gesticulating wildly with his hands. I'm sure Thayer loves that.

With a shake of my head I venture back to the kitchen and finish up my cereal, rinsing out the bowl in the sink.

A text comes through, so I check my phone, finding that it's from Caleb.

Caleb: How are you? I wanted to check on you.

Me: I'm okay. Had a talk with my mom last night. We're going to fight this battle. She's scheduling surgery soon. Her doctors said she needs a mastectomy to have a fighting chance.

Caleb: Damn. I'm so fucking sorry.

Me: We'll get through this.

Caleb: I'm here for you and I mean that. Need to talk? I'm your guy. Need a shoulder to cry on? I can be that too.

Me: Thanks. You're a good guy, Caleb. The best.

I put my phone away and start a fresh pot of coffee. I don't like coffee made at home as much, but with no car and the frigid temperatures it's not like I can take my bike to the coffee shop. This will have to do.

While that brews, I run upstairs to change and grab my laptop. I'm thinking about redesigning the labels for my candles. They've had the same logo for a few years now and it's time for an upgrade.

Setting up my laptop in the kitchen, I fix a cup of coffee dumping in a heaping pour of caramel flavored creamer and sugar.

Sitting down, I get to work. I take a break after about an hour to start the cupcakes and then I'm back at it. By the time the cupcakes are ready to come out of the oven I've completed a logo I'm proud of and excited to switch to. While they cool, I get to work on updating my website with the new logo. I'll have to print new labels later today as well to put on the batch I'm going to work on this week.

A knock on the side door nearly has me jumping out of my seat. Binx watches me with his glowing green eyes like I'm crazy.

Maybe I am.

Opening the door, I let Thayer inside. "Looks like it's only your battery."

I blurt out, "It took you that long to figure that out?"

His expression doesn't waver. Always so serious. "No. I went and got you a new battery and installed it." He drops his gaze, noticing his dirty boots on the tiled floor. "Shit. Sorry about that."

I dismiss his concern. "It's okay. I need to clean the floors anyway." Cocking my head to the side, I add, "You didn't need to go through all that trouble."

"It wasn't any."

I highly doubt that, but I'm learning arguing with Thayer is a pointless endeavor.

"I made you cupcakes." I point at the cupcakes sitting pretty on a cooling rack, waiting for frosting.

The hint of a smile. "Cookie dough?"

"No, I thought this time I'd give you something different. It's peaches n' cream."

He makes a grossed out expression before he can stop himself. Clearing his throat, he says, "Uh ... sounds delicious."

I roll my eyes and start adding the frosting I made to a bag. "They're cookie dough. Calm down, mister."

"Mister, huh?" There's a glimmer in his eyes.

"Don't get any ideas." I roll my eyes. "It won't take me long to frost these if you're willing to wait. But I get to keep three."

"Why three?"

I twist the bag securely closed. "One for now, one for later, and one for tomorrow. Duh."

He chuckles. "Ah, makes sense."

"How much do I owe you for the car battery?"

"Nothing."

"Thayer," my tone is stern, "I'm paying you back."

"No," he insists in an equally severe voice, "you're not."

220

"You're so stubborn," I argue.

He arches a brow. "And you're not?"

Frowning, I focus my attention on the cupcakes. "You admit you're stubborn then?"

He snorts humorlessly. "It'd be pointless to deny it." He pulls out a stool and sits down, still looking warily at the mess he brought in on his boots.

"It's not a big deal. You can't avoid dragging mud in this time of year."

"I should've taken them off outside. My mom would be all over me if she saw this."

I try not laugh, but fail, making his lips rise in a smile. "You're thirty-one, Thayer."

"So? That doesn't mean my mom doesn't still scold me like I'm a teenager."

"We're always kids to them, huh?"

He swipes one of the cupcakes I've done. "Always."

"Hey," I try to smack his hand, "who said you could have that?"

"You did. You made them for me."

Rolling my eyes, I say, "Have you always been this full of yourself?"

"You're the one who said they were for me." He takes a big bite.

Dammit, he has me there.

I finish frosting them and set my three aside before boxing up the rest for Thayer. "There you go. Be nice and share with your family."

His eyes rake deviously over me, sending a shiver skating down my spine. "I don't like sharing."

"Where's your holiday giving spirit?"

He stands slowly, gaze never leaving me as he comes around the counter. He stops when there's less than a foot of space between us. "Can I kiss you?"

I nod, perhaps too eagerly based on the smile that curves his lips. He closes the distance between us, clasping my face between his large hands. I love when he holds me like that. Like I'm the entire world. I've never felt so special. Safe. Protected.

He lowers his head slowly, hovering, waiting for me to close the last breath between us.

Grabbing the back of his head, I pull him down the last bit. His chuckle is silenced by my mouth. We melt into each other, our bodies are desperate for one another since it's been a while since we've been together like this.

Alone.

The taste of temptation on our tongues.

His fingers dig into my hips, trying to pull me closer even though we're already plastered together.

I love this wildness between us. How we can't get enough of each other.

He lifts me onto the opposite counter, away from the cupcakes, and my ass lands on the hard surface. His hands go to my thighs, spreading me wider so he can stand between my legs.

My heart is racing a mile a minute, and yet I feel so utterly calm when I'm around him. It's a strange juxtaposition, but I don't mind it.

"You smell like sugar," he murmurs against my ear. "Pure sweetness." He gently bites the lobe. His lips drift across my cheek, lightly brushing against my mouth. "You taste like it too." His voice is barely above a whisper, raspy.

"Can you shut up?"

I don't give him a chance to answer. With my hand on the back of his neck I press him closer. His body is hot around mine, he's always so warm, like my own personal space heater.

Our mouths move in sync, while my mind chants his name over and over in my head.

It feels like an hour has passed when he pulls away, resting his forehead to mine. Our breaths are shallow, and his heart beats rapidly beneath my palm.

I look up at him through my lashes and I know, all the way down to the depths of my soul, that I love this man. I'll never love someone else as much as I love him. In a short amount of time Thayer Holmes has stolen my heart, imprinted himself in my very DNA, until no one and nothing can ever take his place. He's the only one for me.

It scares me, feeling so much for someone so quickly, but then I think about how many people say when you know, you know, so maybe it isn't so crazy after all.

My fingers play with the hair that skims the back of his neck. He looks at me intently, searching.

"Why do I feel like there's something you want to tell me?"

I swallow thickly, chest shaking with an inhale as I think of my mom. "The lunch you dropped me off to yesterday." I bite my lip, not wanting to say the words out loud. "My mom has cancer."

"Fuck." His head drops. "You let me maul you and you have this shit going on? I'm so fucking sorry, Salem." He wraps his big arms around me, holding me, caring for me. I'm safe. Protected.

"I wanted to kiss you." I don't want him thinking he took advantage of me. "I've missed getting to see you."

He smooths my hair back from my forehead. "What kind is it?"

"Breast. She's going to need a double mastectomy." My chin wobbles.

This is a lot. Unexpected too. I can't imagine what my mom has to be feeling. Her freedom from my father has been so short-lived to now be saddled with something like this.

But she's strong.

Resilient.

I have to believe she'll get through this.

"If there's anything I can do, please let me know."

And I know he would. This man put in an entire home gym in his basement for me. He fixed my car.

"Just be there for me."

It's all I'll ask for. It's all I need.

He kisses my forehead.

Gentle.

Warm.

Reverent.

"I can do that."

And I know he will.

FORTY-TWO

The short holiday break ends, Thayer's family leaves, and my mom has her surgery scheduled for just after the New Year. Apparently, she'd already been doing chemo for months and said nothing to us. I was mad at first when that admission came out, but then I thought about how she must've felt and that she was just being a mom, not wanting to worry us.

"Please come and visit," Lauren says on my phone screen through our FaceTime call. She's walking down the street in Brooklyn, her nose tinged red from the cold. "We can go to Rockefeller Center and see the tree together—remember, we always used to talk about that? We can do some Christmas shopping too. Come on," she pouts slightly, "I miss you."

"I know, and I miss you too. I want to, but it's just not a good time."

"I was afraid you'd say that, so that's why I already spoke with your mom, and she agreed with me that it's a great idea, and she's insisting you come."

I adjust my position on my bed, fluffing the pillow behind my head. Thayer is picking up Forrest from Krista and then he's swinging by to get me so we can pick out Christmas trees. One for his house, one for mine. We figured it would be easiest that way since he has a truck to haul them. "When?"

She grins evilly and I can't help but laugh. "Next weekend."

"Damn. The devil works hard but Lauren Rowe works harder."

"Absofuckinglutely." She sticks her tongue out at me. "I miss my best friend and I want to see you. Besides, with everything going on don't you think getting away for a little bit would be for the best? It's just a couple of days."

I sigh, knowing she's right. "Okay." I smile slowly. "I'm in."

Her squeal is so loud but the people passing her by on the street don't even pay attention like this is a normal every day, occurrence. I guess for them it is.

"We're going to have so much fun, just you wait!"

We say our goodbyes and hang up. Just in time too, since I get a text message from Thayer that he's five minutes away.

Sitting up from my bed, I give Binx a quick scratch around his ears. "See you later, bud."

I yank on my boots and my winter coat, watching out the window for Thayer's truck. When I see it pull into the driveway, I hurry out the door into the frigid cold. Snow is constantly on the ground this time of year, shoved into big nasty gray piles everywhere from the constant plowing.

Climbing into Thayer's warm truck, I smile at Forrest in the back seat. "Hey, Forrest. How have you been?"

"Good. School is exhausting, though. I need a longer break."

Beside me, Thayer tries not to laugh at his dramatic son. "And how are you?" I ask him.

His eyes are heated when he rakes them over me, putting the truck in reverse to back out of my driveway. Just this morning, after I came over for an early run on his treadmill, he pulled me down onto the weight bench, yanked off my pants, and showed me exactly why so many girls rave about oral. I'm still reeling from the intense climax I had.

"I'm ready to get a tree picked out," he says, glancing in the rearview mirror at Forrest. "We're going to decorate it with superhero ornaments."

"It's going to look so cool, Salem, just you wait and see. Do you think you and Binx could come over and help us decorate?"

I look at Thayer, seeing if he's okay with that. I don't want to impede on his time with his son. He gives a gentle nod, so I say, "Yeah, that sounds like fun. Maybe we could make cupcakes, too?"

Thayer chuckles, rubbing his fingers over his jaw. "Only if they're cookie dough."

"Ew cookie dough? I don't want salmon yellow poisoning, Dad."

"It's salmonella, son. And you can make cookie dough without raw eggs so it's edible."

Behind us, in the backseat, Forrest keeps trying to sound out salmonella, but it just keeps coming out as salmon yellow.

"What kind of cupcakes would you want?"

"Oh." He scratches the side of his nose, thinking. "Um, my favorite's chocolate."

"Chocolate is always an excellent choice."

Christmas music plays softly on the speakers, my eyes drift closed, listening with a smile. Despite everything going on right now, I'm trying my hardest to find the joy in the holiday season. When my dad got sick, I vowed to never again let anyone or anything steal joy from me—that even if life was giving me hell, I'd find one good thing in every day to keep me going.

Today, it's Christmas music, the man beside me, and the boy in the backseat.

We arrive at the tree farm, and more music is playing from their speakers when we hop out. Since it's the weekend, it's pretty crowded. There's a line of people at the snack stand and another line for people leaving with their trees.

Forrest runs over to my side and grips my hand, looking up at me with big eyes. "My dad said I either have to hold his hands or yours, so I picked yours."

226

I smile down at the boy, my heart melting. I give his hand a squeeze. "I hope you're ready to pick the best tree for my house too."

Thayer smiles, walking past us to get a saw.

"You want my help?" He points a gloved finger at his chest.

"Of course, I do. You're really smart."

His chest puffs up. "I really am. I got an A on my spelling test and everything."

Thayer returns and the three of us head down the rows and rows of trees, looking for the perfect one to cut. My boots crunch in the snow, my breath fogging the chilly air. But despite the frigid temperature there's no place I'd rather be.

"What about that one, Dad?" Forrest points out a behemoth of a tree.

Thayer shakes his head immediately. "Too big."

"Too big? That's tiny, Dad."

Thayer tries not to chuckle, a huff escaping between his lips instead. "It only looks small because we're outside. Trust me, it's too big. I think we need to head this way for the ones we need." He points to our left. "Watch your step." He holds out a hand to help me and Forrest across a particularly muddy path.

We make it to the more normal sized trees and Forrest pulls free from my hand, running. "What about this one, Dad?"

"Little dude, what have I told you about running ahead like that?"

Forrest drops his head. "Not to."

"Exactly." Thayer ruffles his hair. "It's a great tree, though. Good pick."

Forrest beams up at his father, like a flower blooming beneath the sun. "You think? It's a good one?"

"Yep. This is the one."

It's a tad crooked and a bit sparse in areas, but he's right, it's endearingly perfect.

With a groan, Thayer gets down to cut the tree while Forrest cheers him on. He jumps up and down and says, "You can do it, Daddy! You're so strong!" Turning to me, Forrest grins. "I'm going to be strong like my Dad when I grow up."

"I don't know, you already look pretty strong to me." I give his tiny bicep a squeeze—well, mostly I squish his puffy coat between my fingers but the way he beams I don't think he notices the difference.

"Did you hear that, Dad? Salem says I'm already strong."

"I heard, kid."

Once Thayer has the tree down, he takes it to the front to be wrapped and tagged while Forrest and I search for one for my mom and me.

"What kind of tree do you like?"

I give a shrug, tugging on the branch of one to see if any needles fall. "I'm not sure. I guess I kind of like one a little quirky."

He wrinkles his nose at the unfamiliar word. "Quirky?"

"Different, unique. It's something other people might overlook."

"Oh." He nods his head up and down a few times. "I'll keep an eye out for that."

His feet sink into the snow, causing him to almost trip. My grip on his hand tightens. "I've got you."

"Thanks, Salem."

I smile down at him, surprised at how much I've come to care for this boy in the past few months. "I've always got you."

"I've always got you, too." He wrinkles his nose in contemplation. "Unless you fall. You're too heavy for me to pick up."

I laugh. God, kids. I love the things that come out of their mouths.

"That's okay. You can just call for help."

"I can do that. Hey, what about that one?" He points to a tree that's full and voluptuous on the bottom, but the top is curved downwards. It's whimsical and definitely quirky.

"It's perfect."

"What's perfect?" Thayer walks up to us, saw in hand. His cheeks are red from the cold and his beanie is sitting a tad crooked on his head.

"This one," Forrest and I say simultaneously, pointing at it.

"You guys pick the weird ones," he mutters with a shake of his head, amused.

"They deserve love too," I argue, hands on my hips. "Get me my tree."

228

"I like it when you're bossy," he quips, poking my chilled cheek before he drops to the ground to cut the trunk.

"Can we get some hot chocolate before we leave, Dad? I saw them selling it."

"No," Thayer grunts with the effort of cutting down the tree. "I'm not paying five bucks for watered down overpriced bullshit. I'll make you some at home."

"Mom says bullshit is a bad word."

"It is," Thayer says, "and that's why only adults can say it. When you're an adult you can use them too."

Forrest looks up at me with wide, excited eyes. "Sweet. Being a grown up is going to be so much fun."

If you only knew, kid.

Forty-five minutes later, we're back home with both trees. Forrest runs around the yards while I help Thayer carry the trees inside each house. My mom is still at the shop, so I have Thayer put the tree in the corner where we usually have one and hope she's okay with it.

"Are we still making cupcakes?" Forrest shucks off his coat and muddy boots by the front door. They fall in a pile and Thayer eyes the mess.

"There won't be any cupcakes if you don't clean up your mess."

Forrest looks at the discarded items. "They're fine there."

"Forrest," he warns, pinching the bridge of his nose. "Didn't we have a talk about respecting property? Pick your stuff up and put it where it goes." He groans in a dramatic fashion but picks his things up. "Thanks, kid."

"Whatever."

Thayer fights a smile. "I swear, sometimes I'm reminded he's only six and other times he acts like a teenager."

I rest my hands in the back pockets of my jeans. "I think that's typical."

Forrest comes back into the room. "Now can I make cupcakes? And what about hot chocolate?"

"Lead the way," I tell him, and he runs off to the kitchen.

"I'm going to finish setting the tree up and then I'll make the hot chocolate."

"Take your time. We'll be fine."

In the kitchen, Forrest has already pushed a chair over to the center island and climbed up on top, inspecting the ingredients I swiped from my house. "Can I have one of these?" He holds up a bag of chocolate chips.

I pretend to look around for his dad, then whisper, "Go for it."

He takes the clip off the bag and hurriedly pulls out three mini chocolate chips, tossing them into his mouth. "I love chocolate."

I bop him on the nose. "Chocolate is very lovable and so are you."

He grins at my words.

Bending down, I rifle around in Thayer's cabinets for bowls and everything else I'll need. Despite the fact that he doesn't bake he has a fancy black Kitchen Aid mixer, which helps me out a lot.

I let Forrest help me measure out the ingredients, both of us laughing when he gets flour on his nose. I stick my finger in the flour and draw a smiley face on his cheek, so of course he wants to do the same to mine.

We're a laughing, giggling mess by the time Thayer comes into the kitchen. He eyes the mess we've made. There's flour and sugar all over my green sweatshirt. It's probably in my hair too. I rolled Forrest's sleeves up, but he has flour practically up to his elbows.

But life's boring if you never allow yourself to get a little messy.

"It looks like you two are having a little too much fun."

"Daddy," Forrest giggles, "look, I drew a heart on Salem's cheek. And a smiley face too."

Clasping my hands playfully under my chin, I turn each way so he can see his son's handiwork.

Brows furrowing, he bends down to Forrest's eye level on the counter. "Where's my heart and smiley face?"

"You have a beard on your cheeks. None for you. But what about..." He dips his hands into the flour and brings them to Thayer's cheeks, rubbing them all over Thayer's stubbled cheeks until the thick scruff is white. Giggling uncontrollably, Forrest says, "Now you look like Santa Claus."

Thayer strokes his chin, turning to me for appraisal. "How do I look?"

I look him over, heart somersaulting. "Distinguished."

"You like me with a little white in my beard?"

"It looks good."

His eyes crinkle at the corners with a smile. "Ho, ho, ho."

I squeal when he picks me up around the waist, tossing me over his shoulder and running around the counter. "Thayer!" I laugh, smacking his back. "Put me down!"

"Dad, what are you doing with her?" Forrest laughs. "You're being silly!"

Thayer sets me back down where he first scooped me up, pecking me on the lips. Both of us pause, realizing what he's done. Almost comically, we both turn to look at Forrest. His eyes are wide, surprised.

"Daddy, why did you kiss, Salem?" We're both quiet, floundering for an excuse. "Do you like her *like her*?"

Thayer's eyes drop to me, gauging whether or not I'm comfortable with this. I give a tiny nod, letting him know I'm okay with whatever he says to his son.

"Yes," he makes sure to look into Forrest's eyes, "I do like her. Very much."

Forrest looks at me and back at his dad. "Are you going to marry her?"

Thayer sighs, giving me an apologetic look at his son's prying questions. "Sometimes people like each other a lot but it doesn't mean they're getting married. They might, but they don't have to."

"Oh." He looks confused. "I thought only married people kissed. That's why I asked."

"No. Other people kiss, too. Kissing's nice—but not until you're older."

"You guys are like ... boyfriend and girlfriend, then?"

I hold my breath, waiting for his answer. The worst part is I don't know what I want him to say.

"We're..." He places his hands on his hips. "We're figuring things out, but no, we're not boyfriend and girlfriend. Not yet."

"All right. I like Salem." Forrest's eyes drift to me. "It's okay with me if you want to love each other."

And I think I might cry.

"Thanks, bud." Thayer ruffles his hair. "How about that hot chocolate now?"

WITH WARM HOT CHOCOLATE CLASPED IN MY HANDS, ornaments splayed out across the living room, cupcakes baking, and 'Rockin' Around the Christmas Tree' by Brenda Lee playing softly in the background, I can't help but think that I could get used to this.

Thayer picks up Forrest, lifting him up to add ornaments up at the top of the tree. Watching them makes me happy. Being a part of their little family fills me with a joy I didn't know I was missing in my life.

I had no idea when Thayer moved in that I'd fall so hard for him.

Not just him, but his son too.

I can't imagine my life without either of the Holmes boys. Somehow, along the way, they became mine. I just hope I'm theirs too.

FORTY-THREE

Lauren's waiting for me when I get off the train, exuding cool girl vibes I'm immediately envious of. Her dark hair hangs down well past her boobs in messy artful waves that look like she just rolled out of bed, but I'm sure took her a while to perfect. She wears a pair of light wash jeans, a thick gray turtleneck, black boots, and a black leather trench coat.

I feel severely underdressed in my jeans, sweatshirt, and puffer coat.

"Salem!" She runs to greet me, throwing her arms around my shoulders.

I hug her back, inhaling the scent of her floral perfume. "I missed you."

And God, have I. We talk on the phone as often as we can, but it's not the same as having my best friend in the same town.

"I missed you, too." She pulls back, holding me at arm's length like she expects me to have changed drastically since she left. It's not like she's seen me on FaceTime either. "I'm so happy you're here for the weekend. We have so much to see and do." She starts carting me out of the train station and to the busy, bustling streets. "Are you hungry? Let's get brunch."

"I could eat." My stomach chooses that moment to rumble, but with the noise of the city no one can hear it.

She leads me to the subway and eventually we get off, making our way to a little hole in the wall restaurant. It's narrow and long, but with an open and clean aesthetic that makes it seem much brighter.

We're seated after a thirty-minute wait—one which my stomach vehemently protests to—and I eagerly look over the menu. My mouth waters over the options. I'm pretty sure anything would taste good to me right now.

The protein bar I shoved in my mouth during the train ride has done little to abate my appetite.

Lauren sips her ice water that a waiter dropped off shortly after we sat down and slides her menu to the side of the table.

"I've let you avoid the topic for long enough."

"What topic?" I don't lift my eyes from the menu, but somehow I still know she's rolling hers.

"The breakup with Caleb, duh."

My brows furrow. "It's been a while. There's nothing to talk about."

"Of course, there is. Is there another guy in the picture?"

I swallow thickly. *Did it suddenly get hot in here?*

"Why would there be a guy?"

She snaps her fingers, pointing at me in the process. "You didn't deny it, missy! Spill."

I'm given a reprieve, for the moment at least, when the waiter comes by for our orders. As soon as he's gone though, she's back on it.

"You and Caleb were like the *it* couple. I honestly thought you guys were in it for the long haul and you know how cynical I can be. But at the same time, I can see why you'd end things. You need to grow on your own and not be tied down in the same relationship for all of eternity. Talk about boring." She finally pauses to inhale a breath. "That means you should be out there having fun. Dating other people." She waves her hand through the air lazily at the word *people.*

"Are you dating anyone?" I volley back.

"I'm dating," she supplies. "Having fun."

"Are you being safe?"

She grins, trying not to laugh at my question. "Yes, Mom. I'm being safe."

"Just checking. We don't need an accidental pregnancy here."

She mock gags. "Ew, crotch goblins. No thank you. Not anytime soon, at least."

"What about you? Are you being safe with this mystery man? And don't even try to deny it." Her eyes narrow upon me. "I've had the feeling for a while you're hiding something—or someone, I should say."

If there's anyone in this world I can trust, it's Lauren. I don't know why I've kept it a secret this long from her, but I've been safe and cozy in my little Thayer bubble and since we don't really venture out of that space, I've wanted to keep it to myself.

"You know the new neighbor—"

She gasps, slamming her hand down upon the table and earning us more than a few spare glances in the process. "You mean that hot sexy piece of man meat that mows his lawn shirtless but always looks like such a grump? The man you babysit for? The man who is a dad? Who's *way* older than you? That guy?"

"Yep." I nod slowly, reaching for my glass of water. "That's the one."

"Holy. Shit." She enunciates each word. "You're banging a *daddy* —and I mean that in both the literal and figurative sense."

"Lauren!" I throw a napkin at her, my cheeks flaming red.

"What?" She blinks with mock innocence.

"You know what," I counter, looking around to see if anyone heard her.

"I can't help it." She lowers her voice, leaning across the table. "When did this start?"

And there lies the big reason why I haven't told her.

"It was innocent at first," I explain, nervously picking at my fingers. "Just some harmless flirting. A *feeling*. But then, suddenly, it was more."

Her expression softens. "You were still with Caleb, weren't you? When this something became more?"

I gasp out a tiny, "Yes." Swallowing thickly, I add, "I'm a liar. A cheater. I hate those labels, but they're true."

"Oh, hun." Lauren looks at me sadly. "You're not a liar. And a cheater ... that's just a label, sure, but it's not who you are. I know you. You wouldn't do this on purpose. Be kind to yourself. We're young, Salem. We're going to make mistakes and do things we regret. But it doesn't mean we're horrible people." She stares into my eyes with so much sympathy that I feel tears spring to my eyes. "We're just human. Anyone who thinks they're perfect is delusional. We all make mistakes, do things we regret, just because those things don't all look the same doesn't make someone better over another."

"I hate that I hurt him."

"Did you tell him what happened?"

"No," I admit. "I knew I was already breaking his heart—why shatter it completely? Was that wrong of me?"

"No." She shakes her head steadily. "You were protecting him because you still love him."

"I do love, Caleb. I think a part of me will always love him. But Thayer is..." I flounder, trying to gather my thoughts. "What I feel for him is so much more. I can't explain it. From the beginning there's been a connection."

"Maybe he's your twin flame?"

"My what?"

"Your twin flame," she repeats. "Your soulmate. Other half. Whatever you want to call it."

"You think things like that exist?" I ask skeptically.

"Listen, in a world where the megalodon once existed, I'm not ruling out twin flames."

I hold my hands up like I'm weighing something. "Twin flames, megalodon. Seems comparable."

"Oh, shut up," she laughs, tossing the napkin back at me that I'd thrown at her previously. "So, you're boning your hot neighbor and I'm exploring New York's finest members. We're quite the pair."

I cover my face, trying to hide my laughter. "Lauren!"

"Hey," she presses a hand to her chest, "it's a tough job, but someone's gotta do it. I even keep a notebook. Names, numbers, and score them on performance. Seven and above and you'll get a second call from me."

"You're horrible."

"No, no," she chants as her our food is brought to the table, "I'm organized and prepared, there's a difference. No point in wasting my time on a dude that doesn't know where the clit is or what to do with any of his other appendages."

Thank goodness the waiter has already left before the last part of her speech.

"Listen, no more of that talk. I want to be able to enjoy my meal without thinking about that."

She laughs, digging into her yogurt parfait. "Fine, fine. I'll be on my best behavior. Well, I'll try at least."

"That's all I ask for."

MY WEEKEND WITH LAUREN IS OVER TOO SOON. I DIDN'T want to take the time away from home to make this trip, but now I find myself not wanting to leave. Lauren was right, I needed this break.

She hugs me tight, like she's trying to squeeze the life out of me—or maybe break a bone so I have to stay longer.

"Please, come back as soon as you can. And give your mom all the love and luck from me."

"I will." I hug her back just as fiercely, knowing that once I let go and get on the train it's back to reality.

Christmas is almost here, and then New Year's, and that means my mom's surgery.

The weight of the world is bearing down on me, but I take one more second to hug my best friend and remind myself what it feels like to be young and carefree.

"I love you," I tell her. "You're like a sister to me."

Lauren's shoulders shake with tears. "Don't let Georgia hear you say that. She'll get jealous."

"There's enough of me to go around," I promise.

Pulling away, she wipes at her tear-streaked face. "Don't be a stranger."

"Never." I know I have to go, I can't prolong it any longer. "Be good."

She laughs through her sniffles. "Never."

"Good luck with the job." I toss my bag over my shoulder. Lauren's starting an internship at a media company working in marketing. Apparently, she gave them a pitch on what she'd change with their social media, and they liked what she said enough to give her a chance.

"Thanks." She takes a step back. "Have fun with MacDaddy next door."

I shake my head at the nickname she's given Thayer. "You have to stop calling him that."

"Nope, not happening." She grins, clearly pleased with herself for coming up with the moniker.

"I'll see you soon," I promise.

"You better." She winks, but I can see how much she wants to break down. It's hard saying goodbye. Hellos are so much easier.

Turning, I walk away and don't look back.

FORTY-FOUR

"You're going to do great." I squeeze my mom's hand, fighting back tears. "The surgery is going to go fine, and we'll go home, and you'll heal. You're going to kick cancer's butt, Mom. I know you are. I believe in you."

She gives me a weak smile from the bed. She's in a purple hospital gown, IV in her arm. The nurse waits at the end of the bed, giving me a chance to say goodbye before she's wheeled back to surgery.

They said she'd be in surgery for at least four hours, and then there's the recovery time after but she'll be able to go home tonight. I know she's happy for that, not wanting to stay in the hospital any longer than she has to.

I brush her thinning hair back from her forehead and place a gentle kiss there.

"I'll be waiting."

"Honey, go home for a while, you don't need to stay here."

It's an argument we've been having. "No," I insist obstinately, "I'm staying right here."

She pats my hand. "Stubborn girl."

"I wonder where I get it from?"

The nurse clears her throat. "We really need to get her back and prepped."

"Right. Of course. I'm sorry."

I step away from the bed, holding back tears.

I refuse to cry in front of her. It's not fair if I do. She's the one going through this. Living it. I exit the room before she's wheeled out, because I know if I stay here, I won't be able to hold it together.

The waiting room is sleek and white, with a mix of chairs and couches. I walk out to the cafeteria around the corner and order a coffee before returning to the waiting room. I grab a chair parked in the far corner and sip my coffee, settling in for the long wait. I brought a book with me, one I said I'd read at the beginning of summer and now it's January and I haven't started it yet. Cracking open the book, I read the first three pages before setting it down. I'm too stressed to read. Shocker.

I pass the time watching other people in the waiting room and messing around on my phone. It's slow goings, but I don't want to leave. Not if anything happens. I'd never forgive myself.

Georgia couldn't be here since she wasn't able to get off of work. That leaves me and I won't shirk my responsibilities.

"Salem?"

I look up at the sound of my name, expecting a doctor or someone else, but it's Thayer.

It's.

Thayer.

He stands in front of me, bundled up from the winter cold. His wild hair tries to escape the brown beanie plastered to his head. And in his hands, he holds a bag of food from the Chick-Fil-A a mile or so from the hospital.

"Hi," I say stupidly. "W-What are you doing here?"

"I thought you might want some company, so I brought lunch."

He sits down beside me, opening the bag of food. "You came all

THE CONFIDENCE OF WILDFLOWERS

this way to bring me food?" The hospital is around an hour from Hawthorne Mills.

"I was in the area."

I don't believe him. He pulls out a box and passes it to me. "I wasn't sure what you'd like so I figured I was safe with a chicken sandwich."

"Thanks."

I don't have much of an appetite, but since he went to this much trouble, I'm going to make the effort to try to eat it.

"Here's some Diet Coke." He reaches into his pocket and pulls out a bottle, handing it to me.

He got me food. My favorite drink. He came to comfort me during my mother's surgery.

I'm beginning to think there's nothing Thayer won't do for me. I don't even have to ask him, he just does it—and things I would never expect in the first place.

"Thank you," I say after a few too long seconds, outstretching my fingers to take the drink.

"You're welcome." Lowering his voice, he asks, "Do you know anything yet?"

"No. It's only been about three hours and they said four hours would be the soonest she'd be done."

"Is there anything I can do?" He pulls more food out of the bag, passing me my own box of fries.

"You being here is more than enough."

His lips form a contemplative line. "I'm finding it's easy to be there for the right people."

And I think I understand what he's saying without actually saying it.

That Krista became someone he avoided.

I don't know many details about his marriage to Krista, I try not to pry because I figure he'll share what he wants, when he wants.

Even though I'm selfishly glad that he's mine now, for this moment in time, I do feel bad in a way. Once upon a time he loved Krista and she loved him. They had a child together. But love can change, and theirs did, and in the end they weren't what the other needed.

Biting into my sandwich, I do my best to eat as much as I can, knowing it'll be better for me in the long run if I have something in my stomach.

Thayer stays with me until my mom's out of surgery and I'm allowed to go back to see her. I'm pretty sure he'd hang around even longer if I asked him too.

When I hug him goodbye those three, scary, beautiful words are on the tip of my tongue but I hold them back.

Now's not the time, but I'm not quite sure when will be.

FORTY-FIVE

After my mom takes a pain pill and goes to sleep for the night, I bundle up in my coat and boots before sneaking across next door. I ring the doorbell and wait.

Thayer swings the door open with a confused expression furrowing his brow. His tense features relax when he sees me standing on his doorstep. "How's your mom?" He opens the door wider, letting me inside.

I take off my coat and hang it on the coat rack, setting my boots gently on the rug.

"She's okay. Emotional and in a lot of pain." Biting my lip, I add, "I think it just hit her, the reality of everything." I motion to my chest. "I can't begin to imagine what she's going through."

He shakes his head, his shaggy brown hair falling over his forehead. "It has to be rough. But she has you, and that matters, Salem."

"I'll be by her side every step of the way." It's a vow I don't hesitate to make.

He tips his head, motioning for me to follow him to the kitchen. "I know you will. She's lucky to have you."

"Thank you again for stopping by the hospital today. It meant a lot to me."

I'm not sure he knows how hard that is for me to admit. I don't like depending on people. When you expect too much from someone, you're setting yourself up for disappointment.

Thayer opens the fridge and bends down to pick up a beer. "You want anything?"

"Diet Coke." I grin, holding out a hand eagerly.

"You and your caffeine." He grabs a can and passes it to me. "I wanted to be there, Salem." He lowers his head, long fingers gliding through the chestnut brown strands of his hair. "I didn't like the idea of you sitting there, going through it alone." He twists off the top on his beer and takes a swig. Crossing his legs, he leans back against the counter, letting his eyes drift to the floor. "Everyone deserves to have someone who's there for them. I want to be your someone."

My heart stops beating.

He looks up at me slowly through long dark lashes.

"My ... someone?"

"Yeah," he shrugs, long-sleeve shirt pulling taut over his firm muscles. "I'm thirty-one. I'm too old to be someone's boyfriend. I figure being your someone sounds better anyway."

"I like it." I set my drink down and step up to him, putting my hands on his chest. His heart raps a steady beat against my palm. Guiding my hands up farther, I wrap them around his neck. "Does that mean I'm your someone?"

His brown eyes are warm, a swirl of so many things neither of us will say yet. "No, Salem." He shakes his head slowly. Before I can feel the sting of pain, he says, "You're my everything."

I can't stop the smile the blooms across my face. "I like that even more."

His smile matches mine. "I thought you might."

He sets his beer aside, picking me up. My legs wind around his waist a second before his lips crash to mine. I ache for him. To be held, cherished, *loved* by him. He carries me up the stairs like I weigh nothing. He shoulders his way into his room.

There's nothing rushed, or desperate, or chaotic about either of our movements.

Not this time.

It's different.

He lowers my body to his bed and turns on the light beside his bed. My eyes flick over to it and he must sense that I want to beg him to turn it off.

With his thumb and forefinger, he gently tips my head up. "I want to see you. Let me love you, Salem. The way you deserve. The way only I can."

I nod, perhaps a bit too eagerly based on his small chuckle.

He kisses my jaw, gliding his lips over to my ear. I want to ask him if he does, love me that is, but I keep my mouth shut.

Love is so much more than words.

It's a feeling.

And feelings can't be denied.

He takes his time kissing over my face, like he wants me to know he worships every part of me. He peppers light kisses over the freckles on my cheeks, my nose, beneath my eyes.

"Scoot back," he commands, and I do as he says. "Arms up."

I lift them and he guides my sweatshirt over my head. Dropping it to the floor behind him, he goes for my shirt next. In one smooth move it's off my body, leaving me in my simple white bra. It's nothing special, I picked my comfiest one to wear today, but he stares at me like I have on the sexiest lingerie he's ever seen.

He runs his fingers down my sides and I shiver from his touch. He undoes the button on my jeans and I lift my hips, helping him tug them down my legs. They join the growing pile of my clothes on the floor. He reaches to unclasp my bra, but I shake my head, shoving him back with my foot to his chest.

"You've gotta give me something here. Take your shirt off."

His lips tilt in a wry grin. Grabbing the bottom of his shirt, he yanks it up and over his head. "Happy now?"

"Immensely," I giggle.

With a shake of his head, he's over my body, crowding me.

He pulls down the cups of my bra, his tongue laving at first one nipple and then the next. I moan, my fingers pulling at his hair. He grips my right breast, his touch possessive. With every touch, every lick of his tongue, he's reminding me that I'm his.

"Thayer," I pant his name, holding him against my breast. He sucks my nipple into his mouth, his other hand skimming down my stomach. His fingers breach the edge of my panties.

There's a moment, just a second—less than one really—when horrible memories come flooding back and I freeze. It passes so fast, and I'm back in the moment with him, but he notices.

"Salem?" He blinks down at me, looking over my features to gauge where I'm at. His fingers are on my stomach, no longer under my panties.

"I'm okay." He looks doubtful. "I mean it." I take his face, his beautiful, rugged face into my hands. "I'm here. With *you*."

He looks at me for a moment longer. "Are you sure? I'll stop."

"Please, don't stop," I practically beg. "I need you."

He kisses me long and deep and minutes pass before he starts exploring my body again. He slips my panties down my legs, his fingers finding my pussy.

"Fuck, you're so wet."

"I told you," I wiggle, begging silently for his fingers to push inside of me, "I want you."

He moves down my body, his shoulders pressing my legs open further. "You're perfect, Salem." He rubs his fingers in my wetness.

Not tainted. Not ugly.

Thayer Holmes thinks I'm perfect.

His tongue connects with my pussy and sparks ignite inside me. He sucks and kisses, adding his fingers to bring me over the edge, and then again.

"Please," I beg, not even caring that I sound desperate. "I need you inside me."

Thayer moves off my body, standing beside the bed. He stares at me, right into my eyes, as he undoes his belt, pulling it through the loops on his jeans. The sound of it falling to the ground makes my heart beat faster and I lick my lips in anticipation. Next goes the button. Zipper. And then he pulls his jeans and boxers down in one tug, freeing his erection. He's hot and hard and so ready for me.

"Wait." I find myself climbing off the bed and kneeling in front of him. "I ... I want to try." I bite my lip, looking up at him. "I've never given a blow job before," I admit shyly. "I never wanted to."

He tilts my chin up. "You don't have to do anything you don't want to."

"But I do," I say quickly. "With you. I want to try with you."

He hesitates, then nods.

Wrapping my hand around the base of his cock, I stroke him up and down. I can feel him watching, but he says nothing, does nothing. He's giving me all the power, the control, letting me explore him safely, in my own way, in my own time.

Sliding my tongue out, I lick the head of his dick. He groans, his head falling back.

"Is that okay?"

"Yes, God yes." I do it again, growing bolder. Pumping my hand up and down his cock I add more pressure and take more of him into my mouth. "Holy fuck." He looks down at me with heat in his brown eyes. Gently, reverently, he pulls my hair back away from my face. There's something about that, that I find so sexy.

He gives me little guidance, letting me find my rhythm.

"No more. I don't want to come in your mouth. Not tonight." I let him go, his dick bobbing in front of my face and slick with my saliva. His eyes flare with heat as he looks down at me. Grabbing my face between his fingers, his touch is firm but not bruising. "Open your mouth," he commands.

I don't hesitate and do as he says.

He bends down, slow, steady, his eyes never leaving mine. It takes me by surprise when he spits in my mouth, then covers my lips with his, kissing me long and deep as he pulls me up from the floor with his hand still on my face. Picking me up, he lays me down on the bed. His body is over mine in an instant. Gripping the base of his cock, he slides inside me and both of us moan in relief. Rocking his hips steadily against mine, he clasps our fingers together, resting them beside my head.

"You feel so good," he murmurs into the skin of my neck. "Fucking made for me, Salem."

"God, yes." I squeeze my legs around him. He rests his forehead against mine, our noses brushing, breath to breath.

He makes love to me and I soak in every bit of that, letting it fill me up.

This is what it means to be cared for. Cherished.

Anything less is second best.

FORTY-SIX

"**A**re you sure about this?" Georgia asks our mom for the millionth time.

Mom sits on a stool in the bathroom, a towel draped around her shoulders. Her hair is thin and stringy, bald patches beginning to show.

"Yes." She nods determinedly. "I want it off. All of it. Get rid of it."

Georgia and I exchange a look. We know how hard this is for her. I've never thought of myself as a vain person before, but I can't imagine what it must feel like seeing your hair fall out like this. I've been vacuuming the house like crazy to get it all up so she doesn't see it.

With an inhale, Georgia starts the hair clippers up.

She cries.

I cry.

My mom cries.

And when it's all done, we huddle together and hold on tightly to one another, the hair pooled on the ground around our feet.

"Battles are better fought together than alone," my mom cries steadily. "Thank you, girls, for fighting this with me."

And then we all cry harder.

"You look like you've been crying," Forrest points out, rolling up a ball of snow for our snowman. Thayer has him this weekend but needed to take care of some work things, so that means I get to spend time with his son.

"That's because I was."

"Why?"

"My mom has cancer. My sister came over this morning and we shaved her hair off."

I don't believe in lying or sugarcoating things to kids. They're far more intelligent than most give them credit for.

"Oh." He adjusts his hat, his nose red from the cold. "Is she going to die?"

Out of the mouth of babes.

"I don't know," I answer truthfully. "I hope not, but we don't know."

"I hope she doesn't. I don't know what I'd do if my mommy or daddy died." He wrinkles his nose. "You're a grown up but even grownups still need their mommy."

"You're pretty smart, kid." I tell him, the two of us lifting the middle section onto our puny little snowman in Thayer's front yard. I couldn't turn the boy down when he asked to make one.

"Thanks." He pauses, glancing toward the backyard in thought. I expect him to ask more about my mom, but he's already moved on to another topic of conversation. "When my dad finally builds my tree-house do you think you'll hang out in it with me?"

"You bet. I always wanted a treehouse growing up."

"You didn't get one?"

"No. I didn't ask for one," I add.

"Why not?"

"My dad wasn't as cool as yours."

"Oh." He picks up a ball of snow and packs it together. "He is pretty cool."

"I have to agree."

"You like him, don't you?" He stacks the ball on top for the head and it immediately falls off. He picks it up, frowning at the snow for betraying him.

"I do. Very much."

A car pulls up then, one I recognize, but it's not Thayer.

Krista gets out of her SUV with Forrest's teddy bear in hand, barreling toward us. I can tell she's pissed to see me with her son.

"Where's my husband?" She demands, cheeks flushed with anger.

"He had to run errands, so I'm babysitting Forrest for a little bit. And don't you mean ex-husband?" I can't help but jab.

"This is his time with Forrest. He should be here. If he thinks I won't bring this to the court's attention, he's wrong." She shoves the bear at Forrest who takes it, giving her a funny look. "And who are you to point out that he's my ex? Are you one of his whores?" She looks me up and down like I'm muck stuck beneath her shoe. "Does he make you feel special? Like you matter?" Her eyes are narrow, evil slits. "He cheated on me, bet he didn't tell you that, did he? He'll do the same thing to you. Once a cheater, always a cheater."

I look down at Forrest, horrified she's saying all this in front of her son. She can be angry at Thayer, but he's still her son's dad.

"Have a good day," I say in dismissal, refusing to stoop to her level.

She flips her hair over her shoulde. "You'll get what's coming for you."

She bends down and hugs Forrest goodbye, leaving without a second glance.

Forrest runs over to put his bear on the porch. When he scurries back, he says, "I'm sorry she was mean to you."

"It's okay." I bend down, helping him make the head of the snowman bigger.

"It wasn't very nice. She tells me to be nice to people, but she was mean to you."

"Sometimes adults make mistakes."

"What did she mean about my dad cheating on her? Were they playing a game and he cheated?"

"I don't know," I tell him honestly. "Don't worry about it."

Before I forget, I send a text to Thayer letting him know she stopped by and what she said about court, feeling like he should know. He replies back almost instantly that he'll be home soon.

I'M CHILLED FROM BEING OUTSIDE SO LONG WITH FORREST, but I don't think he's a bit cold. I stir a pot of Kraft Mac n' Cheese for his lunch. I offered him better, healthier choices but he insisted this was the only thing he'd eat. He sits at the kitchen counter with a Marvel coloring book.

The front door opens and Thayer's boots are heavy on the floor. He greets Forrest first, pulling him into a hug and kissing the top of his head.

"Did you ask for Mac n' Cheese, again?"

"It's good, Dad!" Forrest cries, setting his crayon down.

Thayer shakes his head in amusement. With the cheese fully mixed, I ladle some into a bowl and add a fork, sliding it over to Forrest.

"You should have some, Salem. It's really good, trust me."

I don't bother telling him I practically lived off the stuff in elementary school and just do as he says, making myself a bowl before sitting down beside him. Thayer opens the fridge, searching for something. With his back to us, he says, "Your mom stopped by, huh?"

"Yeah, she was in a mood."

I stifle a laugh.

"What did she say?" he asks, pulling out a plastic container of leftovers. Popping off the lid he sticks it in the microwave.

"She said you were a cheater, Daddy. Did you cheat at a game or something? You told me cheating is bad."

Thayer's shoulders stiffen and he flips around from the microwave. "She said that?" he asks me.

I nod, stirring my bowl of macaroni. "Yes."

"You didn't believe her, did you?"

I don't say anything. It's not that I do believe her, but anything is possible.

"I swear to you, I would never ever do that. That's not who I am as a person."

"That's what I said, Dad." Forrest throws up his hand, almost throwing his fork in the process. "Oops."

"Salem," he stares deep into my eyes, leaning his body across the counter so he's on the same level I am, "I swear to you, I didn't cheat on my wife."

"I believe you." Maybe it's naïve, but I really don't think Thayer would lie about it. He doesn't have anything to lose by being honest.

Lowering his voice so Forrest can't hear, he adds, "You're the first woman I've been with since my wife."

And that ... it shouldn't make me happy, but it does.

Straightening, he turns around and grabs his reheated food from the microwave.

"Dad," Forrest speaks up around a mouthful, "will you build my treehouse for my birthday? I really want it."

Thayer sighs. I know Forrest has asked innocently since he moved in about it. "I can't right now, son. It's too cold. I'll build it this summer, I promise."

"You mean it, don't you?"

"I'm going to build it," he vows. "Don't worry about it."

"When's your birthday?" I ask Forrest curiously.

"It's March twelve?" He looks to Thayer for confirmation.

"Twelfth," he corrects.

Forrest looks at me with big eyes. "What he said. When's your birthday?"

"Oh, it was November twenty-eighth."

Thayer's head whips in my direction so fast, I'm surprised he doesn't get whiplash. "You didn't tell me."

I push the noodles around some more. It doesn't escape my notice that it's a statement, not a question. "No."

"Why not?"

"I hate my birthday," I answer simply. "It's not something I celebrate."

"You don't celebrate it." He rubs his jaw. "Why?" He demands, fists clenching. It's like he knows already.

Sliding from the stool, I grab his wrist and drag him from the kitchen away from Forrest's prying ears.

When we're safely far enough away, I drop his arm. "Because," I stare up at him, "it was my birthday. The first night he touched me, it was my birthday." Anger radiates off of him. "I thought he forgot to give me a present. I was so excited when the door opened." I start to cry. Even after all this time I can't help but get emotional for that little girl who endured so much. I told my therapist once that it felt like all of it had happened to someone else. "I was never happy when the door opened after that."

Pain spears his face, but he doesn't say anything to try to make it better. Thayer understands that there's nothing that can. He gently cups the back of my head and pulls me into the protective curve of his chest.

In the warm, safe cocoon of his arms, I quietly weep for the girl who stopped wishing on birthday candles.

FORTY-SEVEN

Time is a scary thing. How quickly it passes. In a blink it's March and Forrest's birthday—well, it's technically a few days after, but it's when Thayer has him to celebrate.

My mom and I are setting up decorations in Thayer's kitchen while he's gone to pick up Forrest. He knows we're here. He asked us the other day if we'd mind setting up and celebrating with them since Forrest loves us so much. Ever since we all carved pumpkins, he's become close to my mom. It's been nice for her to have a kid around. I think his enthusiasm for life has kept her mind off of this round of chemo. She's finishing her last round in another week and then we'll see what happens.

"Does this look okay?" I ask her, climbing off the step ladder to assess the blue streamers I hung across the archway into the kitchen.

She sits at the table taking a break. It's already decorated with a

255

tablecloth, the cake my mom made, balloons, and some presents. Thayer told us not to get anything, that it wasn't necessary, but he's crazy if he thinks neither of us wouldn't do something.

I might've gone a tad overboard on presents, but he's my favorite kid so I'm allowed to spoil him.

"Looks great, sweetie," she says, sipping the glass of water in front of her.

She looks tired. Wary. I wish I could make it all better for her. But there's nothing I can do or say. Georgia has been scrambling to get her wedding planned for June. She might've wanted a summer wedding to begin with, but we all know she's making sure it happens early enough that Mom can walk her down the aisle.

I try not to think about the fact that I might not have the same opportunity.

"They should be back any minute. Is there anything else I should do?" Hands on my hips, I look around the kitchen for anything I might've missed. I sort of blacked out at the party supply store and went overboard. That's what Thayer gets for slipping me his credit card.

"It's perfect honey. Sit down and take a breather before they get here."

Grabbing a Diet Coke from the fridge, I sit down beside my mom. I think Forrest will be happy and that's all that matters.

My mom looks around at the freshly painted walls and renovated kitchen. "Thayer's done a good job with this place. He's doing all the work himself?"

"Most of it."

She sips her water. "You're close with him."

"I babysit for him some, that's it, Mom." I play nervously with the ends of my hair. Her eyes immediately zero in on the gesture. I let my fingers drop. "We're friends."

"Hmm." She hums. "Just friends?"

"Mom!" I blush, looking down at the blue plastic tablecloth covered with dinosaurs. "He's in his thirties. I'm nineteen. It ... that would be crazy."

"Huh." She looks puzzled. "All right."

"What?" I prompt.

She waves a dismissive hand. "Just mom stuff. I thought I sensed something between you two." She smiles, squeezing my hand. "Must've been my imagination."

I clear my throat. God, I hate lying to her. "Must have."

She adjusts the bright green floral scarf she has wrapped around her head. She picked it because it matches the apron she wears today. "Do I look okay?"

My heart softens. "You look beautiful. You always do." She pats the top of my hand. There are tears in her eyes she won't let fall. It happens often these days. "Please, don't cry," I beg. It's not that I'm afraid of her tears, I just don't want her to be sad. I try not to let it show, but I'm so angry this happened to her. If there's anyone in this world who deserves happiness, it's my mom.

"I'm sorry." She dabs at her eyes. "I can't help it. Ugh."

She goes to rise up for a tissue, but I beat her to it. Returning to the table, I pass it to her.

"Thanks, sweetie." She dries her eyes and exhales a weighted breath. "I need to pull myself together. This is a happy day." She motions to the presents and cake waiting for the birthday boy.

"It is," I agree, crouching in front of her and taking her hands. "But you're sad right now and that's okay."

She wipes fresh tears away. "I just started thinking about how one day it might be your kid's birthday, or Georgia's, and I might not be there."

"Mom," I beg, squeezing her hands tight, "please don't say that."

"I have to be realistic."

I lower my head. I know she's right. I know it's a possible reality I have to face. But dammit if I don't want to. I want my mom to always be there and thinking about a world in which she's not is heartbreaking.

"You're strong," I tell her. "A fighter. If anyone can beat this, it's you."

"I'm trying." She pulls one of her hands from mine and tenderly strokes my cheek. "For you, for your sister, I'm fighting every day."

"I know."

And I do. If she loses this battle, I know she'll go out giving it everything she's got. That's just who she is. Because of my father some might view her as weak, but all I see is a survivor. I'll never judge her for that.

BY THE TIME THAYER ARRIVES HOME WITH FORREST WE'VE both managed to get our emotions under control and plaster smiles on our faces for the belated birthday boy. He runs into the kitchen, stopping in his tracks when he sees everything. His eyes go wide, mouth falling open in wonder.

"Wow! You guys did all this for me?"

"We did." My mom smiles at him, and I can tell she's put everything else out of her mind for the moment. "Happy birthday, Forrest."

"It was my birthday a few days ago but thank you."

Behind him, Thayer shakes his head in amusement.

"I know, but we get to celebrate with you now, so it's like your birthday all over again." She tweaks his nose, and he wraps his arms around her in a hug.

"Did you guys get me all these presents? There are a lot here."

"Those are all for you," I tell him. "From me, your dad, and my mom."

He laughs in excitement, eyeing a particularly large box. "You guys must really like me."

"You have no idea." He hugs me next, and I squeeze him tight. It's not just Thayer that took a piece of my heart when he moved in next door. "Can I open my presents now?" he asks his dad.

Thayer chuckles, pulling out a chair. "Go for it, kid. How about pizza after? Are you guys good with that?" He directs the next question to us.

"I'll never say no to pizza." Seriously, who doesn't like pizza? I blush, remembering what happened the last time we got pizza.

Thayer must think of it too because he shoots a smirk my way.

"Pizza would be lovely." My mom picks up her water and I notice she needs a refill. Grabbing the glass from her, I go to fill it up. When I return, she's saying something to Thayer in a hushed tone and he glances at me. His lips quirk up into a smile. There's no worry there, or anything, so I'm assuming she didn't ask him if there's more between us. A small part of me wonders what he'd say if she did question him.

Forrest tears through his presents, oohing and ahhing over the giant remote-controlled T-Rex I got him for his obsession with dinosaurs.

Thayer slips quietly out of the room and down to the basement to get Forrest's final present. Forrest doesn't even notice that his dad has disappeared from the room since he's so enamored with everything he got.

I try to hide my smile when Thayer comes into the kitchen with the Corgi-mix pup. I found her a week ago, abandoned across the street from my mom's shop and when I spotted her, it seemed like fate, considering I found Binx in such a similar manner. I called Thayer and told him, hinting that Forrest would absolutely love to have a puppy and he grumpily agreed to take a look. As soon as he took the puppy from my arms I knew he was a goner for her.

"A girl?" He'd said, holding her out at arm's length. "I don't know how to be a girl dad."

I slapped his arm playfully, and said, "You're going to learn."

Then the next thing I knew he was shopping and buying her all kinds of things—more cushions and toys than any one puppy needs, fitting her into a pink collar, and frankly spoiling her silly.

Forrest gasps when he spots the puppy in Thayer's arms. "Is that a puppy?" He screams loudly. "For me?"

Thayer chuckles and bends down, passing the puppy over to his son. "Yeah. Isn't she cute?"

"So cute." Forrest buries his face in her fur. "I love her so much."

Thayer chuckles. "You just met her."

"Doesn't matter. I love her. What's her name?"

Thayer pets the top of her head. "What do you want it to be?"

"I don't know." He shrugs his little shoulders, looking at the dog with awe. "Salem?" He turns to me. "What's a good name?"

"Oh." I hate being put on the spot. "Name her after something you love. I named Binx after a character in my favorite movie."

Thayer smirks at the mention of the movie. Cocking his head to the side, he says to me, "Do you have a suggestion from that, then?"

"Yeah," Forrest prods, "she needs a good name."

I bite my lip, thinking. "What about Winnie? Short for Winifred."

"Winnie," Forrest repeats. "I like it." He exaggerates the word like, making me chuckle.

Thayer nods along, still petting her head. "Winnie it is. It's perfect."

Over my shoulder, I glance at my mom who's watching us carefully. She doesn't look perturbed, just curious, and I know that despite what I said she still suspects something is happening with Thayer and me. Mother's intuition is a strong force.

Forrest sets Winnie down and laughs as she runs around on her stubby legs.

Thayer orders the pizza, and we settle in for the afternoon spent with the two Holmes boys, and I know that today has just become one of my favorites.

FORTY-EIGHT

itting straight up in bed, I throw the covers off my body. It's been a while since I had a nightmare this detailed, this vivid. It felt so real. Stumbling out of my bed and down the hall to the bathroom, I sink to my knees and throw up. My body heaves, emptying itself of everything in my stomach.

When I'm finished, I flush the toilet and brush my teeth, getting rid of the acidic taste burning my mouth. Sweat still clings to my skin. Grabbing a washcloth, I dampen it with water and pat it over my skin.

Binx meows from the doorway. "I'm okay," I tell him.

He stares at me with bright green eyes like he knows I'm a liar. Pulling off my sweat soaked clothes, I step into the shower and let cool water beat on my skin.

When I don't feel gross anymore, I shut off the shower, and pad across the hall into my bedroom. I quickly pull on my workout clothes and tie my shoes. "I'll be back soon."

Binx looks at me doubtfully.

Slipping out of the house, I head next door to Thayer's basement.

It's been a while since I've had a nightmare, so the last thing I expect is to find him waiting. Well, he's starting back up the stairs when I slip inside but he quickly pauses. He walks back down the stairs, giving me a sad look.

"I had a feeling," is all he says. I give him a weak smile. "What do you need from me?"

I don't hesitate. "Hold me."

His long-legged stride crosses the distance between us, and he gathers me in his arms.

I wrap mine around his strong body.

Safe. Protected. Loved.

His lips press tenderly to the top of my head. "I've got you."

I fist the back of his shirt between my fists, holding on as tight as I can. He lets me hug him for as long as I need to, and when I finally pull away, he takes my cheeks in his hands.

"Better?"

"Yeah."

"Do you still need to run?"

I press my lips together, looking down at my tennis shoes. I want to be stronger than always needing to try to outrun my demons.

"I don't know," I answer him honestly. "I want to try not running."

He gives me a small smile, his eyes warm in the muted light of the basement. "Come upstairs. I'll make you some food and you can help me with something."

"With what?" I ask, letting him lead me to the stairs.

"So nosy," he jests. "I'll show you." In the living room, he takes me to the card table he uses when he works puzzles. "It's not running, but it is a distraction."

I will not cry. Not over a puzzle. Not because of his kindness.

The puzzle is an ombre of colors from a light yellow, to green, to blue. I pick up a piece, rubbing my fingers against it. "You're going to let me help you with the puzzle?"

"Only if you want." He tucks a stray piece of blonde hair behind my ear.

"Okay." I set the piece back down. "But feed me first."

"I can do that."

Despite the early hour, he makes me fresh waffles with eggs. When he sits down beside me to eat, I can't help but think about how much I love this—just existing with him, making breakfast and eating together. These are things we so easily take for granted, but it's the things that matter most.

Winnie nudges her head between us, begging for scraps. Thayer scolds her for begging, but then gives her little nibbles.

When we're finished eating, he rinses off the dishes and I load them into the dishwasher.

So simple. So easy.

He makes us each a cup of coffee before we sit down to work on the puzzle together. We've each added a few pieces to it when I look at him. I take in the slope of his nose, his full lips, the scruff coating his jaw.

Thayer Holmes shouldn't be the right guy for me. He's older than me, he's a father, he's running a business and has his whole life figured out. He's perfectly wrong in all the right ways.

He sets a puzzle piece down. "Why are you looking at me like that?"

And then, because I can't help it, because I'm tired of keeping it locked inside, I say, "I love you."

His warm brown eyes stare deeply into mine and I see the promise of a future there. One I think subconsciously I always thought I didn't deserve.

Picking up my hand, he laces our fingers together, kissing the top of my knuckles.

"I love you, too."

FORTY-NINE

The outside world begins to show signs of spring. The snow melts, trees begin to bud, and the birds chirp excitedly.

But most importantly, the ushering of the spring season brings with it the news we've been waiting for.

My mom is cancer free.

The look of relief on her face when she got the news is something I'll never forget.

"Do you think this is enough cupcakes?" I jokingly ask, loading them into her car.

The flea market in the center of town is opening this weekend and she'll be selling her cupcakes. I have a booth for my candles, debuting some new scents.

"I sure hope so," she replies with a smile, her eyes crinkling at the corners.

I tried to snag a cookie dough cupcake earlier, but she wouldn't let me.

Closing the trunk of her car, we hop in and head off together. Our booths are on opposite ends since they set it up in categories. I hang up my sign and decorate my little tent, trying to make it inviting to draw people in. I brought some of my leftover fall and winter scents, marking the prices down to hopefully get rid of them. I always try not to have too many leftovers carrying over into the next season.

Settling behind the table, I paste on a smile and chat with everyone who stops by. I'm surprised in the first hour how many candles I'm able to sell, but it makes me feel good that my little hobby is making me money. Not that a hobby must be profitable to have merit.

It's near the end of the second hour when I spot Thayer strolling the booths with Winnie on a leash. A pink bandana with polka dots is tied around her neck, her tongue lolling out of the side of her mouth. She's too cute for words.

Thayer approaches my booth and I struggle not to smile when he ignores me at first, pretending to only be interested in the candles.

"You make these yourself?" He plays dumb.

"All done with these little hands." I hold up my hands and wiggle my fingers.

His stoic expression cracks the tiniest bit. "Peony, huh?" He picks up one of the spring candles.

"It's my favorite flower."

His eyes meet mine, the intensity sending a shiver racing down my spine. "I remember." He unscrews the lid and sniffs. "I'll take this one."

"Is it for your mom again? I have gift wrapping." I go to grab a box and tissue paper.

"No." I stop swiveling around. "This one is mine."

"Oh?" I arch a brow, biting my lip to hide my growing smile.

He passes me a twenty, refusing change, so I tell him to grab two of them.

"It's a tip, Salem."

"And I want you to take two. You can pick a different scent if you want."

He grabs a cookie dough one. "Happy now?"

I grin. "Immensely." I put the candles in a little bag and pass them to him.

"You're a stubborn little thing."

"Someone's gotta give you a run for your money." Wetting my lips with my tongue, I ask, "Why the peony?"

I have much more masculine scents he could've chosen from, not that a scent should be categorized by gender, but men can be such sensitive little creatures.

He pauses before leaving my booth, cocking his head to the side. "Because," he looks me up and down and it feels like he's undressing me with his eyes, but not in a gross way, no he's reminding me that he knows me in ways others don't, and more than just the physical sense, "it smells like you."

A tiny gasps flies past my lips. "It smells like me?"

"Yeah." He scoops Winnie into his arms, so she'll stop tugging at his pants with her teeth. "That makes it my favorite." My smile blooms and he answers with a grin. "There's my Sunshine." Tipping his head at me like some old timey southern gentleman, he says, "Now I'm going to go get me some of your mom's cookie dough cupcakes."

"Save some for me," I demand, pointing a warning finger at him.

He scratches under Winnie's chin, her head leaning into his chest with contentment. "No promises. They're my favorite."

It's cheesy, but the words blurt out of my mouth before I can stop them. "You're my favorite."

He sets Winnie down and she scuttles around on the ground excitedly. "You're my favorite," he starts, smiling wickedly, "after cookie dough cupcakes."

I burst into laughter. Second to a cupcake. I guess there are worse things I could be second place to.

"Oh." He shoves his hand in his pocket. "This is for you." He pulls something small out of his pocket, enclosing it in his palm. He holds it out, indicating I should open my hand.

When I do, he drops a ring into it.

It's silver with suns stamped onto the surface.

I look at him in surprise. "What's this for?"

266

"Because, you're my sunshine."

I smile, slipping it onto my thumb. "Thank you."

He dips head. "You're welcome."

I watch him walk away, rubbing my finger against the ring he so thoughtfully picked out for me.

I make a few more sales before I put Thelma of all people in charge of my booth and run across the street to use the bathroom in one of the local restaurants. When I get back to my booth there's a single cookie dough cupcake waiting for me.

"That handsome neighbor of yours left that," she says in a reprimanding tone. "Cynthia," she continues, referring to the elderly neighbor across the street from where I live, "was telling me all about you sneaking over to that man's house early in the morning. She has a weak bladder you see, so she's up all hours of the night peeing." Information I didn't need to know. "She sees you going over there a lot. He's a good bit older than you, you know."

"I wasn't aware," I reply sarcastically, peeling off the cupcake wrapper.

"Mhmm," she hums, undeterred and still firmly seated in my chair. "He sure is nice to look at. Rugged. I can see the appeal. He looks like the kind of man who can throw you over his shoulder and ravage you."

I spit out little pieces of cupcake, choking on the bite I had half-swallowed.

"Virile," she goes on, not at all concerned about me choking and dying. "That's the kind of man in my heyday I would've let knock me up."

"Thelma!" I cry, still clearing my throat. My eyes water and I'm pretty sure there are crumbs lodged in my throat.

"Can you blame me?" She bats her eyes at me innocently. "What is it you do over there so early in the morning? Play Parcheesi?" She winks.

I blush. "I run. He has a home gym I use."

"Is that we're calling it these days? A run?" She mulls it over. "I guess if I saw a man with an ass like that I'd run after him too." I can't help but laugh. She stands up slowly from the chair and pats my hand. "Have fun with that one. You're only young once." She sighs dramatically. "Oh, the stories I could tell you. We'll save that for another day, dear."

I watch her waddle off to another booth and immediately she starts critiquing the price list, insisting they're way too expensive and she'll offer them three dollars for whatever it is that's caught her eye.

Sitting back down, I finish my cupcake and manage not to choke this time.

I'm happy today, happier than I've been in a long time, but the paranoid part of me can't help but think this can't last forever. My mom being declared cancer free, Thayer and I being in a good relationship—something has to give, right? My life is never this perfect. I know my therapist would tell me not to think like this, that I'm just inviting negativity into my life, but I can't help the feeling of dread that sinks into my stomach.

Nothing this good can last. This I know.

FIFTY

The warm weather brings with it my ability to run outside again.

As grateful as I am for the gym Thayer built, nothing beats running outdoors. No nightmare sends me running out the door this morning, just my own eagerness to feel my feet against the pavement.

And there's Thayer, leaning against the lamp post waiting.

He looks me over and I know what he's searching for. "No nightmare. I want to go for a run. That's all."

"Good." He rubs his toned stomach, hidden behind the cotton of his shirt. "You're keeping me in shape with all this running."

"And you're even starting to keep up, old man." With a laugh, I take off, forgoing my normal stretching.

Behind him, I hear his echoing laughter. "Old man, I'll show you."

AFTER OUR RUN, WE RETURN TO HIS HOUSE, SITTING ON THE back porch to eat a breakfast of pancakes made by Thayer and my contribution of a yogurt parfait. The pool cover is off, the water murky and in need of chemicals. It'll still be a few weeks before it's warm enough to swim.

"The greenhouse is going to be thriving once you finish it." He was able to get most of the work done last summer and fall, but there are a few things he still needs to do to complete it.

"I'm looking forward to it. Are you planning on spending time with me in it?"

I bite my lip, thinking about things that definitely don't involve plants and instead consist of me on the table inside and Thayer between my legs.

"I love plants," I say, instead of the thoughts running through my mind. "I'd love to help you with it."

He gives a small, almost boyishly shy smile. "Good." He leans over and pecks me on the lips. It's so easy, the two of us, like it was always meant to be. I hold the back of his neck, deepening it momentarily and smile against his lips.

"I was thinking," I start, ducking my head with sudden worry, "if you're okay with it, I want to tell my mom. About us."

He thinks it over and I expect him to shut down the idea. I don't know exactly why I feel that way. "Okay."

"Yeah?" Excitement almost bursts out of me.

"Sure. We can tell her whenever you want." He glides a finger gently down the side of my cheek.

"Have you told anyone about us?" I ask him, curious.

He chews a bite of pancake. "My brother. You?"

"I told Lauren." He nods like he assumed as much. "Oh, and Thelma knows."

He chokes on his food, spitting out a bite. "Nosy, busybody Thelma knows?"

"Yeah. Apparently, Cynthia told her."

"I knew I shouldn't trust that little old lady," he jokes, wadding up the food he spat out in a paper napkin.

"We're going to do this? For real?" Suddenly I feel nervous about my mom knowing. On Forrest's birthday, two months ago, she suspected, and I lied to her. Now I have to admit that. I might be nineteen now, but I hate lying to my mom.

He arches a brow. "I thought you were ready."

I nod steadily, centering myself. "I am."

"I have to pick up Forrest in about an hour. We can tell her tonight if you want? I can pick up steaks while I'm out and grill."

His thoughtfulness nearly brings tears to my eyes. "That would be nice."

"Good." He swipes a bit of yogurt off my lip, licking his thumb clean. His gaze intensifies, voice lowering. "I didn't think I'd find it."

I give him a funny look. "Find what?"

He traces the shape of my lips with his finger. "Something real. Before, I didn't know what real, true love felt like. Just a weak imitation of it. You've given me this."

My heart takes flight and soars right out of my chest. Grabbing him by the shirt I pull him in for a kiss. I don't think I could possibly be happier.

SITTING OUT ON MY ROOF, I GATHER MY LEGS TO MY CHEST and wrap my arms around my legs. I've missed being able to do this. There's something about sitting on the roof, feeling the heat of the sun that will always make me feel good.

Pulling my hair back into a ponytail, I smile when Thayer's truck pulls into the driveway next door. Forrest gets out of the backseat, stomping away from the truck as Thayer calls after him.

"You're so mean, Dad! You promised! You said you were going to build my treehouse!"

"I am," Thayer insists. "But I can't do it overnight. We're going to work on it. I promise.

Forrest turns, putting his small hands on his hips. "All you do is say you promise but you don't actually do it. I hate you. You're the worst dad ever." He runs to the back of the house, sulking.

Thayer looks crushed. "Love you, too, kid." Lowering his head, he grabs the grocery bags. He must sense my eyes on him because he looks up and spots me on the roof giving me a disapproving but amused look.

I stick my tongue out at him.

With a shake of his head, he walks up the porch and calls for Forrest to come inside but I hear him yell something back about not wanting to.

Lying back on the roof, I close my eyes and let the heat of the sun lull me into a nap. I'm sure most people wouldn't want to fall asleep like this, but it doesn't scare me.

I'm not sure how long I've been dozing when I hear yelling next door.

"Forrest? Forrest? Where are you? This isn't funny!" Sounds Thayer's angry voice. "Don't hide from me!" I sit up, rubbing sleep from my eyes. "Forrest?" Thayer sounds scared, which raises my alarm and I shake off the last vestiges of sleep clinging to my cloudy mind. Thayer storms through the front gate and sees me still on the roof. "Did you see Forrest go inside? I didn't hear him, but he might've snuck in."

I shake my head. "No, I fell asleep."

He looks like he wants to murder me over that tidbit of information and I'm sure I'll get a lecture on almost killing myself by sleeping on the roof, but there are more pressing issues at hand.

"He's not answering me and even if he's pissed at me that's not like him. Forrest isn't a grudge holder." Thayer runs a hand through his hair, the lines on his face stressed.

"Did you check inside yet?"

"A little but I would've heard the alarm say a door opened and it didn't."

Sudden, horrifying clarity washes over me. "Thayer." Ice slides down my spine. It's thick, sticky dread. The kind of feeling you get when you know, know deep in your soul that something very bad has happened. Thayer's eyes meet mine and I think he realizes in the same second I do. "The pool."

FIFTY-ONE

I forgo trying to scramble back into my room, and instead try to reach the ground as fast as I can.

Breath whooshes out of my lungs when I hit the ground, something in my ankle twisting, but it doesn't break.

I watch as Thayer throws open the gate to the backyard. I chase after him as fast I can with my injured leg.

He doesn't hesitate when he arcs his body and dives straight into the murky pool over the fence built solely around the pool itself.

Running to the edge I look down, my hand pressed to my mouth in horror.

Please, let me be wrong. Oh, God. Oh, God. Oh, God.

"Forrest!" I scream for the little boy, panic clawing at my throat.

Please, let him run out from behind a tree. To have snuck into the field of wildflowers. Not this, anything but this.

Thayer comes up for air, flicking his wet hair roughly out of his eyes.

In his hand is a kid's tennis shoe.

I drop to my knees, sobbing.

I can't breathe. I can't breathe. I can't breathe!

He's gone again, under the water, and this time when he emerges he has Forrest's limp body clasped to his chest. He swims to the edge of the pool, heaving the body out before climbing out himself.

Blue.

Forrest is *blue*.

His lips.

His eyelids.

His fingers.

I hate the color blue.

Thayer tilts Forrest's head back and starts CPR.

"Stop," I shove at his soaked shirt. "You're doing it wrong. Call 911."

My phone was in my room, or I would've done it already.

Thayer pulls his phone out of his pocket, cursing and throwing the useless device to the ground.

"Mom!" I scream at the top of my lungs, my fists pumping against Forrest's tiny chest.

He's cold.

Oh, God, he's so cold.

The water was like ice.

And he was ... oh my God.

"MOM!"

Thayer's screaming too. I don't even know what he's saying. My mind can't seem to focus. I just keep screaming and doing CPR and screaming again.

But he's gone.

There's no life left in the boy beneath my palms. It's a shell. An empty one.

A corpse.

My mom runs over, and I hear her scream too.

We're all just fucking *screaming* and it's pointless because Forrest can't hear us. He's not here. Not anymore.

Sitting back on my legs, I look up at Thayer. His hands are behind his head as he paces. When he sees that I've stopped he drops to the ground beside me.

"What are you doing? You can't stop. He needs—"

"Thayer," I choke out through my sobs, "he's gone."

"No," he shoves me away, trying to resume CPR. "No. He's not gone. He's going to be fine. We just have to get the water out of his lungs."

I put my hand on his arm, the sound of my mom crying on the phone in the background. "He's gone, Thayer. I'm so sorry."

When his eyes meet mine, I've never seen pain like this. Heart-breaking, soul crushing *pain*—the kind of emotional anguish someone never overcomes.

He shakes his head back and forth. "No, no. He can't be gone. We were just ... we were going to..." His head falls back, and he screams at the heavens.

I crumble, crying so hard my ribs ache with every inhalation.

Forrest's body lies in front of us.

Empty.

God, it's so empty—so blue.

Wrapping my arms around Thayer's soaked body, I hold him together as best I can, but it's hard to keep someone from breaking when you're shattered yourself.

Death should never happen like this.

Not so suddenly.

Not to a kid.

Not ... just *not*.

"Mom," I say softly, my voice cracking. "Go inside and there's a list of contacts on the fridge. Call Krista."

I can barely function, but I know Thayer is in worse shape than I am, and Krista ... God, she needs to know.

She walks off and I bury my head into the crook of Thayer's neck.

Sirens sound in the distance and then everything happens in a flurry as the paramedics' hurry into the backyard. I know from the looks on their faces they're never going to get over this either.

Death is inevitable—the great equalizer, but it should never happen to a child who has so much to live for.

Thayer doesn't stop crying, and screaming, demanding they do more, try harder.

He doesn't look when they move his body to a bed and cover him with a sheet.

We follow robotically behind them

Krista's SUV flies down the road, the brakes shrieking when she slams it to a stop and runs out of the car.

If I thought Thayer's screams of anguish were bad, they have nothing on Krista's.

The cry of a mother realizing she's lost her child is the most heart-breaking sound in the world.

"My baby! That's my baby!"

An officer on the scene wraps his arms around her when she tries to yank the sheet off of Forrest's body before they put him into the back.

"My baby," she sobs, falling to the ground out of his arms. "Not my baby!"

I close my eyes. I think I'm going to be sick.

It's like everything is happening in a slowed down speed, but somehow incredibly fast at the same time.

I've never heard anything quite like the painful sounds leaving her body.

It's the sound of a mother's soul being ripped in two—half of it forever with her son.

Gathering herself up from the ground she storms toward Thayer and he lets me go, facing her.

"You did this!" She yells, beating his chest with her fists.

Thump.

Thump.

Thump.

Over and over again her fists connect with his chest, like maybe if she beats his heart enough it'll revive Forrest's.

"Our baby!" She sobs. "You let our baby die!"

Thayer sinks to his knees on the ground and she goes with him. He keeps saying he's sorry over and over again as her screams grow louder. Soon her words turn incoherent and only sobs leave her.

Thayer and Krista end up riding in the ambulance. I don't know what the point is. It's not like the answer's going to change once they reach the hospital. But I guess I wouldn't want to leave my child either.

My mom wraps an arm around my body, pulling me away and back toward our house.

Everyone that lives on the street that's home at this hour has been outside watching the entire scene unfold—all of our lives now entwined by this one horrific event.

In my room, I sit on the edge of my bed, numbness spreading through my veins.

This isn't right.

It can't be true.

Wake up.

I slap my cheek.

Wake up.

But this isn't a nightmare I can throw on my tennis shoes and jog away from.

It's real fucking life and you just deal with it.

FIFTY-TWO

'm not sure what makes me get in my car and drive.

I drive and drive until I find myself in Boston on the Harvard campus.

I didn't text him. Didn't call him to say I was coming.

I just show up.

It's wrong of me after we broke up—after all the sins I've committed that he doesn't even know.

It's getting late when I stroll through the dorm and straight to his door.

I hesitate a moment before I knock. He could be in there with a girl for all I know. Not that it matters. We broke up, after all, and it's what I wanted. But right now, I need my friend.

I knock on the door, and my head falls back as the tears come again.

He opens the door with a funny look that turns to concern when he finds me of all people outside his door crying.

"Salem?" He blurts in surprise. "Are you okay? Fuck," he curses, "stupid question. Is it your mom?" I shake my head, my face wet with tears.

"Come here." He pulls me into his familiar arms. His shoulders are narrower than Thayer's but he's well-built from years of playing football. He rests his chin on my head, rocking me back and forth before carefully guiding me into his room. His roommate's bed is rumpled but empty, and I'm so grateful a strange guy isn't there to witness my breakdown. It's not really that I'd be mortified, it's that I don't want to share *this* with a stranger.

"Talk to me." He cups my cheeks in his palms, staring down at me with those caring blue eyes that were always so comforting to me.

My lip quivers and I place my hands on his sides, needing the support to stay upright so I don't crumble apart more than I already have. "Next door," I sob, finding it impossible to get control of myself.

His eyes darken. "Did that bastard do something to you?"

"No, no," I shake my head vehemently. "His son ... Oh God, Caleb, it's so awful."

"Shh," he hushes. "It's okay. *Breathe*, babe." The endearment rolls naturally off his tongue.

"The little boy. Forrest. You know, I watched him some." I gag from my tears, and hope I don't throw up on Caleb.

"What happened?" He brushes hair off my forehead, staring into my eyes. He looks like he's on the verge of tears too and he doesn't even know.

"He ... uh ... he died." I choke on that word. It's my least favorite word in the English language. The worst combination of four letters. "He drowned. He was there, alive, and then he just wasn't. In the blink of an eye." I snap a finger for emphasis. "Like a candle being blown out. Life's so fragile and I just..."

I couldn't go to Thayer, so I went to the next best thing.

Caleb guides me over to his bed and pulls my body down with his. He wraps me in his arms, pulling the blankets over us.

And he just holds me.

It's exactly what I needed, why my subconscious mind brought me here.

He holds me for hours, letting me cry, talk, whatever I need.

And I tell him everything.

About my dad.

About Thayer.

I lay it all out, every truth, every sin staining my soul.

I expect him to shove me out of the bed, to tell me I'm a horrible person. Because I am. I cheated on him after all.

But that's not Caleb.

He holds me tighter, pressing kisses to the top of my head.

"I wondered," he admits, in the quiet of his dorm room, "if you'd met someone else. I didn't think it would be *him*."

"I'm sorry I did this to you."

"It hurts." I like that he doesn't sugar coat it with me. "But I know I played a part in this. With college, and football, my parents breathing down my neck..." He curls his body tighter around mine. "I took you for granted. I thought you'd always be there, so I didn't put in as much effort to make you a priority. That was my failure. What you did was wrong, but it'd be a lie to say that I wasn't a factor in why you did it." Silence falls between us again, and I've almost drifted off to sleep when he asks, "Do you love him?"

"Yes."

"How much?" His body tightens like he's bracing himself for my answer.

I whisper like a confession, "So much."

"More than me?"

"I ... it's different, Caleb."

"So, yes, then?"

I rub my lips together. "I don't know."

"It's okay." He clears his throat and reaches up to turn the light off. "It's not him you're with tonight."

Caleb takes me to breakfast before dropping me off at my car and sending me home. He offers to drive me back himself, but he only has a few days of classes left and he needs to be here.

When I arrive back in Hawthorne Mills the whole town has a somber feel.

It makes sense. It's a small place and a tragedy like this has the whole town mourning together.

I pull into our driveway, noting the fact that Thayer's truck is missing. I don't know where he is and I don't want to pester him. The poor man just lost his son.

Looking at the fence separating our homes, I start to cry all over again. I don't know how any tears are left in my body. Forrest was just there yesterday. Alive and well. He got out of the truck, breathing, moving, running, and now he's not.

Pulling myself back together as best I can, head inside to find my mom sitting at the kitchen table with a cup of tea in front of her.

"You went to Caleb," she says before I even close the door. I sent her a text last night letting her know where I ended up and that I was staying the night.

"I-I did," I stutter, turning toward the fridge. I grab a Diet Coke, but I'm not sure I even want it. I just need to busy my hands.

"Huh." She picks up her tea, emptying out the half-drank liquid. "Isn't that interesting?"

"We were friends, Mom. Before we dated, he was my best friend next to Lauren."

She sighs, looking at the spot where she wishes there was a dish-washer. "But you didn't go to Lauren, now did you?"

She has a point.

"Caleb's closer," I grumble out.

Taking the soda from my hand she sets it on the table and pulls me into a hug. "How are you coping?"

"I think I'm still in shock," I admit, holding onto my mom.

I wish she could make this better, but she can't. "I called your therapist," she says and I freeze in her arms. "I made you an appointment for later in the week if you want it. I thought you might need it."

I swallow past the lump in my throat. "Thank you."

"I know nothing can make this okay, but you have me. You can talk to me anytime you want."

I kiss her cheek. "I know, Mom. I love you."

She touches my cheek reverently, like she's trying to memorize how I look. "You girls are the best thing I ever created. I wish I could've been a stronger mother for you both."

"Please," I beg her, "never doubt, that you were as strong as you could be."

Her lip wobbles with the threat of tears and this time I'm the one pulling her into a hug. And we stay like that for a long time. Sometimes, you have to hold another person and seek comfort and that's okay. It doesn't make you weak to need human touch.

FIFTY-THREE

I hate funeral homes.

You'd think they'd do a better job trying to look a little cheerier. This place has old maroon colored carpet and smells like moth balls.

My mom and I sit in the back. Up front, the small casket is closed.

I haven't seen Thayer all week, but now he stands beside the casket looking despondent. I've never seen someone look so lost, like he's in his body but not. His parents are beside him, his brother speaking to Krista who cries at the casket.

There are two large blown-up pictures of Forrest beside the casket. In one he's holding a baseball bat from little league.

I didn't even know he played.

In the other he's dressed in a blue suit at someone's wedding.

I.

Fucking.

Hate.

Blue.

Blue is lifeless.

It's cold lips and stiff limbs.

It's the color of his death.

I'll never like the color again.

Thayer greets people robotically, going through the motions but not really here, while Krista breaks down in front of the casket. An older couple picks her up and guides her away, out to a side room. I assume they're her parents.

Beside me, my mom puts her hand on my knee. "How are you doing?"

Struggling to hold myself together, I say to her, "I'm doing the best I can." I rub my finger against the ring Thayer gave me, trying to seek comfort in the cool metal band.

She nods woodenly. "It doesn't seem right. Does it?"

"No."

Someone slides onto the pew beside me, and I look over, surprised to find Caleb in a light gray suit with a green shirt underneath. His dirty-blonde hair is brushed away from his face, the slightest hint of stubble on his jaw.

Confusion mars my brow. "You're here. Why are you here?"

His cheeks flush with a hint of pink. "Because I thought you might need me."

The lump in my throat grows heavier and I grip his hand in mine. "I do. I really do." I reach for my mom's hand with my free one. "Both of you."

I look between the two of them.

Somehow, someway, I'll get through this. I have to. And what I feel is nothing compared to what Thayer and Krista are experiencing.

ONLY IMMEDIATE FAMILY ATTENDS THE GRAVESIDE SERVICE, but the three of us do go to the wake held at the community center. I'm pretty sure the entire town is in attendance. At a table front and center so they can watch all the happenings is Thelma and Cynthia.

The side of the room is lined with buffet style dishes. People serve themselves, conversations soft and subdued.

There's a table with a handful of boys. I didn't notice them at the funeral, but they must've been friends of Forrest's. I can't imagine being that age and faced with the tragedy of such a death and the knowledge of how vulnerable life really is.

"You need to eat," Caleb tells me, pulling me toward the food.

"I'm not hungry."

"Fine, you sit, and I'll bring you a plate. Eat what you can. I'll get you something too," he tells my mom.

I open my mouth to protest, but he's already walking away.

My mom gives me a significant look. "He's a good one."

I nod, looking down at the table. "He is."

But he's not the one my heart beats for.

Caleb returns and sets down plates in front of each of us before returning to get one for himself.

I look around, trying to see if Thayer's arrived but I don't spot him or Krista. I do see his brother.

"I'll be right back," I mumble to my mom, pushing back from the table.

I don't hear what she says, because I'm already making my way to Laith.

"Hi." I grip his arm. He turns around to face me. "I don't know if you remember me—"

"Of course, I remember you." His smile is subdued as he pulls me into a hug.

"How is he?" I ask when he releases me.

The small smile he had disappears entirely. "Not good. I've never seen my brother..." He shakes his head, eyes on the ground. "I can't imagine what he's going through right now."

"I can't either. It's awful." My voice cracks and I worry I'm going to fall apart all over again. My mom was right to schedule me to see my therapist again. I can't stop thinking about how Forrest looked when his body was pulled from the water. His limp form when I placed my hands on his chest.

"I know you were there," he continues. "My brother told me. How are you coping?"

I roll my tongue in my mouth, searching for the right words. "It doesn't feel real. I keep waiting to wake up from this bad dream."

His hands flex nervously at his sides. "Me too." He shakes his head back and forth. "This isn't something any parent should have to go through. To outlive their child."

"It's heartbreaking."

"I told my brother he should sell the house."

My heart freezes. "What did he say?"

"That he couldn't. It's the last place Forrest was alive, and he won't leave. He keeps mumbling something about a treehouse too, but there's no treehouse."

A tear leaks from the corner of my eye. "Forrest wanted him to build a treehouse. He kept saying he would and now…"

"And now it's too late."

I drop my head, staring at the plain pair of black wedges on my feet. "I just want you to know I'm thinking of all of you right now."

"We appreciate it." He pats me on the shoulder.

Heading back to the table, I scan the room again for Thayer and find him at a table with his parents. He looks exhausted, like he hasn't slept at all since the accident. I want to run to him, wrap my arms around him, tell him I love him. But something holds me back.

Rejoining my mom and Caleb, I pick up a fork, forcing myself to make an effort to get something in my stomach.

"Thank you for getting the food for me."

"No problem." Caleb watches me carefully, probably looking for signs of imminent break down.

"You're…" I take a deep breath. "I don't deserve you."

"Just let me be here for you."

My mom's eyes flit back and forth between us.

"Thank you."

Caleb Thorne is so much more than I deserve, and I know for as long as I live, I'll never be good enough for him.

FIFTY-FOUR

I t's been a week since Forrest was laid to rest, and I still find the idea that he's really and truly gone to feel so wrong. Like some cruel, twisted joke.

Next door, the incessant banging of a hammer is like a drumbeat. Thayer's working on the treehouse.

With cookie dough cupcakes in hand, I make my way over to the backyard.

"Hey," I say softly, worried about disturbing his workflow. "I thought you might want some cupcakes."

When he looks up at me from his knelt position on the ground it's like I'm a stranger meeting him for the first time all over again. His angry, sullen expression is so much like the first one he ever graced me with.

"I don't want cupcakes."

I shrug, refusing to let his rough words bother me. "I'll set them inside then. You might want them later."

"I won't."

I don't argue with him, knowing it's pointless.

"Do you want some help?"

"No."

"Well, is there anything—"

He drops the hammer down and sits back on his heels. His brows are heavy over his eyes, anger radiating off of him. "Do I look like I want your help, Salem?" I try to say something but he plows on. "All he wanted was this stupid treehouse and I kept putting it off and now...and now..." He breaks down, sobs shaking his entire body. "I-I'm going to make sure he gets it, even if it's too late."

"It's not too late," I whisper, itching to reach out and put a hand on his shoulder but something holds me back.

He surges up, crowding my space. "Not too late? My son is *dead*. If that's not too late I don't know what is. But I'm going to do it anyway. Maybe wherever he is he'll know that I'm sorry, that I love him, and that I'm building him the treehouse he deserves."

"Thayer—" I reach for him but he jerks away from me before I can touch him.

"No." He throws his hands up like he's blocking me. *"No."*

He kneels on the ground, his back to me, and I know I've been dismissed.

The man I love is slipping from my fingers like sand and I'm helpless to do anything but watch it happen.

IT'S FOUR IN THE MORNING A FEW DAYS LATER AND I HAVEN'T been able to sleep at all tonight.

Slipping from my bed, I throw some clothes on and quietly let myself out of the house and over to Thayer's.

The basement is pitch black when I slip inside and for some reason that stings. I know I shouldn't take it personally, but I can feel Thayer pulling away from me.

Taking the stairs up, I'm shocked at what I discover.

His family left only three days ago, and I have a feeling there's no way his parents would've left things in the state of disarray they're in now. It's a *mess*. The rug in the foyer is ruffled, a total tripping hazard, and as I make my way into the kitchen the sink is full, the trash can is overflowing, and Thayer...

Thayer is slumped on the floor, an empty bottle of liquor at his side. There's an ash tray on the kitchen table filled with cigarettes and it *reeks*. It smells like a bar way past closing time.

Thayer groans from his position on the floor, his back leaning against the cabinets.

"Hey." I crouch down beside him, gently pushing his hair back from his forehead. "It's me, Salem. Let's get you up."

He groans again in reply.

Taking his heavy arm, I wrap it around my shoulder and use my arms around his torso to try to pull him up. There's no way I could do it on my own, but by some miracle he manages to get his legs under him and push with me.

Stumbling from the kitchen, he nearly careens into the wall in the foyer.

"How much did you drink?"

I don't get an answer.

Getting up the stairs with a drunk Thayer should earn me an Olympic medal. The man is seriously heavy.

I manage to get him to the bathroom and turn the shower on. I put the water on the cold side, hoping that'll help sober him up.

"You wanna get me naked?" His drunkenness slurs the question as I pull his shirt off.

"Not like this," I mumble.

"You're so fucking pretty." He strokes my cheek with the tip of his index finger. "Too pretty for me. Too young. Too good."

"Shh," I croon, tossing his shirt into the hamper. "I need to get you in the shower."

"I'm a bastard," he continues. "I wasn't a good father. I'm not a good man. You deserve someone better."

I drop my head. "That's not true."

"It is."

He starts crying and I feel my heart breaking all over again.

I don't know how a heart can continue to break like mine does. It would seem after a while it wouldn't be able to sustain more damage, but mine keeps taking beating after beating.

I manage to get his shorts down to his ankles, deciding to leave his boxer-briefs on. Sure, I've seen everything, but might as well leave the man with a little dignity since I'm about to shower him.

"In you go." I give him a push to the shower and strip down to my bra and panties.

He doesn't get in the shower, instead watching me undress with a broken but hungry expression.

"I love you so much," he mumbles, "but I'm not good enough for you."

"Don't say things like that."

I give him another little shove toward the shower and when he sees that I'm joining him, he goes more easily. The icy water pelts his back, dampening his hair. If he notices the cold temperature, he doesn't show it. His hands settle on my hips, fingers dipping beneath the top of my panties to settle on the curves of my ass.

"I have to let you go."

I shake my head, shutting out the words he spoke.

"I want you." I curl a hand behind his neck. "I *choose* you."

His brown eyes swim with tears. "Why?"

"Something inside me knows you're mine."

He looks away. "You're too young to know that."

I shake my head. "Don't say that. It's such a bullshit argument, that someone's age determines their knowledge. What I feel in my heart matters, no matter how old I am."

He presses his forehead to mine, holding my cheeks in his hands. I shiver and he reaches over, adjusting the temperature on the water.

"I need to let you go."

"No." I keep my voice steady, not wanting to show the pain I actually feel at his words. I place my hands on his chest, feeling the pounding of his heart beneath my palm. "Why are you pushing me away?"

"Because," the tendons in his neck stand out, "you deserve more than this." He repeats what he basically already said a moment ago.

290

"More than you?" I arch a brow, doing my best to stay calm.

His chest deflates, shoulders curling inward, cocooning our bodies. "Yes." It's a hesitant, guilty whisper. "I'm a broken man now." His eyes look more coherent, the haze of booze clearing. "You don't need me to hold you back from living your life. Going to college, traveling the world, exploring who you are as a person."

I want to beat and punch his bare, wet chest. I don't. One of us has to remain logical in this situation.

"That's very egotistical of you."

"Huh?"

He looks so genuinely confused it's almost comical, but of course that took him by surprise. *Men.*

"I said, that's egotistical of you. You think you're the reason I'm not at college? Not out there traveling? Exploring, as you put it?" He cocks his head to the side, listening. "I wasn't planning to do any of those things before you came along. College isn't for me. I'm happy here, in this small town, making my candles, working in my mom's shop, and if suddenly that's not okay, then I'll figure something else out." I take a deep breath. "But don't you dare," I grind out between my teeth, "think for one second that it has anything to do with you. You're my choice, just like staying here is one."

I'm not prepared for the crash of his lips to mine.

I taste liquor on his tongue, it's harsh and bitter like the two of us in this moment.

One of his arm winds around my back and he lifts me effortlessly, pressing my back to the shower wall. His erection presses into my core, my hips grinding against him on their own accord.

"Yes," he encourages, guiding my hips with his hands, "get yourself off on me."

He kisses me again, and it's rough, aching, so desperately needy.

My fingers grapple against his slick back.

I rock my hips harder, faster. It feels so good. He feels so right.

My orgasm shatters through me so fast with so much force that I scream.

Ripping his lips from mine, he groans. "Fuck, you're so hot when you come on my dick." He grips one of my breasts through my wet bra. "It hurts how much you look like mine."

"Is that a bad thing?" I pant, still trying to recover from the orgasm.

He looks at me, trying to memorize my features, every sun kissed freckle on my nose. "It is when I can't keep you."

Holding his cheeks in my hands, his stubble rubbing against my palms, I tell him, "You can if I say you can."

He kisses me again, achingly desperate, and turns the water off carrying me from the bathroom. A trail of water follows his steps until he reaches the bed and lays me on top of it.

He strips my wet bra and panties off my body, kissing over my entire body.

"Thayer," I moan his name, my fingers entwining in his damp hair. I rock up into him, my body begging for more, for everything, for the love only he can give me even if he doubts himself.

He swirls his tongue around my clit, and I cry out, my hips rising off the mattress. He grips my hips tighter, holding me down.

His right hand disappears from my hip. Blinking my eyes open, I see his hand shoving his boxers out of his way so he can grip his cock in his hand. I moan at the sight. There's something so hot about seeing him stroke himself while he gets me off.

"Thayer, please," I beg as the high grows closer. "I'm almost there." And when I fall, he catches me, silencing my cries with his lips on mine.

In one sure movement he's inside me.

He holds my gaze, making love to me.

But he's also saying goodbye.

I feel it.

"Don't let me go." A tear leaks out of the corner of my eye and he kisses it away. "We're worth it, Thayer." *I'm worth it. Don't throw me away.*

He kisses and sucks on the skin of my neck, my arms wrapping tightly around his torso like if I hold him tight enough, love him hard enough, he won't leave me.

"I love you," he says, like a vow, a promise, but a curse too.

"I love you," I say back, crying fully now.

"I love you."

292

"I love you."

We say the words and then we say it with our lips against each other's, with our bodies, with our souls.

But deep down I know it's not enough.

FIFTY-FIVE

I sleep for a few hours in Thayer's arms, before I climb from his bed. My panties and bra are in a wet heap on the floor so I pull my clothes on without them. Downstairs, Winnie wags her tail excitedly when she sees me. I turn on the coffee pot to brew, then grab her leash for a walk. Her tongue lolls out of her mouth when I clip it on her collar. Since she has short legs and is still a puppy she tires quickly after a trip around the block.

When I get back to my street, I stop dead in my tracks when I see Thelma on Cynthia's front porch.

The two are kissing.

There aren't a lot of secrets in a small town—but Thelma and Cynthia have managed to keep the biggest one of all.

Thelma turns, catching my shocked expression before I can hide it.

"What? You've never seen two women kissing before, missy?"

"Love is love," I reply.

She smiles back. "That's right, girly. I knew I liked you."

She heads into Cynthia's house, the door closing behind her.

Scooping up a tired Winnie, I let myself into Thayer's house and unclip her leash. Filling her food and water bowl, I hear Thayer's feet on the stairs just as I'm pouring two cups of coffee.

He seems surprised to find me in his kitchen, and I'd be lying if I said it didn't hurt.

He closes his eyes, inhaling a breath. Opening them, he says, "Last night shouldn't have happened."

"W-What?" I stutter, setting down the cup I poured for myself.

He lowers his head. "I shouldn't have fucked you when I know this has to end. We can't go anywhere, Salem, surely you can see that as easily as I can."

"Nothing about what we did was *fucking*," I snap, angry and hurt. "You made love to me and you know it."

He looks at the ground. "You can think what you want."

"No, Thayer." Suddenly I'm in front of him, my irritation propelling me forward. I shove a finger in his chest. "Don't fucking gaslight me. You're better than that."

"No, I'm not." He grasps my wrists. "I'm an almost thirty-two-year-old man fucking a nineteen-year-old. There's nothing *good* about me. We can't be together. What would people think?"

"We were going to tell my mom!" I scream at him. "We were *happy* and you certainly didn't give a shit before, so what changed?"

"My son died!" He yells back and Winnie whimpers, running from the room. "My son died," he repeats, softer. "And that changes everything."

"I know this is devastating. I feel his loss too. But how does this have anything to do with us?"

A long moment passes between us, and I see it, the tether between us fraying. I'm struggling to hold onto it, to keep us together, while he's taking shears to it and ripping it apart.

"Every good, happy part of me died with him. There's nothing left for me to give you."

"I'll take whatever I can get." God, I sound desperate, but I don't care. I might be young, but I know what we have is rare. It's rare and beautiful and too precious to give up so easily.

He tries a new tactic. "What will people think, Salem? You and me? Our ages? I'm a divorced man—that's practically a sentence straight to hell to some of these people."

"Don't give up on us. I don't care how complicated this gets, or what people say. I want you. In this big crazy world, I choose you. Isn't that enough?"

The pity he looks at me with breaks what's left of my mangled heart.

"No, it's not. You have your whole life ahead of you. You'll find someone else."

"Thayer," I grip his shirt in my hands, holding on to him, "you are my life."

He shakes his head sadly, sympathy in those brown eyes that once looked at me with so much love and passion. Taking my hands, he removes them from his shirt. Plucking my fingers off one by one.

It's symbolic in a tragic sort of way.

He's letting me go, letting *us* go, like nothing between us ever mattered at all.

It's then that I know that no matter what I do, what I say, I've lost him.

"Are you really okay with this?" I ask him, feeling the need to say more. I can't let us end as easily as he can. "You want me to leave you? To what? Fall in love with another man? Have his babies? While you what?" I wave a hand around at the mess, the bottles of liquor, the full sink and cigarettes. "Drown yourself in misery? It was a tragic accident, Thayer, one you'll never get over. I know that. I understand it. Do you think I'm not affected by it? But you still deserve to be happy." He stares back at me with a numb gaze. Shutting down. Blocking me out. There are no emotions in that once warm brown. Cold, unyielding. *Dead.*

My Thayer, the grumpy man who I fell so hard for, died that day with his son.

I see that, I know it, but I love him despite it.

But he won't give me false hope.

294

The man standing before me is a weak imitation of the one I first met.

Shaking my head, I turn and walk away.

FIFTY-SIX

t's mind-blowing how fast and slow time can go all at once.

A month passes and I give up trying to communicate with Thayer. He's shut down and there's no reaching him as he spirals into a dark place. He's a shell of the person I love. I keep trying, keep reaching out my hand, but it's not enough. I can't save him if he doesn't want to save himself.

I let myself into his house.

He won't talk to me, completely ignores my presence when I see him, so I've taken to coming over when he's gone just to keep the place tidied up. It doesn't sit right with me, letting him live in filth, and wallow away. So, I do what I can.

It helps me to feel close to him when I'm here and I always feel a little bit better when I leave.

I don't stay long today, I can't.

Georgia is getting married today.

When his house is cleaned up to the best of my abilities in the short time I have, I drive downtown to the local inn that Georgia and Michael are having their ceremony and reception. I'm running late, so I'm not surprised when those words are the first thing out of my sister's mouth.

"You're late," she accuses, pointing to a chair. "You need your hair and makeup."

My mom shoots a worried glance my way. Parking my butt in the chair, I let the makeup artist and hair stylist go to town on me and do whatever it is Georgia requested. When that's done I slip into my dress and everything happens in a flurry.

One of Michael's friend's walks me down the aisle and I find myself scanning the crowd of guests. I know Thayer's not here. He wasn't even invited. Why would he be? He would've been if we'd gotten the chance to tell my family about us, but we didn't, and now it seems like we never will.

The music changes and everyone rises for my sister to make her grand entrance.

Michael clears his throat, crying before she even emerges. Maybe I should give the guy more credit, he clearly loves my sister.

The French doors open and my sister steps into the room holding our mom's arm. Her hair is starting to grow back but it's short and fuzzy. She was going to wear a hat, worried her shorn scalp would embarrass Georgia, but my sister merely kissed her on top of the head and shot down the idea.

Watching them exchange vows fills me with a strange sort of melancholy. I stupidly thought I might marry Thayer one day and now ... now I know nothing.

It seems like the whole wedding happens in a blink but like I'm watching in slow motion.

It's how I've felt ever since that morning I left Thayer in his kitchen. Without him time ticks differently. I'm a witness, a bystander in my own life now as I watch everything take place around me.

I give my speech at the wedding robotically, but no one must notice how out of it I am, or at least Georgia doesn't. She cries, hugging me when I've finished.

Caleb's there and when he asks me to dance I say yes, because I see no point in turning him down. He spins me on the dance floor, and I end up laying my head on his shoulder.

"He hurt you." It's not a question, but an accusation.

"Yes."

"I should kill the bastard."

I smile, perhaps my first genuine one in weeks. "He'd probably thank you."

He sighs, holding me tighter. "It's horrible, what happened to his son." His hand on my waist tightens.

"I don't want to talk about him."

He clears his throat. "Okay. What do you need?"

I answer him honestly. "I don't know." We sway back and forth, only half-dancing at this point.

Clearing his throat, he asks, "When you figure it out will you let me know?"

On my tiptoes, I press a kiss to his cheek. "You'll be the first to know."

CALEB DRIVES ME HOME FROM THE WEDDING. I INSISTED I could drive myself, but I think with as checked out as I am it really worried him, so I finally agreed. Plus, with the late hour I figured it might be safer anyway.

We pull up outside my house, and he puts the car in park. "Are you okay or do you want me to come in for a while?"

"I'll—"

I plan to tell him I'll be okay, but then I see Thayer getting out of his truck.

He's not alone.

A lump lodges in my throat when I watch a woman giggle and press her body all over him.

I climb out of Caleb's car before I know what I'm doing.

"Thayer!" I yell after him. I feel like my body is being painfully carved apart. "What are you doing?"

He turns, looking surprised to see me.

Bastard.

The woman giggles, swiping a finger down his chest. "Who is this? Your sister?"

Sister? Gag me.

"What are you doing?" I repeat.

Why is my face wet? I touch my cheek, realizing I'm crying.

Thayer doesn't respond, he seems frozen, stunned.

"Come on, Salem." Caleb wraps a hand around my arm to pull me away.

Thayer snaps to life. "Don't fucking touch her!"

Caleb steps in front of me, shoving me behind him in protection. "Who the fuck are you to tell me not to touch her? Huh? You're the one that fucked her when she was my girlfriend."

I don't know who throws the first punch, but suddenly both of them are on the ground, throwing fists and kicks.

"Stop!" I scream, hiccupping. The other woman watches in confusion.

"This is too much for me," she mutters. "I'm calling a cab." She walks down the street, phone pressed to her ear.

"Stop it!" They ignore me. "Oh, God." I slap a hand to my mouth and turn sharply, throwing up right in the bushes Thayer painstakingly planted and trimmed last summer. My body heaves as I get sick. Cool fingers touch my neck, pulling my hair back.

When I look, I stupidly expect it to be Thayer at my side, but it's Caleb.

"Hey." He rubs my back. "I'm sorry I snapped. Are you okay?"

I ignore his question, searching for Thayer in the darkness. He's watching me, staring back.

Something in me just snaps, finally breaks.

I'm not perfect. I make mistakes. I hurt people. But I'm a strong girl, one who's been made weak by Thayer.

I wipe my mouth with the back of my hand and straighten up, holding onto Caleb while I let go of Thayer. I take the ring off my thumb finger, the one he gave me months ago at the flea market, and shove it against his chest. It falls to the sidewalk, and he looks down at it.

"Goodbye, Thayer." My voice cracks.

For the first time in weeks, his face shows some sort of emotion other than confusion.

He knows.

I'm closing the door on us.

Ending the chapter.

We're a period on the end of a sentence.

Full stop.

I thought our love story was written in the stars; destined, remarkable, once in a lifetime.

Turns out we're nothing but a memory gone up in flames, ashes scattered in the wind.

FIFTY-
SEVEN

Lauren's squeals fill my ear drums when she opens her door. "I know you're going through it right now, girl, but I'm so happy you decided to move in with me."

I've never liked big cities. Hawthorne Mills has always been more my speed. But I needed a change of scenery, so the day after Georgia's wedding I called Lauren, and now two days after that here I am.

I can't be in that town with Thayer. It's only big enough for one of us and I know he'll never leave, not after what happened to Forrest, so that meant my leaving.

So here I am.

New York City will be an experiment of sorts, I guess. It'll certainly push my boundaries, that's for sure.

"Thank you for letting me come."

She locks up behind me as I look around her tiny space. It's hardly big enough for one person, let alone two, but that's New York City for you.

"I would've loved for you to move with me from the start."

I give her a wobbly smile. "This will certainly be an adventure."

She gives a small answering smile, leaning against the butcher block countertop of the small kitchen. "I'm sorry, you know. About you and—"

"Don't say his name," I beg, closing my eyes. "Please, don't."

She nods. "Can I hug you?"

I open my arms and let my best friend hug me. "There's something I need you to hold my hand through."

"Oh?" She gives me a puzzled look. "What?" I bend down and open my purse, pulling out the plastic bag. Passing it to her, she takes it and looks in the bag. "Salem." She gives me a worried look. "No."

"I think so."

"What are you going to do?"

"I don't know. That's what the test is for."

"Oh, Salem." Her eyes fill with tears. "It's his?"

"Are you serious?"

"I'm sorry, I didn't mean it like that. I just thought maybe you'd slept with someone else since then."

"I haven't." I take the box from her.

"You're doing this now?" She sounds so surprised.

"I have to know."

She nods. "I'd have to know too. All right," she claps her hands together, "let's do this."

She waits outside the bathroom while I go, and I lay the pregnancy test on the porcelain sink while I wash my hands.

I'm torn on what I want it to say.

I'm only nineteen—I'd be twenty when the baby's born if I am pregnant, but that's so young to become a mother. On the other hand, if I'm not... I know I'll be sad. It'll be like losing Thayer all over again.

"Are you done? Open the door," she pleads, so I crack it open.

"It said it would take five minutes for results."

"God, that's so long."

Closing the toilet lid, I sit down on top, chewing at my thumb nail. I miss my ring. I went out to get it from the sidewalk the morning after throwing it at him, but it was gone. It's for the best, I suppose.

"I want you to know, if you are pregnant, everything's going to be fine. We'll get a bigger apartment and I'll help you. We'll sister wives this shit. We've got this."

Laughter bubbles out of me and I'm shocked by its genuineness. "Thank you."

"That's what friends are for."

"How long has it been?"

She glances at the test. "Nothing yet."

I lean my head back, waiting.

Another minute passes, and I get up. Lauren watches me pick up the test and look at the results.

I close my eyes, tears leaking out of the corner of my eyes.

I said goodbye to him, and I meant it. I don't deserve to be half-loved by someone, shoved aside. He's grieving, I know that, but I would wait—I'd help him through this if he only let me.

The universe doesn't want us to have an end, but a new beginning, because I'm still a little bit his.

Thayer and Salem's story continues in The Resurrection of Wildflowers.

ALSO BY MICALEA SMELTZER

Outsider Series

Outsider

Insider

Fighter

Avenger

Second Chances Standalone Series

Unraveling

Undeniable

Trace + Olivia Series

Finding Olivia

Chasing Olivia

Tempting Rowan

Saving Tatum

Trace + Olivia Box Set

Willow Creek Series

Last To Know

Never Too Late

In Your Heart

Take A Chance

Willow Creek Box Set

Always Too Late Short Story

Willow Creek Bonus Content

Home For Christmas

Light in the Dark Series

Rae of Sunshine

When Stars Collide

Dark Hearts

When Constellations Form

Broken Hearts

Stars & Constellations Bundle

The Us Series

The Road That Leads To Us

The Lies That Define Us

The Game That Break Us

Wild Collision

The Wild Series

Wild Collision

Wild Flame

The Boys Series

Bad Boys Break Hearts

Nice Guys Don't Win

Real Players Never Lose

Good Guys Don't Lie

Standalones

Beauty in the Ashes

Bring Me Back

Temptation

A Love Like Ours

The Other Side of Tomorrow

Jump (A 90s novella)

Desperately Seeking Roommate

Desperately Seeking Landlord

Whatever Happens

Sweet Dandelion

Say When

ACKNOWLEDGMENTS

Salem and Thayer's story hit me out of nowhere a few months ago and I knew I had to drop what I was doing and write it. When I sat down to plot this story, I quickly realized this was going to be way more emotional and angsty than I originally thought, but I knew this was going to be one of those stories that stays with me long after I finish writing it. Thayer and Salem still have a ways to go and I hope you'll enjoy the rest of their journey in book two.

Emily Wittig, not only do you continue to wow me with your creativity with cover design, I mean seriously this duet is stunning, but you're the realest friend I could ask for. Who would've thought this is where we'd be ten years after you sent me that first message? I'm so thankful to have a real, genuine friend like you. So many people aren't blessed enough to have someone as kind-hearted as you are in their life. You're always there to cheer me on, talk me off the ledge, or make me smile when I'm feeling down. Love you lots!

Kellen, thank you for your friendship and unwavering support. I'm so thankful to this book world that we met. You're one of the real ones.

To my doggies who are always by my side with every book I write; I love you, Ollie, I love you, Remy, I love you, Romeo, and yeah, I even love you too, Tucker, you moody smoosh face.

To my family, I know I suck and don't acknowledge you in every book, but I am so blessed to have your support. I know not everyone that strays from the traditional life path and decides to take a risk with writing has the kind of support I do, and for that I'm grateful.

The teams at Barnes and Noble in Ashburn, VA and Fairfax, VA I have no idea if you'll ever see this, but thank you for taking the risk and stocking Sweet Dandelion in your stores. I've been thrilled that it's selling, but more importantly you helped me realize my dream of seeing one of my books in your stores.

Thank you to the bloggers, bookstagrammers, booktokers, and every single one of you I've met along my journey since 2011. I'm inspired by your passion for books and the love you spread through the community. It's so appreciated.

And lastly, to you dear reader, whether it's your first time reading or your twentieth, or maybe even more than that, thank you. Thank you. Thank you. Thank you. Because of you I get to live my dream, write the worlds and characters in my head, and that's the greatest gift I could possibly ask for.

THE RESURRECTION OF WILDFLOWERS

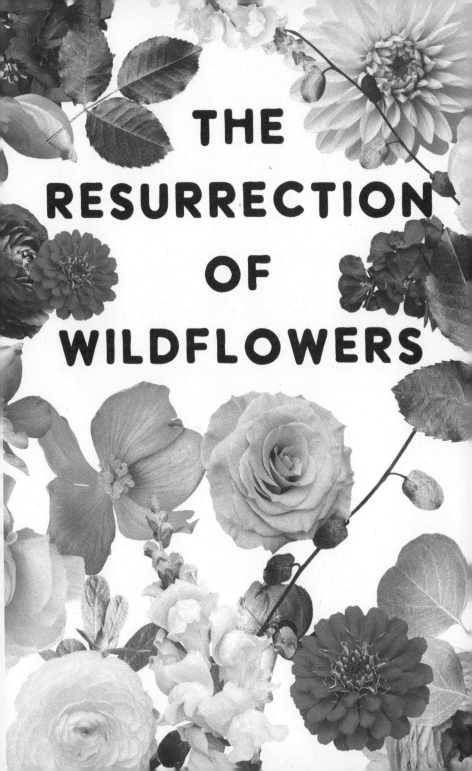

THE
RESURRECTION
OF
WILDFLOWERS

THE RESURRECTION OF WILDFLOWERS

The Resurrection of Wildflowers

Cover Design: Emily Wittig Designs
Editing: KM Editing
Developmental Editing: Melanie Yu
Formatting: Micalea Smeltzer

For anyone who has had to live through unimaginable pain and had to become stronger because of it.

TRIGGER WARNING

Cancer and death.

"Flowers grow out of dark moments."

—*Corita Kent*

PROLOGUE

Salem

t took me a while to learn that sometimes no matter how much, or how hard you love someone, or something, you have to let them go. You can't save a sinking ship.

Sometimes, you have someone else you have to be strong for, who needs you more.

You make a choice.

A devastating one.

And you hope, maybe one day, they'll come back to you.

ONE

Salem

Spring in Hawthorne Mills is my favorite. I haven't spent any time here since I left six years ago. I came back a few times that summer, hoping the man I loved next door would snap out of it and see me, come back to me, but he never did.

Thayer Holmes was lost to me, so I tucked my tail and moved on.

Got a job waitressing at a diner close to Lauren's apartment. I stored away every penny I could. Caleb and I started talking more, and then we started dating again, it was almost a year to the day of Georgia's wedding that he asked me to marry him, and I said yes. We married two months later. He finished college and we moved to California. I loved it there, almost as much as here, but he got a job offer a year ago in Boston, so we returned.

And still I never set foot back here at my childhood home.

He knew why and it hurt him.

All I've ever done is hurt him.

So, I let him go.

Our divorce was easy, just like everything with us. I know he'll always be in my life, but now he's free to find the kind of love I knew once. Once you've had it, nothing else compares no matter how much you try and how much work you put into it.

It's like trying to fit a puzzle piece in a space it doesn't belong.

Opening the car door, I step onto the driveway.

As much as I swore I'd never come back here, to this place, to *him*, only one thing could bring me back. Letting myself into the house, I find my mom in the makeshift bed set up in the living room.

"Hi, Mom." It takes everything I have in me to stave off the tears. I don't want her to see me cry.

"There's my girl," she smiles, beckoning me forward with a swish of her pale thin hand.

My mom's dying.

The cancer found its way back and nothing has worked this time. No matter how hard she fights, it's stronger, and now she has two months, perhaps not even that, left to live.

My steps sound so loud to my ears as I make my way into the living room and bend down to hug her.

"You just missed Georgia," she tells me, her hug weak. There's not much muscle or fat on her body. She's withering away right before our eyes. "I'm sure I'll see her later."

"The kids were asking about you guys."

I smile, brushing my fingers over the papery skin on her cheek. "They'll see us soon." Georgia and Michael have two kids now and another on the way. To say they have their hands full is an understatement, but they're happy. "Do you need anything?"

"I'm okay right now. Maybe we could watch a movie or something after you bring your stuff in?"

"That sounds good, Mom."

Caleb and I have remained living together since the divorce. It just made sense while I figured out my next step, but with my mom's condition deteriorating I knew it was time to return home. To take care of her in her final days, give Georgia a break, and when the inevitable happens clean out the house and figure out what comes next.

It's hard, knowing my future is a big question mark at the moment. I'll be twenty-six later this year and just like at eighteen, I still don't have shit figured out. But maybe that's the truth of adulthood no one wants to tell you—we're all out here winging it.

Outside, I steadfastly ignore the house next door. I know he still lives there, my mom mentions him from time to time. Sometimes I wonder if she does it trying to gauge my reaction. I've never told her about what happened with Thayer. With my heart so broken, and accepting that him and I were truly over, I didn't see the point.

I manage to get all of my stuff brought inside without stealing a peek next door.

That's a lie.

I take a small one.

Just long enough to see the completed treehouse in the backyard and the hint of the roof of a greenhouse.

"Did you get everything?" My mom's croaky voice sounds so small from the living room.

"I did. I'll carry some of it up now."

"All right. I think I'll just ... rest my ... eyes ... for a bit."

She can't see me in the kitchen, but tears spring to my eyes.

She's slipping away. What could've been a long life is now measured in weeks, hours, minutes, *seconds*, and every single one is precious.

TWO

Salem

My room is a relic.

It's literally exactly the same. For some reason, I expected my mom to have changed it in some way. It's clean since both Georgia and I pitch in to pay a cleaning lady to come by weekly. There's not a speck of dust anywhere. The bed is freshly made, the corners of the covers crisp.

Since my mom is sleeping and not going to be ready to watch a movie anytime soon, I unpack my clothes and toiletries, then call Caleb.

"Hey," he says, his voice deep. "Did you make it in all right?"

"Yeah, thanks for asking."

"How's your mom?"

I sigh, rubbing my forehead. "Sleeping. She's frailer than I expected."

"I'm sorry." I can hear the genuineness in his voice. Despite us falling apart, Caleb remains to be one of the kindest people I know.

"It is what it is," I reply softly, sitting on the end of my bed facing the window I used to sit out on, often with Caleb himself.

"Someone's trying to steal the phone from me," he chuckles.

I laugh too. "Put her on."

"Mommy!" My daughter's voice is like a balm to a wound. With just one word she makes me feel better, more grounded.

"Hi, baby. How's your day been?"

"Good. Daddy picked me up from school and we went to the grocery store. I got a lollipop."

I hear Caleb laugh in the background. "That was supposed to be our secret."

"Oops," she giggles.

Seda was the unexpected surprise Thayer left me with. She's been the gift I didn't know I wanted or needed. Being her mom makes me feel like a superhero.

"I miss you already," I tell her.

"I miss you, too, Mommy. Give grandma kisses—you always say kisses will make it better."

Oh, fuck. I'm going to cry. I wish tears would make my mom better, but I don't think magical kisses can fight cancer off.

"I will," I say to my daughter. "I love you."

"Love you, Mommy!" She hangs up the phone, the line going quiet.

When I make my way back downstairs, my mom is still asleep so I decide to go ahead and start on dinner. Georgia says Mom isn't eating much these days, but I have to at least try.

Searching the cabinets I come across a bottle of wine, probably something Georgia stashed before she got pregnant again, and open it. Filling the glass, I drink as I cook. I'm not a huge drinker, but today calls for a little wine to soothe my nerves.

"Salem?" My mom calls and I turn away from the simmering pot.

"Yeah?" I call back, surprised she's awake. I expected to have to wake her.

"Could you bring me some water?"

Filling up a cup with a straw, I carry it in to her and hold it to her lips. She drinks greedily, her eyes grateful. Setting the cup down, I ask her, "Do you need anything else? I'm making dinner."

"No, the water was all." She pats my hand lovingly. "I'm sorry I fell asleep before we could watch a movie."

"It's okay. I'll put one on while we eat."

She watches me, her eyes sad, and I wonder what she's thinking about. "Are you happy, Salem? You don't look like it."

"I'm as happy as I can be right now."

"I guess that will have to do."

I smile sadly at her, backing out of the room to finish dinner.

When it's ready I carry two plates of spaghetti and garlic bread into the living room. Propping her up, I fix a tray across her lap and get her comfortable before I sit down myself to eat.

The movie plays but I'm not paying attention.

I leave it going while I clean our dirty dishes. My mom barely touched hers, but I know she tried to eat as much as she could.

By the time I return, only a handful of minutes later, she's fallen asleep again.

It's getting late anyway, so I switch off the TV, cover her more fully with the blanket, make sure she has water, and that her phone is where she can easily access it if she needs me.

"I love you, Mom." I kiss her forehead.

A tear leaks from the corner of my eye. Swiping it away, I quietly take the stairs and shower before heading to bed myself. It's been a long day and I need my rest.

RETURNING FROM MY MORNING RUN, I LET MYSELF IN THE side door into the kitchen and smile when I see my mom at the table. There's a little more color to her skin this morning, more pink than gray, and I hope that means she got a good night's sleep.

"Hey," I smile, adjusting my ponytail. "Are you hungry?"

"I had some cereal," she explains, flipping through a magazine.

"You know," I say gently, "you're not supposed to walk around without someone to help you."

She's a fall risk and she knows this.

But I guess if I was in her situation, I might be a little stubborn too at times. It has to be difficult coping with needing another person to help you do basic things like use the bathroom or wash your body.

"I had my non-slip socks on."

"Mom," I say in a warning tone, starting a pot of coffee. "You know that's not going to cut it."

She sighs. "I felt okay this morning. I wanted to move on my own."

"Just be careful," I beg.

"Salem," she says my name softly, carefully. My back is to her, grabbing a mug for my coffee so I turn around. "You know I'm going to die, right?"

I lower my head. I know. Georgia knows. We all know.

"Yes."

"I just want to still feel like me with as little time as I have left. All right?"

I give a tiny nod in understanding, damming back the tears that beg to burst forth. It's the worst feeling mourning someone while they're still alive.

"I was thinking," she continues, "that we could bake some cupcakes together today. Since I'm feeling okay."

My shoulders stiffen. I haven't baked cupcakes since whenever the last time was I made them for Thayer. Afterwards, it hurt too much. They only make me think of him.

"We—uh—we can do that."

I'm not about to tell my dying mother no.

"I thought we could make cookie dough. They were always your favorite. Thayer, next door—they're his favorite too. I always took some over when I made them, you know, before I got too sick to bake anymore."

My shoulders tighten with tension.

"Y-Yeah," I stutter. "I remember he loved those."

She's watching me carefully, with this assessing look, and I stare back. "He's a nice man. It's a shame what happened all those years ago. His poor son. I think I would've had to leave, but he hasn't moved."

"Mom," I try to change the subject, "do you want a drink or something?"

"Not really." She closes the magazine and slides it away from her on the table. "He mows the yard for me, you know?" She continues on, still talking about Thayer. I don't want to hear about him. I don't want to know. It hurts too much, but I can't say that to her. With my back to her, I add some cream and sugar to my coffee. My hands shake, but from where she's sitting I know she can't see. "He comes over sometimes, I think he's lonely, and we'll have a drink—"

"Are you into him?" The question rushes out of me before I can stop it and I immediately cringe.

I don't even want to consider the possibility of Thayer and my *mom*. I might throw up.

"God, no." She laughs, but it turns into a cough. I sit down across from her, watching with a careful eye to make sure she's fine. "But it was nice to have someone to talk to. You moved clear across the country and Georgia was busy with work and her family. I needed a friend."

"Well, I'm glad you had each other."

Fuck Thayer Holmes. He can talk and be friends with my mother, but he can't talk to me?

I think of all the time I spent trying to get him to open up to me. I knew he still loved me like I loved him, but it wasn't enough apparently, and I gave up trying. I couldn't be the only one trying to fix what was broken. He needed to put in some effort too and he wouldn't.

"When we finish the cupcakes, you can take some over to him."

I tap my fingers on the table and force a smile. "Sounds great."

It's been six years. I should be over him. Moved on.

But I'm not sure you ever really move on from your one true love.

THREE

Salem

The kitchen smells of cupcakes and I'd be lying if I didn't admit I'm weak and cave to the need to eat one. They taste just as good as I remember, and baking felt good too. It was like riding a bicycle. I don't think I let myself realize how much I missed it.

"I need to ... go sit down for a while." My mom sounds out of breath, the weakness creeping back in.

"No problem." I rush around the counter to her side, giving her my arm to hold on to. I guide her into the living room, feeling her rest more of her weight against me as we go. "Do you want to sit on the couch or the bed."

She thinks for a moment. "Bed."

"Okay." I help her into the hospital bed and cover her with blankets. "Rest, Mom." I kiss her forehead.

"Don't forget to take cupcakes to Thayer."

I stifle a groan. "I won't."

I send up a silent prayer he won't be home when I take them over.

Her eyes grow heavy and she's already dozing off asleep before I leave the room.

My phone rings and it's Georgia.

"Hey." I put her on speaker so I can clean up the kitchen as we talk. "What's up?"

"How's Mom today?"

"She had some energy this morning but she's taking a nap now. We made cupcakes."

"Oh." I hear the smile in her voice. "That's good. That's really good."

"I thought so too." I load the dishwasher.

"Thank you for coming and staying with her. I know you didn't want to, and I don't blame you, and I understand not wanting to have—"

"Georgia, she's our mom. You don't need to thank me. I want to be here. I need to be."

She clears her throat and I know she's getting a bit choked up. "I have to get back to work. I'll call you later."

"We're fine." I know my sister's the nurse and I'm not, but I'm not incapable of taking care of our mom and she has enough on her plate without worrying about what's going on here.

"Maybe I could drop by after my shift with some fast-food or something."

"Just let me know."

We say our goodbyes and hang up. The kitchen is spotless once more, so that leaves me with no choice but to take the plate of cupcakes over to Thayer.

I know it shouldn't, but it annoys me learning he's been friends with my mom. He spoke to her and never reached out to me.

Asshole.

I plate the cupcakes and cover them with saran wrap. The frosting gets smashed a bit, but I don't care.

Taking a deep breath, I prepare myself to face Thayer for the first time in years.

I can do this.

I'm a strong, powerful woman. I won't let any man make me feel down.

Only, when I go around the side of the fence, there's no vehicle in his driveway.

That's good … I guess.

But as long as I'm staying at my mom's place it doesn't matter. I'll run into him eventually and I'm not sure how that makes me feel.

GEORGIA COMES IN THE SIDE DOOR WITH BAGS OF FOOD. HER scrub top is stretched over the swell of her belly, and I can't help but smile.

"Oh, look at you," I coo. "Can I feel?" I ask, taking the bags from her and putting them on the table.

She sighs, jutting out her belly. "Go for it. This one is just like his dad. Never still. I'm exhausted. He keeps me up all night kicking."

"You found out it's a boy?"

She grins from ear to ear. "Yeah, just the other day. Three boys, can you believe it? I always thought I'd be a girl mom, but you know, I wouldn't have it any other way." She places her hand on her stomach by mine. "Don't you want another?"

"I think I've got all I can handle right now."

"I don't know how you can stand being away from her," she goes on, "I know your reasonings, but…" We both look to where our mom still sleeps in the living room. She's slept ever since she laid down.

"It's killing me being away from her, but she doesn't need to see her grandma like this." I motion to all the medical equipment and our mom's sleeping, frail form. "She's too young. I know she's in good hands with Caleb anyway and we FaceTime any chance we get."

Georgia shakes her head and pulls out a box of fries from Wendy's shoving around five in her mouth at once. "I was shocked when you said you guys were getting a divorce. I always thought you had it together so well. I mean, that boy stepped up to the plate and married you when you had someone else's kid."

I lower my head. It was no secret to any of our families that my daughter wasn't Caleb's. We didn't want to lie to them or to her either about her parentage, but no one except Caleb and Lauren know who her real father is.

I still remember the hate Caleb's mother spewed at him when we told her. She couldn't understand him taking me back, *marrying* me, when I was having a child that wasn't his.

She stopped talking to him right after that. Didn't even come to the wedding.

I've never forgiven myself for that. I was never her biggest fan, but she's Caleb's mom. I haven't had the heart to ask him if she's contacted him since our divorce.

"Caleb's a good man," I tell her, rifling through the bags of food. "But he's not the right man for me."

She shakes her head, clucking her tongue. "Forgive me, but you're stupid."

I laugh, pulling out a wrapped burger. "I know."

Believe me, I'm all too aware of my mistakes and sins. Caleb being at the top of the list. The worst part is, he's still my best friend. But I guess that makes things easier in a way with Seda involved. My daughter is just as much his as she is mine. It's not only DNA that makes a parent, it's how you behave, and Caleb is the best daddy to our little girl. He's never, not once, treated her like she's not his.

She lowers her voice to a whisper, "Do you think you'll stay here or move back to Boston after mom...?"

"I won't stay in Boston," I answer quickly. I've never been a city girl and I've had enough of them in the past few years. "But I don't know if I'll stay here either."

She looks around, pondering. "This is a good house. If you decide to stay."

"I don't think I could live here."

It's not just about Thayer, though he's a factor, but this is our mom's house, and I don't think I'd ever feel like it was mine.

"Yeah." She lowers her head sadly, eyes flicking to where our mom slumbers in the next room. "I understand. I'm not sure I actu-

338

ally could either." Pulling her hair over one shoulder, she says, "Christy, one of my nurse friends said she could stay with mom for a day and night this weekend. I thought you might want to use the time to see Seda, but I wanted to run it by you first before confirming with her."

"That would be great," I tell her honestly, feeling relief flood my chest.

I know Seda is in great hands with Caleb, but I hate being away from my little girl. I didn't want her to be around my mom while she's dying. Death is inevitable, but no child should see someone they love disintegrate right before their eyes. It's not that I won't let her see my mom at all, but I don't want her staying here around this twenty-four-seven. Besides, she has school and she's currently enrolled in Boston. I wasn't going to yank her out with only a few weeks left of the school year.

"Awesome, I'll let her know. She's a great person and a wonderful nurse so you don't need to worry. Mom will be in great hands."

That's Georgia—she might be a bit of a wild card, but she's always taking care of us.

"I love you," I tell her.

"Aw, I love you, too. And I'm so happy you're back for however long as that is."

"Thanks. It's good to be back."

And surprisingly, it's not even a lie.

FOUR

Salem

Driving down to the local grocery store, I park and hesitate before going inside. The fridge at home isn't well-stocked and I want to get some things for meals, but I'm dreading this trip because I'm bound to run into someone I know, and small towns love drama. Me returning to town after my divorce—that's huge news for them.

I made a list before leaving the house, so that once I get inside, I won't need to think over what I might need for cooking meals.

Regardless, I can only go so fast.

Grabbing my purse, I hop out of my SUV and scurry into the store with my head ducked low. Swiping a cart, I make my way to the produce section. If anyone's watching me, I'm sure they're amused with how fast I move. But the quicker I go, the sooner I'll be out of here, and the less chance there is of someone interrupting.

I make it all the way to the frozen section where I'm looking at the ice cream when someone says my name.

"Thelma," I smile, and it's genuine—even if she is a nosy busybody. "How are you? And you too Cynthia. It's good to see you guys. And together."

Thelma shrugs, leaning over to kiss Cynthia's cheek. "We're too old to stay in the closet anymore. You're back in town for your mother?" I nod. "It's just awful. She's so young—well, young to someone my age, you see, and—"

"I'm actually finishing up shopping and heading back to her so —" I quickly reach inside and grab a random tub of ice cream. "I'll just be going."

"Have you seen that man of yours yet?"

I cock my head to the side. "Who?" My heart thunders. I know exactly who she's talking about.

"Don't play coy with me, girl," she snaps a finger, eyes twinkling. "You know exactly who I'm talking about."

"No, I haven't."

"Huh." She clucks her tongue. "Interesting."

I shrug. "He's moved on." It's been six years, I don't for a minute think he hasn't.

She laughs like I've told the funniest joke she's ever heard. "Oh, that's a funny one, girl. That man..." She shakes her head. "He hasn't moved on. I'm not sure you have either." She looks me up and down. "If you had, you would've come back sooner."

With that, her and Cynthia walk down the aisle away from me.

I look down at the ice cream I picked.

Peanut butter Oreo.

Gross.

I put it back and grab cookie dough.

Much better.

"Mom, I'm home," I call out, bringing in the first load of groceries. I tried to get it all in one trip, then quickly realized that was next to impossible. "Are you hungry? I thought I'd make chicken sandwiches for dinner?"

I set everything down, poking my head around the corner. She turns her head weakly and yawns.

"I'm not that hungry."

"What about ice cream?"

She wrinkles her nose, and I can tell the idea alone displeases her. "No."

"That's all right." I refuse to be deterred. "Is there something, anything you'd like?"

She shakes her head, her gaze drifting to the front window.

It hurts knowing she's slipping away second by second.

"If you change your mind, let me know." I won't push her on the matter right now. Maybe I'll be lucky and get something in her a little bit later.

I finish bringing everything in, exhaling a sigh of relief when I manage to do it without bumping into Thayer. I know it's not something I can avoid forever, but I'm going to try for as long as I can. That's the wimpy way out, but when it comes to him, I've never claimed to be strong.

I put the groceries away and start dinner, making some for my mom too so there's something to eat if she gets hungry.

"Should we watch a movie?" I ask, sitting down on the couch with my plate.

"I was wondering..." She starts, clearing her dry throat. I immediately hop up and hold out her water for her to sip. "Would you read a book to me? There's one I've been wanting to read, but—"

"Which one?" I look around for it.

"It's right there." She points to it on the coffee table. "I had Georgia pull it for me, but never picked it up."

Scooping up the book, I sit down and curl my legs under me. I balance my plate on the arm of the couch and open the book.

When I start to read, she smiles.

I take a mental picture of this moment, knowing it's one I'll cherish forever.

FIVE

Salem

"**M**ommy!"

Seda runs straight for me when I open the door to the brownstone.

I crouch down, catching her just as she launches herself at me. "My girl," I breathe, inhaling her scent. She smells like grass from playing outside mixed with her watermelon shampoo.

"I missed you so much, Mommy." She cups my cheeks in her soft hands. "Is Grandma okay?"

"She's all right." I put my hand over one of hers. "But she doesn't have much time left with us."

"When can I visit? I miss her. I made a drawing for her. I'll show you." Then she's running off, presumably to locate the drawing.

I stand up, just in time to see Caleb walk out of the kitchen and lean against the archway. "She's talked about your mom non-stop."

I blow out a breath I didn't even know I was holding. "I've tried to explain to her, but I don't think she fully grasps what's happening."

"She's five," he reasons, tossing a rag over his shoulder. "Are you hungry? I'm getting ready to put leftovers away."

"Starving." Seda comes running back to me with a piece of printer paper.

"Look, Mommy." She holds it up. "See that's grandma in her bed," she points at the stick figure with yellow hair, "and that's my brother. He's an angel and he's waiting for her."

I grind my teeth together, so I don't burst into tears. Caleb and I have made an effort to talk about Thayer and Forrest with her. She knows that Caleb is her dad, but that she has another one too who was sad when her brother passed and wasn't capable of being in her life because of it. It's a whole complicated situation and trying to explain it to her in a way she understands is hard at times.

I put her in swim safety lessons as a baby too. I wanted to make sure she knew every tool she could use in case anything happened.

Reaching for her, I pull her into a hug and rest my chin on top of her head. "Yeah, baby girl. He is."

Her little arms wrap around my neck—well, they're not so little anymore, but I think I'll always see her that way. "He'll make sure she's okay, so you don't have to cry, Mommy." She holds my cheeks, looking into my eyes with ones the color of Thayer's. Warm and chocolatey. "Crying isn't bad," she repeats back to me what I tell her all the time, "but I don't like it when you're sad."

I kiss her cheek. "I'm not sad, baby. Just so proud of you." Standing, I hold on tight to her drawing. "Mommy's hungry. Do you want to sit with me while I eat?"

"I want to draw some more before I go to bed."

I laugh when she runs off. Clearly, I missed her more than she did me.

Caleb's already plating some of the dinner he made and popping it into the microwave.

"I could've done that." I grab a soda from the fridge.

"I know." He braces his hands on the counters, his muscles flexing. "How's your mom doing?" His voice is low so Seda can't overhear.

I shake my head, sliding onto the barstool. "Not good, which is expected, but she's talking and still getting around somewhat on her own—mostly because she's stubborn and tries to refuse help every chance she gets."

Caleb chuckles, pulling the plate out of the microwave and setting it in front of me with a fork. "Sounds like Allison."

"I promise once all of this is over, I'll be out of your hair." I can't help but look around the kitchen, the cabinets I picked out when we remodeled, the polka dot cannisters for flour and sugar I chose for a pop of whimsy.

Caleb rolls his eyes at me, grabbing a beer. "We're still friends. We'll always be friends. And," a shadow flickers over his face, "even if that idiot comes back into the picture, I'll always be in Seda's life. You can't take her from me, and neither can he."

"Calm down," I tell him, forking a piece of meatloaf. "We've talked about this. I would never do that to you. Seda loves you—you might not be her father by DNA's standards, but you are her dad by all the ways that count. I understand more than anyone that DNA doesn't make a father."

Caleb's head lowers and he looks at me from beneath his lashes. "Thank you."

The one and only thing we argued over during the divorce was Seda. Caleb was terrified that I'd take her from him and he'd never see her again. I could never be that cruel. Caleb stepped up to the plate, for me, for her, when Thayer was too lost in his grief for me to reach. I wouldn't only be punishing Caleb if I took her away, I'd be hurting her.

"I'm sorry," he adds, running his fingers through his blond hair. "I guess with you back there, it has me feeling uneasy."

"Hey," I say softly, reaching across the counter to place my hand on his. "You have nothing to worry about. Not with Seda."

He clears his throat, and I can tell he's getting a bit choked up. "I'm going to watch TV."

"All right."

I finish eating in silence, then put my plate in the dishwasher. The kitchen is already spotless, so I go to the playroom on the first floor where I'm sure I'll find Seda.

She's scribbling madly on a piece of paper, creating another masterpiece. "It's bath time, missy," I tell her from the doorway.

"Ugh, but Mom—"

"No buts." I shake my head, letting her know not to argue. "After you finish your drawing its bath time and then to bed."

She gets a mischievous look. "Will you read me a bedtime story?"

"One." I hold up a finger and wiggle it. "And only one. You're not sweet-talking me into more tonight." I stick my tongue out at her, and she giggles. We both know I'm weak when it comes to her. Not that I'm a pushover, but I love spending time with my girl. These moments when she's a child are so fleeting. I want to enjoy them and make special memories with her. Especially since I'm not sure I'll have more kids. That was a big factor in the divorce. Caleb wants more kids, and I won't keep him from that.

While Seda finishes her drawing, I head upstairs with my bag to the guestroom where I moved my things months ago. Caleb tried to get me to stay in the master, saying he was fine with the smaller room, but I reminded him I don't plan on living here like he does.

"Hi, Binx." I pet my beloved cat on the head where he snoozes on the covers. "I missed you."

He opens one green eye, glaring at me. I know he's pissed at me for leaving. He's needy like that, but instead of wanting love and attention now that I'm back he gives me the silent treatment. Cats, man.

I unpack the clothes I washed at my mom's and repack some different items. I might as well have a little variety to spice up my life. I'm tired from the week and can't wait to get into bed, but I really do want to spend time with Seda first.

I'm walking out of the bedroom when she tops the steps. "I finished. I guess that means I'm ready for my bath." She sounds anything but.

"Go pick out what pajamas you want to wear and I'll start it."

"Okay!" That excites her.

Flicking on the bathroom light, I push the plug in the tub and start the water, making sure the temperature isn't too hot or cold.

Seda comes running into the bathroom with her bright pink princess pajamas. "These." She drops them onto the floor and quickly strips out of her clothes without any prompting on my part.

"Do you know what book you want?" I ask, wetting her hair so I can suds it up.

"The one with Princess Seda," she giggles, tilting her head back. She loves when I massage the shampoo into her scalp.

"Why am I not surprised?" I smile at her, giving her cheek a small pinch. When she was a baby my mom gifted us one of those books with your name in it and it's been her favorite since she was a toddler.

"It's my favorite, Mom," she says dramatically like I'm not already aware, throwing in an eyeroll for good measure.

She's five going on fifteen.

When her hair is clean and she's scrubbed her body thoroughly with the cloth I pass her, I scoop her out and wrap her in a towel.

"Egg game!" she cries, feet pounding on the floor as she runs into her room.

I chase after her, pajamas in my hands. She falls to the floor, covering her body with the purple towel.

"What is this?" I say, circling her body. "Is this an egg? What an unusually large egg. And purple too? Hmm." I tap my finger against my lips. She starts to wiggle her body. I gasp loudly. "Oh my God, it's moving." I grin when I spot Caleb watching us from the doorway with his own smile. "Do you see this mysterious egg? Look at it moving!"

"I'm cracking!" Seda cries, wiggling more. *"Crack."* She throws off the towel and stands up. "Look, Mommy! It's a Seda!" She shakes her wet hair like a dog.

"Would you look at that? Who would've guessed that's what was in the egg." She giggles. "Pajama time." I hold up the top and she takes it from me, putting it on. She spots Caleb and smiles. "Did you see, Daddy? I was an egg!"

He chuckles. "I saw. You're my favorite egg." His eyes find mine and I feel his heartbreak still. Even though we're on good terms, it doesn't change the fact that he didn't want the divorce and he's still in love with me.

"Mommy's going to read me a story. Will you help her? I love it when you both do the voices."

He meets my eyes, seeing if I'm okay with it. I nod.

"Sure, baby girl." He picks up her wet towel and drops it into the hamper.

Seda grabs her book and climbs into bed with Caleb and I on either side of her.

She holds the book, flipping the pages and doing her best to read along with us.

By the time it's finished, her eyes have grown heavy.

We each kiss her forehead and tuck her in for the night

Out in the hallway, Caleb looks at me like he wants to say something but decides against it.

I watch him head down the hall and back downstairs.

I'm a coward, because I don't follow him and ask him what's on his mind.

Instead, I go to bed, because it's the easier option.

SIX

Salem

"**M**om?" I call, letting myself into the house.

Christy called me about thirty minutes ago during my drive letting me know everything was okay, but she had to head out instead of waiting for me to arrive.

When I pulled into the driveway, I steadfastly ignored the truck parked next door. It's bigger than the one Thayer used to have, but I still managed to act like I didn't see it, using my hair as a shield.

"In here, honey," she calls from the living room.

"Hey." The word leaves me in a relieved breath. Her skin tone is a little warmer today, slightly flushed and she looks less tired despite being in the bed. There's a tray across her lap and she's coloring. "Looks pretty," I comment, looking at the floral design she chose.

She's filling it in with shades of purple and teal. "Seda sent these for you." I dig in my bag for the drawings.

"Oh." My mom takes them, smiling and looking over each one. "How sweet of her. Was your time with her nice?"

I nod, sitting down on the couch so I can remove my strappy sandals. "Yeah, but it always is. Even when she's driving me up a wall, I love her so much."

My mom smiles, her eyes crinkling at the corners. "Being a parent is the most amazing thing you'll ever do in your life. It's not for the faint of heart, though."

"That's for sure." I shudder, thinking of Georgia's young boys and how she told me once that the oldest caught a mouse and brought it into the house. Not even Binx does that.

"Is Caleb all right?"

Although my mom fully supported my decision on the divorce, she loves Caleb and likes to keep check on him.

"He's good."

"Is he dating anyone?" she inquires, continuing to color like she didn't ask me a monumental question.

"I don't know." I pick up some of her coloring books from the pile on the floor. "We don't talk about that kind of thing. He's free to date if he wants."

"Is he still in love with you?"

My shoulders lock, my body tensing. "Mom," I beg.

"It's a genuine question, Salem." She gives me that motherly look —the one with the arched brow daring me not to answer.

"Yes." I flip through the pages, looking for a page to color myself. Her eyes try to bore a hole through me, but I steadfastly ignore her.

"You did the right thing, you know." Her words take me by surprise, my head jerking up. She looks back at me with a tiny smile. "You love him, I know you do, but he loves you more. So, you did the right thing in letting him go."

I exhale a shaky breath. "I thought if I just tried harder, put in more effort, I could love him like he loved me."

"But you never could."

"No," I answer even though it wasn't a question. "When he started talking about having kids, I just…" Rubbing my lips together,

350

I search for the right words. "I couldn't do it anymore. He's amazing, the greatest guy, and I love him, but not in the way he deserves to be loved."

I look down at the page I stopped on, the black and white image blurred from the tears flooding my eyes. I never, ever wanted to hurt Caleb. Not back then and not now, either. But I'm not a perfect person, no one is and if they think they are then they're delusional. We all do things we're not proud of. I will never regret my time with Caleb. It's not possible. But I do regret not loving him enough. The worst part is, if I'd never met Thayer, and known what soul-crushing, all-consuming love felt like, then I think Caleb and I would've been a good match.

But I did meet Thayer, and that single moment forever changed the trajectory of my life.

"Please, don't cry," she pleads, reaching for the box of tissues on the table beside her bed.

I reach for the tissue, taking it from her to dab my eyes. "I'm a horrible person, Mom. The shittiest. He loves me so much. Why can't I do the same?"

She looks at me sympathetically. "Honey," she says softly, her eyes pitying, "you have to forgive yourself. You did the right thing."

"It doesn't matter if it was right or not." I dry up more tears. "I still hurt him."

"Hurt is temporary."

"Yeah?" I laugh humorlessly, thinking about how it's been six years since Thayer broke my heart. That hurt certainly hasn't been temporary, but maybe things would've been different if I didn't have our daughter. She's the best thing in this world, but she's also a constant reminder of him.

"You're so strong."

"Mom." I shake my head. "You're the strong one."

She laughs. "How about we're *both* strong?"

"That works." I wipe the tissue beneath my nose.

Her face sobers, and she looks at me with worry. "I want you to be happy, Salem. It's what I've always wanted."

"I am happy," I argue, because it's true. Could I be happier? Yes. But I'm not unhappy.

"You're content. There's a difference."

She has a point. "I'll find what brings me joy one day."

"You will." Her smile is sad. "I just wish I'd be alive to see it."

Another crack is added to my already mangled heart.

I WAKE UP AT SEVEN IN THE MORNING AND THROW ON MY running clothes for a jog. I don't have nightmares anymore—well, rarely, thanks to my return to therapy and sticking with it—but some habits are hard to kick and I do love running early. I just don't do it before five A.M. anymore.

Popping in my ear buds, I turn on my cardio playlist while I stretch on the driveway. Instead of turning to jog in front of Thayer's house in the direction I used to go, I turn and head the opposite direction. I never liked this loop as much, it's hillier, but I'm being petty not wanting to take my old route.

By the time I turn to head back, I'm drenched in sweat and my hair doesn't want to stay in a ponytail.

I turn onto the street that brings me home when I spot a jogger heading toward me from the opposite direction.

Tall, big build. Obviously, a man.

My steps falter as we both slow—me in front of my mom's house, him in front of—

I pull my ear buds out, my lips parting as I get my first look at the man I left behind.

"Thayer," I breathe his name into existence.

He cocks his head, taking me in. Surprise fills his brown eyes.

"Salem."

SEVEN

Salem

The man standing in front of me is so different, and yet so similar to the one I left. He's thirty-seven now, almost thirty-eight if I'm doing the math right in my head. I'm too stunned to think coherently. There's a hint of gray at his temples, subtle but it's there, and there's some of that same color sprinkled into the scruff on his cheeks. I didn't know gray hair would be a turn on for me, but with Thayer I think everything is. His brown eyes are taking me in as greedily as I do him. The lines around them are more prominent now. His eyes are brighter, clearer than the last time I saw him.

It was the end of that summer, and my hope had waned. I went over to his house one last time, begging and pleading for him to get up, to *live*, because that's what Forrest would want. He was drinking his life away, slipping through my fingers. And nothing I did was good enough. In the end, I called his brother and told him Thayer needed him, and I went back to New York City with Lauren. I had a baby to think about and that meant being strong even when I wanted to fall apart too.

I take in his running clothes and shoes, trying desperately to fight my rising smile.

"Hi," I say stupidly.

His eyes continue to rake over me. "Hi."

I keep expecting to feel an awkwardness settle in my chest—after all, this is *Thayer* and I haven't seen him in ages, but it just feels natural. Like it always did.

He doesn't look like what I expected.

After the way I last saw him, I guess I expected him to look even worse than he did then. But that was a man that was grieving, and this is one who somehow pulled himself out of that and has healed.

He looks *good*.

Healthy.

Somehow, that makes the last six years even worse.

"H-How are you? How has life been?" He asks in an uncharacteristic way for him—flustered and taken by surprise. I suppose, despite his friendship with my mom, she didn't mention me coming back to town.

I take my sweaty ponytail down, brushing my fingers hastily through the strands before putting it back in a low bun on the nape of my neck. His eyes watch my movements and I wonder if he senses how nervous I am. So many things are running through my head and it's on the tip of my tongue to blurt out, *"I had a baby and it's yours!"* But I think *that* situation needs to be handled with a little more grace.

"I ... it's been ... life."

Wow, so eloquent of you, Salem. Of course, life has been life. Could you sound any dumber?

"Heard you got married." He squints down at me, lifting his hand to shield his eyes from the rising sun.

It's not a question.

354

I hold up my left hand, showing my empty ring finger. "And divorced."

"He's an idiot."

I laugh, a full belly laugh that feels so good to let loose. "No, I'm the idiot." I look down at the ground between us, toeing my shoe against a piece of loose gravel on the sidewalk. The giddy eighteen-year-old girl inside me is screaming right now in excitement like I'm talking to my crush. But the twenty-five-year-old I am now is screaming at her to stand down, that we have to guard ourselves against this man. "I'm the one that asked for the divorce."

"Why?" His lips purse, eyes narrowed. He's surprised, but also curious, and trying to hide those feelings. I wish he wouldn't do that. He's so hard to read, and I value any insight he gives me into his thoughts.

"Because, I could never love him like he loves me. Caleb is a great man. But he's not my forever. I already gave my heart away."

Oh, God! Why did I blurt out that last part! I couldn't keep my mouth shut?

Thayer's eyes flicker with curiosity, and a flash of heat. "That so?"

"Yeah." I try not to smile and fail. "Now that guy? He was an idiot."

Thayer throws his head back and laughs and laughs and *laughs*. It's music to my ears.

"I assume you mean me."

I don't hesitate when I say, "Yes."

He drops his head, the smallest of amused smiles on his lips. "I deserve that."

Now that the surprise is wearing off, panic is setting in. This is *Thayer*. The man I gave my heart, my soul, my everything to. I was a broken mess when I left him.

My marriage to Caleb might be over but *he* helped put me back together.

Clearing his throat he says, "It's ... uh ... good seeing you."

"Yeah, you too."

Awkwardness sets in and we stand in front of each other, waiting for the other to do or say something first.

I'm the one to break the silence.

"I need to check on my mom."

"Right." He nods, backing a step away, closer to his side of the property line. "She invited me over for dinner tonight. I already said yes—I didn't know you were going to be here, she didn't say—anyway, I'll call her later and cancel."

Rolling my eyes, I inhale through my nose and out through my mouth. "I'm an adult, Thayer. Don't treat me like broken china. Just because you shattered my heart, doesn't mean I'm still damaged. You're welcome to come for dinner."

I'm glad I sound stronger than I feel.

"Oh." He looks at me surprised—did he really expect me to just crumble and cry at his feet seeing him again? "If you're okay with it, then."

"I'm fine." I don't give him a chance to respond, turning on my heel. Before I reach the door, I stop and whip around. He's still standing at the corner of the driveway. "Don't be later than five."

He wets his lips with a smooth slide of his tongue, hiding a growing smile. "Do you want me to bring anything?"

"Just yourself."

"I can do that."

I dip my head, reaching for the doorknob.

"Good."

I let myself in and lean against the closed door.

What the hell? I went from not seeing the man for years to finally laying eyes on him again and now we're having dinner tonight—all thanks to my mom.

It's just weird.

EIGHT

Thayer

close the front door behind me, standing in the foyer shell-shocked.

Salem's back in town.

She's back.

She's divorced.

And I have no fucking idea how long she's going to be here.

Now, I'm supposed to have dinner with her and her mom. I can't help thinking Allie planned this on purpose. She's known about Salem and me since Forrest's birthday that year. I guess now that Salem's divorced, she's playing matchmaker.

Rubbing a hand over my jaw, I head into the kitchen and grab a bottle of water. I gulp down half of it in just a few swallows.

I'm having trouble wrapping my head around the fact that Salem's here.

Moving on from her should've been easy in theory—I was with her less time than I was with my ex-wife. But it didn't work that way. I never expected it to, either, not with how intense my feelings were for her.

I moved on though—not in the physical sense, but mentally. I accepted that she had married and her life would carry on as it should, while I'd still be here.

That's not the course things have taken, and that means, maybe, just fucking maybe, I have a second chance to get our love story right.

NINE

Salem

I set the table for three and then lay out the dishes I made across the counter so Thayer and I can serve ourselves buffet style—I'll make a plate up for my mom so she's not on her feet too long—and that way the table won't be too cluttered.

"It smells good."

My mom's voice comes from the doorway, my head jerks up quickly in response.

"Mom, you're supposed to ask for help before you get up."

She waves a dismissive hand. "I'm not dead yet." This is her only argument.

My shoulders collapse. "And I'd like to keep it that way for as long as possible."

"I had to pee," she argues.

"Since you're already up, go ahead and have a seat. I'll fix your plate." There's no point in arguing with her. Unless she absolutely has no energy to do something, there's no getting her to cooperate.

"I'm not very hungry."

I narrow my eyes on her as she pulls out the chair where there's only one place setting, meaning I'll be forced to sit beside Thayer or move the placemat and everything, which would look weird if I did.

"I'm going to put a little of everything on your plate. At least try to take one bite of each." She looks grossed out at the thought, but nods. "Why did you invite Thayer over for dinner if you don't even want to eat dinner?"

"I was being neighborly, Salem. He's a nice man."

My shoulders stiffen and I turn away, washing my hands in the sink. "Do you *like* him?"

She snorts a laugh. "I'm dying, Salem. I don't have time to like anyone in the way you're implying. But I do like him as a person."

"Hmm," I hum.

There's a knock on the side door at 4:59 and I turn the lock, letting him in. I can't help myself when my eyes rake over him. His hair is freshly washed, still damp from a shower. I greedily take in the light stubble on his jaw, up close and personal this time. His brown eyes are warm chocolate that I want to melt in. He even smells of cologne, like he put in a little extra effort tonight.

No! Stop it! You can't let this man make you all weak in the knees again! He's done enough damage.

But I can't help it.

I'm looking at him with new eyes, older eyes. I'm no longer that freshly pregnant nineteen-year-old who was scared out of her mind. Looking back, I know I made the decision I thought I had to. Was it the best choice? In hindsight, probably not, but life is a series of choices and at the time you don't always know whether it's good or bad. You just do what you can with the information you have.

Back then, I was terrified to be a mom, but there was never a question in my mind about keeping the baby.

But Thayer was spiraling after losing Forrest, understandable yes, but I couldn't pull him out of that—not on my own. *He* had to do it, and I knew it. But I had to make sure my baby was going to be safe and taken care of, so I did that the best way I could, and that meant giving Thayer space.

I thought ... I thought he'd find me.

Call me.

Text me.

Send a fucking carrier pigeon for God's sake, but he never did, and I felt used and thrown away.

"Is something on my face?"

"Oh!" I jump away, knocking my hip into the corner of the counter. "Ow!"

"Careful." He grips my wrist, steadying me. Electricity shoots up my arm at his touch.

"I'm okay." I pull gently from his grasp, not wanting to betray my true feelings.

He lets me go and holds up a bottle of wine I didn't know he was holding. "I wasn't sure what we were having, but I didn't want to come with nothing."

"Oh, how sweet." My mom smiles. "Thank you, Thayer. Isn't that nice, Salem?"

"So nice," I mimic woodenly, turning away. "Let me grab glasses," I mutter, distracted.

If I didn't know better, I would swear my mom is trying to play matchmaker with Mr. Broody. I wonder what she'd say if she knew he broke my heart or that he's Seda's father. I wonder, since they're friends, if he knows I have a child. I'm guessing not or I think he would've brought it up when he mentioned my marriage.

I add wine glasses to the table while Thayer chats with my mom. I make her a plate and set it in front of her.

"You can get your own plate," I tell Thayer.

"Salem!" My mom scolds.

My cheeks flush. "I just meant he can pick and choose what he wants."

Turning my back on them, I grab my plate and start piling food onto it. I don't pay attention to what I'm doing and it's only when Thayer says, "I don't think chicken goes on top of mashed potatoes," his long finger pointing at the gravy I made and should have been spooning on instead, that I jolt back to reality.

I close my eyes, mortified. It has to be obvious to him, that even after all this time I'm still affected by him. Still hopelessly enamored for God knows why.

He broke your heart!

He broke it, and yet, that stupid organ races in my chest at an accelerated rate for him.

I hate him.

I hate myself.

I hate *this*.

That he's here, in my mom's kitchen. That she's dying. That Seda is in Boston.

I just—

"Here, let me help you." He takes my plate from me, raking the roasted chicken off my potatoes and fixing my plate.

"Maybe I wanted my chicken on my potatoes," I grumble.

He arches a brow. "Do you?"

"Well, no."

He doesn't wait for me to say anything further. He finishes my plate, carrying it to the table. He places it on the spot in front of my mom. Pulling out the chair, he turns to me with a tilt of his head. "Are you going to sit down?"

"Um, yeah."

I really hate that he has me so disoriented. It's like I can't tell up from down or left from right.

Sitting down, he scoots my chair in and I let out a tiny squeak of surprise at the gesture.

Does he not see how weird all of this is?

My mom looks down at her plate, but I don't miss the flash of a smile.

"What are you smiling about?"

"Nothing."

"Liar," I grumble.

She mock-gasps, and it turns into a cough, which instantly has me on alert. Luckily, it stops before I become too worried.

"You can't call a dying woman a liar."

362

"Why not?" I'm aware Thayer can overhear our entire conversation, but I don't care. "If the shoe fits..."

She cracks a smile. Thayer pulls out the chair at my side, his arm brushing against mine as he sits down. My treacherous body shivers —visibly so.

"Are you okay?"

I press my lips into a flat smile. "Splendid. It's just a bit chilly."

He gives me a funny look because it's anything but cold in the house. My mom is cold almost all the time these days and doesn't want the AC on.

"Dinner smells amazing. Did you make it?"

I turn to him, raising a brow. "Obviously. *Ow.* You kicked me."

My mom blinks back innocently. "I did no such thing."

Thayer's eyes flicker back and forth between us in amusement. "I really appreciate you inviting me over, Allison."

"I've told you—" she coughs and instantly my hand holding my fork lowers, "—call me Allie."

"Allie," he repeats. "Right, sorry."

"Are you all right?" I ask her.

I know Georgia mentioned with our mom's immune system being non-existent at the moment that she'd be more susceptible to illnesses.

"I'm fine. My throat's just a tad ticklish tonight."

I eye her skeptically. Even Thayer looks worried.

It hits me, in moments like this, that she's dying.

That no matter what I do, or how hard she continues to fight, this is her final battle and there is no happy outcome.

It's one thing to know something, it's another to witness it.

"Do you want to go lay down?"

She pushes the food around her plate. "I'm fine."

"Mom, if you'd feel better laying down—"

She looks between the two of us across from her. "Maybe that would be a good idea."

I stand up to help, but Thayer urges me back down. "I'll help her," he says in a hushed tone.

Before I can protest, he's moving around the table and helping my mom up and into the family room.

I stay seated, staring at my plate so she can't see the tears pooling in my eyes.

Thayer returns, his chair squeaking as it slides back on the linoleum floor.

"You don't have to stay," I mutter, not looking at him.

"I'm hungry," is his gruff reply. "I'm not about to walk away from a home-cooked meal. I'm too tired and lazy to cook most days and end up ordering takeout."

My head whips in his direction, appraising the lean body beneath his clothes. "Doesn't look like you eat unhealthy."

His brow arches, lips twitching when he fights a smile. "Checking me out?"

"Don't flatter yourself."

He chuckles, taking a bite of mashed potatoes. "You made these from scratch."

It's not a question, but I answer anyway. "Yes." I force myself to eat a bite, then another.

"Would you happen to know anything about cupcakes showing up at my door a few days ago?" He asks it in a way like he already knows the answer, so there's no point in lying.

"I made them with my mom and she asked me to drop some off. That's all."

Aka: Don't read into it.

He nods, rubbing his lips together. "Salem, I—"

"Not right now." My words are biting, cutting, but I *can't* do this right now. Not with my dying mother in the next room. She's my focus right now. Not Thayer. He can't be.

"We need to talk."

We need to talk about way more than he thinks we do.

I mentally start building a wall around my heart. It's the only way I can operate around Thayer. I can't—*won't*—let him get to me so easily. Not this time.

"Do you remember?" I snap at him, my tone icy. "Do you remember the last time I saw you? What you said to me?"

His forehead wrinkles and he looks confused. "I—I'm not sure."

"You told me you hated me." He pales, horror stricken. "That was the least of what was said, if I'm being honest. And listen, you were drunk and grieving, but I survived a different kind of abuse before and I wasn't going to let you hurt me with words."

"Salem—" His Adam's apple bobs. "I didn't … fuck, I can't believe I said that to you." He shakes his head.

"I know we need to talk," I continue like he didn't say anything at all. "But I can't do it right now. Not after just seeing you for the first time in so long." Pushing my plate away, I stand without looking at him. "I'm not so hungry anymore. Lock up behind you."

I walk out of the kitchen, past my sleeping mom, and upstairs. I lock my bedroom door behind me and hastily close the blinds. Doing everything I can to block out the hateful words he lobbed my way that night.

You're the reason he's dead.

I was distracted thinking about you and he's gone. You did this. It's your fault.

I hate you. Get out.

I wish I'd never met you.

That last one was a massive blow to my heart. The others hurt, God did they hurt, but I knew they were the words of a broken father.

Curling up on my bed, I fall asleep.

In the morning, all the leftovers are put away and the kitchen is spotless.

There's a note left on the counter.

I'm sorry.—T

TEN

Thayer

When I crack my eyes open in the morning, my first thought is; *I told her I hated her?*

What a fucking bastard I am.

Salem has every right to hate me. I know I lost myself to my grief after Forrest's passing. It was something no parent should ever have to live through. There are days where the grief comes back full force and cripples me. On those days I end up calling my guys and telling them I won't be in to work, and I sit in the treehouse or visit his grave.

If only I hadn't been such a lazy fuck and gotten it built for him.

Maybe then ... *maybe then.*

"Fuck," I groan aloud, crossing my arm over my eyes.

I try not to let myself go down that path with my thoughts, but sometimes it's hard not to.

Shoving my sorry ass out of bed, I hop in the shower.

My body yearns with the need for a release. It becomes impossible for me to ignore my aching cock. Seeing Salem again has awakened desires in me I long thought dormant. Gripping the base, I stroke up and down, rolling my wrist around the tip.

I don't mean to, but I can't help it when I picture Salem in my mind.

It's always her. Even when it shouldn't have been. Even when I broke us.

My release comes fast and hard. When it's over, I lean against the shower wall.

I finish washing up and get dressed for work. Tugging the Holmes Landscaping shirt down over my torso, I reach for my cap and sunglasses.

The very same pair of sunglasses Salem bought me.

They're loose and beat up, I need a new pair, but I refuse to part with these. I guess I'm a sentimental fool like that.

Lacing up my boots, I head downstairs and scarf down a bowl of cereal. It's not the healthiest breakfast—especially with my choice of sugary cereal in the form of Fruity Pebbles—but it'll have to do. I don't have the time for anything else this morning.

Normally, I'd head out to my greenhouse before leaving, but thanks to my extra time in my shower I can't afford to spare time for that either.

Quickly rinsing my bowl, I swipe my keys from the counter and head out to my truck.

Before I can back out of the driveway, a phone call comes through the speakers. Laith's name flashes across the large display.

I don't really feel like talking to my brother right now, but I have a forty-five minute drive to the site so I might as well get this over with.

Pushing the button on my steering wheel to answer his call, I greet him with a simple, "Hey."

"Are you sober?" He laughs after he asks it.

It's his standard greeting.

I roll my eyes. He knows I've stayed away from alcohol for years. I don't have a drinking problem, but I did rely too much on it after Forrest died. It became a drug that could numb my feelings and put me to sleep.

Now, I choose to stay away because it's not worth feeling like shit to drink it.

"I'm always sober."

"Can't blame me for checking."

"Why are you calling?"

"Because I can."

"I'm on my way to work, so if it's something important get a move on with it."

He chuckles. "Have some patience, Thayer. I can't call and check on my big bro?"

"Sorry, I'm running late this morning and it has me on edge."

What really has me on edge is how I can't get Salem off my mind.

"Somehow I don't believe that's what's on your mind."

I groan, pinching the bridge of my nose when I roll to a stop at a red light. "Salem's back."

It's all I have to say. After she was the one to call Laith all those years ago and he came to the rescue, I had to fill him in on what was going on with her.

The fucker laughs and laughs and laughs. "Oh, you're fucked."

"Why?" I bite out through clenched teeth.

"Don't play stupid, bro. You've been hung up on her all these years. She's still married?"

"No," I sigh.

"No? Well, that's good then. Why do you sound pissed?"

I'm quiet for a moment. "What if I fuck up again?"

"Easy, don't fuck it up."

"I don't want to, but I have a feeling we have a lot of baggage to wade through."

This time he's the one who's quiet. Then he asks, "Is she worth it?"

"She's worth everything."

"Then I say, don't let this chance pass you by. You deserve to be happy—more than anyone I know."

My brother's support surprises me, but I guess it shouldn't. He's always had my back.

"Thanks. I gotta go."

"Sure. Talk to you soon."

He ends the call and I spend the rest of my drive wondering if it's possible to right my wrongs and finally get the girl.

ELEVEN

Salem

"I miss you," I tell the sweet face on my phone screen as I lock up my mom's shop behind me. It's been permanently closed for a few months now, once my mom got too weak and tired to work, but there are still things to move and clear out before we figure out what to do with it. Selling the store makes the most sense—Georgia's a nurse, she's not going to open a store, and I'm ... well, I don't know what I'm doing. Stupidly, though, I hate the idea of getting rid of it. It was the first thing our mom ever really did for herself.

"Miss you, too, Mommy." She smiles into the phone. "Daddy says we can have pizza for dinner!"

"Mmm, that sounds yummy." I unlock my car and set a box of my old candles in the back. I doubt they even have much smell to them at this point, but I didn't want to leave them there. Silly, I know. I stopped making candles when I left town and felt this ache when I saw the box.

I'm not ready to go home yet, so I walk across the street. Georgia picked Mom up and took her to her house for dinner. I was invited, but bowed out to come to the store instead. Since I don't have to hurry back to the house yet, I think a walk around our quaint downtown area will be nice.

"What are you going to have for dinner?"

"I don't know yet."

"I wish you could have pizza with us."

"I know, baby."

"When can I come visit Grandma?"

I press my lips together. "I don't know." Maybe I can finagle a way to bring my mom to her. I can't have her coming here, risk Thayer seeing her, before I say something.

Though, with her blonde hair, it's hard to tell that Caleb *isn't* her father. At least from a distance. But I know. I see bits of Thayer in her every day. From the shape of her lips, to the curve of her cheeks, down to the look on her face she gets when she's thinking about something.

But especially in her eyes.

The same warm, intelligent brown as his.

"Daddy says the pizza is here!" She jumps up, running with the phone in her hand. "I love you, Mommy!"

"Love you, too." She ends the call, my screen returning to normal.

I walk down the street, taking in shops old and new. One beckons to me and I open the door, inhaling the scent of lavender and eucalyptus.

"Hang on, I'll be right there!" A cheery voice calls.

I pick up a homemade bar of soap, giving it a sniff.

The sound of swooshing fabric has me looking up just as a tall woman, probably in her late thirties or early forties, rounds the corner of the table. Her hair is a wild mass of dark curls, and she's wearing fitted bell bottom jeans with a plain white t-shirt. Bracelets adorn her wrists, jangling as she moves.

"Hi." She looks me over. "I haven't seen you here before."

371

Gotta love small towns—if people don't recognize you, they're quick to call you out on it.

"I lived here as a teenager. I'm back taking care of my mom. She owns A Checkered Past Antiques."

"Oh." Her smile falters a bit. "Allison is such a lovely woman. It's such a shame about the cancer."

"Yeah." I lower my head, picking up a glass jar of bath salts with lavender in it. "Your shop is lovely."

"Oh, thank you!" Her energy returns, lighting up with excitement. "It's been a dream come true owning my own shop."

"What would you recommend I get?" I motion to the table in front which seems to be a variety of all sorts of bath products.

"If you enjoy bubble baths, definitely this and this." She grabs two items and holds them out to me, one is the salts but this one says it's orange scented. The other is a bar of some sort. "This one is shampoo." She points to the weirdly shaped soap. "It looks strange, I know, but it does wonders for your hair."

Looking at how beautiful and full her hair is, I have to believe her.

"All right. I'll take both then."

"Great!" She smiles and takes them over to the register. "Feel free to look around some more if you want. I didn't mean to ambush you."

"It's okay." I pick up a jar of lotion in the same orange scent. "I'll take this too." I place it by the register and she rings me up. I slide my card onto the counter while she wraps everything in brown paper, placing it in a bag. She swipes my card and puts the receipt in the bag.

"I hope you'll be back. I'm Jen by the way."

"It's nice to meet you." I take the bag from her. "I'm Salem."

"Wow, that's a different name. Unique. I like it."

"Thanks. I'm sure I'll be back in."

Letting myself out, I walk around a little longer before going into the local Italian eatery. The town is so small that there's no such thing as waiting for a table.

The hostess sits me at a table in the corner. It's small, only room for two, with a small candle lit on the table.

She sets the menu on the table and I offer a mumbled, "Thanks."

Going out to eat by myself was something I started making myself do during the divorce. I'd always had my mom, or sister, Lauren, Caleb, and even Thayer to do things with and I knew it was important for me to get comfortable doing certain things on my own. So, I'd take myself out to eat, or go to the movies, anything that I'd always felt self-conscious about doing alone.

And I've come to enjoy it—these pockets of time that are only for me.

I place my order and the waitress returns a few minutes later with a glass of wine and bread with dipping oil. My stomach rumbles at the smell of the bread. Tearing off a chunk, I dunk it in the oil and take a bite.

"Is this seat taken?"

I cough, choking on the bread.

Thayer looks down at me with drawn brows, clearly worried he might have to give me the Heimlich.

"What are you doing here?" I reach for the water glass the waitress dropped off when she first came by for my order. A couple of sips seems to help clear my throat.

Thayer looks down at me, his hand on the chair across from me—still waiting for a yes or no. That's Thayer. He won't push me or do anything I'm not comfortable with. If I say no, he'll leave or at least go to another table, and won't make me feel sorry for it.

His mouth twitches almost imperceptibly, but I'm honed in on the gesture, always searching for his smiles. "One usually eats in a restaurant."

"I meant at my table." My fingers shake the tiniest bit when I lower them from the water glass. I hate that it's been so long since I've seen him and the man still has the ability to put me in knots. Tucking my hand under the table, I lace my fingers together.

He shrugs, still holding onto the chair like it's some sort of lifeline. There's a ring around his pinky. He never used to wear one before and I can't help but be curious why he does now. "I saw you and I thought maybe we could eat together."

"We had dinner the other night."

"With your mother." He points out, straightening. "It's okay. I'll grab mine to-go."

He turns to walk away. Lowering my head to stare at the red and white checkered tablecloth I can't help but feel like such a complete bitch.

"Thayer." I sigh, shoulders drooping. He freezes, not turning fully around but giving me the side of his handsome face. "Sit down."

He turns, facing me. "Are you sure?"

I nod. "Please."

He pulls the chair out and sits. The plain gray tee he wears shouldn't look so nice, but it hugs his chest in all the right places.

This feels so much more awkward than the other night at my house. Then, my mom was there as a buffer. Now, it's only us.

"Oh, I didn't know someone was joining you. What can I get you, Thayer?"

Of course the waitress knows him—that's how it is in small towns. I've been gone long enough that there are enough people who don't recognize me.

"The usual," he says easily, dismissing her. He doesn't take his eyes off me the entire time. "What are you thinking?"

"You come here a lot."

"They have good food." He leans forward, lowering his voice. "Besides, I told you I usually eat out."

I take a deep breath, my chest shaking when I exhale. I hate that he makes me so nervous. I'm an adult now. A full-grown woman. Thayer Holmes has no right having this hold on me.

Clearing my throat, I grab the stem of the wine glass and take a sip. "How's life been?"

He chuckles. "That's a loaded question."

"How so?"

"It's been six years, Salem," he says like I don't know how long it's been since I saw him. "A lot happens in that time. Good. Bad. Happy days. Sad ones. That's what makes it loaded. I don't even know where to start."

"At least you seem sober." I wince as soon as I make the comment.

He clears his throat. "I'm sorry you ever had to see me like that."

"I don't want you to constantly be apologizing for the past." I look away from him, watching an elderly couple get seated a few tables over. "I can't imagine what kind of shape I'd be in if that were—" I bite my tongue. "If I had to lose a child," I correct myself.

"I went to therapy. I still go once a month." He ducks his head, trying to get me to look at him. I relent, meeting that brown-eyed gaze I fell so hard for as a teen. "You inspired me to do that."

"Me?" I nearly choke on my tongue. "How?"

"You told me that you went to therapy for..." He clears his throat. "Well, you know." I appreciate that he doesn't say it out loud. "I knew if you could survive your trauma and go to therapy for help then I could as well. My brother helped too. He moved in and lived with me for over a year."

"Really?" I'm shocked. I might've been the one to call Laith, but I certainly didn't expect him to go to that extent.

"He ... I think he was scared of what I was turning into and didn't want to leave me on my own until he was certain I was in a better place. He told me you were the one to call him."

I roll my tongue in my mouth. "You wouldn't let me help you—and someone had to."

"I know." He leans across the table. "It kills me that I pushed you away. That I hurt you the way I did."

"Then why did you?" The question rolls off my tongue. It's something I've wondered about over the years. It seemed so unlike Thayer.

The waitress appears with a tray containing our food and a glass of water for Thayer. "Do you need anything else?"

"No, we're good," I tell her. "Thank you." I arch a brow at Thayer. "So?" I prompt. I swirl a bite of linguine around the fork.

"I was a broken man, grieving for my child. I had no idea how long I was going to be in that dark place and you were this beautiful, caring woman and I didn't want to drag you down with me." He rubs a hand over his stubbled jaw, his eyes haunted from days gone by. "I thought I was doing the right thing, Salem. I know now it was the completely wrong one, but you were nineteen and I wanted to set you free. You would've waited for me, however long it took for me to pull myself out of that dark place, I know you would've been there and I just ... didn't want you to do that. You deserved more than me."

I say it calmly, but there are tears in my eyes. "You had no right to decide that on your own."

"I know." He sounds choked up, his eyes watery as well.

"You broke my heart."

His eyes close. "I know."

"You made me hate you."

His Adam's apple bobs. Again, those two words. "I know."

We eat our meal in silence after that.

TWELVE

Thayer

"You're not paying," she argues when I pull out my wallet at the end of the meal.

"Yes, I am." I keep my tone calm and even.

"I can pay for my own," she grumbles, reaching for her purse.

I try to hide my smile. "I never said you couldn't."

I hand enough cash to cover the meal and tip the waitress when she passes by. Salem blinks at me open-mouthed.

"Thayer," she groans my name, her nose wrinkling with irritation.

I don't know what it says about me that blood rushes straight to my dick at her tone. Even her annoyance is sexy.

"It's too late now." I shrug easily, sliding the chair back.

"You can pay me back in some other way."

Her cheeks flush red. "I'm not sleeping with you."

Arching a brow, I look down at her where she still sits. "Did I say anything about sex?"

She grows redder. "Well, no. But—" She sputters, trying to dig herself out of this hole.

I jerk my head toward the exit. "Let me walk you to your car."

Her tongue rolls around her mouth and I expect her to protest, but she surprises me by replying with a simple, "Okay."

She gets up from the table and my hand goes to her waist. It's automatic—like my body can't help but touch hers. She eyes my arm with narrowed, uncertain eyes. She's guarding her heart from me, I feel it, and I can't say I blame her.

Letting my hand drop, I hold open the door for her and follow her out onto the street. The sun has gone down, stars shining brightly in the night sky. It's one of my favorite things about living in such a small town. You always see the stars.

"My car's down this way in front of my mom's store."

I walk beside her, my hands in my pockets so I don't touch her. Being around her again makes it all too easy to fall into who I was with her before.

"Thank you," she says after a minute, "for buying dinner."

I can't hide my amusement and she rolls her eyes playfully at my grin. "You're welcome."

I spot her car and disappointment floods me that our evening is over. When I saw her in the restaurant I couldn't help but approach her table. I can't resist her. Even after all this time.

She looks up at me briefly, a soft flush coloring her cheeks. I wish I knew what she was thinking, but I don't ask. I don't have the right to know, not anymore.

Stopping by her car, I wait for her to say something. She's quiet, but she doesn't make a move to get in the car either.

Blowing out a breath, she unlocks her car. I expect her to get inside and not say another word to me, but she surprises me.

"Seeing you again ... it's different than I expected."

"A good or bad different?" I wet my lips nervously, waiting for her response.

She shrugs, opening the door. "I'm still figuring that out."

I stay on the sidewalk, watching as she starts up her SUV. She waves before she drives away.

My truck is in the direction we came from so I head back that way.

Driving around for while, letting my thoughts wander—mostly to Salem because I'm a sad fucker when it comes to that woman—I pull into my driveway an hour later.

Shutting my truck off, I don't go right inside my house. Opening the fence gate, I head out back to my greenhouse. Easing the door open, I step into the place that has been my safe harbor and my greatest torment.

The entire interior of the greenhouse is filled with intricately petaled, pale pink peonies.

Originally, I meant to use my personal greenhouse to grow a variety of plants.

But after that year when Laith moved out, and the reality of my actions began to set in when I learned Salem was getting married, I started growing them and I just couldn't stop.

They became my last connection to her.

I've treasured growing them, nurturing them.

Grabbing the small shears, I start cutting.

It's the first time I've ever cut any of them—except for spent blooms that needed to be removed—and lay the stems out on the table.

I swore I would never cut any.

Not unless they were for her.

I honestly didn't think this day would come, so I smile to myself as I put together the bundle of flowers.

THIRTEEN

Salem

"What are you doing?" My mom asks from the doorway of the kitchen, her voice groggy and her eyes still half asleep.

"Mom," I admonish for the millionth time, "you're supposed to let me help you."

I scurry around the island to help her into one of the kitchen chairs. I understand her need for independence but dammit if it isn't going to be the death of me.

"You didn't answer my question."

It doesn't matter how old you get, mothers will always be mothers.

"I found some of my old candles at your shop. I was just taking them out of the box." I point to the few already on the counter.

"Oh, I had those pulled for someone."

I laugh, not sure I've heard her right. "What? For who?"

"That doesn't matter." She waves a dismissive hand. "Take them back to the store."

"Why?"

"Because they're already paid for."

"Oh, right." I shake my head, loading the candles back into the box. "Sorry, I didn't know. I was surprised you still had any left."

She shrugs. "I held back some. That was the last of it."

"Huh." I put my hands on my hips, wondering why someone would pay and have her hold old candles. "Are you ready for some breakfast?"

"Maybe some scrambled eggs." She looks a bit queasy talking about food. I can't imagine what it must be like to be in her position —little to no appetite but knowing you need to get something in your system.

"I'll whip those right up."

She gives a forced smile, but I know she appreciates I'm here and helping. "I was thinking." She clears her throat. "I'd like to do something with you today."

I pull a carton of eggs from the refrigerator. "Are you up for that?" She was out at Georgia's for a few hours yesterday evening. I don't want her to overdo herself. "I'd like to get out for a while. It's a nice day."

"What do you have in mind?"

She toys with the tie on her robe. "I thought we could visit Seda and Caleb."

I gape at her—not because of her asking to visit, that's understandable, but—"Mom, are you sure you're up for that kind of trip?"

It's a few hours there and back and she's ... well, she's not in the best shape to put it lightly.

"It might be easier if we stayed the night," she acquiesces, with a nod, her slender fingers still rubbing against the material of her robe. She smiles sheepishly. I know she feels guilty because of the situation with Caleb, but I can't deny her request to see her granddaughter.

"Let me run it by Georgia and see what she thinks about you making the trip and I'll ask Caleb too."

"All right."

I finish her eggs and add a piece of toast just in case she ends up wanting some to nibble on some before I step outside to make the calls.

It's warm outside with a slight breeze, the birds chirping merrily. I missed this place. This house. The town. Even the people in it.

"Wha—" I gasp when my foot hits something it shouldn't.

My eyes shoot to the last step, a startled gasp passing through my lips.

A bouquet of fresh pink peonies wrapped in Kraft paper lies there waiting.

I know without looking at the note attached that they're for me from Thayer. Bending down I pick them up. Each one is perfect, not one discolored petal or imperfection to find. I look around, like I expect him to be lurking somewhere, but I don't see him. I hold the flowers close, not sure how to feel about the gesture. I'm not mad, but I am confused.

Six years.

I moved on.

Started a new life.

I *never* heard from him again.

He didn't reach out, but now he acts as if he wants to pick up where we left off—well, maybe not exactly there, but—

Shaking my head, I set the flowers back down and walk away from them.

I don't have time to think about Thayer, to contemplate how and why he does things.

Do you want things to pick back up?

I pinch the bridge of my nose.

Yes.

No.

I don't know.

And not knowing is the scariest part of all.

After all this time, I think I expected to see him again and for the attraction to have lessened but that's not what happened at all. If anything, the pull is only stronger and that *terrifies* me. I can't allow myself to be broken by him again.

Once was enough and the only reason I survived was because I was growing our child.

For her, I was stronger.

For her, I didn't give up.

Inhaling a deep breath, I shove all thoughts of Thayer out of my brain and focus on the task at hand—calling my sister and Caleb.

I'm not on the phone long with either and pick up the flowers again, carrying them inside with me.

"Everything's a go." I set the flowers on the cabinet, searching for a vase in the cabinet above the stove. "We'll head out in about an hour."

"Where are the flowers from?" Her tone is suspicious.

"No idea," I reply, sounding equally as mystified.

"Was there a card?" I conveniently slide the note away, planning to read it later.

"Nope. It must be from your secret admirer."

She rolls her eyes. "Ah, yes, I get a lot of those. That makes total sense."

"Smartass," I snicker, filling the vase with water.

She laughs. "Don't sass me."

"Can't help it." I unwrap the flowers gently, putting them in the water one at a time.

"Those are your favorite flower," she remarks. "How interesting."

"I know. What are the odds?"

She shakes her head, fighting a smile. I narrow my eyes on her, but she's not looking my way. I can't help but wonder if she knows something about Thayer. I don't see how, but—

"You better get my stuff packed up if we're going to leave in an hour."

I set the vase in the center of the table. "When did you get so bossy, Mom?"

She grins at me, her lashes non-existent. "When you're dying, you don't have the time to be any other way."

I swallow past the sudden lump in my throat. Clearing it, I say, "Right. I'll pack your bag and we'll head out."

383

"Salem?" She calls after me before I can leave the kitchen.

"Yeah?" I pause, turning to look back at her.

"I know..." She wets her dry lips with a swipe of her tongue. "I know I didn't let myself love again, after your dad, but promise me you won't close your heart off forever? If there's anything we all deserve in this world it's to love and be loved."

My mouth twitches as I hold back tears. "I promise."

I'm not sure how easy of a promise it'll be to keep, but I'll try, if only for her sake.

FOURTEEN

Salem

We pull up outside the brownstone, the car barely in park when the door opens. I expect it to be Seda, but instead it's Caleb. He walks down the steps, through the front gate, heading straight for my mom's door on the passenger side.

"Allie," he says, smiling at her. "It's so good to see you."

She pats his cheek. "It's always nice to see you too."

"Do you need some help?"

"I'll never turn down help from such a fine gentleman," she jokes.

He chuckles, helping her with the seatbelt and out onto the street. Since he has her under his care, I hop out and grab her bag. I didn't bother packing a bag for myself since I have everything I need here.

Caleb helps her inside with me following behind.

385

"Where's Seda?" I ask.

He chuckles, looking back at me over his shoulder. "Believe it or not, passed out napping. She went to the trampoline park with Maddy," he mentions one of her good friends, "and came back exhausted."

"Sweet girl," my mom croons. "I can't wait to see her."

Caleb looks back at me, worry in his eyes. Worry for me and worry for her. He knows that losing my mom is going to be hard on me. It doesn't matter how far you know in advance, losing a parent isn't easy. She's been my rock and my sounding board. She's gotten me through some of the hardest times of my life. And now when I wish I could repay the favor more than anything, I can't, because nothing can overcome death.

Caleb settles her on the couch in the family room.

"Can I get you anything to drink?" He asks her.

"Maybe just some water."

He smiles and passes her a blanket. "Make yourself comfortable and I'll be back with your water."

Caleb leaves and I help her lay down. Wrapping the blanket around her, I prop her legs up with a pillow beneath. "Are you tired?"

"A little," she admits reluctantly.

"Just rest." I kiss her forehead and back away.

In the kitchen, I lean my hip against the counter watching Caleb fill up the cup with ice and then water.

"How's she doing? For real—no sugarcoating things."

I sigh, running my fingers through my hair. "She has good days and bad days. I feel so helpless, Caleb. It's like watching the sand in an hourglass and I know at some point the sand is going to run out. And when it happens, I'm going to lose my mom. And I just," I pause, catching my breath. Feeling the tears burn my eyes. "I don't know how to live life without her."

"Come here." He flicks his fingers, pulling me into the safe embrace of his arms.

I lay my head on his chest, his fingers gently combing through my hair. I can't stop it when the tears come, soaking into the cotton of his t-shirt.

"It's okay," he croons, continuing with the gentle strokes of his fingers through my hair. "Just cry. I've got you." And I know he does. He always has. Caleb is my rock, my safe place. "You're strong," he reminds me, "but even strong people need to cry now and then." His arms are tight against me, holding me together.

"Why are you so good to me?" I only cry harder at the question. Caleb should hate me. He should be pushing me away instead of pulling me into his arms. But he's so good. He's not the kind of person that will shove you away just because you broke his heart. I know that there's someone out there for him. It's not that I'm bad for him, but I'm not good enough for him. And that thought makes me cry a little harder. I'm not deserving of him. Even though I might have asked for the divorce. Even though I'm the one walking away from him. I still love him and a part of me always will.

"Because," his voice rumbles against my ear where the side of my head is pressed firmly to his chest, "you're a better person than you think you are."

"Caleb—" I pull away from his chest slightly, angling my head back to look up at him.

He playfully covers my mouth. "Don't say whatever it is you're about to say."

When he lets his hand drop, I ask, "Why don't you hate me?"

He cocks his head to the side, eyes narrowed. "Why do you hate yourself?"

His question is like a bullet to the heart, one I've never stopped to contemplate.

"I—"

Lowering his head, he whispers, "I forgive you, Salem. It's *you* who has to forgive yourself."

Picking up the glass of water, he retreats from the kitchen. I cover my face with my hands, knowing he's right.

There are so many things I haven't forgiven myself for. I drag those things along behind me everywhere I go like deadweight I can't seem to shake. Because of his question, I realize I'm the only one holding those things over my head. Not him, he never did, and if Caleb can forgive me, surely, I can find a way to forgive myself.

Taking a deep breath, I steady myself and brace my shoulders.

My mom settles into the guest bed, her eyes heavy from exhaustion.

After she woke up from her nap, and Seda too, she played with her granddaughter until dinner time. Caleb ended up picking up food from one of our favorite restaurants since neither of us felt like cooking. I wasn't surprised when my mom picked at her food, hardly any of it making it into her mouth. Her body is giving up on her—frankly, I think it gave up on her a long time ago, and it's been her sheer tenacity and will to live that has kept her going.

"This was nice," she yawns, her eyelids growing heavy. "Thank you for bringing me. I love that little girl so much."

I brush my hand over her forehead like I'm comforting a child. "She loves you too."

"You're a great mom. I didn't do a lot of things right in my life—".

"Mom—"

"Let me finish." Her breath is rough, her hand shaky when she reaches up to touch my cheek. "But you girls ... you turned out amazing, despite my mistakes."

I close my eyes, feeling tears leak through my lashes.

"I'm sorry," she whispers, her fingers feather light on my cheek.

Clearing my throat, I say, "I am too." Lowering her hand, she yawns. "Go to sleep, Mom. I love you." I kiss her forehead just like I do Seda's when I tuck her into bed, flicking the light off beside the bed.

Easing the door shut behind me, I creep down the stairs and fix up the couch to sleep on. We only have the one guestroom, and I wasn't about to make my mom sleep on the couch all night. The nap was bad enough.

I brush my teeth in the bathroom downstairs and change into my pajamas. Padding into kitchen I'm surprised to find Caleb there, sitting at the kitchen table with a bowl of fruit.

"I thought you went to bed."

He shakes his head, picking up a piece of watermelon. "Nah, I have a lot on my mind."

"Work?" I probe, opening the fridge to swipe a can of Diet Coke.

He nods. "This case is taking a lot out of me."

"I'm sorry." He's not allowed to talk about cases with me or else I'd ask him if he wants to talk about it. Instead, I say, "Do you want me to stay up with you?"

He shakes his head. His blond hair is cut shorter on the side, slightly longer on top. He normally keeps it neatly slicked back but since he's fresh out of the shower it's damp and wavier than normal. "I'm okay. Get some rest. I'm sure you need it."

"Thank you for letting my mom come visit."

He rolls his eyes, looking genuinely pissed. "I'm not going to tell your mom she can't visit—besides, this place is still half yours, too."

"Caleb—"

"Look," he stands up from the table, putting the Tupperware lid back on the container, "I know you're way more eager to be done with me than I am you—but you don't have to remind me all the time, okay?" There's genuine hurt in his voice that stings my heart like an open wound.

"That's not what I meant." I shake my head, hair falling forward to shield my face. "You're just … you're so good, Caleb. You're not the bad guy. I know that, and that makes this so much worse, because I am, and I never want you to think I'm taking advantage of your kindness."

He sighs, swiping a bottle of water from the fridge. "Did you ever stop to think that you're not the villain either? Sometimes relationships aren't built to last and there is no bad guy. It's just two people who weren't meant to be."

"No." I shake my head. "I didn't."

"I don't blame you for the divorce, Salem. I know you love me even now, but sometimes that's not enough and I get it. Am I hurt? Yeah, of course I am. I pictured it all with you—a house, cars, pets, kids," he waves his hand around at the house over our heads, "but this isn't the end of those things for me. I still have that little girl upstairs asleep in her princess room." He smiles, probably thinking about the day we spent together turning it into her dream space. "And one day, when the timing is right, I'll meet someone else." He shrugs, twisting the cap on the water bottle back and forth. "Life goes on. I'm not broken."

"I just want you to be happy."

"I know. And I want the same for you—but you can't put my happiness on a timeline just so you feel better."

His words smack me across the face. I didn't realize that was what I was doing, but he's completely right.

He slips from the kitchen, and I listen to the soft sound of his feet on the stairs before I go to the family room and lay down on the couch.

Sleep never comes.

FIFTEEN

Salem

When I pull into my mom's driveway, Thayer is in his unloading groceries. He raises his hand, shielding his eyes from the sun. Putting my SUV in park, I silently curse when I see Thayer in my rearview mirror. He walks up to my side and taps the window. Putting the window down, I can't help my sarcasm when I blurt, "Solicitors aren't welcome here."

It's obvious he wasn't expecting that. His lips twitch, trying not to laugh, but he finally gives in. Putting his hands up in front of his chest, "No soliciting here. I wanted to see if you needed some help."

My mom leans around my body. "How sweet. We'd love some."

I have to bite my tongue to not growl out, *"Mom."*

391

Thayer crosses his arms, leaning into my car. He's *right there*. I can smell his familiar scent. It reminds me of the outdoors, woodsy and rugged. All man. He smiles at me. He knows what he's doing, pushing himself into my space and he's going to keep doing it. Our roles are entirely reversed from six years ago and I'm not sure I like it. I must've been so annoying. He should've told me to take a hike.

"Why don't you give me the keys and I'll get the door unlocked for you?"

"Huh." I blink, stunned.

"The keys." He grins slowly. "To the house."

My mom reaches over, turning off the ignition. She holds the keys out to him. "Thank you, Thayer. That's so thoughtful of you."

He takes the keys, retreating from the inside of my car and taking his intoxicating scent with him.

It's really unfair that it has been this long, and he still has a way of making me drunk off his presence. He could bottle that power up and sell it like a lethal weapon. It might only work against womankind, but let's be real the men are useless without us.

While Thayer unlocks the door, I get out of the car, taking a deep breath to help clear my head. It gets unreasonably foggy around him.

I make my way around the car to get my mom, but he's already getting her door and offering his hand.

It shouldn't make me mad that he's helping.

But it does.

He broke me—shattered my heart, and now he's acting like the past didn't happen.

Since he's helping her inside, I grab her bag and follow them, all the while keeping my grumbling to myself.

He helps her into one of the kitchen chairs, saying something to her I can't hear as he does.

I'm annoyed—that he's here. That he's helping. That he's in my space. And most importantly that he still makes me feel things. This is why I was scared to come back here. I worried my feelings for him were still just as strong. Turns out, I was right to be afraid.

Yanking open the refrigerator more forceful than necessary, I swipe a Diet Coke and turn around, popping the top on the can. Thayer's eyes flicker from the can to my eyes.

"Water's better for you."

"I've been told a time or two."

"You really should drink more water, Salem." Now my mom's joining in on the let's slander Salem for her love of soda.

"Right now, this what I want. I could have worse vices, you know? I could be a homicidal maniac."

Thayer's chuckle is amused. "I thought most people used the drug addict analogy."

"I'm not most people."

He ducks his head, unable to hide his growing smile. "No, you're certainly not."

"I'm feeling really tired," my mom announces. I quickly set my drink down and rush to her side, but I can't get to her with Thayer's big body blocking me. "Do you want to lay down?" I ask from behind Thayer, trying to peer over his big shoulders but it's impossible unless I stand on my tiptoes and use his arm for support and I'm *not* touching him.

"That might be a good idea."

"I've got her." Thayer dismisses me, helping my mother up. She moves on her own two feet holding onto his side, but I know he'll scoop her up in a second if she shows signs of needing it.

She settles in the hospital bed, her eyes heavy. "Why don't you two go do something? I'm going to be napping anyway."

"Why would we—" I start, but Thayer swoops in and cuts me off.

"That sounds like a great idea, Allie. You sleep and we'll be back soon. Call us if you need anything."

Steam practically shoots out of my ears.

"You can't just—" He puts a hand on my lower waist, guiding me away from my mom back to the kitchen. "I'm not going anywhere with you," I snap.

"Why not?" He argues back, a stupid little smirk on his lips. I hate more than anything that this *amuses* him. "We still have plenty to talk about."

I square my shoulders. "I know that, but I don't want to talk about it right now."

"I have a feeling you won't want to talk about it ever. Why don't we just go for a drive?"

393

"My mom—"

"Get out of here and leave me alone! I need my beauty sleep!" she yells in a croaky voice, overhearing us.

I glower at the man who towers above me. "Fine," I bite out. "Lead the way."

He saunters out first, and I almost slam the door shut and lock it behind him.

Almost.

The only thing that stops me is my mom's demand for us to leave. I know her time is limited, but I can't imagine how I'd feel in her position with people always hovering. She should be allowed to have *some* time to herself. Even if it'll worry me sick.

"I want to be back here in thirty minutes." I point a finger forcefully at the driveway to drive home my point.

"All right." He walks backwards, hands in the pockets of his cargo shorts. "Then walk faster. We have twenty-nine minutes and—" he looks at the watch on his wrist "—forty-eight seconds left."

I don't think I've ever met anyone more infuriating.

"Were you always this annoying and I was too dumb to see it?"

A flash of pain pierces his face, but he quickly schools his expression back into place. I can't help but feel bad for letting that comment slip. I find it particularly difficult to bite my tongue around him.

He unlocks his truck, the scent of brand-new leather hitting my nose. He lets me climb inside but doesn't shut the door right away. "Do you hate me, Salem?" He's not asking it in a joking way. He's serious, and worried to.

I duck my head, my blonde hair falling forward to shield my face. "No," I admit softly. "I could never hate you, Thayer."

He was my first *true* love—maybe my only one.

He's the father of my child.

I don't have it in me to hate him.

But that doesn't mean any of this is easy.

"Good. That means there's a chance." His eyes are relieved. He closes the door and moves around the front of his truck.

I let his one comment go, not wanting to touch that. "Where are we going?"

He cranks the engine, turning the AC all the way up.

"Like I said, for a drive."

"All right." I look out the window at my mom's house. The hydrangea bushes in the front are lush and full. I can't help but wonder if the man at my side has anything to do with that. But I won't dare ask.

We drive away and it isn't long until we're out of the town limits, cruising the roads.

"I thought you wanted to talk," I prompt stupidly.

A tiny grin graces his lips. "And I thought you didn't."

"I'm locked in a car with you, I might as well speak."

He rubs at his jaw. "Tell me something, anything about the past six years."

It's on the tip of my tongue to ask him why he cares, but I bite back the words. I'm being defensive and it's stupid. I'm a grown woman now and I swore to myself I'd leave the past in the past, so I need to do a better job of actually practicing that. It's just that seeing him, being around him, leaves me feeling conflicted. I hate being thrown off balance.

"Well," I clear my throat, "there's not a whole lot to tell."

You know, except for the kid bomb I need to drop on you at some point.

I don't want to keep Seda a secret from him. That was *never* the plan. I've imagined a million different ways of telling him and none of them seem right. I don't think there is a right way to tell him. I just have to do it.

"Give me something. Anything." He sounds almost desperate to know about my life without him.

"I lived with Lauren in Brooklyn for a while, got a job waitressing. Came back to Boston and lived in an apartment with Caleb when we got engaged. We ended up moving to California for him to finish school and start practicing law. Then he got a job offer back in Boston that was too good to pass up. That's about it." I shrug, my eyes glued out the window, ignoring his gaze on me.

"Did you ever go to college?"

"No."

"What about jobs?"

I was a stay-at-home mom.

"Just some random things from time to time. Nothing really stuck."

"You just ... huh." He scratches his jaw, contemplating.

"You really thought you were holding me back?"

"I guess even after your passioned speech, it made me feel better to think I'd cut you loose so you could do something with your life."

A flash of anger erupts in my veins. "Just because I didn't go to college or have a steady job doesn't mean I haven't done anything with my life."

"Sorry," he sounds sincere, "I didn't mean for it to sound like that."

I sigh. "No, I'm sorry. I seem to be a tad defensive when it comes to you."

He smiles over at me, his fingers flexing against the steering wheel. "A tad?"

"Okay, a lot. I'll work on it."

"I like your anger."

I look at him like he's lost his ever-loving mind. "You like my anger?" I volley. "Are you insane?"

His eyes meet mine for a brief moment before they're back on the road. "If you're angry at me, it means you still care."

He has a point there. I look down at my legs, bare since I wore a pair of high-waisted shorts. "I don't want to be angry at you," I admit in a whisper.

"Then why are you?" I notice the way the muscle in his jaw twitches, waiting for my response.

"Because it's easier than admitting the truth."

The God-awful disgusting truth.

"And what's the truth?"

"Don't make me say it," I beg with a shake of my head. I don't want to say it out loud. That makes it all the more real and makes me an even shittier person than I already am.

"I think I need to hear you say it."

I bite my lip, holding back tears. My voice is barely above a whisper when I say, "I never stopped caring about you. I moved on, but my heart didn't."

He pulls the truck abruptly off to the side of the road. Gravel and dirt kick up behind us as he slams the vehicle into park. He turns slowly in his seat to look at me.

"Thayer—" I start to question, but he doesn't give me a chance to finish my thought. He cups my cheek in one hand, his mouth descending on mine in less than a heartbeat.

There's a second there where my brain wants to fight back.

He hurt you! It cries out, wanting me to push him away, but I can't. My body doesn't get the memo. It sinks into him, sighing in relief at the feel of his mouth on mine. I think I'd convinced myself that our connection wasn't as strong as I believed, but it was—it *is*. There are all kinds of different loves in the world, but the kind I share with Thayer can't be broken by time, or distance, or anything else. We could be on separate continents, and it would still exist in this form.

His name is a whisper on my lips when he deepens the kiss.

A part of my brain is convinced this is a dream.

There's no way this can be real.

But then I take inventory—the scratch of his scruff against my face, the fabric of his shirt scrunched in my hands, the rough feel of his hands on my face—and I know that this is very real.

He pulls away, just slightly, our breaths still mingling together. "You come back here, to this town, and it's like you never even left."

I close my eyes, exhaling shakily. "But I did."

His tongue slips out, moistening his lips. "But you did," he echoes. I wait for him to pull away, to put a pin in this. I didn't come back here thinking we'd have a second chance. Instead, he shocks me when he says, "Date me."

"What?" I stutter, convinced I couldn't have possibly heard him right.

"Date me," he repeats, scanning my face. "We ... *I*," he corrects, "never did things right with you before. Let me change that. Go on a date with me."

My eyes narrow stubbornly. "Are you asking me or telling me?"

He grins, shaking his head. I stupidly love the way his hair falls over his forehead. I itch to brush it back, but clasp my hands together instead.

"Will you go on a date with me, Salem? A real date?"

I hesitate, my heart skipping a beat. But there's only one answer I can give Thayer.

"Yes."

SIXTEEN

Thayer

Salem climbs out of my truck with a quiet goodbye, walking back over to her mom's house. My phone is still lit up with her contact information where I put in her new number.

I can still taste her mouth on mine. Smiling, I rub my fingers over my lips.

I'm not sure what overcame me when I pulled my truck off the road and kissed her, but I don't regret it. I've been starved for the taste of her for too long.

And she said yes to dating me.

That gives me hope—that even through her hurt, she might find her way back to me. As for what kind of date I want to take her on, I have no idea. I don't want to just take her to a restaurant—there's nothing wrong with that, but I want to put more effort into it, show her that I'm thinking of her and want to do something special.

Locking my truck behind me, I get out and head inside to get Winnie out of her crate in the laundry room. My good girl yawns and stretches before showering me in kisses. I let her out into the back-yard to go pee. As soon as she does, she scurries back in, grabs her treat from me, and dives into her cushion.

Shaking my head, I open the fridge and grab a bottle of water, guzzling it down.

It's obvious Salem still has feelings for me, even if those feelings might only be attraction. I'm hoping with her giving me this chance to take her out on a date, do things right this time around, there's a chance for us.

Passing by Winnie, I give her head a scratch and swipe up the remote. Turning the TV on, I flip through the channels, settling on the sports channel. It's a golf tournament—not really my thing, but I'm not planning on paying too much attention anyway.

Pulling out the chair at my puzzle table, I sit down and pick up a piece.

I'm not sure what it is that first drew me to puzzles. I liked to do them even as a kid. It's a dorky hobby, but who gives a fuck. I only do shit I enjoy.

Winnie waddles into the living room with a bone in her mouth, plopping at my feet.

Despite the sound of the TV in the background, it's eerily quiet in the house. It's something I haven't been able to get over in the last six years. I might not have had Forrest all the time after the divorce, but the quiet was different when he was alive.

I miss his endless chatter, the million and one questions he would ask me, the sound of his feet running through the house.

Sometimes it feels like I've been stabbed between the ribs, the pain feels so real, knowing I won't hear or see him ever again. He's forever stuck in my memory as that little seven-year-old boy. He'd be thirteen now, at the start of his teenage years. I'm never going to help him learn to drive a car, or watch him graduate, or see what he decides to do with his life beyond that.

It feels like some cruel cosmic joke.

The worst is when I dream about him and wake up and have to realize all over again that he's gone.

After he passed, Krista begged and begged for us to have another child. She didn't even care if we got back together. She just wanted another baby. She thought that would make things better for her, but I knew it wouldn't and rebuked all her advances. She's not who I wanted, and I didn't want to bring a child into this world with someone I no longer loved.

Last I heard, she's married again, but I have no idea beyond that and don't care. Our lives are separate now.

For too long, it's only been me.

Well, me and Winnie—can't forget her.

I think of Salem, next door, close but so far away.

I told her I wanted to date her and I meant it. I knew all those years ago she was the woman for me—now I have to prove that I'm the man for her.

SEVENTEEN

Salem

Georgia stops by to spend some time with our mom, so I use the reprieve to my advantage and go for a run. It's later in the day than I normally go, and the heat is killer, but I know it'll do me good to get a workout in.

I don't really know or understand where I'm going until my legs carry me to the cemetery. I search out his grave and stop in front of it with a wildflower clasped in my hand that I plucked along my way just because I thought it was pretty. Maybe my subconscious knew I'd end up here before I did.

I lay the flower across his name and sink to my knees.

Tracing my fingers over his name, I cry, my tears splashing on the clean marble marker. Someone takes care of his grave, it's more well-kept than the others around him and I wonder if it's Krista or Thayer who does it.

"You would be thirteen now." My chest shakes as I cry. "A teenager. A little man." I tilt my head back toward the sky.

I've thought of Forrest every day since he passed. I see him in his sister. In her smile and laugh, in her zany personality, and her love for dinosaurs. Forrest is gone, but there are still pieces of him earth side.

It's not fair that such a young life was cut short.

He deserved more.

Accidents happen, it's true, but it doesn't make it any easier to deal with.

Death is just so fucking final and no matter how hard we try; we don't really know what waits for us beyond.

When I signed Seda up for swim lessons I learned exactly how common water accidents are and how silent drowning is. It's *terrifying*. And yet every time I've taken Seda to a public pool or we went to the beach, I see parents glued to their phones, oblivious to the horror that could so easily snatch their beloved child from them. Ignorance isn't always bliss. Sometimes ignorance is dangerous.

"You have a sister," I tell him, wiping my damp cheeks. "I think you'd love her so much. Even though you're older than her, I know you'd be kind to her, let her tagalong with you. I named her after you, you know? Seda," I whisper her name into existence, tracing my finger over his again. "It means spirit of the forest." I hang my head.

Forrest's death was hard enough to cope with before I found out I was pregnant. And once I held my baby in my arms, I couldn't imagine the pain of laying a child to rest forever.

"You're a good kid, Forrest. The best." I know I'm talking like he's still here, but it's easier to pretend that he is when I'm talking to him like this. "I miss you." I press my fingers to my lips, kissing them before I press them to the stone.

Standing back up, I dust grass off my shorts.

I don't much feel like running back now, so I decide to walk instead.

Making a pitstop into the coffee shop, nearly colliding with someone when the door opens at the same time I reach for it.

"Oh, I'm so sorry!" The woman carefully balances her iced drink. "Hi," she smiles, "it's you again. Salem, right?"

"It's nice to see you, Jen."

The apothecary store owner beams. There's an airy warmness to her that can't help but draw you in. "I hope you're enjoying the salts and everything."

"Very much. I need to stop back in."

"Come in any time." She starts to walk away, saying over her shoulder, "I hope you have a good day."

"You, too."

Inside the coffee shop, I place my order and grab a table while I wait. The place looks exactly the same as when I lived here before. I don't think they've changed a thing, not even the art on the walls. It feels like no time at all has passed since I left town and yet so much has changed in other ways.

When my name is called, I grab my iced coffee and head back onto the street, circling back to the house.

It's been a few days since Thayer asked me on a date and I haven't heard from him at all, despite the fact I gave him my new number. It makes me nervous that he's changed his mind, not to mention I'm still trying to figure out the best way to drop the kid bomb on him. I'm not sure there *is* a best way, and I don't know that he'll understand my reasoning for not telling him or if he'll believe me that I tried.

Letting myself in the side door, I walk in to find my sister crying.

"Georgia?" I set down my coffee, going to her side where she paces by the counter. "What's wrong?"

"I'm sorry." She fans her face, emotional and trying to contain it. "She's sleeping," she adds in a whisper. "I just..." Her hands go to her round belly. "I got to thinking about how she might not live long enough to meet the baby and how this baby won't know her and I just ... it's not fair and I'm angry."

I pull my older sister into my arms, letting her cry and get this off her chest. I can't imagine dealing with the emotions of this on top of being pregnant.

"Cry as long as you need." I hold her even tighter.

"How are you keeping it together so well?"

"Trust me, I'm not. I have my moments too."

"Life's so unfair and she's been failed so many times." She pulls away from me, grabbing a paper towel to dab at her eyes. "Ugh," she groans, motioning to her smeared mascara. "I'm a mess." Sniffling, she leans against the counter for support. "I just don't know how to live life without her. She's our mom. What am I going to do when I can't pick up the phone and call her? Ask her for advice or what ingredient I'm forgetting in the cupcakes I'm making?"

I hold her arms gently in my hands, making sure to look her in the eyes. "You'll feel sad. You might cry a little bit. And then you'll call me, and we can cry together. And I'll always tell you what ingredient you're missing."

She says no more, just yanks me back into a hug, the swell of her belly in our way. "Please, move back here. I don't want you to leave again."

Rubbing my hand against her back, I bite my lip. "I'm thinking about it."

"What?" She jerks back in surprise. "Are you serious?"

I nod. "Now that I've been back here ... I feel different about staying. But nothing is decided," I warn her, not wanting to get her hopes up.

"Well," she smiles despite the tears still lingering in her eyes, "you have to do whatever feels right, but I hope you stay."

EIGHTEEN

Thayer

Parking my truck, I grab my thermos of hot chocolate, my lunch cooler, and head into the cemetery. It's too hot out to enjoy the hot chocolate, but it's sort of become my tradition when I come here.

I navigate my way through the gravestones. I'm pretty sure I could get to my son's grave blindfolded by this point. I come by once a week, sometimes more if I find myself really needing to talk to him.

I used to think that people who came to cemeteries to speak with their loved ones were crazy. It's all just a bunch of grass and stone—it's a place where Forrest was never alive—but I still like coming here. It's peaceful and I feel closer to him.

My eyes narrow when I approach his marker. There's a single

purple flower laid above his name. Cocking my head to the side, I look around in search for whoever left it. Not that it's much mystery. Krista doesn't find the same comfort here that I do, so she doesn't visit. Which means Salem most likely left this. Recently too since the wind hasn't blown it away.

I don't know what makes me do it, but I pluck the flower off and put it in my lunch box. The urge to keep it is stupid, but I can't help it. It's tangible proof of her heart, of how even after all this time she still cares about my son, and maybe me too.

She wouldn't have kissed you back like that if she didn't still have feelings for you.

Getting comfortable on the grass, I unwrap my sloppily made peanut butter and jelly.

"How are you doing, kid?" I chomp into my sandwich. "I wish I could hear your voice—that you could tell me what it's like wherever you are. I want to know you're okay and taken care of. That's one of the hardest parts, you know?" I wipe my mouth with the back of my hand. "When you're a parent you just want to know your kid is being treated right and safe, but I have no way of knowing that now with you." Grabbing my thermos, I pour a little into the lid. "Here you go, kid. Enjoy." I tip the canteen back and take my own sip.

"I've played that day over and over in my head so many times, trying to figure out every little thing I could've changed that would've resulted in a different outcome, but I still don't know if it would've made any difference. Even if you weren't mad at me, you might still have ended up in that pool." Sighing, I take a deep breath. "I don't know what's worse—thinking I could've changed something and you'd still be alive, or thinking this was some cruel twist of fate and I couldn't do anything about it anyway."

I'm rambling now, it's usually what happens to me when I'm here. I word vomit my thoughts at him and Forrest, of course, says nothing.

"I miss you. So much. You are the best seven years of my thirty-seven years of existence on this planet. You made me a dad. I thought for a while that I stopped being one when you died, but I realize now you don't stop being a parent just because your child is gone. No matter what, I'll always be your dad, Forrest, and when I meet you on the other side I can't wait to feel your arms around me again."

While I finish my lunch, I fill him in on mundane things in my life—like what's going on at work, the latest movie I watched that reminded me of him—all of the silly day to day things he misses out on.

I have to get back to work, so I pack my trash away, and place my hand over his name.

"I love you, kid."

Standing up, I brush the dirt and grass from my shorts.

I have to get back to work, because no matter what, life keeps going.

NINETEEN

Salem

The next night after helping my mom bathe—she sits on a shower chair and I take care of the rest—and into bed, I slip out the side door for some fresh air, discovering another bouquet of peonies.

I pick them up, inspecting the petals. Each one is so delicate and perfect.

There's no note this time. When I finally read the one he included before, it said;

For my sunshine.

—T

Setting them back down, I walk to the end of the driveway and peek at Thayer's house. The sun is beginning to set and I see him sitting on the front porch swing that I helped him put up a lifetime ago.

Hesitating for a moment or two, I finally make my way up his front walk onto the porch.

He saw me approaching and his eyes study me as I stand in front of him. He pushes his feet, the swing swaying lightly.

"Hi," I say softly, hesitant to approach.

The tiniest of smiles dances across his lips. "Hi. Do you want to join me?"

I nod and he scoots over so there's enough room on his left side for me to sit with him.

The blue and white stripped cushion is soft beneath my butt. I have to fight my body's natural desire to want to curl into him. It's like my body has forgotten all the time that has passed and that he's not mine to touch freely anymore.

He arches a brow, noticing the way I incline away from him. "I'm not contagious. You can touch me."

I ignore his comment. "You don't have to bring me flowers. But thank you. They're beautiful."

"I'm glad you like them. They're all for you anyway."

My brows narrow in confusion, not quite sure what he means by that comment. If he got me flowers and left them, then of course they are for me, but I feel like there's a deeper meaning I'm not catching onto.

"I have to ask you something."

"Okay?" He sounds unsure.

"Why didn't you call me?"

A heavy sigh rattles his chest. He looks away from me, at the setting sun that paints the sky in a watercolor of pinks, purples, and oranges.

"For a while, I convinced myself that I'd accomplished what I wanted. I pushed you away to live a life without me and it would be weak to break the promise I made to myself to give you a chance to grow on your own." He rubs his jaw, looking pained. "By the time I realized what an idiot I'd been, it was too late."

My voice is barely above a whisper when I prompt, "What do you mean?"

"Your mom had been gone a few days, so when she came back, I asked her if everything was okay." He pauses, rubbing his brow like it still pains him to remember this. He continues to look away from me, like it's too much to meet my eyes. "She said she had been gone for a wedding. I don't know what made me ask whose wedding, but I did, and she said it was yours." His voice grows weak with emotion. "I had just made the decision to find you—I tried calling and texting, but I think you'd changed your number at that point. I was too late." He finally looks at me, and I see years of pain, regret, and even love in his brown eyes. "It's what I deserved."

"How did we let everything get so messed up?"

He runs his fingers through his hair, blowing out a breath. "Hubris gets all of us at some point. I tried to convince you, and myself, that you were better off without me and hurt both of us in the end." He stares down at his hands, flexing his fingers. "I knew you were it for me, though, that I'd never love another person the way I love you. So, it's just been me, here," he waves a hand at his house, "alone. I decided that was my punishment—to have tasted something real and to be denied it for the rest of my existence because I pushed it away."

I stay fixated on the fact that he used love in the present tense. "Do you still love me then?"

"I don't want to scare you."

Shaking my head back and forth rapidly, I plead, "I just want you to be honest."

We've both spent too much time not saying what we really mean and I'm tired of it. So much can be wasted by keeping things to yourself.

"I never stopped loving you, Salem. Not once. Not for a minute, not even for a second."

Tears burn my eyes. I moved on thinking he truly didn't want anything to do with me and all this time...

"Why are we like this?" I ask the heavens more than him.

"Not everything is clear cut in life, Salem. Sometimes things blur and we fuck things up. We're all human."

"I still loved you, but I married someone else. I thought you were over me and that I had to move on, so I did—and this whole time ...

411

this whole fucking time." I stand up, facing him. "Do you not see how fucked up this whole thing is?"

"Believe me, I know."

I cover my face with my hands. "We're quite the pair," I mutter.

"You had every right to move on," he says softly, carefully. "I didn't leave you with any hope that we'd get back together. I know you loved Caleb ... it makes sense that you went back to him."

"He deserved better."

I loved Caleb, still love him in a certain way, but that doesn't change the facts. He wasn't Thayer, he never could be, some loves are only once in a lifetime. I know he made his choices, just like I did, but it doesn't mean I don't regret feeling like I dragged him along. I never meant to, but I'm not sure that makes it any better.

"Sit down," he pleads, pointing to the spot beside him I got up from. "You're getting worked up."

"Of course, I am!" I throw my hands in the air. "I'm a shitty person. I ruined his life."

"It doesn't make you a shitty person to move on with your life. I know you, Salem, and you wouldn't have married him if you didn't have genuine feelings for the guy so stop punishing yourself. I loved Krista and even though we didn't make it, I don't think for a minute I ruined her life, or she did mine. We weren't meant to last but that doesn't mean there wasn't something valuable in what we had. Stop punishing yourself."

Stop punishing yourself.

His words strike deep, like they were meant to, and he's right—my time with Caleb might not have been meant to last forever, but that doesn't mean it was cheap. I did love him, we had a good life together.

"I've hated myself so much," I finally admit out loud.

He reaches for my hand and takes it, tugging me forward. "You have to stop."

"I don't know how."

"It's not always easy to forgive yourself—there is no step-by-step process. Just remember no one is perfect." He lightly touches my cheek with his other hand. "At the end of the day, we're all human, and not a single one of us is better than another."

I know he's right, but it's easier said than done.

"Sit down," he says again, softer this time. "Life's too short to constantly be stuck on the past or obsessing over what ifs. We have this." He waves to the world around us. "We have now."

I know he's right, but that doesn't make it any easier.

Settling beside him, I rest my head on his shoulder and we watch the last of the sun disappear together.

TWENTY

Salem

S taring at the text from Thayer, something sinks in my stomach.

"Is something wrong?" My mom notices my expression change from normal to worried.

"Oh, yeah, I'm okay. Nothing's wrong." I put my phone back in my pocket and return to folding laundry.

"You can't bullshit your mother, Salem. Out with it."

Those mom senses really are too good sometimes. "It's nothing, really."

"I'll pry it out of you eventually." She coughs, her throat dry. "You might as well tell me."

I know she isn't going to let it go. "I got asked out on a date. He just texted a day and time to see if it was okay."

"So, why did you look so ill? Is he not a good guy?"

"It's not that." I add a shirt to my stack.

"Then what is it? You're not giving me a lot to go on here. I'm dying, time is of the essence."

I pick up a pair of cutoff shorts. "I wish you'd stop saying that."

"Why? It's true. Tell me about this guy, please. I need the distraction."

I've decided maybe her constant need to remind me that she's dying is her own coping mechanism. It doesn't make much sense to me, but I guess whatever makes her feel better.

Lowering my head, I whisper, "It's Thayer."

"Thayer? Next door Thayer?"

Shockingly, she doesn't sound that surprised. More excited than anything else.

"The one and only," I reply, moving the shorts to the growing pile.

"He's a good man, but what's the problem?"

I look up at the ceiling, fighting the burn of tears in my eyes. "It's too soon," I say, which is partially true.

The other reality is, that there's a stone sinking in my gut because I can't, not in good conscience, go on a date with Thayer before I tell him about Seda. I'm tired of this hanging over me, I have to put the truth out there, but I don't know how.

I don't say any of that to my mom, though. She doesn't know about my past with Thayer, and I'm not ready to divulge that. I'm aware I might never get the chance to tell her, but again, there's no way I can tell her the truth before I tell Thayer.

"It's never too soon to open your heart to love again. I made that mistake, thinking I couldn't, now look at me." She shrugs her bony shoulders. "I'm going to die, never know true love, never knowing a *good* man. I had you girls, and my store, and other dreams realized, but sometimes I do wish I'd allowed myself to open my heart to someone."

"I'll think about it." My phone sits like a heavy weight in my pocket.

I know I technically already agreed to this date, but now that he's put a day and time on it, it's so much more real.

But I have to tell him.

I just don't know how.

RAIN POUNDS AGAINST MY BEDROOM WINDOWS, TREES blowing relentlessly. I wish I could say it's the summer storm keeping me awake, but it's not. My thoughts keep going around and around. There's no silencing my mind.

Throwing the covers back, I toss a jacket on and shove my feet into an old pair of flip-flops. Slipping down the stairs and quietly past my mom, I let myself out the door. As soon as I step from beneath the cover of the porch, I'm pelted with rain. By the time I make it next door I'm drenched.

Are you really going to do this?

Yes.

I pound my fist against the door. I don't stop either. I just keep knocking and knocking until it swings open, revealing the man on the other side.

My eyes eat him up and I allow myself this moment because after I say what I have to, he might hate me. I wouldn't blame him for it either.

He stands before me with sleep tousled hair, his chest on display for my eager gaze. There's that smattering of chest hair I loved so much that grows thicker beneath his navel, disappearing into his sweatpants that it looks like he haphazardly pulled on. He takes me in as well, looking confused. I'm sure I'd be equally confused if he showed up at my door looking like a drowned rat.

"Why are you—"

"Can I come in?" My voice is soft, cracking on the end.

"Yeah." He steps back, opening the door wider. "Are you all right? You didn't answer my text earlier."

He closes the door behind me, but we don't move away from it. It feels weird, standing in this foyer again. It looks exactly the same, like no time at all has passed. Six years is so short but so long all at the same time.

"I'm fine, but I ... uh..." I start get choked up. I don't want to get overly emotional telling him this. Fortifying myself, I look into his eyes and say the words that have been long overdue. "I can't go out on a date with you, not in good conscience, without telling you this first."

He cocks his head to the side, eyes narrowed and skeptical. "Tell me what?"

I clench my hands together, my fingernails digging into the skin of my palms.

Spit it out, Salem.

"I have a daughter."

There. It's out there now. I can't take it back.

He gives me a funny look. "You were worried I'd be mad you had a kid? Do you think so little of mine?"

"No." I exhale a weighted breath. "It's not that."

"Then what is it?" He crosses his arms over his chest, leaning against the wall behind us.

I'm thankful for that bit of extra space between us. It allows me a second to breathe air that isn't intoxicated with his presence.

I'm realizing there's no good way to say this. No right words. Nothing to make it easier or better.

"Do you remember—that last time we had sex? You'd been drinking and—"

His eyes narrow further until I can't even see the brown anymore. "Yes."

I wet my lips, nerves sending a bead of sweat down my spine despite my wet clothes. "I got pregnant."

"You got pregnant?" he repeats, slowly, carefully, making sure he's grasping what I'm saying. "With my child?"

"Yes." I'm surprised the word comes out so sharp and clear when I feel so jittery on the inside.

He looks away, a surprised sound leaving him. It's almost a laugh, but not quite. "Pregnant?" His eyes drop to my stomach like he expects it to find it rounded and full. It's not, but it is squishier than it used to be with stretch marks on my stomach and hips. "Why didn't you tell me?"

I cover my face with my hands, letting my arms drop back to my sides. "A million different reasons and none of them are good enough. I was terrified. You were drinking yourself into oblivion and deep into grieving and I just ... I guess I thought if I couldn't manage to pull you out of this, then how would a baby? And I didn't want you to fake it for our baby's sake either." Swallowing thickly, I add, "You said you didn't love me anymore, didn't want me, and that scared me too because what if I told you and you thought I was trapping you." I'm rambling at this point, but that's how my thoughts were back then—all over the place. I was a terrified nineteen-year-old, practically a kid myself. "I stayed as long as I could—until I realized I wasn't the person who could help you."

"That's when you called Laith," he fills in the blanks. "Did he know you were pregnant?"

"No. Just Lauren at that point."

He tugs on his hair, shaking his head lightly. "Wow. This is a lot to process."

"I'm sorry. I should've told you a long time ago. I wrote you a letter one time and then chickened out and didn't send it. You'd already rejected me, and I was so scared of what it'd feel like if you rejected her too."

He rears back, almost knocking his head into the wall. "You thought I'd do that?"

"Thayer," I say his name slowly, "you turned into an entirely different person when Forrest died."

His head lowers and he nods like he knows I'm right. "I'm so fucking sorry."

Now I'm the one stumbling back. "You're apologizing to me? Why?"

Warm brown eyes meet mine. "Because, I was an asshole to you back then. I *wanted* to push you away, and ultimately, I did, and fuck if it doesn't piss me off at myself that it was when you needed me most."

"You needed to grieve."

He clears his throat. "We both really fucked things up, didn't we?"

I don't answer him so he goes on, "You said she's a ... I have a daughter?" A tiny smile fights for space on his lips.

"You have a daughter and she's perfect." Clearing my throat, I add, "I know I didn't tell you about her, but I didn't keep you a secret from her. She knows about you and Forrest too. She talks about her brother a lot."

"What's ... uh ... what's her name?" He's getting choked up talking about her, and even though this is going *way* better than I anticipated, somehow this makes me feel worse. I deserve his anger, for him to yell and scream, to cuss me out.

"Seda," I reply, not being able to help myself when I smile at her name. "She's perfect and beautiful. Funny and creative. She's everything."

He rubs his jaw, brown eyes pooling with tears. "Can I see a picture?"

"Yeah." I push my wet hair out of my eyes, shivering. "I have a million on my phone."

He notices me shaking with cold. "Fuck, I should've offered you a shirt."

"It's okay. I'm fine." I shiver again.

Rolling his eyes, he mutters, "Liar," and heads up the stairs leaving me in the foyer.

He isn't gone long before he returns with a cotton shirt, extending it out to me.

We both seem to remember at the same moment another time I showed up at his door completely soaked from rain. Only that time I had Binx with me and I was confessing something entirely different, telling him about my past.

"Thank you." I let myself into the downstairs bathroom and shuck off my wet jacket and tank top beneath, tugging the plain shirt down over my body. My nipples stand erect thanks to being in my cold, wet clothes so long. There's nothing I can do about it, so I just have to hope the looseness of his shirt helps camouflage it.

Stepping out of the bathroom with my wet clothes in hand, I set them by the door and find him in the living room sitting on the couch waiting for me.

A bottle of water sits in front of him with a Diet Coke beside it.

Pointing at the soda before I take a seat, I say, "You don't drink that stuff."

"No." He eyes the can, then me. "But you do."

"You just keep Diet Coke on hand in case I show up?"

He looks away, like he doesn't want me to see him vulnerable in this moment. "Ever since you came back."

Why—why does that one gesture want to send me into a fit of tears?

Picking up the soda, I take a sip and settle beside him. Unlocking my phone, I bring up all my albums of Seda. Deciding to start at the beginning, I show him a few photos from when I was pregnant with her. His smile is sad, but wistful. He's handling this extremely well, but that doesn't erase all the guilt eating away at me.

I never wanted things to end up like this.

I certainly didn't expect to get pregnant. But when I did, there was a moment when I imagined us together. The three of us. A family.

I show him a few of the sonograms I had saved into my phone before I move onto newborn pictures. I have all her photos organized in my phone in different albums by year, so I let him take it and flick through them. He zooms in from time to time, studying her little face as it grows and changes. Laughing when her bald head gains one tuft of blonde hair that I insisted on putting a bow in. I watch her grow up through the photos alongside him, but I know it's so different from actually watching her turn from a baby to a toddler and into a child.

"She's perfect." He smiles lovingly at a photo of her on her first day of kindergarten this past August. "She looks like you."

"Like you, too." I don't know how it happened, but I've ended up with my head resting on his shoulder. "She's the perfect mix of both of us."

"Seda," he says her name softly, carefully, rolling it over in his mouth to test the sound. "That's an unusual name. Is it a family name of yours?"

I shake my head slightly since I'm still resting against his bare arm. "No. I wanted to honor Forrest. I wasn't really sure at first how I was going to go about it, but one day when I was searching for names Seda came up, and I loved how it sounded. Then when I read what it meant it felt like maybe Forrest was giving me a nudge in the right direction."

"What does it mean?" He's still looking at the last photo he stopped on. She's on her princess bike with a hot pink helmet. Caleb is running behind her since she was nervous with no training wheels.

"It means spirit of the forest."

Goosebumps pop up on his arms. "Whoa. Wow." He shakes his head, rubbing a hand over his mouth. "That's ... wow."

"I know it's unique, but I knew then that it was supposed to be her name."

"You said she knows about me, about Forrest?"

"She doesn't know you specifically, but she's aware that while Caleb's raised her and he's her dad, that she has another dad too because she's doubly special." He smiles at that. "Only Caleb and Lauren know you're her biological father. To everyone else I decided it was best if I just said it was a one-night-stand."

"That ashamed of me, huh?" He says it in a joking tone, but I can see in his eyes that he believes that might be a little bit of the reason why.

"It just seemed easier. I was still heartbroken and convinced you never wanted to see me again. I guess just being young and stupid I decided on that course. If I could do it over again—"

"Life doesn't have do overs," he says gently. His big palm comes over my knee and he gives it a squeeze. "We all make choices in moments that we might come to regret. There's no point wasting time in the here and now dwelling on it. Life's too short, too precious, for that. Forrest taught me that." He touches his fingers gently to the side of my face. A soft sigh escapes my parted lips at the caress. "It doesn't mean it doesn't hurt, knowing you didn't tell me. It's fucking painful. But I can't change either of the decisions we made. That's why I choose to go from here. From this moment." He holds my gaze, my heart beating rapidly in my chest. "You know, after you got married, I didn't think we'd have another chance, but we *do*. In all the time we've been apart, what I feel for you has never lessened, and that ... it was honestly fucking terrifying at times—realizing I was never going to get over you and have to figure out how to live life without you. Now that you're back here, now that I know we have a child together,

I'm not throwing this second chance away. I'd be a fool to do such a thing when I've begged the universe to give me another chance with you." He clears his throat, eyes clouded with barely withheld emotion. "I lost Forrest in a way that there's no getting him back, but I lost you too in the process, but you're something I can fight to get back." He grabs a piece of my hair, gently tucking it behind my ear and letting his fingers skim my cheek. "If you want me back. You can tell me to get lost any time, Salem, and I will. I know it's been a long time and you might not feel the same way—"

I press a hand over his mouth, silencing him. "When you asked me to date you, I said yes because I want that."

I feel him smile against my hand. "Good." His voice is muffled by my hand, so I let it drop. He looks back at my phone, but the screen has gone black. I quickly unlock it and pass it back to him. "When can I meet her?"

"Whenever you want. I just have to arrange it with Caleb."

"I want to meet her soon. But I don't want to scare her. I know you said she knows she has another dad, but that doesn't mean she knows *me*."

"I think she'll handle it better than you're expecting. She's a smart kid."

"Can you send me some pictures?"

"I'll get them all to you." I lean against the back of the couch, watching him look at her. "I should've tried harder."

Slowly, he looks away from the photo. "I gave you no reason to. You were protecting yourself and protecting her from what you thought I could be. And let's face it, Salem, I could've reached out to you sooner than I had wanted to. But I didn't. We've both made a lot of mistakes and we can sit here and continue to rehash them, but it doesn't change anything. I just want to move forward."

"I want that too."

"Good." He passes my phone back to me. "Now are you ever going to reply to my text?"

"Oh, right." I quickly bring up my text messages and type out a reply. His phone buzzes in his pocket.

With a grin, he pulls it out and nods at my response. "See you tomorrow."

He leads me to the door, opening it and waiting for me to step onto the front porch. The rain has lessened, mostly a drizzle now. I pause, turning back to look at him in the doorway of his home.

A moment passes between us, a thousand words said without a single spoken aloud.

A second chance, he said before, but do we really deserve one?

Selfishly, a little voice in my head whispers, *I hope so.*

TWENTY-ONE

Thayer

I can't go back to sleep, not with this news dropped on me.

Salem went home about an hour ago and I've been in the basement ever since.

My fist slams into the bag over and over again, alternating left then right.

I'm drenched in sweat, like I can exile all my thoughts and demons.

I have a daughter.

I have a child with Salem.

We ... we made a baby.

And she never fucking told me.

Over and over again I slam my fist into the bag. Tears mingle with my sweat and I wipe at the dampness on my face.

I keep picturing that little girl's face in my mind.

Her eyes are brown, just like mine.

I wish so badly I could've been there, for Salem, for my daughter.

I didn't get to see Salem grow round with our child, or give birth, or get to be there for any of Seda's milestones. It wasn't a lie when I told her I didn't want to dwell on the mistakes of our past, because it's true, I want to move on and start fresh, but I need this fucking moment to wallow.

Both of us made mistakes and horrible choices, not just her. I know I'm equally at fault for this outcome and I'm just as mad at myself for it as I am her.

I'm going to let myself feel that—the anger—and then move the fuck on.

When I've exhausted myself, I trudge upstairs to my room and take an extra-long shower. It's still early when I get out so I lay across my bed and check my phone. Salem's sent me albums of photos to download.

I look through them slowly, picking apart details and learning everything I can about my daughter. Like how she must love all colors, but especially pink. How she likes to dress up as a princess and have tea parties but also likes to run around outside in the rain, getting covered in mud. There are photos of her in a ballet tutu. I wonder if she takes lessons or she was only playing dress up.

I learn many things from the photos, but my questions grow too.

Light starts to peek through the blinds. Laith is living in Denver, so he's hours behind the east coast, but he's going to have to deal. I need to talk to him, and I've waited long enough.

"What the fuck, man?" He groans into the line.

"I need to talk to you."

"It's like..." He must look at the time. "Four in the morning."

"Salem came over last night."

"Ugh, you are not waking me up at the ass crack of dawn to give me a rundown on your booty call."

"Salem is *not* a booty call, and we haven't been together since she got back."

425

There's rustling and I know he must be sitting up in bed. "You mean to tell me your celibate ass hasn't been all over that, yet? Come on, bro, you'll be in a lot better shape once you get laid."

"Don't talk about Salem like that. She's not just ... she's more than that, okay?"

My brother knows all about Salem. All the gory details. He thought I was a fucking idiot for pushing the love of my life away—and he was right. I was the dumbest fucking idiot. I thought I was doing what was right. I didn't know how long I'd be grieving and I just ... didn't want her to see me like that. *I* ruined us. Not her.

"Right, right. I know. But it's *four-fucking-o-clock-in-the-morning*. Cut me a break. I'm not a morning person."

"I have a daughter. With Salem. We have a child."

He's silent for a minute and then there's a whistle of air escaping his lungs. "Holy fucking shit."

"That about sums up how I feel."

"That kid has to be what? Like six?"

"Five."

"Fuck. That's crazy. No wonder you called me this early. This is a lot to process. Have you told Mom and Dad?"

"I just found out. You're the first person I called."

"Aw." I hear him slap a hand to his chest. "I feel special."

"Don't let it go to your head," I grumble, raking my fingers through my hair.

"Oh, I am," he chortles. "Admit it, I'm your favorite person."

"No."

"That's right—second favorite, behind Salem. I'll take it. But a kid, Thayer? A whole ass child? Wow. Fucking insane."

I scrub my hand over my face. "I think I'm in shock."

"Of course you fucking are. She kept that a secret from you all this time," he rambles, barely taking a breath. "It's a lot to take in."

"She knows about me—well, not me specifically, but that the guy Salem was married to isn't her biological father."

As much as it hurt me that she went back to Caleb, right now I'm actually kind of grateful for the dude. It's weird, I know, but he didn't steal her from me. He was there for her when she needed someone the most. He was young, but he did what I couldn't with my grief—he stepped up to the plate and became a husband and father.

"What does this mean for you and Salem?"

"What do you mean?"

"I mean, she kept a whole ass child a secret from you. That's kind of a big deal."

"I'm not saying it isn't, but I'm not throwing this chance with her away." Laith has never met his Salem—he doesn't get how fucking lucky I am to have a chance to do things over with her, to do it *right* this time.

"All this time and you still feel the same about her?"

"Yeah. I do."

When you know, you know.

I knew then but I wouldn't let myself believe it. I believe you should learn from your mistakes, so that's what I'm trying to do.

"So, what's your daughter's name?"

I smile before I even say it. "Seda."

"That's a weird name."

"Shut the fuck up," I growl at my younger brother. "It's a beautiful name."

"Sorry, my bad—need I remind you it's *four in the fucking morning*."

"Right, right. You're not a morning person. My bad."

"When do you get to meet her?"

I sigh, nerves rattling my stomach. "I don't know. Soon, I hope."

"You know, despite this early hour I've learned something valuable from this conversation."

"What?" I ask hesitantly. I never know what's going to come out of my brother's mouth.

"Always wear a condom before I go to pound town."

With that final statement he ends the call, presumably to go back to sleep, and I get ready for work.

TWENTY-TWO

Salem

I'm a jittery mess all day counting down in anticipation to my date with Thayer.

A date.

A real date.

I act like I've never been on a date at all with the way my palms keep sweating.

"Would you stop pacing?" My mom scolds with an amused smile. "You already spilled water on me earlier and now you're going to wear a hole in the carpet with all that walking back and forth." She mimes walking with her fingers. I open my mouth to reply but she silences me again, adding, "And don't you dare try to use me as an excuse not to go again. I'm living vicariously through you right now."

I've already tried three different times to back out. Not because I don't want to go, I definitely do, but the guilt eats me up over leaving my mom even though a nurse is stopping by for her weekly checks and Georgia will be here with her—apparently Georgia likes to supervise these visits.

"What if you need me?" I argue, still pacing.

She huffs, adjusting the blankets on her lap. A rom-com plays softly in the background, but she's been paying more attention to me than it. "Your sister is going to be here with me, and believe me, she's a hoverer. Besides, I do know how to work a phone to call or text. You worry so much about everyone else. Go out, Salem. Enjoy yourself. Have a nice time with a nice man."

I cease my pacing, planting my hands on my hips. "You make it sound so much easier than it is."

She laughs, but it quickly turns into a cough. I move forward like I can help her and she's quick to wave me off. Once she's recovered, she says, "That's the thing it *is* easy—it's overthinking and making your brain run through every possible scenario that complicates things."

She's totally right. Smoothing my hands down the blue and white floral dress I put on, I take a deep breath and do my best to silence my scattered thoughts. "Do I look okay?"

She crooks a finger, beckoning me forward. I bend down closer to her, and she grabs a piece of my hair, tucking it back behind my ear. The short pieces keep slipping free of the low bun I twisted it in.

Touching her hand gently to my cheek, her skin cool against mine, she says, "You look beautiful, Salem. You always do."

"Not as beautiful as you."

She snorts. "Stop trying to flatter me."

"It's not flattery." I kiss her cheek. "You're the most beautiful person I know, inside and out."

When I straighten, there are tears shining in her eyes she tries to hide.

The side door in the kitchen creaks open and Georgia calls out a hello. I hear the thump of her purse hitting the floor, or maybe it's the kitchen table. She waddles into the room, glowing and all smiles.

"Hey, Mom." She bends down as much as she can, wrapping her

arms around mom's neck. "Little sis." She hugs me next. "How's the day been?"

"Good," I tell her, meaning it. Mom's been more alert and not in as much pain. It's all we can ask for, especially when I know it's so short lived.

"Feeling okay?" She reaches for our mom's wrist, and I know she plans to check her pulse, but mom quickly tucks her arm against her chest.

"Georgia, that's what the nurse is for. Why don't you take a seat?"

Georgia pouts her lips but does as she's asked. "Do you want anything to drink or a snack or something?" I ask, wanting to busy myself with something.

"I can get it myself—" She starts to stand, but I wave her back down.

"You're pregnant, working, and chasing after two kids already. Sit while you can."

She laughs, shaking her head but she can't help but smile. She loves those boys with her whole heart. She's truly a good mom. "Fine, grab me a water then and some crackers."

In the kitchen, I give myself a chance to take a few deeps breaths to calm my racing heart. Despite the fact that I know Thayer so well, and my confession is out in the open, my nerves are at an all-time high. This feels so different. Official in a way we never were before. It's out in the world, knowledge for everyone, that we're going on a date. Not some sneaky secret.

I fix Georgia a glass of water and grab a pack of crackers from the tiny pantry. She takes both from me with a smile.

"How excited are you for your date?"

"She's worn a path in the rug if that tells you anything," my mom interjects before I can say anything.

"It's been a long time since I've been on a date," I defend.

There's a mirror above the small table near the stairs, that I use to check my reflection yet again, trying to slick back stray hairs. Maybe it would've been a better idea to keep my hair down, but I had wanted to do something different.

The doorbell rings and a legitimate scream flies past my lips, making both my mom and sister laugh.

"Oh, yeah, she's nervous," Georgia cackles. "Oh, no." She looks down at her lap. "I think I peed a little."

I stick my tongue out at her playfully before opening the door.

Thayer stands there looking ridiculously good—if he had any idea just how much I'm attracted to him he'd laugh. Or run the other way.

He's clearly put more effort into his hair than usual, it's brushed back and not as unruly. His facial hair is trimmed and neat. I was worried I might have overdressed—even though my dress is far from fancy—but I feel better seeing him in a nice pair of jeans and a pale blue button-down shirt with the sleeves rolled up.

"These are for you." He holds out yet another bouquet of pink peonies. I wonder where he's getting them all. I can't imagine our local florist has much.

"Peonies are going to take over the house," I warn him with a smile, taking them and cradling them in my arms. "Lucky for you, I don't mind."

He chuckles, shoving his now empty hands in his pockets.

"Here, I'll take those." I didn't even notice my sister get up from the couch. She holds her hands out for the bouquet and I pass it over. "You two kids have fun now." She smacks me on the butt before waddling toward the kitchen.

Thayer holds out a hand for me to take before poking his head in the door. "I'll bring her back soon, Allie."

She smiles, her eyes crinkling at the corners. "Just take care of her for me."

His gaze moves down to me, his smile growing. "I will."

Shutting the door behind me, I let him hold my hand on the way to his truck that he's moved into our driveway.

"I would've walked over. You're literally right next door."

"Nope." He shakes his head forcefully. "This is a date. That means it starts with me picking you up from your house, not mine." He opens the passenger door of his truck, offering a hand to help me up.

Once I'm safely inside he closes the door, walking around the front of the truck to climb in the driver's side. He cranks the engine, grinning at me before he puts it in reverse.

"What?" I ask, wondering why he's staring at me like that.

"I'm making a memory right now."

My heart tugs at his statement. "I am too," I whisper.

He leans over, cupping the back of my neck. "I refuse to let you be the one who got away."

"What does that mean?" My eyes zero in on his lips, thinking of the kiss we shared in his truck only a week ago.

"I don't want you to be someone I think about for the rest of my life, wondering what if? What if I'd tried harder? What if I had just told you how I felt?" He lowers his forehead to press gently against mine, our breaths sharing the same space. "I want you to be *the one*. That's it. No second guessing. No wondering. Just a sure thing."

"I—"

"Don't say anything," he pleads, pulling away. "I want to do this right. Get to know who you are now, date you for real, and I want to take my time."

"Take your time with what?"

He wets his lips, looking at me like he's afraid I might disappear. "Making you fall back in love with me."

I don't say anything to that as he backs out of the driveway, but I can't help thinking that I'm not sure I ever fell out of love with him.

TWENTY-THREE

Salem

'm surprised when Thayer turns into the parking lot of the local park. I'm not sure what exactly I was expecting but it wasn't this.

"What are we doing here?" I turn around, looking for any sign of why he would've chosen this spot for our first date. But it looks the same as it always did. Lots of open fields, a wooden playground for the children, and a walking trail along the perimeter.

"We're having a picnic."

"A picnic?" I brighten, never having thought of that.

"Originally, I planned for us to eat on a blanket in the grass, but the storm last night kind of ruined that. But there's the gazebo so I figure that can work."

Somehow, I had forgotten about the storm, but that explains why it's mostly empty at the park today with no one wanting to risk the muddy mess of grass.

Thayer reaches to open his door, quickly looking back at me. "You wait there."

"Wha—"

He doesn't let me finish before he's out and closing his door. He comes around the truck and opens my door, holding out his hand.

"I'm doing things right with you."

My heart does a somersault.

I accept his help without protest. When my feet land on the ground, his hands go to my hips. He doesn't say anything, and I don't either. But I wonder if he's thinking the same thing I am—that I never thought we'd end up here. When I got back together with Caleb, I made myself say goodbye to this part of my life, to *him*. I mourned the loss of what we could've been.

But now, here we are with this second chance, and even though this, *him*—has the capability to obliterate me all over again—I can't turn away. Some things are worth the risk if you're brave enough to take the leap.

Thayer opens the back door and pulls out a packed basket—a literal basket like you see in movies when the couple goes on a picnic —and a blanket he drapes over top of it. Closing and locking up the truck, he offers his hand to me, and we trek across the muddy grass toward the gazebo. I'm thankful I wore a pair of Converse sneakers instead of the sandals I had planned on. I'll have to wash these later, but it's worth it.

The gazebo is white with vines of flowers crawling up the sides. It matches the one in the middle of town but is larger in size.

Letting go of my hand, he sits the basket down and spreads the blanket out.

"Is this okay?" He looks a bit unsure of himself which is unusual for Thayer. Normally nothing ruffles his feathers.

"It's great." I hold onto the side of the gazebo and take my shoes off, not wanting to get mud all over the blanket. Thayer does the same, then opens the top of the basket, pulling out covered dishes of food.

"What did you make?" I gather my skirt up, tucking it under me as I sit down.

He uncovers a bowl and passes it to me. "Pasta!" I cry in delight. "Is that lobster in it?"

He laughs softly, ducking his head as he rummages through the basket. "Yes."

"Wow, you really went all out. I feel special."

"You are." He says it so simply, like it's a fact I should already know.

He sets out bread and dipping oil on top of a cutting board along with a knife. He passes me a fork before uncovering his own bowl.

"This is amazing." I look at the spread of food. "You thought of everything. You could've just taken me to a restaurant, you know?"

He swirls pasta around his fork. "And what's special about that? We've already eaten at a restaurant together." Lowering his head, he adds in a deeper voice, "After everything, you deserve something different than that."

I don't much feel like rehashing the past now, so I don't remark on that. Besides, we've established that I was hurt by his silence after everything. We're adults, we both know we could've made different choices.

"Truly, this is ... well, honestly, it's perfect."

It's simple, sweet. The thought that went into him planning this for us means everything.

"Do you think you would've come back here, to Hawthorne Mills, if it wasn't for your mom?"

I wrinkle my nose, contemplating his question. "Eventually." Picking up a piece of bread, I dip it in the oil to busy myself while I sort through my thoughts. "I think I would've had to. As much as I've avoided this place, it's always called to me."

"You stayed away because of me."

He makes it a statement, but I answer anyway. "Yes and no. Because of everything this place became somewhere I dreaded to be. And I think, even after I got married, I was afraid of what it would feel like to see you with another woman."

He clears his throat, his cheeks pinkening. "About that..."

"Yes?" I prompt curiously.

"I haven't been with anyone."

"For a while?"

"A long while." He looks out of the gazebo at the trees, mumbling, "Not since you."

"Since me?" I blurt loudly, taken by complete surprise. "Thayer," I laugh, more from shock than any genuine humor, "that's ... you have to be joking. I mean, don't you remember that night after my sister's wedding? Caleb brought me home and you were there with a woman. Granted, she left," I ramble, talking animatedly with my hands, "but I saw you."

He lowers his head, but not before I miss the shame swimming in his eyes. "I was in a bad place. A really fucking bad place and I was being an asshole because I was hoping you'd see. I *wanted* to push you away. I didn't want you wasting your love on me when I felt like all the good in me had left. I wouldn't have gone through with it. I never planned to." He rubs his jaw, the muscle clenching at the memories. "I'm not saying I haven't gone on any dates in all this time —mostly in a vain hope that maybe I'd feel some sort of spark—but I haven't had sex with anyone."

I blink.

Blink again.

Surely, I haven't heard him right.

There's no way.

He gently pushes my jaw back up. "Don't want you catching flies like that."

"You haven't had sex in six years?"

Stunned. I'm completely speechless. There's no way. This has to be a joke, right?

"No."

"I ... whoa ... *wow*." I'm having a hard time wrapping my head around this and then I start laughing, because this means— "The last time you had sex you got me pregnant. You really went all out, didn't you?"

Even he has to snicker at that. Sobering, he clears his throat. "Were you alone when you found out?"

Shaking my head, I stretch my legs out fully and adjust my dress around my legs. "I was with Lauren."

His eyes drop to the blanket. "Good. I'm glad you had someone. You had to be scared."

"Terrified," I laugh, and I'm glad I can find the humor in the situation now. I was so worried about becoming a mom so young, especially pregnant by a man who was going through such a tragedy. "I never missed my birth control, but Seda didn't get the memo. That girl is a force of nature."

He smiles, sadness in his eyes. "I can't wait to meet her."

"I don't know what I'd do without her."

"And Caleb ... he's been good to you? Good to her?" He looks away from me as soon as the words leave his mouth. He never liked Caleb much before, so I can't imagine how he feels now, but he's handling it, all of this, better than I could've ever expected.

"The best."

His eyes shoot back to mine, brows furrowed. "I remember what you said before, but I have to ask again, why did you get divorced?"

I rub the blanket between my thumb and index finger, seeking a small amount of comfort in the gesture to get me through this. "I didn't lie to you then—when I gave my heart away to you, I never fully got it back, and I realized that I would never be able to love Caleb the way he loved me. It was infinitely unfair to him, and I couldn't do that. I was already planning to file when he told me he was ready for us to have a baby. He wanted Seda to be a big sister and I just—" I close my eyes, treacherous tears leaking from the corner. I feel his fingers collect my tears in a gentle caress, but I don't dare open them. When his touch disappears, I continue on. "Caleb is a better person than I am, and I couldn't..." I shake my head. "He deserves to find the love I had once, because he won't have that with me. I think if I had never met you, we could've had a beautiful life together, but the fact of the matter is, I did meet you and that changes everything." He flinches like I've slapped him. "Oh, Thayer." Now I'm the one reaching out to touch him. I place my hand on his cheek and he puts his over mine.

"I've really ruined your life, haven't I?" He says it with a hint of humor, but I know he's aching at the thought of it.

I shake my head. "No, Thayer, that's not what I meant at all." Stroking my thumb over his cheek, I go on. "You taught a broken, abused girl what love is *supposed* to feel like. Before that, I had no idea what to base it on. Falling for you was the most confusing, all-consuming, thing I've ever done. I don't regret it. I never have."

He exhales a breath and it's like he loses a hundred pounds with it. "I've worried a lot, over the years, about how you felt toward me—if you ended up feeling like I took advantage of you or something. Especially with your history." He shakes his head sadly. "I didn't want to have been a cause of more trauma in your life."

"Trust me, Thayer—" I'm not sure I'll get used to being able to say his name again. "You're one of the best things to ever happen to me. No regrets." Dipping a piece of bread in oil, I venture to ask, "After Laith came ... what happened? You were in a bad place. It worried me. Leaving you was the hardest thing I've ever done."

He sets his food aside and lays down on his side, propping his head in his hand. A curl falls over his forehead, my fingers twitching with the desire to push it back, but I keep my hands to myself. I want to take things slow. Thayer and I ... it's so *easy*, so right with him, and that makes it feel difficult to go at a speed that's necessary.

"Mostly he yelled at me—which I needed. Told me I was a waste of space and a shame to my son's memory." He takes a deep breath, the pain of that loss always hard to bear. "It worked. I started grief counseling and learned to channel my emotions in healthier ways."

"Like what?" I ask, curiously.

His cheeks turn the barest hint of pink. "Crafts ... and stuff."

"Crafts?" I repeat, trying not to smile. "Care to elaborate for me?"

The pink in his cheeks deepens until he's full-blown blushing. "Well, my therapist had me try out some different things until something stuck."

"You're really going to make me pull this out of you, aren't you?" He says something in a rush of words that is impossible to decipher. "Huh?"

Slowing down, he says, "Sewing, okay? I started sewing dog bows for Winnie and that morphed into dog clothes."

I stare at him, stunned.

Did this lumberjack looking man just tell me he sews clothing for his dog? I can't possibly have heard him right.

"She said I had to find something that wasn't already something I enjoyed, so that knocked out a lot of things like carpentry, plants, puzzles," he starts ticking things off on his fingers, "camping—"

"You like camping?"

I hate that I'm practically panting at the visual of Thayer in the outdoors. A shirtless Thayer chopping wood? Sign. Me. Up.

I suddenly have a desire to go camping.

"I love it," he says with a grin, his eyes lighting up. "I go a lot. You should come with me sometime?"

"Are there bathrooms?"

His smile grows bigger. "There are trees."

I sigh dramatically on purpose, fighting a smile. "I guess that could work."

"You'd seriously go camping with me?" Now, he chooses to look doubtful.

"Sure, why not?" I set my plate aside and lay down on my side, mimicking his pose.

"Huh. I guess I thought that wouldn't be something you'd enjoy."

"You don't know until you try."

"You never went camping as a kid?"

I snort at that. "No, definitely not."

"I'll take you sometime. I know it's hard right now with your mom, but I promise someday we'll go."

"I'd like that."

And it's crazy, but I really would.

The sun starts to set in the distance, and I'm surprised by how much time has passed. Thayer must be too, because he sits up and starts gathering our plates up.

"I better get you home before it gets any later."

I help him pack everything away and we make the trek back through the muddy grass to his truck.

"I want to see those bows and outfits of Winnie's sometime."

He shakes his head. "Never gonna live it down, am I?"

"No," I laugh lightly, "definitely not."

In the truck he holds my hand, our fingers wrapped firmly together. I keep looking at them, his skin a golden-tan against my paler tone, and I can't help thinking to myself how I never want to let go again.

Thayer drops me off in my driveway, giving me a peck on my cheek. A part of me is disappointed after the kiss we shared previously, but I realize he's trying to take things slow with us.

Letting myself into the house, I find my mom asleep already and Georgia sitting in the chair crocheting a pair of baby booties.

Never thought I'd see the day that my sister was doing such a thing, but here we are. It makes me smile, seeing her so happy and content with her family. She deserves all the happiness in the world.

She makes a shushing motion with her finger when she sees me in the doorway, as if I hadn't already noticed mom's sleeping form.

"How'd it go?" She mouths the words.

"Amazing," I mouth back.

She smiles, tucking the booties back into her bag. She stands up, pressing a hand to her lower back. She points to the kitchen, and I follow her.

"It's not even that late and I'm ready to crash." She yawns, covering her mouth with her hand. "But I expect a full report on this date later, you hear me?"

"Yes." I stick my tongue out playfully. "How was Mom?"

"The usual." She shrugs, biting her lip. "I don't think she has much time left." Her eyes dart helplessly to the living room. "I know she's fighting to hang on as long as she can, but ... I think it's coming soon. Doing what I do, you start to sense it after a while."

I close my eyes and nod. "I hate this."

"Me too."

I open my arms and my sister returns the gesture. We hold on tight, united in our pain and grief. It's so difficult mourning someone who isn't even gone yet—it feels like a betrayal in a way, even though she knows it's coming too.

"I've gotta go." She pulls away, dabbing beneath her eyes with a finger. "I'll talk to you tomorrow. Probably stop by too. I want to spend as much time with her as I can."

I open the door and see my sister out to her car.

Standing on the driveway, I watch her pull away. Before turning to

THE RESURRECTION OF WILDFLOWERS

go back inside, I hear the clinking sound of a dog collar and spot Thayer with Winnie across the street.

A big pink bow is around her neck.

Like he can feel the weight of my eyes, he looks over at me and lifts a hand in a wave.

I smile, and it feels good despite the heaviness in my heart.

TWENTY-FOUR

Salem

The next morning, I'm sitting on the front porch with my mom after eating breakfast, knowing I have to drop a bomb on her. Despite the already warm day, there's a blanket draped over her lap. She rubs the material between her fingers like she's trying to memorize the sensation. Across the street, she watches some kids playing in the front yard with their golden retriever. I wonder what she's thinking, but I don't want to ask.

"Mom," I say softly, getting her attention. I wrap my fingers tighter around my cup of orange juice, trying to brace myself for what I'm about to tell her. "There's something I have to tell you."

Her eyes slowly move to where I sit in the rocking chair beside hers. "What is it?" She looks curious, alert.

"You know Seda isn't Caleb's biological child, but I never told you who her father is."

"And you've waited until I'm on my deathbed to tell me?" She's amused, not a hint of anger, but I still feel bad.

"It never seemed like the right time," I admit. "It's stupid, I know, but I don't think I knew how to handle a lot of this. Getting pregnant wasn't a part of my plan, and then I got back with Caleb, and we were married, and it all just…"

"Life passes in a blink." She covers my hand with hers, her skin cool to the touch despite the warmth of the outdoors. "Time is strange, the way it feels like not much has passed but then you realize it's actually been an entire lifetime."

"Yeah." I tuck a piece of hair behind my ear with my free hand.

"Why do you want to tell me now?"

"Because it should've never been a secret." I duck my head with shame. "I was scared, and angry, and I just … I didn't handle things the way I should have."

"You were young, Salem. We all do stupid stuff, even when we're older, what matters is that you *learn* from it."

I swallow past the lump in my throat. "I fell in love with someone older than me," I start the story, "he didn't take advantage of me, I promise you that, but it was intense. I had never felt anything like it before. I didn't *know* I could feel things the way he made me feel them. I thought I knew love, but he showed me everything I thought I knew was wrong." I take a deep breath, this is harder than I thought it would be. "I fell hard and fast. I thought I'd get over him, but I never have." I wipe away a tear that tracks down my cheek. I make myself say it, put it out into the universe and make it real. "Thayer is her father."

She stares at me for a long moment, never breaking my gaze.

Nothing at all could possibly prepare me for the words that come out of her mouth.

"I know."

"You know?" I flounder to understand how she could possibly know. "How?"

She shakes her head. "Well, I couldn't be certain he was Seda's father, but I did notice resemblance and as far as your relationship with him ... honey, I'm your mother. I know you thought you were being sneaky, but you really weren't. I figured it out pretty quickly."

"And you never said anything because?"

"Because you were happy. After everything, why would I try to take that away from you? I'm not saying I *liked* it, but I understood it."

"And you ... all these years you've been friends with him since I left, why?"

"Because he needed a friend." She shrugs like it's so simple. "And he knew that I knew, so I think he felt safe talking to me."

My jaw drops at that. Here I thought I was the one who was going to be dropping bombs on my mom and it's reversed. "When did he know?"

"Forrest's birthday that year."

I sit back in the rocker, stunned. "Wow. I wasn't expecting this."

"I never told him about Seda or that I suspected she was his. It wasn't my secret to tell."

"I told him. He knows now. He wants to meet her." I run my fingers through my hair, trying to gather my breath. "I really made a clusterfuck of things, didn't I?"

She doesn't say anything for a moment, so long in fact that I think maybe she's not going to say anything at all. But then she says, "We all make messes, Salem. It's how we deal with them that matters."

I lower my head. "I'm trying to make things right."

"You'll get there, my girl." She rubs my hand, trying to soothe me. She's the one dying, but she's comforting me, because even now she can't stop being a mother. "I believe in you." She grows quiet after a while and I think she might doze off, so it surprises me when she speaks again. "I know we don't talk about what your father did, but trauma like that lingers. For you, for me, for Georgia. It affects your mind and choices you make. I don't think it's something therapy can fully erase. That means, sometimes, you're not going to handle things the way a normal person would. Trauma is deep-rooted and some-times we don't even realize how it's influencing us."

"I never thought about it like that."

"Just don't let it affect you too much. I see the way that man looks at you and you look at him. A love like that ... it doesn't come around again. You deserve to be happy. Let yourself have that—because that's another effect of trauma."

"What is?"

She looks down sadly and I think she might be thinking of herself. "Self-sabotage. Thinking you don't deserve certain things because you're dirty, tainted."

"Mom." My heart breaks for the woman at my side, who dealt with a bastard like my father and now sits at the end of her life much too soon.

She sniffles, her eyes watery. "Don't worry about me, baby girl. But when I'm gone, promise me you'll remember the things I say."

"I promise." My voice is soft, barely audible. It's like my voice has fled me. I hate talking about this, the inevitably of her death. But it's here. Staring all of us in the face.

You have to be strong, I tell myself.

I'm tired of it, though, always being the one who has to keep myself together.

Eventually, we all have to break.

TWENTY-FIVE

Salem

My nerves are at an all-time high when Caleb's Mercedes pulls into the driveway. I've had a whole week to prepare for this moment, even made a drive back to Boston to explain in person to Seda that she was finally going to meet her father.

"And my brother too?" She had asked me, and I promised to take her to his grave so she could say hello.

"My hands are sweating," I whisper to my mom at my side on the front porch.

"Mine would be too."

"Mommy!" Seda rolls down her window and waves.

I smile despite my nerves. That girl can quiet every ridiculous thought in my head. I talked to Lauren on FaceTime for over two hours last night while she tried to calm me down through intermittent fits of laughter. I warned her if she didn't stop laughing at me, I wouldn't be her maid of honor for her wedding in a few months. She only laughed harder since we both knew it was an empty threat.

Seda unbuckles her seatbelt, launching herself out of the car and into my arms before I can reach her.

"There's my girl." I wrap her tight in my arms, inhaling the scent of her kid shampoo.

"Daddy said this is where you grew up. He said you both used to sit on the roof."

"We did." I tweak her nose playfully. "But don't think I'm going to let you sit on it."

She giggles, spinning in a circle. "Daddy! Show me the roof!"

Caleb comes around the side of the car, tucking his phone in the pocket of his pants. He gives me a small smile, ruffling Seda's hair. "She wanted to hear all about us when we were teenagers the whole drive," he explains. "It's right there, sweetie." He points out the spot on the roof to her and she smiles.

"That's so cool. I wish I could do that."

"And give me a heart attack?" I counter. "I don't think so."

Behind me in her chair on the porch my mom laughs. "Payback," she says loud enough for me to hear.

Caleb scoops Seda into his arms, her eyes round and big as she continues to look around. "Whoa, Mommy! Look! That house has a treehouse!" She points out the structure in Thayer's backyard. "That's so cool. Do you think I could play in it?"

Caleb's eyes meet mine, but he says nothing.

"I'm sure we can ask." I brush my fingers through her blonde hair.

I've waited for this day for a long time, for her to meet Thayer, for him to meet her. I always knew it was inevitable and as much as it terrified me, I looked forward to it too. And now that day has come.

"Do you need to use the potty?" Caleb asks her, setting her back on her feet.

"No, Daddy." She rolls her eyes with a huff. "I peed before we left and I don't have to do number two either, so don't ask."

My mom cackles. "I hope you two are ready for the teen years with her."

Caleb salutes her jokingly. "Thanks for the vote of confidence, Allison."

Seda starts up the front porch to my mom, hugging her tightly. "Hi, Grandma. I missed you. Did you make cupcakes?"

We all laugh, because of course Seda has sweets on the brain. "Your mom and I might've made some." She winks at her grand-daughter. "Why don't we go get one?" She starts to get up, struggling a bit. I move to help her, but she waves me off. She heads inside with Seda, Caleb and I watching them go.

"She doesn't look good," he says mournfully beside me. "She already looks way worse than when you guys visited."

"I know."

He can hear the raw pain in my voice and quickly wraps his arms around me, rubbing his hands up and down my back. "I'm sorry, Salem." He rests his chin on top of my head. "I wish I could make this better."

"I have to enjoy what time I have left." It's a shitty fact, and the worst part is every day my mom is in more pain. I'm not sure there's any joy in her final days for her at all.

"I'm going to head over to my parents. I don't want to be in the way for this."

"You're not in the way." I step back from his embrace. "I'm not going to send you away either. If you want to be here you can stay."

He shakes his head. Clearing his throat, he says, "I think it'll be better for me if I'm not."

"All right." I won't push him to do anything he's not comfortable with. As long as he knows I'm not pushing him away from Seda, that's all that matters.

"Hey."

We both turn at the sound of Thayer's deep voice. He stands at the end of the driveway. His hands are in his pockets, eyes watching us curiously. But he doesn't look jealous or irritated seeing me standing so close to Caleb.

"She's inside," I tell him. "Caleb's getting ready to leave."

"I'm glad I caught you then." He walks closer, stopping in front of my ex-husband.

Caleb gives me a curious look and I shrug, because I truly don't know what's going on.

Thayer holds out a hand to Caleb. My ex eyes it warily, like a snake he's not quite sure is poisonous or not. He looks back at me, gauging my reaction. With a sigh, he takes the offered hand and I think we're both more than a little shocked when he pulls Caleb into a hug.

"Thank you," Thayer says, an overwhelming amount of emotion in those two words. "Thank you for taking care of them."

"I didn't do it for you," Caleb responds, not in offense but more as a statement—a reminder that he did it for us.

"I know, but that doesn't mean I'm not grateful."

Caleb nods, clearing his throat. I think he might be a little choked up. "All right … okay … you're … welcome, I guess." I press my lips together, so I don't laugh. It's kind of cute how flustered he is. "I'm going to head out."

He points at his car and says goodbye. Thayer and I stand on the driveway side by side watching him back out.

"Fancy car," he remarks, watching the Mercedes disappear down the street. "Yours, too." He points at my Range Rover.

"It sure beats my old clunker, but I did love that thing."

He looks at the spot where it used to be parked in front of the house on the street, like if he stares hard enough, he can bring it back.

"I sold it," I ramble, feeling the desire to fill the silence for once with him, "I didn't need it in Brooklyn, and it made sense to have the extra money since I was…"

"Since you were pregnant," he fills in the blanks for me.

"Are you ready to meet her?"

He looks at me through thick lashes, nervous excitement in his brown-eyed gaze. "Yeah." A tiny smile graces his lips. "Yeah, I am."

"Come on then." I hold my hand out to him. He takes it, holding on so tight it's like I'm a buoy and he's been adrift at sea, desperate to find something to keep him afloat.

Up the porch steps we go, the screen door creaking when I open it.

"Mommy!" Seda comes running from the kitchen, cupcake in hand and frosting all over her face. "This one is my favorite! Grandma said it's cookie dough!"

Thayer's hand goes limp in mine.

He's seen photos. He knows what she looks like. But there's a vast difference in looking at an image and staring at the living, breathing person in front of you.

When I was pregnant with her, I used to think about what would happen if I was able to reunite with Thayer before I gave birth. How he might look at her when she entered the world.

He wears the exact expression I dreamed of now—one of wonder and surprise, like someone who has just discovered one of the world's greatest secrets.

I can almost hear his thoughts—how she looks like us, how she's this beautiful little light in the world. She's precious, the world is infinite in the eyes of our child. She's the reminder that there's always good somewhere in life.

Thayer looks at me, his eyes filled with awe. I can tell he doesn't know what to say to her.

But Seda doesn't need prompting. Tilting her head to the side, her small pink tongue licking the icing from around her mouth, she blurts, "Are you my Dad? My mommy said I was going to meet my dad today. Did you give me DVD? No … that's not right, what did you call it, Mommy?"

"DNA," I correct. I move behind her, pulling her soft blonde hair behind her shoulders and facing Thayer. "And, yes, baby. This is him."

Thayer clears his throat, crouching down on one knee so he's more her height. "Hi." He offers his hand to her to shake if she wants.

She stares at his outstretched hand. I don't urge her to take it. That's her decision to make. Slowly, carefully, she shakes his hand and lets hers drop quickly back to her side.

"Mommy said when she had me you were in a bad place and weren't ready to be my dad."

Thayer looks up at me briefly and back to her. "That's right. You

450

know about your brother?" When she nods, he goes on. "I was in a bad place after he died. It's not easy for parents to lose their child."

She reaches out, placing her small hand gently on his cheek. "It's okay. I'll help you."

He smiles, putting his hand over top of hers. His big hand completely swallows the small one beneath it. "I'm sure you will."

Seda's eyes flicker up to meet mine before she refocuses on Thayer. "Mommy says I'm so special I got two daddies to love me. Is that true? Do you love me?"

Thayer visibly swallows. "Yeah." I can hear how choked up he is in the way his voice breaks. "It's true. I love you."

The love of a parent is so beautiful in that way—how you can look at your child and see *everything*. It makes me wonder how people like my father ever exist. It feels like it goes against the laws of nature.

He reaches out with his other hand, giving her plenty of time to step away or say no to his touch when he puts his hand on her cheek the same way she has hers on his.

My heart beats rapidly and I fight back tears.

Turning away from the sight, I step outside to catch my breath. I don't want Seda to see me break down and think she's done something wrong, because it's the complete opposite. She's so kind and open-hearted. She's able to trust and understand so much and I love that about her. I love that she'll never be tainted by the darkness my own childhood endured.

Sitting down on the porch steps, I glance over my shoulder when I hear the door open. Thayer steps out and settles beside me.

"Why did you come out here? You didn't have to follow me."

He drapes his arms over his knees. "I know."

"Then why did you?"

"I was worried about you."

"About me?" I laugh incredulously. "Why?"

"You tell me." He nudges my arm with his. "What's on your mind?"

"Just mad at myself," I mumble, watching a bumble bee buzz near some marigolds around the walkway.

"Mad at yourself?" His face twists in confusion. "Why?"

"Because I kept her from you. It wasn't right. Not for her and not to you, either."

Thayer sighs, leaning back on his elbows and stretching his legs out on the stairs. "I've lost out on six years with our daughter." I wince at that. It's a punch to the gut but it's a truth and those are always the hardest to hear. "That fucking sucks, Salem, and yeah, it's shitty that you kept her from me—but we all have our reasons for the things we do. I can't go back in time and change your mind, so things work out differently. This is the reality we're dealing with and I'm not going to waste my time being mad about the past. You're *back*, Salem —and that's a chance I swore to myself I wouldn't throw away. And that kid in there? She's a miracle as far as I'm concerned. Let's not linger on the could-have-beens, okay? I want to move forward—do you want that?"

"So much."

"All right, then." He holds his hand out to me. "Let's shake on it. The past belongs to the past and the future is ours for the taking."

I slip my hand in his with a wobbly smile. "Ours."

With his hand still on mine, he helps me up and we head back inside to our daughter.

TWENTY-SIX

Thayer

"This is the best spaghetti I've ever had, Mommy." Seda chews on a meatball on the end of her fork.

"I'm happy you like it, sweetie." Salem eyes the takeout containers in the trash from the dinner I had delivered to her house. My lips twitch with the threat of a smile. I can almost hear her mind spinning from here, wondering why our daughter prefers restaurant spaghetti over something she'd make from scratch.

"Seda," I say, getting her attention. "What's your favorite color?"

She wrinkles her nose. "Rainbow, but mommy says that's a thing not a color, so pink then."

My heart beats a little faster. Just like I had guessed. It makes me feel good that even from some photos I was able to guess something about her.

"What about your favorite food?"

She sticks her tongue out in thought, but it takes her no time to decide. "Strawberry ice cream. Ooh, Grandma, do you have strawberry ice cream?"

Before her grandma can reply, Salem says, "You already had a cupcake, remember?"

"That was before dinner. It doesn't count."

My shoulders shake with laughter. Leaning into Salem, my lips brush her ear. "She really is my kid."

Her eyes sparkle. "Definitely."

As we eat, I continue to ask Seda questions to get to know her. I can't help but smile when she starts turning questions around on me.

"You have a treehouse." She pushes her empty plate away. "Can I play in it?"

Salem looks at me, worried about how I might react to this question. It doesn't upset me. If anything, it makes me happy. I think Forrest would like knowing his little sister is as excited about it as he was. "Sure. Yeah. Let's clean the dishes and you can come over and check it out."

"Really?" Her eyes light up.

"I want you to see it," I insist. Beneath the table, Salem's hand finds my knee, giving it a light squeeze.

Seda can't clean things quick enough then. She jumps up, helping to clear the table and even tries to do the dishes but Salem helps her when water starts immediately sloshing on the floor. She does let her load the dishwasher on her own.

When the door closes on the dishwasher she starts jumping up and down. "Treehouse now?" Her eyes bounce between Salem and me. I helped get Allie settled in her bed while they cleaned up.

I look at my daughter, never wanting to take my eyes off her. "We can go now."

"Sweet." She grins up at me, grabbing my hand. I look down in surprise at her small one wrapped around my larger one.

Seda is so open and loving. She doesn't hesitate with her affection.

I expected her to be shy, maybe even to be intimidated by me. But she's not. Kids are so much more resilient and accepting than we give them credit for.

Salem turns away, but not before I see the tears in her eyes. I hope they're good tears.

The three of us walk next door to my house and into the backyard. Seda looks around, taking in all the details. Her eyes grow round with excitement at the pool. "I love swimming!"

Salem senses the fear sliding through my veins.

"She's had extensive lessons since she was a baby and understands water safety. It was important to me."

Taking Salem's hand I give it a small squeeze, silently acknowledging my thanks. She smiles back, but it's a bit wobbly, and I know she's thinking about Forrest. That day left a scar on more people than just Krista and me.

Seda runs ahead of us to the treehouse. Her blonde hair is wavy, hanging halfway down her back. I see myself in her, but mostly she's a mini Salem. Looking at the woman beside me, my heart warms. She's been through more in her life than most people endure in a lifetime. She's strong and fierce—a fighter through and through. As much as I wish I could've been there for her when she was pregnant, been the man she needed, I think she was right in knowing that I wasn't capable of it. Not truly, anyway. I imagine I could've pretended for a while, but I was so checked out from myself, from *life*, for a long while after Forrest's passing. I hate that someone else had to step up to the plate that should've been mine, but I'm also so fucking glad she wasn't alone.

"Can I climb up?" Seda grabs onto the ladder that's secured to the treehouse and cemented into the ground.

"Go for it." I let her climb up on her own, but hover behind her in case she slips.

I'll be there to catch her—from now on that's where I'll belong, at my daughter's side guiding her through life.

She reaches the top and gasps. "Mom! There are bean bag chairs in here!"

Salem laughs, her hands in the back pockets of her shorts. The sun is almost completely set, behind her fireflies start to glow sporadically.

"She loves bean bag chairs."

I arch a brow. "That so?"

"Yeah." She shakes her head, smiling at a memory. "She begged for one for her bedroom. I kept saying no, but I ended up giving in. She has a reading nook and so I put it there."

Seda pokes her head out of the entrance. "Are you guys coming up?"

"It's big enough," I tell Salem, in case she wants to go up.

"All right." She starts her climb, and I don't mean to, but I can't look away from her ass. It's perfect and round. I want to grab it and pull her back down, kiss her long and slow and make love to her. My body aches with the need, it's been too fucking long—six years too long—but I want to take things slow with her.

Once Salem is inside ,I climb up.

With the three of us it's crowded, but there's enough space for me to rest my back against the wall and spread my legs out.

Salem looks around taking it all in. It took a while to get it built since I took my time with every detail, but I'm proud of how it turned out. "This is really nice."

"Thanks."

"Forrest would love it."

"Forrest?" Seda asks curiously. "Is this his treehouse? Can I say hi?"

Salem brushes her fingers through Seda's blonde hair. "Forrest is your brother."

"Oh. So, he's … gone?"

Salem nods sadly. "Yeah, baby, he's gone."

Seda turns her intelligent brown eyes to me. "Can I see a picture of my brother? Mommy didn't have any."

"Sure." I sit up, pulling my phone from my pocket and flip through my photos. "Here he is."

Seda studies the picture. "Do you think he would've liked me?" She addresses me, not Salem.

"I know he would have. He always wanted a sibling and a dog."

Her eyes light up. "Do you have a dog? We have a cat. He's kind of old though and sleeps a lot. His name is Binx."

My eyes find Salem's. She still has Binx. She gives a half-smile and shrugs.

"I have a dog. Her name is Winnie."

"That's cute. Can I meet her?"

"Sure."

Salem watches our interaction with a smile, tears shimmering in her eyes. I'm sure this is as emotional for her as it is for me.

"Can we go now?"

"If you want."

"I do."

She starts to move to climb out, but I shake my head. "Let me go first."

That way if she has any trouble I can help.

"Okay." She waits for me to crawl—yeah I have to fucking crawl—to the opening and climb out. As soon as my feet touch the ground she's already on the second rung. She handles it like a champ, never needing my help. "Come on, Mommy. We're waiting for you."

Salem starts down the ladder, her foot catching on the second to last step.

"Oh," she cries, losing her balance.

I'm right there though, wrapping her in my arms and helping her down before she falls. She turns in my arms, her hands on my chest. Her big eyes look up at me and I see the desire in them—I'm sure she can see the same in mine.

I've wanted this woman ever since she brought me cupcakes and rambled her way into my heart. When I look at her like this, it feels like no time at all has passed, like we were never separated. I think that's how you know a person is yours—when not time, or distance, can lessen the love between you.

"Are you okay?" I ask, brushing a stray hair back from her forehead.

"Y-Yeah," she stutters, breathless.

The urge to kiss her is almost too much to bear. I think I'd give in if it weren't for Seda.

"Hurry up you guys. I want to meet the doggy."

I set Salem fully on her feet. "Our daughter beckons," she says, her eyes never wavering from mine.

"I love the sound of that."

She wrinkles her nose in confusion. "Of her beckoning us?"

I shake my head. "Our daughter."

TWENTY-SEVEN

Salem

I wake up with a mouthful of Seda's hair.

"Ew," I gag, trying to get away from the wild tangle of hair in front of my face.

I put her in Georgia's room for the night, but at some point she climbed into bed with me and I let her. Soon, times like these where she comes to me for comfort will be long gone. I want to cherish them while I have them.

Rolling over, I pick up my phone from the nightstand and peer at the screen. There's a text from Thayer and Caleb. I open Caleb's first.

Caleb: I'll pick Seda up at noon if that's okay.

I type back a reply.

Me: That's fine.

I open Thayer's message next.

Thayer: I thought I could pick you two up for breakfast and visit Forrest's grave. You mentioned last night that she wanted to go by. If it's a bad idea it's fine.

Stifling a yawn, I look over my shoulder at her sleeping form.

Me: That's a great idea. I just woke up. I have to get Sleeping Beauty up too.

Thayer: Take your time.

Me: Caleb is going to pick her up around 12.

His reply takes a little longer this time.

Thayer: Okay.

Setting my phone back down, I ease from the bed and go to the bathroom. I pee and brush my teeth, then quietly go downstairs to check on my mom. After I've helped her into the bathroom and dressed for the day, I go back up and wake up Seda.

"I want to sleep," she grumbles, holding on tighter to the pillow.

"We're going to go get breakfast and visit your brother's grave."

Her eyes pop open at that. "Really?"

"You said you wanted to go. Is that still true?"

She nods soberly. "I'm going to shower, so don't fall back asleep," I warn, tapping her nose.

She giggles, wiggling around. "I won't."

"Get dressed and go talk to grandma if you want."

"Okay!" She grins, kicking off the covers. She runs from my room to Georgia's where her overnight bag is.

Taking a quick shower, I hop out and wrap myself in a towel. I apply a bit of mascara to my lashes and gloss on my lips. I don't have time for anything else since I need to get dressed and check on Seda and my mom.

Pulling on shorts and a red tank top, I slip my feet into a pair of white sneakers. My hair is wet from my shower, so I decide to leave it down to air dry until we leave. Then I'll pull it back into a bun.

Downstairs I find Seda sitting beside my mom's hospital bed. They're both coloring and talking quietly. I can't help myself when I take my phone out and snap a photo to catch the sweet moment.

"Mommy!" Seda cries when she sees me. "Are we ready to go? I'm hungry. I want pancakes with chocolate chips and syrup and—"

I chuckle at her enthusiasm. "Take a breath, girl."

She pauses, inhaling a deep breath. "Grandma, are you going with us?"

My mom shakes her head. "No, sweetie. Not this time."

"Aw, that's too bad. But it's okay, I'll bring you back something."

My mom pats her hand gently. "You do that, sweetie."

"Can we keep coloring when I get back?"

"Sure, if you want."

"Your dad is picking you up at noon to go back to Boston," I tell her, padding into the kitchen. I open a yogurt for my mom, setting her pills in a bowl. It's mostly pain pills at this point, just trying to keep her feeling the best she can.

"Aw, man. I like it here," she says when I come back into the room.

"You'll be back. Don't worry."

My mom takes the pills with the yogurt, and I silently encourage her to eat the rest of it.

I can tell she doesn't want to, but she obliges.

When the yogurt cup is empty, I throw it away and send a text to Thayer that we're ready.

"We'll be back soon, Mom. Behave yourself. Georgia will be here in about fifteen minutes."

She sighs. "You two don't trust me by myself, do you?"

I laugh, kissing the top of her head. "No, we don't."

She studies the page she was coloring. "Have a good breakfast."

"I love you, Mom."

"I love you, too."

Seda wraps her arms as best as she can around her grandma. "Love you, grandma!"

"I love you, peanut." My mom kisses her cheek.

Taking Seda's hand, we step outside onto the front porch. I lock the door since Georgia will come in from the side.

"Mommy?"

"Yeah, baby?" I drop my keys in my purse.

"Why does grandma have to die? Why did my brother have to die?"

Having this conversation with a five-year-old is hard. I don't want to lie to her, but I have to explain it in a way she'll understand.

Crouching down, I grasp her arms gently in my hands. "Life is beautiful." I brush her hair back from her forehead. "It's running through fields of flowers, catching butterflies in the summer and snowflakes on your tongue in the winter. Death is just another part of life. It's inevitable for each of us. The great equalizer." She listens intently, taking in every word I say. "Death doesn't have to be seen as this scary thing. It's a beautiful reminder that each of our breaths, each heartbeat," I point to her chest, and she places her hand over her thrumming heart, "is a gift to cherish."

She stands before me, and I know she's thinking over what I said. "So, I should be happy for grandma?"

"You should be understanding—death is scary, especially for the people left behind. We feel the sadness and pain of loss."

"And grandma?"

"I'm sure she doesn't want to die, but she won't be in pain anymore."

"So," she twists her lips back and forth, "death is nicer than life then, right?"

"What do you mean, sweetie?"

"Well, I get a boo-boo and feel it. I cry and I get sad. But death takes that away so it can't be so bad."

I smile at her. "That's a great way of looking at things."

Stepping off the porch, I hold her hand and walk next door to Thayer's. He's coming out of his house. His hair is damp from a shower, curling around his ears. He's dressed in a pair of khaki cargo shorts and a green shirt. Butterflies take flight in my stomach just looking at him.

"Are you ladies ready for breakfast?" He pushes the button on his keyfob to unlock his truck.

"Yes! Yes!" Seda jumps up and down. "I want pancakes with chocolate chips and syrup and whipped cream and—" I place my hand gently on her hand to stop her bouncing around. She giggles, smiling up at me. "Sorry."

Thayer is grinning at the whole thing, his eyes lit up as he watches us. "Pancakes, got it."

"Oh, shoot," I smack my forehead, "let me grab her car seat." I turn to walk next door, but Thayer stops me.

"Already taken care of." He opens the back passenger door, revealing a booster seat almost exactly like the one in my own car. Except this one is bright pink. I picked one that matched my car's interior, but Thayer's chose one that's Seda's favorite color—well, second favorite after rainbow.

I am not going to cry over a car seat! I admonish myself.

"Oh, wow. Okay. When did you get this?"

"Last night." He says it so casually, like he didn't run out late at night and buy a whole booster seat for Seda. It's such a little thing in the scheme of things, but it means everything.

"Hurry up, you guys. I'm hungry." Seda climbs up into the back and in her seat. She buckles herself in, but just like I always do Thayer tightens the straps, making sure she's secure.

He closes the car door, arching a brow when he finds me standing there staring at him. "What? Did I do something wrong?"

"No." I shake my head slowly. "You do everything right. That's what is so annoying."

He laughs, crossing his arms over his chest. "Annoying? How so?"

"Because nobody else can measure up," I mutter, skittering around him to get in the car.

He doesn't let me go that easy. His warm hand closes around my wrist, spinning me around until I collide with his chest. "I don't do these things for that purpose. I would never try to ... to *bribe* my way into your good graces."

Shaking my head, I can't take my eyes off his hand around my wrist. "I know that, Thayer."

He doesn't say anything, but I see it in his eyes.

He loves me. He still loves me as much as he did back then. It's never changed, but he won't say it because he won't push himself back into my life.

"We better go," I say, breaking the moment and gently pulling my arm from his. "Seda's hungry."

He nods, turning away with a mumbled, "Okay."

The two of us are quiet on the drive to the diner, but Seda entertains us telling Thayer stories about her school and her best friend

Maddy. He takes in every word, memorizing every detail she gives him.

Thayer parks behind the diner. Almost immediately Seda is unbuckling herself, reaching for the door but it has kid safety locks so she can't get out.

"Open sesame," she groans, trying to force the door open. "I want pancakes in my tummy!"

Soberly, I warn Thayer, "She's a monster when she's hungry."

"It's too bad I ate my emergency Snickers."

"Chocolate chip pancakes, please!" She shakes the door handle again.

Putting her out of her misery, I get out of the truck and open her door. She climbs down, staying by my side since she knows better than to run off.

Thayer locks up the truck, the three of us heading inside the diner. This might be a small town, but this place is always busy. Several people look our way, and I know they're probably figuring out what's going on here.

It'll be all over town soon that not only did I just come back to town, but I had Thayer's love child at nineteen. This will fill the town's gossip quota for the next five years—at least.

You seat yourself, so Thayer leads us to a booth in the back. He slides in one side and I know he's expecting Seda to sit opposite him with me, but instead she chooses his side. His eyes dart from her to me with surprise.

I take my spot across from them and I know this is one of those times I'm taking a snapshot in my mind. I don't want to forget this, how perfect they look side by side.

"Can someone get me chocolate chip pancakes in this place?" Seda asks loud enough that almost the entire building hears. If they weren't already staring, they would be now.

"Seda, that's not how we ask for things we want."

"Oh, I forgot the please. Sorry."

I shake my head, she's right on forgetting that but I was thinking more along the lines of using her inside voice.

"Well, well, well look at you. I thought I'd never lay my eyes on *the* Salem Matthews again."

I smile up at Darla who was always my favorite waitress here. "Hi, how are you?"

"I'm good." She nods, her eyes bouncing around the three of us. "This one yours?" She points at Seda.

"Yeah." I grin proudly. "She's mine."

"And ... Caleb's?" It's a presumptuous question, rather rude actually, but I know she doesn't mean any harm. That's how people in small town's are—your business is everyone's business.

"I assume you mean biologically?"

"Y-Yes?" She stutters it out as a question.

"Then the answer is no. Thayer," I wave my hand at him, "is her biological father. If everyone must know he wasn't aware of that until very recently. Caleb is her dad too, he's raised her, and that's that."

I keep my chin high, refusing to cower from these people.

Across from me, Seda's lips puff out with frustration. "Why do all these old people care who my daddy is? I have two daddies because I'm twice as special as all of you. *Now* can I have my chocolate chip pancakes?"

And with that statement from her, the volume in the diner picks up as people return to their food and coffee. Leave it to Seda to put people in their place.

TWENTY-EIGHT

Thayer

The situation at the diner wasn't the best, but Salem handled it like a champ just like she does everything.

Once all of us are full, I take my girls to the local flower shop to let Seda pick out flowers for Forrest's grave. I expect her to run around excitedly looking at all the pretty flowers, but I'm learning Seda rarely does what I expect. Instead, she quietly meanders the tiny shop, carefully peering at every flower and being careful not to touch.

"You're smiling," Salem says at my side. "What are you thinking about?"

Tilting my head her way, I tell her, "That I'm a lucky bastard. I got

466

to have breakfast with my girls—and I fucking love the sound of that. My girls," I repeat, my smile growing when Salem blushes.

She tucks a piece of hair behind her ear. "You think I'm yours, huh?"

"Think? No, baby, I know. I knew then and I know now—you're mine in the same way I'm yours. I don't own you, but you're my perfect fit—the puzzle piece I didn't know I was missing."

Her eyes soften, lips curling into a soft shy smile. She likes what I said and I meant every word.

Up ahead, Seda points at a bunch of flowers. "These."

It's a ready-made bouquet filled with sunflowers, eucalyptus, and small purple wildflowers similar to the one I suspect Salem left on Forrest's grave.

I grab up the bunch and carry it to the checkout counter. "We'll take these."

After it's paid for, I hand them over to Seda for safe keeping.

Salem stands off to the side, watching me interact with our daughter. I can see the guilt in her eyes, the worry that she really fucked things up. I wish I could get rid of those thoughts for her. Because no matter what happened before, we're here now.

Caleb has her past, but I have her future. That's all that matters to me.

"Come on, ladies, we don't have much time."

We load back into my truck, heading the short distance to the cemetery. We were at the diner longer than I expected and since Caleb is picking Seda up at noon I want to make sure we're back on time. It irks me to know I have to hand off my kid, but I don't want to step on Caleb's toes. I know in the long run it's better to keep our relationship cordial.

At the cemetery Seda hops out of the truck and stands there stoically. "It's quiet here," she whispers.

"Cemeteries are almost always quiet. I guess that's why they call it the final resting place."

"Hmm," she hums. Salem reaches across Seda's car seat and grabs the flowers, passing them to her. "Can you hold them?" My little girl asks me. "They're too big for my little hands." She holds up her hands, wiggling her fingers.

I take the flowers from Salem, surprised when Seda fits her hand into my empty one and her other into one of her mom's.

Seda doesn't know me—not really, anyway—but she has such an open loving heart that she doesn't hesitate to show affection.

The three of us walk hand in hand through the freshly mowed grass. I spot Forrest's grave up ahead and point it out to Seda.

"That one right there. That's your brother."

She looks up at me with big brown eyes—*my* eyes. I'm not sure I'll ever get used to that.

"Do you think he would have liked me?" She's already asked this before. It must be a question weighing on her mind.

"I know he would have loved having a little sister like you."

"I wish I knew him," she says softly as we finally reach the gravestone. She lets go of our hands and takes the flowers from me with a grunt. "Here you go, Forrest." She puts the flowers beside the grave. "I picked these out just for you. They're so pretty. I hope you like them." Seda looks up at us for support, like she's questioning whether or not she's doing this right. When I nod, she goes on. "I love dinosaurs—my mommy says you loved them too. That's cool. Do you have TV where you are? You probably don't, but if you do there's this show—"

Salem and I sit down in the grass a few feet away, giving Seda space to talk to her brother. I stretch my legs out, Salem scooting close enough to me that our legs touch and she rests her head on my shoulder.

This ... it feels like a dream.

I accepted my fate, that she'd never be mine, but the universe has given us another chance and I can't help but think it's because it was always supposed to be us.

"She's pretty amazing, huh?" She whispers the question so only I can hear.

I smile, watching our little girl sit cross-legged with Forrest, chatting animatedly like he's right there beside her.

"She's perfect."

CALEB'S SHINY MERCEDES SITS IN THE DRIVEWAY WHEN WE get back. I try not to let that piss me off. I need to be a mature ass adult about this.

"Daddy!" Seda cries excitedly from the backseat.

I feel a tiny sting in my chest, because that excitement isn't for me. I have to earn it, just like he did.

I park my truck on the street in front of my house. Caleb walks over, scooping up Seda when she jumps out.

"There's my girl." He spins her around.

My frustration melts a tiny bit, because I see how much he loves Seda. He loves her as if she really was his own—that's more than a lot of people are capable of.

He sets her down and turns to me, holding out his hand. "How's it going?"

I know I blindsided him yesterday thanking him for taking care of them, because let's face it, when he was a teenager heading off to college I wasn't exactly his biggest fan. But I guess we're both trying to put our best foot forward and be decent about this.

"I'm good." I shake his hand. "How was your night?"

"Good," he laughs. "My mom was happy to see me." I turn just in time to see Salem roll her eyes. "My mom doesn't like Salem," Caleb explains.

Salem huffs. "She liked me just fine when she thought we weren't that serious. But when you didn't break up with me that summer after senior year she got scared." She looks up at me, and finishes, "She's one of those boy moms that can't let go."

Caleb laughs more fully this time. "You're not wrong."

Salem goes on to add, "She definitely didn't like it when Caleb took Seda on as his own."

Caleb squeezes Seda's shoulders lightly. "Her loss, because this is the most awesome girl in all the land." He picks her up again, spinning her. Seda's giggles fill the air. When he sets her back down, he says, "I haven't seen my parents much the past few years so I'm trying to make some effort, but it isn't easy."

Salem gives him a sympathetic smile.

"I'm sorry she's the way she is."

Caleb shrugs. "Don't be, she could change. Anyway," he taps Seda on the head, "are you ready to go?"

"Yeah! Can we go to Target? There's a new princess toy I want and—"

"I'll think about it."

To me, Salem whispers, "He's going to stop. He's a sucker for whatever she wants."

"Hey," Caleb chortles, "I heard that."

"Well, it's true." Salem lets her hair down from the bun she had it in, and I must be a fucking pervert because even her hair turns me on, swaying around her shoulders.

Or maybe it's just that I really need to get laid.

Six years is a long time to be celibate, but honestly it didn't seem so bad until I saw her again. Now, I'm horny twenty-four-seven. Going to job sites with a boner is kind of awkward and hard to explain.

"I'll go get her bag so you can be on your way."

"I already got it. Georgia let me in, and I wanted to say bye to your mom anyway."

"Oh, okay." She bends down and opens her arms up to Seda. "Bye then, my little munchkin."

Seda dives into her, wrapping her arms around Salem's shoulders. "I love you, Mommy. I'm gonna miss you so much."

Salem lets her go and holds her fingers up. "How much is so much? This much?"

"No, more!" Seda giggles. "Like *this* much." She opens her arms wide.

Salem pulls her into a hug again, burying her face in Seda's neck. "I love you, baby girl."

"Love you too, Mommy. Now let me go. You're squishing me."

Salem releases her, standing back up. "You guys better go so you miss traffic."

Caleb rolls his eyes. "There's always traffic."

She laughs. "This is true."

Crouching down, I say to Seda, "Be good. I hope you can come back soon."

She nods eagerly. "I want to go in the treehouse again. That was fun."

"When you come back I promise you can play in the treehouse as much as you want."

"Awesome! Thanks, Dad!"

I don't expect a hug goodbye from her, but she wraps her little arms around my neck and squeezes me.

Fuck, I'm getting choked up.

With the goodbyes said, Caleb loads her in the car with Salem and I watching from the sidewalk when he backs out and leaves. He gives a honk of his horn before the car disappears from view.

Salem lets out a heavy sigh. "I miss her already. It's like a limb is missing."

"I know," I murmur, thinking not only of Seda but Forrest too.

Sympathy fills her eyes, no doubt thinking about Forrest now. Her hand finds its way to mine and she gives a small squeeze.

She doesn't say anything. She doesn't have to. Sometimes saying nothing is just as meaningful as saying everything.

TWENTY-NINE

Salem

t's late and I'm exhausted. I want nothing more than to fall face first into my bed, but I want to see Thayer more.

The last week with my mom has been rough.

The time is coming.

She knows it.

I know it.

Georgia knows it.

I'm terrified for her to take her last breath, leaving this realm for good, but I don't want her to hurt anymore. She's in so much pain that even morphine isn't doing a great job masking it, but it does make her sleep a lot which helps.

Walking next door, I climb his porch steps to ring the doorbell.

The urge to sneak over here was hard to resist, but I reminded myself I'm an adult now and there's nothing to hide. I'm single, Thayer's single—I'm twenty-five, he's thirty-seven.

The door opens. He doesn't say anything, just steps to the side to let me in.

"Hi." I rock back on my heels, suddenly feeling awkward now that I'm here.

"Hi," he says back, fighting a smile. "Do you want a glass of wine?"

I let out a soft laugh. "I'd love one."

I don't drink much, but right now it's exactly what I need.

Following him into the kitchen, I stare at the spot where we had our first kiss.

He stops in front of a cabinet. "Red or white?"

"Red."

He pours a glass, sliding it across the counter to me. Sitting on the barstool, I watch him pour his own glass and then make us a plate of crackers and cheese.

He settles beside me, his arm brushing mine in the process. A shiver runs down my spine. It's been so long since I've been touched by him in the way my body craves. Just one touch from him sends my body into flames. He notices the way I start to wiggle, his eyes narrowing. He sucks his cheeks in, I'm sure his ache is even worse than mine.

This man hasn't touched another woman for six whole years.

I wouldn't be mad if he had. I would've expected it. But the fact he didn't is one of the biggest turn-ons.

"Do you ... uh ... wanna talk?" He tries—and fails—to inconspicuously adjust his hard-on.

My mouth waters—and not because the wine is delicious, or I really like cheese.

I know he's asking about my mom, so I answer with, "Not really, but I probably should."

"You don't have to." He picks up a cracker, putting a slice of cheese on top.

"I know."

Thayer has never pushed me to do or say anything I didn't want to. I know people might look at our age difference and assume other-wise, especially with our past, but it's not true. Thayer is an alpha-male, but he understands my past and has always made sure I know who really has the control in our dynamic.

Sipping at the wine, we're quiet for a little while before I say, "I don't think she'll make it through the week."

Thayer hisses through his teeth. "Fuck." He scrubs a hand over the scruff on his cheeks and jaw. "I'm sorry, Salem. I don't really know what to say."

"We knew it was coming, it's not like it was a secret, but it feels so different now that it's here."

He surprises me when he puts his hand around the back of my neck, gently tugging me toward him. The ring on his pinky finger is cold against my skin.

"No matter what, Sunshine, I've got you."

A breath shudders through my whole body. It feels good—more than good—to hear him say that. His lips press tenderly to my fore-head. My body sinks into him on a sigh. Thayer has this way about him that makes me completely melt. I feel *safe* with him.

When he releases me, I grab for his hand. "What's your ring?" As soon as the question is out of my mouth, I already know. The suns stamped onto it look up at me. "I thought I lost this," I murmur, tears burning my eyes. I trace my finger over the cool surface. "I threw it at you." I'm lost in the memory. "I went back the next morning, and it was gone."

There's a lump in my throat, because Thayer took it. He *kept* it all this time.

"I always meant to give it back."

"But I left for good," I fill in the blanks.

He nods, taking his hand from mine. He slips the ring off his pinky and grabs my left hand. I hold my breath when he slips it on my bare ring finger, bringing it up to his mouth to press a tender kiss to it.

"That stays on," he says with a low growl, "until I'm the one to take it off and replace it."

I wet my lips. "Is that so?"

"Yeah." His voice is deep and husky. I wiggle in my seat, pressing my thighs together. I'm aching to be filled. "Just to make things clear, Sunshine, so we don't have any misunderstandings—I fully plan to make you my wife."

My heart beats loudly and rapidly. "You want to marry me?" My voice is high and squeaky.

"I want more than to marry you."

"W-What does that mean?" The man has me so flustered I'm stuttering now.

"It means, I want to have more babies with you. I want to go on vacations with you. I want to cook meals in this kitchen and do stupid mundane shit like clean the fucking house together. I want your clothes with mine in the fucking laundry. I want to laugh and cry together. I want to hold you every night when you sleep. I want to kiss you goodnight and good morning. I want to make love to you slow and fuck you hard. I want to sit out on the front porch and rock on the swing. I want, not only to grow old with you, but to live life with you. I want it all."

I tackle the man.

Literally jump out of the stool I'm sitting in, where it falls with a loud bang to the floor and wrap my arms around his neck so I can kiss him. He holds me tight against him, kissing me back.

He stands up with me in his arms, my legs going around his waist.

His lips never leave mine as he sits my butt on the counter.

My hips grind against him and he puts his hands on them, forcing me to still. I mewl in protest.

Need. I need him.

"Thayer," I plead between kisses.

His lips glide softly, delicately to my ear. "I want to take things slow," he reminds me.

Leaning back, I grip his shirt in my hand forcing him to look at me. "Fuck slow. I went six years without you. I want you. Today, tomorrow, fifty years from now, and even when we've turned to stardust." He smiles at my words. "Now, *please*, for the love of God—"

I don't have to finish my sentence. His mouth slants over mine, stealing my breath.

My hands skim beneath his shirt, feeling the heat of his stomach. His abdominals flex at my touch. I pull him closer, between my legs.

Kissing his way over to my ear, he murmurs, "You are everything to me."

Gliding a hand down my chest, between my breasts, he gently guides me to lie back. The stone is cold against my back, but I don't feel that way for long when he quickly undoes my jean shorts, sliding them down my legs to drop them on the floor.

I cry out at the first swipe of his tongue against my pussy. I slap a hand over my mouth, stifling my sounds. He senses this somehow, grabbing my arm to pull it away from my mouth. He wants to hear me. He works his tongue against me like a man who's been starved too long—which I guess in a way is true. His hand moves and I see him palming himself over his sweatpants. I whimper at the sight. Thayer touching himself is a ridiculously big turn-on.

With his freehand he rubs my clit and between that and the stimulation of his tongue, my orgasm spirals through me.

"Yes, yes, yes!" I cry out, the orgasm feeling never-ending.

When I finally come down from the high, my legs shaking, I climb off the counter and drop to my knees in front of Thayer.

I don't waste any time in freeing his cock from his sweatpants. He's big and hard and ready for me.

Biting my lip, I look up at him from beneath my lashes. "For the record, you're still the only man I've done this with."

I don't give him a chance to respond. Swiping my tongue over the bead of pre-cum and letting the slightly salty taste settle on my tongue.

His eyes are dark and hooded, his head dropping back with a soft, *"Fuck."*

Swirling my tongue around his tip, I take him deeper, stroking his length with my hand. From the sounds he's making I must be doing an okay job. I haven't been sucking him off long when he pushes me back.

"I'm not coming in your mouth. Not tonight."

He gets on his knees, taking my face between his thumb and forefinger he pulls me into a rough kiss. He bites my bottom lip, quickly soothing the sting with a swipe of his tongue.

We rid ourselves of the last of our clothes, and then he's laying me down on the floor. He bends one of my legs, and slides into me with one hard thrust.

"Oh my God!" My nails scratch at his back searching for purchase.

His eyes are molten, taking me in beneath him. He traces his fingers lightly over the stretch marks on my stomach.

"I fucking love these." I blush at the compliment. He lays his hand over my stomach. "You grew our child in there. Your body loved her so much it always wanted to remember her." He trails his finger over the line of one and I nearly shiver. "You feel so good, baby. You've always felt like mine." He buries his head in my neck, pressing open-mouthed kisses to the sensitive skin there. I hold him tight, never wanting to let go—never wanting to forget this. The weight of his body on mine is a reminder, that this, *us*, is real.

"Keep going," I beg, tugging on his hair. "I'm almost there again."

He moans when my pussy squeezes around his cock. "Keeping doing that and I won't last long, Sunshine."

"Can't help it." I do it again. "You feel so good in me."

"Fuck, yes, I do." He rises above me, taking my neck in his hand and squeezing lightly. "That's because I was made for you. And—" He pumps into me harder—"you were made for me."

The sounds he's making are such a turn on. Knowing he's enjoying this, *hearing* his pleasure, is enough to send my second orgasm rattling through me.

"Fuck, baby." He squeezes my throat a little tighter. "I can't—" He grits his teeth, trying to stave off his release. "I have to—" He throws his head back, flicking his hair out his eyes. "Oh, *fuck*."

He comes long and hard, his body shaking from the force of his release. His sweat-dampened body drapes over mine, his hold on my neck slackening.

He rises up slightly, placing a tender kiss on my swollen lips.

"Wrecked," he struggles to get a breath. "You have completely, and utterly wrecked me."

We fall asleep like that, right on the floor—a tangle of limbs and promises of a tomorrow.

THIRTY

Salem

Georgia sleeps soundly on the couch, her hands cradled under her head, mouth hanging open. She can't be comfortable. I knew she wouldn't go home, so I told her to at least go upstairs and lay in bed. She didn't listen. She wanted to be here.

My mom inhales a struggled breath.

This last week, we've known this time was coming, and I feel it now.

I had dozed off asleep, but I woke up—sensing the time is imminent, probably within the next hour. Nudging Georgia awake, we climb awkwardly into the hospital bed on either side of her. I rest one of my feet on the floor. I want to be close to my mom, for her to know she's not alone.

Her eyes crack open the tiniest bit. "Hey, Mom," Georgia sniffles.

"M-y my girls," she says groggily, the two words so quiet they're barely audible.

"We're here." I take one of her hands, her skin paper thin. Georgia takes the other. "We're not going anywhere."

"L-Love you b-both."

"We love you too." Tears stream down my face.

"D-Don't be m-mad at the world g-girls." Her chest inflates with a breath, making her cough. "Be h-happy b-because I l-lived."

Georgia and I hold onto her tiny frail form, both of us crying, and less than twenty minutes later, the alarms on her monitors that she's been wearing the past few weeks sound, alerting us to the fact that she's really and truly gone.

"Bye, Mom," I sob brokenly. "I'll miss you every day."

"Love you," Georgia cries. "I hope you're not hurting anymore, Mom."

Our mom suffered so much in her life, a life that was much too short, and all we can do is hope that there really is a better place out there, because if there's anyone who deserves it, it's her.

THIRTY-ONE

Thayer

The sound of sirens wakes me up from a dream, returning me to a nightmare. Every time I hear them now, I'm transported back to that dreadful day with Forrest. My stomach rolls as I get up from bed. Stumbling into the bathroom, I relieve myself and realize I still hear the sirens and they're *loud*.

Salem.

I yank on a pair of shorts, shoving my feet into a pair of shoes as I rush down the stairs. I don't even bother grabbing a shirt.

Rushing out the door, I see the ambulance is next door at her house.

I don't think, I just run over.

And there she is, standing on the driveway in her pajamas with her sister. They cry holding onto each other like if they let go one or both of them will completely crumble.

"Baby," I whisper, and somehow Salem hears me.

She opens her tear-streaked eyes, and I see the instant relief when she realizes it's me.

While she holds her sister, I hold her. She needs my support right now and I'm more than happy to give it. I'd give this woman anything.

Her body sinks against mine, inhaling audibly like she can breathe for the first time.

"I've got you," I murmur, kissing the top of her head. "I've always got you."

They roll her mother's body out of the house, loading it into the back of the ambulance.

"She's gone," Georgia cries loudly. "She's really gone."

"It was time."

"She didn't get to meet the new baby."

"I know. I'm sorry. I know you wanted that."

Salem's the youngest, but here she is comforting her older sister. Salem's always been that person though—putting everyone else above herself. But she has me now. I'll be her rock, her support when she needs it. With me, she doesn't have to be the strongest person. I'll help her weather any storm.

The ambulance leaves, the street getting eerily quiet once more and very dark. Across the street, my two favorite nosy neighbors, Thelma and Cynthia, stand on their porch watching. Thelma throws her hand up in a wave before the two of them scuttle back into their house.

"I need to take Georgia home," Salem whispers up to me.

"I'll take her."

"No." She shakes her head. "I need to do this."

"Are you sure? I can drive you both."

She hesitates, struggling to let me help, but finally she nods. "Okay."

"Let me grab my keys"

I run back over to my house, swiping my truck keys. Salem sits in the back with a crying Georgia while quietly giving me directions to her sister's house. I park out front and hop out to open the door. Salem gets out with her sister, walking her up to the door and unlocking it. I stand outside by my truck, waiting. She's in there for about fifteen minutes before she comes out. Her blonde hair hangs in her eyes, her shoulders hunched with exhaustion. I want to take her in my arms and hold her. I want to make this all go away.

And I realize, with stunning clarity, that when Forrest died that's all she wanted to do for me and I wouldn't let her.

I was such a fucking asshole.

I know I was grieving. I know I was in the darkest place imaginable. But I still think I should've been more understanding that she was only trying to help me because she loved me. You don't go out of your way for people who you don't really care about.

I meet her halfway on the driveway, wrapping my arms around her. She's nearly swallowed whole in my arms, but she doesn't seem to mind. I still didn't put a shirt on when I went back for my keys, I was in too much of a hurry, and her warm tears coat my bare skin.

"Don't worry, Sunshine," I cup the back of her head, "I've got you."

Her fingers grapple against my sides like she's having trouble holding on, but I know it's not that, it's just that her hands are shaking too much.

"She's gone," she hiccups. "She's really gone. I know it's for the best. She's not in pain anymore, but I just want my mom."

"Shh," I croon, resting my chin on top of her head. "It's okay."

"Why do the people we love have to leave us?" She forces my head back, looking up at me with a tear-streaked face.

Wiping away her tears with my thumbs, I say, "I don't have an answer for that. I've searched for one for years and come up empty."

Eventually I get her in my truck and drive her home—and by home I mean to my house.

She's fallen asleep on the drive, so I ease her from the truck, into my arms. Carrying her inside and all the way up to my bedroom, I lay her beneath the sheets and cover her up. Her breaths are even, her face still red and splotchy from crying.

She's beautiful, though. She always is. Staring down at her, it feels like every beat of my heart is saying *mine*.

I get into bed beside her, wrapping my arms around her and holding her to my chest.

Kissing the skin of her neck, I murmur, "I love you."

I swear, even in her sleep, she smiles at those three words.

I HEAR HER BEFORE I SEE HER. HER FEET QUIETLY TIPTOE down the stairs. Leaning against the kitchen counter, I sip at my morning cup of coffee. I smile against the rim when she pops around the corner. Her hair is messy from sleep, her shirt rumpled —but I fucking love seeing her like this, just out of bed, in my house.

"Hi," she says quietly. "You got anymore of that?" She points to the mug in my hand.

"Sure thing. Sit down."

While she sits I pour a cup, adding her specified amount of cream and sugar. Sliding the mug across to her, I ask, "Can I make you anything for breakfast?"

She frowns, wiggling her nose. I itch to reach out and run my finger along the freckles dotting the bridge of her nose. "I don't think I can eat."

"I understand."

"Do you want to talk about it?"

"No." She shakes her head. "Yes. I don't know." She takes a sip of coffee, wrapping her fingers around the warm cup. "Is it okay if I stay here? I don't think ... I'm not ready to go back to the house yet."

"You can stay here as long as you need." *Stay forever.* I don't say that though. "Want me to grab some things for you?"

She bites her lip, looking unsure. She looks up at me from beneath her lashes, her green eyes hesitant. "You don't mind?"

"Nope."

"That would be great. All of my stuff is upstairs in my old room and the bathroom." She runs her fingers through her hair, trying to straighten the messy strands. She sighs in frustration when she decides it's a futile effort. "I knew this was coming. We've known it for months, and this last week it was obvious her body couldn't fight anymore and yet … it feels so sudden." She shakes her head. "That sounds so stupid."

"I think death, even when it's expected, still feels sudden. It's so final."

She nods woodenly. "Most everything is already taken care of as far as funeral expenses and all that, but I just—" She rests her head in her hand. "I don't want to deal with any of it. Even the small decisions, but I can't burden Georgia with all of it. She's already pregnant and with two little ones."

"I'll help you. Whatever you need, I'll help."

"I know."

"I'm going to make breakfast, then I'll go get your things. If you decide you want to eat, that's great, but right now I won't force you."

She arches a brow. "Meaning there might come a point where you do force me?"

"Coerce might be a better word. I can be very persuasive."

"Is that so?"

"Mhmm," I hum, turning away from her to open the refrigerator, searching for something to make. "I have my ways."

She gives a soft laugh. I'm glad I can manage to bring her some sort of amusement through her grief.

Pulling out the eggs and some vegetables I already have chopped I get to work on some omelets. I don't ask her how she'd like hers. I just make one, then slide it in front of her. Grabbing a fork from the drawer I set it beside the plate, take one for myself, and sit down beside her.

"It smells good. Thank you."

"You're welcome." I dig into mine, not pushing her to eat. Surprisingly, she takes a bite and a few more until half is gone. That's all she manages to get down, but it's way more than I expected so I count it as a win.

Cleaning up the dishes, I let her sit quietly. After washing my hands, I nod upstairs. "Why don't you go up and shower? I'll go get your clothes and stuff."

"That'd be great, thanks."

She slides off the barstool, slowly leaving the kitchen. I wait to leave until I hear the shower start up.

The front door is unlocked to her mom's house. In some places, that would be a scary thing. But Hawthorne Mills is a town with so low of a crime rate it almost doesn't seem real. Small towns might be filled with nosy people, but they're good for some things too.

Upstairs, I find her room easily since I know it has to be at the front of the house. I scoop up a bag, tossing random clothes inside, and then head to the bathroom. Her toothbrush and toothpaste are on the rim of the porcelain sink. I stuff those in the bag along with some hairbands. I shove the shower curtain aside, swiping her shampoo and conditioner.

If there's anything else I missed, I'll have to come back later.

When I get back to my house and upstairs, she's still in the shower. I pull out her shampoo and conditioner figuring she'd prefer that over my man smelling ones.

"Salem?"

She eases open the glass door. "Yeah?"

"I brought these for you."

"Oh, thanks." She takes them from me.

I grab her chin before she can shut the door.

"Your eyes. You've been crying again." She nods, lower lip trembling. "Baby," I murmur, cupping her cheeks in my hands.

"Will you get in here with me? No funny business." She laughs brokenly, lifting her hands innocently. "I mean it. I'll be on my best behavior."

"All right." I let her go and step back, slipping out of my sleep pants. My dick is already hard, but I mean with a naked wet Salem right in front of me what do you expect? "Ignore him." I point at my cock. "He has a mind of his own."

She giggles, the sound surprisingly genuine. "I don't want to be alone."

Taking her face in my hands, I press my forehead to hers beneath the spray of the rain shower. "As long as my heart beats, you are never alone in this world."

She swallows thickly. "I love you too, Thayer."

She heard me last night.

"No funny business," I promise, "but I really need to kiss you."

She nods eagerly, like that's exactly what she needs. I kiss her. "I love you." I kiss her again. "I love you." I kiss each of her cheeks, murmuring those three words. "I love you." I kiss her forehead and then I just hold her for a few minutes.

When I let her go, I motion for her to turn around. She doesn't protest. Grabbing her shampoo bottle I lather the soap in my hands and then gently massage it into her scalp.

Sex is intimate, there's no denying it, but these are the raw, real, intimate moments that build your foundation. When you love someone, you take care of them in whatever way they need. Once her hair is washed, I grab my body wash since I didn't see hers back at her house and pour it onto a loofah. I wash and clean her body, making it completely non-sexual because that's not what she needs right now. She just needs to be cared for.

Stepping out of the shower I wrap her in a clean towel. I wrap another around my waist.

She exhales a shaky breath. "Thank you."

"You don't have to do that—thank me for everything."

"But I want you to know what it means to me."

"Believe me," I say slowly, carefully. "I know. I see it in the way you look at me. In how you say my name. The way you smile when I say something. I know, baby. I've always known."

She waddles forward in her towel. I know what she wants without asking. Wrapping my arms around her, I hold her. She soaks in my touch like it's a lifeline. I would be lying if I didn't say I wasn't doing the same with hers.

Six years ago, this smiley blonde woman wormed her way into my cold, angry heart and made it hers. I've never wanted it back. I still don't. But I do want to give her even more. When she's ready.

THIRTY-TWO

Salem

step inside the funeral home—the same one Forrest's service was held at. A shiver runs down my spine. I hate it here. I didn't think I would ever set foot in this place again. I didn't want to. I guess the universe had other plans.

Thayer's hand tightens against my waist. This is hard for him, but he refuses to be anywhere but at my side. I told him repeatedly that he didn't need to come for this, but he was adamant that he was going.

I'm thankful he's here, for his support, but I would understand if he couldn't face this.

The casket sits at the end of the aisle, the seats full of people. I expected no one to show up and instead the whole town is here.

I was supposed to be here earlier, but I just couldn't do it.

So, now I'm late. My sister sits at the front with her family but stands when she sees me.

"Hey." She eyes Thayer behind me but says nothing. She looks pleased though. "I was getting worried about you."

"I'm sorry." I reach to push hair behind my ear and realize that it's all pulled back in a low bun. I let my hand fall awkwardly to my side. It's not left hanging for long. Thayer entwines our fingers, giving my hand a small squeeze. "I didn't mean to be late. I just…"

"It's okay. I get it."

"Caleb and Seda will be here soon."

There's still twenty minutes until the service is set to begin.

"If we need to wait, we will," Georgia assures me. "Do you want to see her?"

I glance for a second at the open casket. "N-No," I stutter.

I know for some people it brings them comfort seeing their loved one, but not me. That's not my mom. That's a shell. Everything that made that body my mom is gone. Her spirit has left this realm. I hope she's saying hi to Forrest and carving pumpkins with him. Maybe they're looking down at us right now while drinking cups of hot chocolate.

"All right." Georgia doesn't argue with my choice. "You guys are to sit right there. Caleb and Seda will sit with you." She points out the spot reserved for us, and I nod gratefully.

My sister knows now all about my past with Thayer, that he's Seda's biological father. She wasn't surprised. She said she never knew for sure, but she had suspected. Apparently I'm way more of an open book than I thought.

Thayer and I take a seat. I blow out a breath, grateful so many people turned out for my mom, but at the same time I'm hoping I don't have to talk to them. I can't put on a smile right now and make small talk. I think it's wrong for people to expect that of those who are grieving. This is all so hard.

Thayer squeezes my hand again, reminding me he's here.

I love this man so much. And I know, even with the horrible tragedies we've gone through, I'd live it all again and again if it meant it led me to him.

When Caleb and Seda finally arrive, she cries out a loud, "Mommy!" when she sees me, diving into my arms.

"My girl." I hold her tight. She's getting so big. Soon the days of her saying mommy and letting me hold her like this will pass, becoming nothing but a memory.

She takes a seat between me and Caleb, with Thayer on my other side.

When the service begins, it feels like I'm not even in my body. I've checked out. It's the only way I can deal with this.

And Thayer had to do this for his child. His son.

I hold Seda's hand a little tighter.

A basic speech is given by some man, I can't even remember who he is, maybe a preacher, or maybe he works at the funeral home, but then Georgia gets up to speak. I didn't even know she was going to say anything.

She clears her throat, angling the microphone to her mouth. She shuffles some index cards, nodding like she's giving a mental pep talk to herself.

"My mom was a wonderful, tough woman. She endured things no person should ever have to. As did my sister and I." She taps the cards against the podium. "When my father died, she moved us to this town to get away from it all. A fresh start. She'd always dreamed of having something of her own and so she opened her shop. A Checkered Past Antiques was her special place, her calm against the storm. The name of her shop was a reflection of herself, just like many of the things she carried to sell. All beautiful and unique in their own away, a little battered and scarred, but still worthy of love." She sniffles, wiping beneath her nose. "My mom deserved the world, but the universe is rarely fair. When she got cancer the first time it was hard enough, but the second time around? She'd done everything right, so why was it back?" Georgia sighs, shaking her head. "Even when you do everything right, it can still go incredibly wrong. My mom's time came all too soon, and even if her past was speckled in darkness, she made the most of things when she got out. She loved us, my sister and me, with every beat of her heart, right until the end. She made us cupcakes, and braided our hair. She tucked us into bed at night with kisses on our foreheads. There was ... was a monster who haunted the three of us." She wipes at tears wetting her cheeks. "She thought she failed us. Thought she wasn't good enough. But she tried. She tried so many times to protect us, to get us away, and she couldn't. She was trapped in a marriage to a monster. Many of you don't know that, but now you do. Now you know that Allison Matthews was a victim of domestic violence, of marital rape, and so much more. But that's not *who* she was. She was light. She was happiness. She was *love*. She was a store owner. A baker. A grandma. Our *mother*. She might be gone, but she lives on in every beat of our hearts and those of our children." She pauses, taking a breath to gather herself. "Thank you."

She returns to her seat, and Michael pulls her into his arms, kissing her forehead.

I know I should probably get up and say something, but I can't.

Besides, Georgia said it all anyway.

The service comes to an end, and Thayer drives Caleb, Seda, and me to the cemetery for the graveside portion of the service. I feel emotionally drained and exhausted, but I know I have to make it through this part as well. Then I can crash.

At the grave side, it's only Georgia's family, Caleb, Seda, Thayer, and me. It seems like such a small amount of people, but I know my mom would only want us here.

Seda stands with her cousins, happy to see them.

"Are you okay?" Thayer whispers in my ear, his lips brushing my sensitive skin.

I force a smile. It's on the tip of my tongue to lie, but I don't want to lie to him anymore. "No." He wraps his arms tighter around me. His gaze drifts in the direction of Forrest's grave. "You don't have to stay." I know how hard this must be. I'm not expecting him to stay glued to my side if this is too much.

He shakes his head. "I'm not leaving you." Warm brown eyes meet mine and I instantly feel comforted. "Wherever you are is where I belong."

Luckily the graveside service is short and sweet, and we all start to head back to where we parked our cars.

Seda tugs on Caleb's hand. "My brother is over there." She points in the approximate location of Forrest's grave. To me she says, "Don't worry mom, he'll look after grandma."

I pull my black skirt up slightly so I can crouch down to her level. I stroke her soft cheek. "You think so?"

"Mhmm. They're family." She looks at me, then Caleb, and lastly Thayer. "We're all family."

"Yeah, we are." Caleb scoops her up, her arms going around his neck.

It's unconventional, the three of us raising Seda, but we are a family and we're going to do the best we can.

THIRTY-THREE

Thayer

Caleb heads back to Boston, leaving Seda behind since she's out of school now and she wanted to stay with her mother. I could tell it bothered him leaving her, but he didn't fight it since it's what Seda wanted.

The three of us are on the couch in my living room, watching some PIXAR movie Seda loves. She rests her head on Salem's leg, her body draped in a blanket, snoozing away. But neither of us makes a move to change the movie or turn the TV off all together.

"I was thinking," I start, and Salem turns her eyes up to me. She looks exhausted, her eyes red from crying off and on today. "Do you think ... I mean, would it be okay if I turned a room upstairs into a bedroom for Seda?"

She smiles slowly, stretching slightly. I'm sure she's stiff from not being able to move with Seda sleeping on her leg, but she never complains. "I think that's a great idea."

"You do?"

"You look so worried." She pokes my cheek. "Don't be. She should have a room here."

"I don't want her to feel obligated to stay here if you're not here, but I'd like for her to have a space that's her own."

"Trust me, Seda doesn't do anything she doesn't want to do."

"We can go furniture shopping tomorrow. I'll get whatever she wants."

Salem laughs lightly. "You're such a pushover."

Her phone vibrates on the coffee table. I lean over and grab it, handing it to her.

Her brows furrow at the screen. "Wha-?"

"What is it?" I ask.

"It's Lauren. She said she had something delivered and I need to grab it right now."

"What do you think it is?"

"I have no idea, but I better go see."

"Let me go."

"No." She shakes her head. "It's fine."

Somehow, she manages to get up without disturbing Seda. She heads quietly to the front door and opens it, looking around. I get up too, joining her. I put my hand on the back of her neck, massaging my thumb into the skin there.

"She probably meant your mom's house, love."

"Oh," she blushes, "right, of course."

Barefooted, she scurries off my front porch and runs next door. A moment later I hear a shrill, high-pitched scream. I look back at my house for one second and close the door before I take off in a run.

Is she being attacked? What's happening?

I get my answer seconds later when I run onto the driveway and find Lauren and Salem jumping up and down hugging each other.

That was a happy scream? I thought she was being murdered.

The two girls can't stop shrieking and my eardrums hurt. "Ladies," I interrupt, "do you mind if we head over to my house?"

Salem lets go of her best friend.

Lauren is tall with dark hair and tan skin. She's Salem's complete opposite, at least in looks, I can't say anything about her personality.

"Oh, look," she looks me up and down for emphasis, "it's Baby Daddy."

Salem busts out laughing while I shake my head.

"Seda's sleeping, come on," I encourage.

Salem grabs Lauren's hand, dragging her with her. "Thayer, grab Lauren's bag from her car will you?"

With a sigh, I unload the massively large suitcase from the back of the rental and wheel it behind me.

The girls' excited chatter grows softer as we approach my house since Seda is still asleep on the couch. I take Lauren's suitcase upstairs and put it in the first guestroom. It has an attached bath which I'm sure she'll prefer.

When I get back downstairs, I find both of them in the kitchen drinking wine with Salem gushing over a diamond ring on Lauren's finger. Salem hears me approach, looking over her shoulder with a smile. I'm glad Lauren came. She needs a friend during this time to help lift her spirits.

"Hi, Baby Daddy," Lauren says again. "It's nice to finally meet you."

Salem stifles her laughter. She's a little too amused at her friend's nickname for me.

I hold a hand out to Lauren. "It's nice to meet you, too."

She shakes my hand, squeezing a little tighter than necessary. "Hurt my bestie again and I have diplomatic immunity in six countries."

Salem snorts. "Don't listen to her."

Lauren releases my hand. "I mean it." She points a warning finger at me. "The minute you make her cry again—you're out." She makes a slicing motion across her throat. "I've seen *Dexter*."

"*Lauren*," Salem admonishes with a giggle. To me she says, "She's not serious."

"Like hell I am," Lauren grumbles.

Some guys might be turned off by Lauren's forward defensiveness, but I'm glad Salem has someone like her. Lauren has every right to be wary of me. I *did* break Salem's heart.

"You ladies have fun. I'm going to grab a water and carry Seda up to bed." I smack a kiss on Salem's cheek. "Don't get into too much trouble. I'm not sure I have enough bail money."

Lauren makes a yikes face and whisper hisses, "If he doesn't have money for bail you better run now."

"Lauren!" Salem playfully slaps her friend's arm.

Leaving them to their antics, I scoop Seda up off the couch and into my arms. She wiggles a bit and I still, praying she stays asleep. Luckily, she keeps snoozing. Upstairs, I lay her down in the other guestroom, carefully pulling the covers back and up over her.

I can't help but take a second to look at her.

It's unreal how perfect she is. I still have a hard time wrapping my head around the fact that this is my daughter. I have a little girl. My heart feels full for the first time in a long time.

Before Krista and I knew Forrest was a boy, I couldn't imagine myself having a daughter. I knew I'd be happy either way, but I hoped for a boy. I knew I could handle that. Being a boy dad would be easy. I'd had a brother and always done traditional guy things.

When Salem told me she'd had our child, a girl, there was no disappointment in any way. Seda is a gift, one I didn't know I even deserved. This little girl was created from the true love Salem and I have—a tether to always tie us together and bring us back.

Smoothing her hair off her forehead, I tell her I love her and slip out of the room I fully plan to redecorate from the generic furniture I put in there for the rare occasions I have visitors.

I DON'T KNOW HOW MUCH TIME HAS PASSED WHEN SALEM gets into bed. She snuggles up to me, pressing her cold toes against my legs. I crack an eye open.

"That was mean," I joke.

She wiggles her toes. "I need you to warm them up." She puts her hand on my cheek. "I'm sorry about Lauren," she whispers, then hiccups. "Too much wine, me thinks." With another hiccup she adds, "She means well."

"She loves you. I like that she's protective of you."

Salem smiles. "She really is a great friend. Can you believe she's getting married? He's a billionaire too. Yeah, with a B. Billionaire. Lauren would fall in love with a rich guy. She gets to live out all her billionaire romance lover dreams now." She slaps her hand over her mouth, stifling a yawn. "I'm drunk and rambling." She giggles.

Tracing my finger over her lips, I say, "There's something I want to talk to you about."

Her eyes widen. "Oh no. Am I in trouble? I swear I'm not that drunk."

"You're not in trouble, baby. But it's not something I want to talk about when you're drunk and sleepy."

"In the morning then?"

"In the morning," I promise.

Wrapping my arms around her, she rests her head on my chest just when I think she's asleep, her tears wet my skin.

"Sunshine," I whisper, holding her closer.

"She's gone, Thayer. She's really gone," she sobs. "I'm never going to see my mom again."

I press my lips to the top of her head and say, "I'm here. If you want to cry, scream, whatever you need to do, I've got you."

And so she just cries, because sometimes that's the only thing you can do.

THIRTY-FOUR

Salem

Waking up, I press a hand to my pounding temple. I drank way too much wine last night. I didn't mean to, but I stayed up late chatting with Lauren, catching up, and frankly just trying to forget about the events of the day. Since I'm not a big drinker it's caught up to me this morning.

Not to mention my eyes are practically swollen shut from crying myself to sleep.

My mom is really gone.

I can't walk next-door and see her.

I can't call her and hear her voice.

I'm never going to hear her laugh again or see her smile.

Rolling out of bed—*Thayer's* bed—I stumble into the bathroom.

There's a separate space for the toilet so I relieve myself—my bladder damn near bursting—while he's in the shower.

"Toothpaste," I mutter to myself, wanting to get rid of the fuzzy feeling in my mouth.

Thayer gets out of the shower, and I shamelessly ogle him in the mirror's reflection. My mouth literally waters. I hastily spit out my toothpaste before I make a fool of myself.

Only Thayer has the ability to completely ransack my thoughts and make me forget how sad I am just by looking at him.

Thayer swipes a towel from the rack, wrapping it around his waist.

I whimper as he approaches me, squeezing my legs together. Apparently hungover me turns into horny me.

He wraps his arms around me from behind, kissing the sensitive skin of my neck. I lean back into him, inhaling the scent of his woodsy body wash.

Just being held by him instantly makes me feel better.

Rinsing out my mouth with mouthwash, I spit it back into the sink and then reach for my hairbrush.

"My drunk memory might be hazy, but I think I remember you wanting to talk about something."

He leans his hip against the sink. "I did."

"And?" I prompt, setting my hair brush down.

My mouth waters just looking at him. He really needs to go put some clothes on because Thayer still wet from the shower with only a towel is my kryptonite.

His eyes narrow on me. "Stop looking at me like that."

"L-Like what?" I lick my lips. I can't help it, I'm so insanely attracted to him, and something about my grief has me wanting to be held and loved by him.

"Like you want me to fuck you."

I lift my chin defiantly. "Maybe I do."

I don't know who moves first, but suddenly I'm in his arms, his hand cupping the back of my head. Our tongues tangle together, and he backs me into the bedroom. He lets me go, a soft cry leaving me at the loss of his body heat. He checks that the door is locked and then he's back in front of me.

"God, I fucking love you," he growls, devouring me.

Some people wait a lifetime for a love like this.

I found it at eighteen in my grumpy, plant loving, lumberjack of a neighbor. Our paths diverged for a while there, but we were always meant to end up back here.

Thayer lays me down on the bed. Sitting up, I tear off my top. He hungrily takes in my bare breasts, leaning over me to suck first one nipple and then the other into his mouth.

I undo his towel, letting it drop and quickly grip his hard cock. His breath hisses between his teeth. Grabbing my boy short underwear I slept in, he yanks them down my ankles and drops them on the floor. His fingers find my core, rubbing my clit.

"Right there," I beg, rolling my hips.

He keeps rubbing just like I asked him, while I stroke his length.

"Need to be inside you," he begs. "You're gonna make me come just like this."

I guide his cock to my pussy and he doesn't waste any time sinking inside. His head falls back with a moan. I fucking love hearing his sounds. It's the biggest turn on knowing he gets so much pleasure from my body.

My nails dig into his ass cheeks, urging him on.

It's hard, fast, and a little bit wild. But I love seeing him let go.

"Fuck, baby," he groans, gripping my hips tighter. "You're squeezing my cock so tight."

He stands at the edge of the bed, wrapping his arms around my legs to pull me impossibly closer. He lifts my hips higher and the change in position is all I need for my orgasm to rip through me. He pumps his hips harder, faster, until he spills inside me.

He collapses on top of me, holding his weight up by his hands positioned on either side of my head.

"I love you," he whispers in my ear. "I love you so goddamn much."

I cup his scruffy cheeks in the palms of my hands, staring up into his eyes. "I love you, too."

I cherish being able to say those three words to him.

He pulls from my body, his cock still half-hard. "Stay here."

I watch him unabashedly as he pads into the bathroom. The

faucet runs and he returns a minute later pressing a warm, damp cloth between my legs. I move my hips, unable to help myself. I just had him, but I already want him again. Thayer has this way of turning me into a fiend.

He bites his lip, still wiping gently at my core. His eyes flick up to mine and I'm surprised when he asks, "Do you want more kids?"

I used to wonder if I did want more, it's something that's been in the back of my mind more as of late. Especially with Seda turning six in a matter of months. When Caleb approached the topic of having a baby I didn't freak out because I didn't want more kids, but over the fact that it felt wrong to have a child with him when I felt like he deserved more than me.

"Yes." I feel sure of the answer this time.

He sets the cloth aside. "Do you know..."

"Do I know what?" I prompt when he grows quiet.

He yanks a pair of boxer-briefs out of the dresser drawer and tugs them on. "Do you know when?"

"I'm not sure." I look away from him nervously. "Soon, I guess. Seda will be six and I know she'd love to be a big sister."

He leans over my body, cupping my face. Gently, he rubs his thumb over my bottom lip. "You can say no, I won't be mad..."

I narrow my eyes. "Okay?"

"I'd like for you to go off your birth control."

What?

"I ... like now?"

He nods. "I love being a dad, and I want to have more babies with you. I want to watch our kids grow up in this small town with its quirky traditions. I want to smell you baking cupcakes for school events. I want ... I already told you I want everything with you, and I want that future to start now." I can't help it, I start crying. "Fuck, baby," he wraps my naked body in his arms, "I didn't mean to make you cry."

"They're happy tears, I promise," I hiccup.

I didn't expect to have this kind of talk this morning, and I know it's fast, but it feels ... right. My mom would be happy, she'd want this for me. She wanted both Georgia and me to understand that life's short even if you die old and in your bed. You can't let fear hold you back. You have to *live*.

He doesn't look convinced as he brushes the wet droplets from my cheeks. "Are you sure? I know this is kind of out of left field, but I want everything with you, and fuck waiting. But I never want to push you if your timeline isn't the same as mine."

"Y-Yes. You want to have another baby with me?"

"Another and another and as many as you'll let me."

I laugh, my body shaking. "Let's get through one more first before you start planning on kid number three and beyond."

"Deal."

His smile sets my soul on fire—it's cheesy, but it's true.

"I'll stop taking my birth control today." His smile grows impossibly bigger. "Don't look so happy at the idea of knocking me up."

He chuckles. "I already did that once *with* birth control, excuse me for being a little cocky."

I poke his side. "Get off me. I need to shower and get dressed. Seda will be up soon. Lauren will probably sleep for half the day."

He eases up and I start to stand but he scoops me around the waist, spinning me into his body. My hands land on his hard torso.

"Are you sure you want this?"

I roll my eyes. "If it wasn't, I'd tell you."

"This is all happening faster than I planned. I wanted to do things right, take it slow with you—"

I press my hand over his mouth. "This is *our* right. You can't put love on a timeline. I've waited what feels like a lifetime to call you mine. I don't want to waste a single second more."

"Fuck, I love you."

"I love you, too. Now, let me go. I smell like sex. and I have birth control to throw in the trash."

He lets me go with a swat on my ass. I smile at him over my shoulder.

"Wait," I pause in the doorway of the bathroom, "was that what you wanted to talk to me about? The baby thing?"

He opens another drawer on the dresser and pulls out a pair of cargo shorts. "It wasn't, actually."

"Oh?" I wait for him to elaborate.

He shakes his head. "Don't look so scared. We'll talk about it later."

He swipes a shirt from the closet and heads out of the bedroom, closing the door behind him and leaving me no choice but to wait for that conversation, whatever it might be.

THIRTY-FIVE

Thayer

raid my pantry for the ingredients to make homemade waffles for breakfast. I figure it'll help soak up the last of the alcohol in the girls' systems.

I didn't mean to spring the baby thing on Salem, but it just kind of happened. I love her, I want to spend the rest of my life with her, and it seems like she wants the same, so what's the point in waiting?

But as sober as she seemed this morning, I still want to bring up the conversation again when I know for sure she has a clear head and ask her about moving in.

I've just finished stirring up the waffle batter when Seda pads into the room in her footy pajamas, rubbing her sleepy eyes.

"I'm hungry."

"I'm making waffles—do you want those or something else?"

Her brown eyes light up. "Waffles!"

"Do you want to help spoon it onto the waffle maker?"

"Yes, please." She nods eagerly.

I lift her onto the counter and pass her a spoon. She ladles the batter on, and I close the lid.

"When the light turns green that means it's done."

"Can I have chocolate chips in mine?"

I chuckle. I should've known she'd want chocolate chips. "Yep. Let me grab them."

It only takes me a second to swipe them from the pantry and set them on the counter with everything else.

"The light's green!" She cries excitedly, pointing at the waffle maker.

"Let me do this part," I tell her, grabbing a rubber spatula. "It's hot." I take the waffle out and set it on the waiting plate. "All right, time for more batter."

We work together, finishing all the waffles by the time Salem and Lauren come down.

Salem's freshly showered, her hair damp, and dressed for the day in her usual shorts and tank top. Lauren looks like she got run over by a car. Her hair is an untamed mess, there's drool dried in the corner of her mouth, and she's still wearing a pair of matching pajamas.

"Auntie Lauren!" Seda shrieks, climbing off the counter.

Lauren presses her fingers to her temples. "Quiet down my favorite little gremlin."

"I didn't know you were here," Seda jabbers, wrapping her arms around Lauren's legs. Poor Lauren looks like she's about to throw up. "Are you hungry? My dad made waffles. I helped."

"We'll see, kid." She ruffles Seda's hair and sits down at the table, laying her head on the surface.

Salem grabs the bottle of orange juice, pouring a glass for all of us. She carries one over to Lauren and says something about going to grab ibuprofen for her.

Lauren raises her hand, giving a thumb's up.

I plate up waffles for everyone and Seda helps me set the table.

Salem returns, handing Lauren two pills. She gulps them down and mutters something under her breath. Salem laughs, pushing the plate closer to Lauren.

"Eat," she admonishes. "It'll make you feel better."

"When I throw it all up in your lap don't say I didn't warn you."

Salem rolls her eyes, mouthing to me, "She's being dramatic."

Breakfast goes relatively smoothly, despite the glares Lauren sends my way every other minute. I don't let it bother me. I know she's being protective of Salem, and I'm glad she has a friend that cares so much.

Once the kitchen is all cleaned up, I join Salem and Lauren out on the deck while Seda plays in the treehouse.

I pull out a chair and sit down. Lauren has a big pair of sunglasses on her face, shielding her eyes. Salem props her legs up on the deck railing, tilting her head back to absorb the sun.

"Are you still up for taking Seda furniture shopping?"

Salem nods, wiggling her toes. They're painted a blue color. "Absolutely. I think she'd like having her own space here."

"Good. I might have to run by the hardware store too."

"For what?"

"Paint—I'm sure she'll want to change the color."

Right now, it's just a beige color I put in the guestroom because I had it leftover from a project.

Lauren snorts. "Pushover."

I shrug. "If it'll make Seda happy I don't think that makes me a pushover."

"Ignore her, she's just grumpy because she can't party like she used to."

"We didn't even party. We *drank* and now my brain hates me because it's literally pounding against my skull." Lauren points at her head to drive home her point. "I only just turned twenty-six and my body apparently has decided I'm forty and my life is over."

"Your life isn't over at forty."

Lauren lowers her sunglasses, her lips twitching when she tries not to smile. "You'd know, Old Man."

Salem shakes her head. "I need a babysitter for you. You're more of a handful than Seda."

Lauren tips her sunglasses like they're a hat in some old timey movie. "Happy to be of service. Someone has to keep you on your toes."

"Yeah, because life hasn't already done that to me yet."

Lauren wags a finger. "Touché."

"Seda!" Salem calls out. "Come down from there. We're going to run some errands, get some things to decorate your room!"

"Really?" Seda pokes her head out of the treehouse window. "Can I get a princess bed?"

"You can get—" Salem slaps her hand over my mouth, trying not to laugh.

"You are such a pushover. You can't tell her she'll get anything she wants. She might only be five, but she'll take full advantage of that."

"I wasn't going to say that." I grin when she lets her hand go.

"Oh, you weren't?"

My smile grows bigger. "Maybe."

She shakes her head, and I tug her into my lap.

Before Salem came back into my life, I was living every day just to make it through. Now, I'm living *for* every day.

It's like I can finally breathe again.

THIRTY-SIX

Salem

I'm exhausted by the time we get home from shopping. I've never grown into a love of shopping and I doubt I ever will. But Seda has a brand-new furniture set on the way, along with a new bedspread, and what she's dubbed Perfect Princess Pink paint for her room's walls. It's actually called Melted Ice Cream, but try telling her that.

"I normally love shopping," Lauren says, lugging in a bag of décor items, "but your daughter is making me question it."

"She's something," I agree.

Seda let loose to shop is like trying to wrangle a wild bunny. She runs and hops all over the place—skips too—says hi to almost every stranger she sees, and dances in aisles if she likes the music the store is playing.

Basically, my child is the complete opposite of what I was. Then again, I'm not really sure what I would've been like as a child if it hadn't been tainted by a monster.

We unload all of the bags while Seda runs around the front yard singing a made-up song.

"Don't go near the street," I warn, walking up the porch steps to set bags in the foyer.

"I won't, Mom. You don't have to worry so much."

She has no idea but that's like half of being a parent, maybe even more, constantly worrying.

"Do you think you'll have kids?" I ask Lauren when she sets down a bag of throw pillows beside my bag of blankets—because Seda can't just have one blanket, she needs twelve. *That* she did get from me.

"Maybe when I'm thirty." Lauren wrinkles her nose, pursing her lips like she tastes something sour. "No, not even then." She glances out the open door to where Thayer is now chasing Seda around the lawn. "I like your kid, but that's it. I'm not sure I'd be a good mom."

"You'd be a great mom," I assure her, because she would be if that's what she chose. "But not everyone wants to be a parent and that's okay, too."

She shrugs. "We'll see in the future. Right now, I like it just being me and Anthony." She glances down at her ring finger. "Gotta get through the wedding first."

"I can't believe you're getting married in the Hamptons," I bump her shoulder playfully, "you boujee bitch."

She cackles. "Anthony's parents' place is there and it's stunning. It's perfect."

The way she lights up talking about her fiancé makes me happy. She deserves that. For a while there I wasn't sure she'd ever settle down. There's nothing wrong with that, but I could tell she was searching for someone to tame her. Not that Anthony has completely tamed her wild side, but when she's with him she is a slightly calmer version of her normal self.

I have to head up to Manhattan soon for the final fitting of my

Maid of Honor dress. The wedding is at the end of the summer, and in just a few weeks we're headed to Vegas for her bachelorette. With the loss of my mom, I don't know how much fun I'll be on that trip, but I wouldn't miss it.

"Speaking of the wedding, now that you're with Thayer I assume you'll be bringing him?" She asks as we head back out to my SUV for more bags.

"I mean, I guess, yeah. I hadn't even thought about it."

"I'll add him to the list." I reach for a bag when she catches my arm. "You know, I love to give you a hard time, but I'm happy for you. You and him..." Her eyes drift to where he has Seda draped over his shoulder, spinning her around, "anyone can see it's special. I'm glad you got this second chance. Not everyone gets that. You deserve to be happy more than anyone I know."

I throw my arms around her, squeezing my best friend tight. I miss living closer to her. "Thank you."

"Ew," she playfully shoves me off, "you're giving me cooties."

I stick my tongue out at her. "You wish."

"Save them for Thayer. I'm pretty sure that man *loves* your cooties."

"Lauren!" I shriek, swatting her arm.

She just grabs a bag and cackles all the way into the house.

THE NEXT DAY, LAUREN'S HEADING BACK TO MANHATTAN. I'M so happy she was able to come out—she said she had intended to be in early enough for the funeral, but her flight from Chicago got delayed; her fiancé has another place there where they stay sometimes depending on what he's doing with work.

I hug her tight beside the rental car—already loaded with her suitcase thanks to Thayer.

"I don't want you to go."

"I don't want to go either, but I'll see you soon for dress fittings and then it's Vegas time, baby!" She lets me go, doing a little wiggle.

Thayer arches a brow. I haven't had a chance to fill him in on the wedding and all the details, but with Lauren heading back to New

York we'll have more time. Plus, we're taking Seda back to Boston today. I wanted to keep her longer, but Caleb and I are still trying to figure out this whole system. Plus, I need to start cleaning out my mom's house and it'll be easier if Seda isn't around, just because she'll get into everything. Regardless, it already feels like a piece of my heart is missing and she isn't even gone yet.

"Love you, girly," I kiss Lauren's cheek, "see you soon."

"Don't be a stranger." She winks playfully, trying to mask the tears in her eyes.

Standing on the driveway, I wave as she backs out and drives away. Thayer comes up behind me, putting his hand on my shoulder. Winnie barks in the yard, chasing after Seda. They both wear matching rainbow tutus that Thayer sewed himself—talk about swoon.

"I'm sorry she had to leave so soon." His voice is deep and husky beside my ear.

I exhale, trying not to be too upset about it. "It's okay. I'm happy she came at all."

That's what means the most, knowing my friend came to support me during this time.

"We haven't had a chance to talk about the other thing."

I turn to face him, brows wrinkling. "What thing?"

"The one I wanted to talk to you about."

"Oh." Clarity comes to me. "Right. What was it?"

"When we drop Seda off, I was thinking you could get more of your things, Binx too, and..."

"And what?" I prompt.

He ducks his head, his shaggy hair hiding his eyes from my view. "Do you want to move in with me?" His cheeks turn bright red like he's embarrassed and nervous. I think I love seeing him flustered way too much. Thayer is normally the definition of cool, calm, and collected, but this has him feeling floundered.

"You want me to live with you?" He nods. "Like share the same bed? My hair clogging your shower, clothes on the floor, my crap taking over yours—that kind of live together?"

He nods again. "It makes sense, right? Why wait?"

He has a point. I mean, I did throw my birth control away. We had

510

another conversation about it that night. He wanted to make sure I was clear headed and making a sound decision. I wasn't that drunk that morning, I drank way less than Lauren it just makes me feel foggy-headed, but it made me happy that Thayer always puts me first and understands how important my consent is.

I glance next door at my teenage childhood home. I don't want to live there. It's not that it holds bad memories—my dad never lived there—but it doesn't feel like mine. It reminds me of her, and I don't think I could ever do anything to change that. The best course of action is to clean it up, fix some small things, and sell it. Georgia and I can split the money and it'll help out both of us.

The store is a different situation. I know it's stupid to keep it, makes no logical sense, but I have way more trouble parting with it than the house.

"Yes," I say softly, then a bit louder I add, "I'll move in with you."

His smile starts small, then it grows into a full-blown grin. He doesn't say anything. Instead, he scoops me into his arms, spinning me around and around. My feet lift off the ground and I giggle.

He sets me down, cupping my cheeks. "I swear to God, Sunshine, I'm going to make you the happiest woman on the planet." He doesn't give me a chance to respond. Slanting his mouth over mine he kisses me deeply.

Some people never find this kind of love in a lifetime. I found it at eighteen, lost it for a while, and now I'm never letting it—letting *him*—go.

THIRTY-SEVEN

Salem

I could tell Caleb was sad when I packed up more of my stuff and took Binx with me. I told him why and there was the briefest flash of pain in his eyes before he forced a smile and said he was happy for me. I don't like that I'm always breaking his heart, but I remind myself we're divorced now, and we were both going to move on eventually.

One day, he'll find his person, and then he'll understand.

I'm hanging up a dress in Thayer's closet when he comes in, wrapping his hands around me from behind. He smells like sweat, earth, and cigarette smoke from his day on the job site. He doesn't smoke anymore, at least that's what he says, but some of the guys he works with do.

"I missed you." He lays his head on my shoulder. His hands go to my stomach. "Do you think you're pregnant yet?"

I giggle, swaying out of his arms so I can turn to face him. "You're obsessed with knocking me up out of wedlock, aren't you?" I can't help but joke. Truth be told, I don't feel the need for him to propose. Now that we're together again I know everything will happen in the timeline it's supposed to.

He looks me over with a half-smile. "Fuck yeah. I love the thought of you round with my child." I roll my eyes. He grabs my hips, gently pulling me into his space. He towers over me, so I angle my head back to see him. "I didn't get to see you the first time. I didn't get to feel her kick or take you to doctor's appointments. I want that."

I wet my lips, feeling shame.

He cups my cheek, forcing me to look at him when I try to drop my gaze. "Don't do that. Don't hide what you're feeling from me. I want us to be honest with each other, always. That's when things get tough, when you hide things, or lie about how you feel."

I sigh, my shoulders feeling impossibly heavy. "I wish you could've been there too and I feel awful that you didn't get to be."

"You did the best thing," he reminds me for the umpteenth time. "I wasn't ... I couldn't have been the man, the father, I needed to be back then. You knew that." He rubs his thumb over my cheek. "I refuse to let you have regrets, because we have right now. I get to wake up every day with you in my arms. I get to hear Seda running in the halls when she's here. Winnie and Binx get to be best friends." I laugh at that, because surprisingly they are. My black cat and the corgi like to sleep together on the couch. "And one day, whenever it's meant to happen, I'll get to hear our crying baby down the hall."

A tear leaks out of the corner of my eye. He quickly swipes it with his pointer finger.

"Now," he grabs my hand, "come shower with me." He grins wickedly, eyes dark with desire.

I let him tug me along and when he presses my naked back against the shower tile, sinking inside me, I finally let go.

AFTER A FACETIME CALL WITH SEDA WE SETTLE ON THE couch with a bowl of popcorn for a movie night. Thayer lays down, plopping his head in my lap.

"What are you in the mood to watch?"

"To be honest," he yawns, "I'm probably going to fall right to sleep, so whatever you want is fine."

I flick through the movies I have saved on my account, settling on a rom-com. If he's truly about to fall asleep then I'd like to watch Matthew McConaughey's Benjamin Barry get tortured by Kate Hudson's Andy Anderson in *How To Lose a Guy in 10 Days*.

Thayer doesn't protest when it starts. I rub at his scalp with one hand, popping bites of popcorn into my mouth with the other. On the other end of the couch Winnie snoozes with Binx curled up against her.

It's only fifteen minutes into the movie when I look down and find Thayer fast asleep. He works a lot of long days. He might be the owner and therefore the boss, but when it comes to his business he likes being as hands on as possible.

Not to mention he's spent the past couple of days painting the room that's now Seda's, as well as putting together her furniture.

When she comes back in a few days she'll have her very own princess room.

Thayer even went back to the store and got the bean bag chair I had previously convinced him to leave behind.

There are a total of three spare rooms upstairs, one is Seda's now, and I guess, if Thayer manages his goal of getting me pregnant, another will be turned into a nursery.

The idea of watching Thayer rock a precious newborn in his arms at night has me feeling all kinds of warm and gooey.

Then almost immediately another feeling overcomes me, one of sadness and pain when I think about Forrest's old room that Thayer did away with a long time ago. I asked him about it and he said he left it for a while but seeing it just became too painful so he packed most things away, sold the furniture, and moved some of Forrest's more prized possessions like his favorite dinosaur and a toy car to different spots around the house. It says it makes him smile seeing those little pops of Forrest but that the whole room was just too much.

I look down at him, his face calm in his sleep.

The pain he's had to live through must be unbearable.

He told me his therapist described grief as a ball in a box. When the pain is fresh that ball is large, constantly hitting the sides of the box, but then the ball grows smaller over time and hits the box less.

Right now, for me, that ball is pretty large. It's why I'm avoiding going back over to my mom's house.

I don't want to touch her stuff. I don't want to pack it away in storage or donate it or—

I wipe away my tears with the back of my hand.

When I do that, it'll finally feel real.

Right now, I'm in this state of pretending she's still in that house baking cupcakes or watching a movie or just sitting at the kitchen table eating a bowl of cereal.

Grief is strange that way—how it tries to defy logic.

I saw her die. I went to the funeral. The grave.

I did all those things, and yet my mind is still holding onto the illogical hope that she's in that house.

The movie continues to play, but I'm not paying attention anymore. When the end credits roll, I turn the TV off and gently wake Thayer. He takes one look at me and knows that the grief is consuming me. He doesn't say anything. He doesn't have to. He just wraps me in his arms, letting me grab onto him in a koala hold, and carries me upstairs to bed. He doesn't let me go even then and I wonder if he thinks he can hold me tight enough that I don't fall apart.

THIRTY-EIGHT

Salem

Two weeks pass before I'm ready to start clearing out the house. Georgia insisted on helping when I let her know I was finally taking on the job, but I was more persistent in getting her to let it go since she could go into labor at any time. With this being her third she's more likely to come before her due date and she definitely doesn't need to be doing anything strenuous despite her stubborn behavior.

"Where do you want to start?" Thayer asks, hands on his hips.

We stand on the front lawn since I haven't made the first move to step inside yet. Thayer's been keeping the lawn immaculate so at least we don't have that worry.

I open and close my mouth, no words willing to come out.

Thayer doesn't let my silence deter him.

"Maybe we should go around and mark the bigger furniture items with different colored tape. What you want to keep, donate, and trash. That might make it easier with those things."

I nod steadily, willing my tears not to fall. It's just a house. It's just things. So why is this so emotional?

"That's a good idea."

"All right." He nods to himself. "You wait here, and I'll grab tape from my truck."

I wrinkle my nose. "You keep tape in your truck?"

"I keep lots of things in my truck."

While he gets the tape, I wander closer to the side door. It feels easier to go through there than the front door. That puts me too close to the living room and I'm not ready to tackle that.

Thayer returns, finding me fumbling with my keys by the door.

He swipes them from me, juggling three different rolls of tape in colors of yellow, blue, and green. "Which is it?"

"That one." I point to the one with the white daisy rubber holder on the end.

He slips it easily into the lock and turns it. The door squeaks loudly, in desperate need of some WD-40 on the hinges—another thing to add to the to-do list—and steps inside first.

"Are you coming?"

He doesn't ask it in a taunting way. It's more like he's trying to gauge how I feel about this and whether or not it's a good idea to start today.

But if I don't cross this threshold now and start this process, I don't think I ever will.

I do it, I put one foot forward and keep going until I'm standing in the kitchen. I flick the switch to turn the ceiling light on, bathing the room in a yellow tone.

Thayer wastes no time, I think he wants to distract me, so I don't get lost in my thoughts, and starts spewing out questions. "What about the table? Keep? Donate? Or trash? It's in pretty rough shape, but it could be sanded down and painted, so I'm thinking donate. And what color tape do you want to put with each category?"

I can't help but smile at his need to keep my mind from wandering. "I think yellow for donate, green for keep, and blue for trash."

"Okay, got it. Committing it to memory."

"We'll donate the table."

He rips off a piece of yellow tape and applies it to the table.

"Chairs?"

"Also donate."

He tabs each of the chairs with tape. "You can just point and tell me what you want to do with each thing."

"Okay," I sigh, looking around the space.

"Trash." I indicate a picture across the room. It was a yard sale find shortly after my dad died. I thought the picture was so ugly—a muddy looking watercolor that reminds me of some kind of ugly wallpaper, but my mom loved it for some reason, or maybe she just loved it because it was something she could buy with her own money for the first time. "Actually, I want to keep it."

Thayer doesn't even question why I'd want to keep the ugly painting, he just switches the tape color and moves on.

It takes us a few hours just to go through the kitchen. I end up keeping all of the baking supplies. Despite not baking for years until I came back here, I want to keep them, and I even want to bake on my own again. I think it'll do me good and help me feel close to her. There are a few things I put in the keep pile for Georgia as well, things she already asked for—like the cookie jar that's shaped like a circus tent and a set of plates.

"How do you feel?" Thayer asks me, picking up the last of the donate boxes to load in his truck to drop off. We figured it would be easier to take the smaller items as we go and then when it's all finished, we'll rent a truck to pack up the home's bigger items to get rid of.

"I think we made good progress, but I'm also worried about how long this will take. We spent *hours* on one room."

"I don't mean about this." He looks around the room. "I mean about *you*. I know this isn't easy."

I pull out the kitchen chair and sit down. "Exhausted. Both emotionally and physically. But strangely ... happy." I shake my head. "That sounds so strange but it's true. So many of these items hold memories and it's like I get to relive them all over again." I pick up the wooden spoon I'm keeping. "Like this." Tears pool in my eyes. "It's just a wooden stirring spoon to you, but I remember stirring up cupcakes with my mom when I was little and sneaking licks of the batter when she wasn't looking. I think she knew anyway." I set the spoon back down. "It's nice, remembering the things I forgot."

Thayer sets the box back down, joining me at the table. "It doesn't sound strange. I felt the same way packing up Forrest's room. It was the hardest decision I've ever had to make, but I knew for my mental health I needed to change the space. As I packed up his clothes, toys, I remembered so many good things I'd forgotten because that one day put a dark cloud over my memories." He clears his throat, getting choked up. "Losing him was ... the worst fucking day of my life. But every day he was alive was also the best day and I realized then I was letting one day overshadow all the others. Remembering didn't feel so painful anymore after that." He shrugs. "So, yeah, I get it."

"Grief is weird."

He gives a soft laugh. "Yeah, it is."

"Do you ever wonder..." I pause, biting my lip—unsure if I should say it or not, but I decide to just go for it. "Do you ever wonder what would have happened if..."

"If Forrest hadn't died? If we'd told your mom?"

"Yeah." I look down at the table, not wanting to meet his eyes. "I know it's stupid, to waste time wondering when there's nothing you can do to change the outcome but..."

"I used to," he says softly. "All the time. But I stopped doing that a long time ago, because it was driving me insane. I'd like to think that if things had gone according to plan that your mom would've understood, but she also might've been pissed. I mean, she already knew, but making it official is different." He sighs warily, sinking further into the chair. "And then maybe we would've dated a few more years. And I would've gotten down on one knee, proposed, and we would've gotten married with Forrest as my best man. But there's also the chance that because of how young you were that the pressure would've been too much. Society looks much differently on the ages we are now, than what we were." He flicks a finger between us. "That might've torn us apart. We don't know."

"You're right." I look around the kitchen, the walls now bare, the drawers empty, cabinets and countertops completely wiped down. "I guess this just has me dwelling more than usual."

He reaches across the table, squeezing my hand. "Come on," he stands, still holding onto my hand and using it to tug me up with him. "Let's go drop this off and grab something to eat. I think we deserve it."

My stomach rumbles in answer. "Good idea."

THIRTY-NINE

Salem

We work on clearing out the house as much as possible. With Thayer working, he's not around to help during the weekdays so I do what I can that doesn't involve heavy lifting. After that first day it's gotten easier. I think I've managed to put blinders on and not think too much about it, which has helped. Plus, I know this needs to be done. We can't just leave the house sitting here. Sometimes, you have to set your grief aside and take care of what has to be done.

I'm elbow deep in dust, cleaning out a storage closet when my phone rings. I can't grab it right now, so I let it go to voicemail.

It rings again right away.

"Huh." I set down my cleaning supplies and get up off the floor, my body groaning in protest since I've been in a hunched position for too long. I knew I should've gotten up and taken a break, but I didn't bother.

I don't make it to my phone in time before it stops, but it starts up yet again just in time for me to find it under a pile of trash bags. Lovely.

Georgia's name lights up the phone.

"Hello?"

"I'm in labor," are the first words out of her mouth, "I know we didn't talk about this, but mom was with me both other times and I want you to be there this time. Are you okay with that?"

My heart warms that she wants me there, that she trusts and loves me enough to be there when she brings her third child into the world.

"Yeah, of course. Are you at the hospital?" I start gathering up my stuff and trying to leave things in some sort of order, but quickly realize that's a futile effort since everything is a mess.

"We're dropping the boys off with Michael's parents and driving straight there. Oh, fuck," she curses. "This hurts. I don't remember it hurting this bad before. Was it always like this?"

Michael answers her and I hear his reply of, "Yeah, and you just always forget," through the speaker phone.

"I'll be right behind you guys."

"Thank you." I can hear the tears in her voice. "I just don't want to be alone."

"What am I? Chopped liver?" Michael asks.

"You know what I mean," she argues, and they launch into a back and forth.

"All right, I'm going to hang up now so I can finish up and head to the hospital."

"Okay," my sister replies. "I love you."

"Love you, too."

I turn the lights off, set out the garbage, and run over to Thayer's to have a quick shower since I'm covered in dust and change my clothes.

When I get into my car to head to the hospital, I shoot him a quick text to let him know what's going on and that I won't be home.

He texts right back as I'm backing out of the driveway.

Thayer: I'll head to the hospital when I'm done with work.

The local hospital isn't far, only twenty minutes away, so I call Michael through my car's Bluetooth speaker.

"Hey, I'm on my way. How is she?"

"Uh ... for the moment, calm. But as soon as she has another contraction, she'll be demanding that I get a vasectomy. As soon as that has passed, she'll threaten me that I better not because she wants one or two more. Honestly, Salem, if she keeps this up my balls are going to shrivel up and die."

I can't help but laugh. The poor guy. "Sounds like my sister. Let her know I'm on my way and I—"

I don't finish my sentence, because in that exact moment someone runs a red light, and the sound of screeching metal fills my ears. My head slams against the window, the airbag exploding, and then there's only blackness.

FORTY

Thayer

Saying goodbye to my crew, I hop in my truck to head home. I'll take a shower and grab a bite to eat before going to the hospital.

I'm halfway home when my phone rings and it's Georgia's name on the screen.

"Hello?" I answer skeptically, wondering why Salem's sister would be calling me. Maybe Salem's phone died, though, and she's wondering where I'm at.

"Thayer," Georgia says my name in a rush of relief. "Oh, ow! Son of a bitch! Fuck, I better not say that, because that makes me the ah!" She screams in my ear. "Michael, take the phone."

A moment later, her husband comes on the line. "Uh, hey, man."

"What's going on? Is something wrong with Salem's phone?"

He's silent for a moment. I know it's only seconds, but it feels like minutes.

"Salem's been in an accident."

I drop my phone. It falls somewhere on the floor between my feet. Making a very illegal U-turn, I speed back in the opposite direction toward the hospital.

My brain keeps repeating two words over and over again.

Salem.

Accident.

Salem.

Accident.

I'm fucking hyperventilating by the time I get to the hospital and park my truck, rushing inside through the emergency entrance.

The lady at the front desk is startled by my sudden appearance.

"Salem Matthews. Was she brought in?"

Fuck, they could've taken her to the city. Life-flighted her. What if it was really bad? What if she's in surgery? What if she's—

No. I won't fucking go there. I won't think that. She's not. She can't be. I would *know* if she were dead. I'd feel it. I have to believe that.

"Who's asking?" She sounds peeved, and I guess that's my fault for coming in here acting like a mad man.

"Her fiancé," I lie, but it does the trick.

"Security will take you there." She nods her head at the guy in a black and white uniform.

He hands me a sticker and I quickly slap it on my shirt.

He walks as slow as fucking possible through the emergency section. I count the seconds. All two-hundred and sixty-three of them so I don't fucking murder the man and never find her in this maze of sectioned off rooms.

"Salem Matthews. Right here." He taps on a door.

I don't say thank you. I push past the man and into the room. "Salem?" I shove aside an ugly blue curtain, preparing myself for the worst.

She sits on the end of the bed in a gown. There's a gash beside her eye that looks like it'll need stitches and she cradles her arm tenderly.

Her eyes widen with shock when she sees me standing there. "Thayer? How did you get here? How did you know?"

"Your sister and Michael. I rushed right here."

The adrenaline flees my body and I drop to my knees in front of her. I don't even feel the pain of my kneecaps hitting the hard surface of the floor, because I'm so fucking relieved she's okay. I thought ... well, I thought the worst. I didn't want to believe she was gone, but my brain couldn't help going to the worst-case scenario.

Her fingers delve into my hair, and she leans her body over mine. "Don't cry," she begs.

I didn't even realize I was, but she's right. I'm shaking with the sobs.

The fear that I might lose her just when I got her back was overwhelming.

But she's here. She's alive. Breathing. Sitting up. Not seriously injured.

My feelings are raw, though. Nothing makes you feel more helpless than someone you love being hurt and knowing you can't do anything about it.

"Shh," she croons. "I'm okay. I'm sore. And I think my arm is broken. But I'm okay."

She keeps saying it over and over—that she's okay.

I manage to pull myself up off the floor, gently taking her face in my hands. She lets me look her over, appraise her for more bumps and bruises. After I've finished a thorough inspection she arches a brow, fighting a smile.

"What's the verdict, Dr. Holmes?"

"The verdict," I brace my hands on the bed, bending so I'm eye-level with her, "is that you tried to give me a heart attack, Ms. Matthews. I'm an old man now, you can't do that to me."

"You're not even forty yet." She rolls her eyes. It makes me want to spank her. She's in the fucking hospital after a car accident and she's rolling her eyes at me? The nerve. "And forty isn't even old so cut the shit."

"Are you okay?" I ask her. "Not just physically, but mentally."

She exhales shakily and I place my hand on her knee, trying to instill some warmth and comfort into her body.

"Shaken up," she admits. "It happened so fast, and I blacked out when I hit my head." She points to the side of her face where the cut is. There's a lump on her skull as well. "My arm is killing me though."

Her left arm is already swollen and there's a purplish bruise near the elbow.

"Have they X-rayed yet?"

"No." She shakes her head tiredly. "That's what I'm waiting for. Poor Georgia, she wanted me here to help with her labor and now this happened."

"Don't stress about it, Sunshine," I beg. I don't like seeing her like this.

"I'm just upset." Her bottom lip wobbles with the threat of tears. "It seems like it's always something and I can't catch a break. I'm just exhausted from life." She sniffles and I grab a tissue from the box by the bed, handing it to her. She smiles gratefully, wiping beneath her eyes. "I'm being dramatic. I know I'm so blessed and lucky in so many ways—"

"Don't degrade your feelings." I cup her cheek in my palm. "A car accident is traumatic for anyone. Don't feel guilty for being upset. You've been dealing with a lot already."

She nods, swiping the tissue beneath her nose. "You're right."

"Ms. Matthews? I'm here to take you to our X-ray department."

A nurse enters the room pushing a wheelchair. I glance from it to Salem. "Why do you need a wheelchair? Are your legs—"

"It's just standard hospital procedure, sir." The nurse interrupts my line of questioning. "Nothing to worry about."

In other words, I need to calm my ass down.

Got it.

Salem gets into the wheelchair, and I'm forced to stay behind. Luckily, she isn't gone more than fifteen minutes.

"A doctor will be in shortly after the images have been reviewed."

"Thank you," Salem tells the nurse, settling onto the bed and lying down. When the nurse is gone, she says to me, "I'm so tired now."

"It's the adrenaline." I'm feeling it too, to be honest, but I don't tell her that because I don't want her to think I'm trying to lessen how she feels. "Close your eyes and go to sleep. I'll be right here. I'm not going anywhere."

"You're not?"

I take her hand in mine. "I'm going to be right here."

Despite all the beeping machines, her eyes close a few minutes later, her breaths evening out and I know she's fallen asleep.

I'm glad she's able to doze off. The rest will do her body good.

An hour later a doctor finally comes in and I'm forced to wake her up.

He doesn't waste any time telling her that her arm is broken, but doesn't need surgery, so they'll be fitting her into a cast and that the cut by her eye won't need stiches, but the nurse will apply butterfly bandages. Thank God it doesn't need stitches since she's already been here for roughly two hours. If she had needed them, you'd think they would've taken care of that already.

When the doctor leaves, Salem says, "I've probably missed the baby being born."

"You don't know that."

Her lips pout out. "I feel so bad that I disappointed Georgia."

"Oh, fuck," I curse. "I should've called her and let her know you were okay." I yank my phone out of jeans pocket, but I don't have any cell service. "I'll go outside and call her."

She grabs my arm, yanking me back down into the chair. "I had the nurse call her and let her know since I was on the phone with Michael at the time. I didn't want her in labor and freaking out about me."

I brush her hair back from her forehead, looking at her in awe. "Do you have any idea how remarkable you are, the way you always put everyone else first?"

She shrugs like it's no big deal.

Luckily, the wait to get a cast put on isn't long and she lights up like a little kid when she gets to pick the bandage color. She chooses a light pink, saying that Seda will love it. I don't think she realizes it but I'm pretty sure pink is her favorite color too.

It's dark out by the time she gets discharged and we head up in the main elevator to the maternity level.

528

"Do you think she's had the baby yet?" Salem looks up at me, eyes wide with excitement.

"I don't know. I guess we're about to find out."

The elevator opens and we step out onto the maternity floor. Salem strides up to the desk, giving her sister's name.

"Down that hall. Room 216."

Salem books it in that direction. With my long legs I'm able to keep up with her easily, but I am more than a tad amused at her enthusiasm.

She reaches the door and gives a soft knock. We wait a minute and then Michael eases the door open.

"Hi." His eyes are lit up with happiness and I already know before he says it that the baby is here. "Do you want to meet the baby?"

Salem jumps up and down excitely. "Yes!"

"How's your arm?" He eyes her cast.

"It's fine, now let me see the baby."

He chuckles, stepping aside. "You can come in too, man. Everyone's decent."

I follow Salem inside, watching her light up when she sees her sister lying in the bed. Tired, but glowing as she holds her sleeping newborn.

"Oh my God." Salem's hands go to her chest, her mouth turning down in a frown when she smacks her boob with the fiberglass cast. Undeterred, she goes on, "Look at him and that sweet little face."

"Her."

"Her?" Salem reels back, stunned. "What do you mean *her*?"

Georgia smiles from ear to ear, perhaps the happiest I've ever seen her. Michael moves to her side, his chest puffed out with pride. "Apparently the doctors got it wrong. We have a little girl. A daughter." She smiles up at her husband and he leans down to kiss her.

There's a pang in my chest. Not exactly jealousy, but I want that. I want *this* with Salem.

One day, I remind myself. *In due time.*

"Oh my God." Salem moves closer to the bed, peering down at the squished face of the newborn, her head covered with a pink and blue hat. "What's her name?" she asks softly so as not to disturb the sleeping baby.

"Victoria Allison."

"Oh." I settle my hand on her back, her eyes filling with tears when she looks up at me. Focusing back on her sister, she whispers, "It's beautiful. Perfect."

"Do you want to hold her?"

Salem's eyes widen with excitement. "Can I?"

Her sister doesn't say anything more. She lifts the baby up for her to take. Salem cradles baby Victoria carefully in her arms. I don't think she even realizes it, but she immediately starts rocking her.

"Look at you, precious one. So little. Your brothers are going to adore you." She lifts her gaze to her sister and brother-in-law. "Do the boys know yet?"

Georgia smiles, shaking her head. "No, we thought we'd surprise them tomorrow when they come to visit."

"They're going to be so excited." Salem turns to me. "They wanted a sister and were a tad disappointed it was another boy."

Georgia laughs, rolling her eyes. "Disappointed? Jackson, our oldest, fell to the ground crying when we told him."

Michael rubs her shoulder. "They're going to think we lied to them."

"We *all* got played with this one." She points at the baby. "Only a few hours old and she's already giving us a run for our money."

"How are you feeling?" Salem asks her. "How was labor?"

"Once I got my epidural it was fine and dandy."

Salem shakes her head in amusement, still rocking the baby. "Do you want to hold her?"

"Me?" I ask shocked.

"Go ahead," Georgia encourages.

Salem passes the baby to me. She looks so tiny in my arms. Like a little potato or something. Her small pink lips are parted in sleep, her eyelids a light shade of blue. One little fist is curled up by her face, having escaped the swaddle she's in.

There's a loud sniffle, drawing my attention to Salem. She sobs openly watching me hold the baby. I don't ask her what's wrong. I can see it written all over her face. She's thinking of Seda and what could have been. I want to tell her not to cry, that it's in the past, but I think she needs to feel this. I want her to let her pain go.

I hold the baby a little longer, until she starts to stir. She's probably hungry so I hand her to Georgia.

"We better be going." Salem hugs her sister, kissing her cheek. "It's late and you need to rest and love on your new baby. Let me know if you need anything. Especially now that this sweetie is a girl, not a boy." She lightly taps the baby's nose.

Georgia beams at the newborn in her arms. "I wouldn't mind a few new outfits. All I have is boy stuff and I'd like something cute to bring her home in."

"You got it. I'll bring a few options." She hugs her sister again and then we're headed out of the hospital.

We exit through the emergency room since that's where I parked.

She sighs when she sees my truck, a frown marring her lips. "I'll have to get a new car."

"Yours was totaled?"

"The whole right side was really messed up. I doubt it's going to be worth fixing." She rubs at her forehead, and I grab her hand so she doesn't mess up the bandage. "I need to call Caleb and let him know what happened. He probably wonders why I haven't called to say goodnight to Seda."

"Call him on the way home."

"Yeah," she says sleepily, "I will."

The day has clearly caught up with her. She speaks with Caleb for a while, he's clearly worried—I can't hear what he says, just the rapid speed at which he shoots questions at her. She assures him she's all right while I swing by a drive-thru and pick up something for us to eat.

"I'm okay, I promise. Seriously. It's just some scrapes and bruises." There's a pause on her end of the conversation. "Yes, I realize a broken arm is more than a scrape, but—" Caleb's voice gets a bit louder, more animated. "No, we're not suing the other driver. Caleb, I swear I'm fine. The car isn't, but I am." She shakes her head, trying not to smile. "I know you don't care about the car, but I'm telling you I'm okay. I wouldn't be talking to you if I wasn't."

I pull up to the speaker and order a bunch of random things. Pulling around, I sit up to pull my wallet out. Salem is already waving her card at me, and I push her hand gently away.

She sticks her tongue out at me, but slips her card away.

"Mhmm, I'll call you in the morning. All right. Bye." She ends the call. "Caleb worries too much."

"He cares about you."

"You actually don't sound jealous saying that. I'm surprised."

I shrug, handing cash over at the window. "I'm not. Not anymore at least."

She grins, her eyes crinkling at the corners. "So, you admit it? You were jealous of him at one time?"

I grunt, taking my change and driving up to the next window. They hand over the bag of food and I pull out of the lot.

"Use your words, caveman," she bosses.

"Stupidly so, yes. At the time I didn't even realize that's what it was. I rationalized that I was only looking out for you. Someone had to."

She shakes her head, her lips twisted in amusement. "Lumberjack caveman," she mutters softly.

"What was that?" I try not to smile, rubbing my hand over my mouth to hide any hint of one.

"You're such a lumberjack. The beard. The plaid shirts. The muscles. And you act like a hulking caveman sometimes. So, you're a lumberjack caveman."

"Well," I turn onto the street and pull into my driveway a moment later, "that's a new one."

"Hey, if the shoe fits wear it."

I'm not even touching that one.

Grabbing the bags of food, we head inside to immediately be greeted by Winnie and Binx. I let Winnie out back and set out the food on the counter.

"I didn't think I was hungry, but this actually smells really good." She picks up a fry, biting off the end.

After I let Winnie inside, we sit down to eat and head upstairs to bed.

I pull her into my arms, burying my head into the crook of her neck. I inhale her scent, thinking about how I could've lost her today. But I didn't.

I hold her that much closer.

FORTY-ONE

Salem

"Y our cast is going to be a unique accessory to your bridesmaid dress," Lauren says with amusement, signing her name to the hard pink arm cast.

"I know," I sigh, frowning at my reflection in the mirror of the dress shop. The light pink of the cast seems to stick out like a blinding light against the sage color of the bridesmaid dress. "I'm sorry. It totally clashes."

She rolls her eyes. "I don't care about the cast. I care about *you*."

"I know, but I feel bad." I frown at my reflection in the massive floor length mirror. The cast is thick and bulky, sticking out like a sore thumb.

"Stop." She waves her hands through the air, flapping them in my face. "Nuh-uh. We're not doing this. None of this feeling bad shit. No moping. I mean it."

"Okay." I paste a smile on my face. "As long as you're okay with it, that's all that matters."

"You act like I'd kick you out of my wedding for a broken arm. Do you think so little of me?" She jokes, heading behind the curtain so the seamstress can help her into her dress for the final fitting. Two weeks from now we head to Vegas for the bachelorette party and her wedding is the weekend after that.

So many things are happening this summer. The good thing is, between the birth of Victoria and Lauren's wedding it's been a nice distraction from losing my mom.

Stepping off the riser, I take a seat on the couch by one of Lauren's other bridesmaids named Holly. She works with Lauren. On her other side is Elizabeth, Anthony's sister. The wedding party is rounded out with two other friends—Kelsey and Sabrina whom she met through an art gallery she loves.

When Lauren steps out from behind the curtain, we all collectively gasp.

Lauren is stunning. Her dress is sleek and form fitting, modern and yet classic at the same time.

She grins at our reaction. "Isn't it beautiful?"

She went with only her mom to pick out her dress and ended up having something custom designed since nothing suited her taste, so it's the first time any of us are seeing it.

"You look stunning!" Holly cries.

"So beautiful." Elizabeth wipes a tear from her eye.

"You're an absolute looker," this is from Kelsey.

Sabrina adds, "Anthony is going to lose his mind when he sees you."

That leaves me for last. "You're beautiful, Lauren. You're a ... well, you're a bride."

She beams from ear to ear, clapping her hands together. She launches into a detailed description of what she has planned for her hair and makeup. I love hearing her so happy and excited for her wedding. Anthony's the perfect guy for her.

When the fitting appointment is over, we all head to brunch at one of Lauren's favorite restaurants in the city.

After our orders are placed, Lauren turns to me. "Tell me, how are things going with Caleb?"

"The usual, I guess."

Her eyes narrow and she picks up her mimosa, taking a sip. "You guess?"

I sigh, not really wanting to get into it, but Lauren is like a dog with a bone, and I know she won't let this go easily.

"It's just hard trying to figure out custody. Neither of us really wants to get a mediator involved, but with school getting ready to start I want her to live with me during the week and I'd like to have her some weekends too, but Caleb is arguing that her school is in Boston, and she's used to it so we shouldn't change her."

Lauren squeezes my hand sympathetically. "No offense to Caleb, but you're her mom. I don't just mean that in the DNA sense. You're the one who's stayed at home with her and all that. Besides, he works long hours. I don't think he can be as stable for her as he'd like to think he can be."

I pull my hair back into a ponytail, more from the need to busy my hands with something than an actual need to get my hair out of my face. "I think he assumed I'd move back to Boston and none of this would be a big deal, because even if I moved out of our place I'd still be in the city, but with me staying in Hawthorne Mills that puts us a few hours away."

"I know you probably won't like me saying this, but honey, he's being selfish. Seda needs to be with you, and he can have her some weekends."

She makes it all sound so simple, but there's *nothing* easy about sharing custody of your child. It doesn't matter how well things ended, it's a complicated situation.

"We'll figure it out," I say evasively.

"I'm not letting this go." She wags a finger. "If she's going to be with you, she has to get enrolled soon. You know this. Stop being a wimp and tell him like it is."

I pick up my mimosa with my good hand, downing it like a shot.

I think I'm going to have to be drunk to make it through the rest of the day.

I MAKE IT BACK HOME FAIRLY EARLY THE NEXT MORNING. IT'S Sunday, the street quiet. I let myself into the house, expecting to find Thayer still asleep but he's in the living room at his puzzle table, quietly putting together the Disney Princess puzzle Seda picked out for him. He promised to have it finished by the time she comes back since she's excited to see it.

"Hey." I wrap my arms around him from behind. "I missed you." I kiss his cheek.

"Mmm," he hums, "missed you too." His voice is still gruff and deeper than normal from sleep. His hair is a mess too, so I doubt he's been up long.

"I want some coffee. Have you had any yet?" I head out of the living room, toward the kitchen.

"Not yet," I hear him mutter.

I set the coffee to brew and make myself a bowl of cereal.

Thayer comes into the kitchen, Winnie and Binx on his heels. "I told you I could get you from the airport."

"I know, but it would've been silly to drag you out so early. The taxi was fine."

"We need to go to a dealership today."

"I know." I frown, my stomach rolling at the idea of the car buying process, but what's a girl to do? My car was declared totaled like I figured it would be, so it's time for a new one. "I don't even know what I want."

"That's what test drives are for. I've already researched some good options. I don't know your budget, so I picked a few different ones in different price ranges."

"Well, look at you," I say in amusement, grabbing a coffee mug from the cabinet, "doing all your research like a proper boy scout."

He eyes the cast on my arm. It's now adorned with all of the girls' signatures from the bridesmaid's party. Lauren signed hers with, *I licked it so it's mine,* above her name. I'd expect no less from her.

"I just want to keep you safe."

"I know, and I appreciate that." I pour coffee into my mug, then fill another for Thayer. "I wish you didn't worry so much."

He shrugs, fighting a smile. "Can't help it."

Sitting down at the table with my coffee and cereal, I say, "Show me these options."

A FEW HOURS LATER I FIND MYSELF AT A TOYOTA dealership.

"What do you think of this one?" The salesman shows me a white 4-Runner. It's beautiful, the paint a pearly finish with a beige interior.

I don't say anything, though, not wanting to indicate I like the looks of it. Thayer launches into a series of questions for the man who struggles to keep up.

There's something insanely hot about Thayer taking charge. He stands with his arms crossed over a gray t-shirt, a pair of athletic shorts hugging his toned backside.

I swear everything about this man turns me on.

Not that he complains.

Thayer has always made me feel safe to be myself with sex. I don't feel the need to downplay my desire and I know I can talk to him about what I like and don't like.

As a teenager I used to feel ashamed of my sexual urges, worried that it wasn't normal because of my past. Little did I know that being a teenager means almost all of you are raging hornballs whether you act on it or not.

"Let's take it for a drive."

"All right, sir. Let me grab the keys for this one," the young salesman replies, heading back to the dealership a short distance away.

"Do you like it?"

"It's pretty," I reply. "I don't know much about cars to be able to comment on anything else."

We've already been to three different dealerships, and I wasn't crazy in love with anything, so right now I'm feeling pretty neutral about the whole thing which is probably for the best anyway. That way I won't make any hasty decisions.

Thayer launches into different specifications about safety and handling, but finishes with, "This one is the Limited model, so it has an extra two seats."

I arch a brow. "And this is important because?" I try not to smile while I wait for his answer. Yes, I'm baiting him. Sue me.

He pulls me against his chest, lowering his head to rub his nose against mine. "We have to have room for all our future kids. Winnie and Binx need space too. They're important family members as well."

"How dare I forget the dog and the cat." I shake my head in mock shame and he clucks his tongue playfully.

"I've got the keys and the license plate." The salesman returns, holding both up.

Thayer somehow manages to convince the salesman to stay behind while we take the SUV out for a spin. I roll the windows down, letting fresh air blow throughout. My hair whips around my shoulders and I can't stop smiling.

"I like this one."

Thayer laughs. "I had a feeling this might be the one."

I miss my old car, but there's no getting it back and I can't afford that kind of luxury vehicle on my own.

We return to the lot, and I let Thayer handle making the deal.

It takes forever, but two hours later I'm the proud new owner of a car.

Thayer walks out with me to the SUV. I hop inside the driver's seat and roll the window down so he can lean inside.

"Where do you want to go?" he asks. "I'll follow you."

There's only one answer. "Home."

His eyes light up. "I like the sound of that."

"Me too."

FORTY-TWO

Salem

The back room of A Checkered Past Antiques is full of a mixture of empty boxes and ones that are filled with random items that never made it out front.

This ... this is harder than the house.

This was my mom's love, her passion. This was the thing she made her own after my dad passed away. She worked so hard to make the store a reflection of herself. Filled with items that were beautiful but maybe a little broken, in need of some TLC and a little elbow grease.

I let myself cry instead of keeping the emotions bottled up.

Packing this up is like saying goodbye to the last substantial piece of my mom.

"What do you need me to do?" Thayer asks from across the room.

I know he's concerned about me, but he also knows I need to feel these things. I remind myself that every tear is filled with love. I didn't shed a single one for my father. There was no love in my heart for him. Now, my whole-body weeps with this loss.

Sometimes I think if I close my eyes tight and think hard enough about it that I can conjure her image and bring her back to the living.

Is that how Thayer felt? That if he tried hard enough, he could undo what happened?

"Just cut down the empty boxes for now and set them outside. Bring any full ones to me and I'll go through it."

"All right." He pulls a box cutter out of his pocket and gets to work.

I sort through the things, tagging some as I go. There's a flea market in town soon so I figure I can try to sell some of the smaller items that are in good shape.

I pick up the box with my candles, the one I brought back when my mom said someone already bought them. Only I have no idea who that was, and no one's ever tried to contact me about getting them.

I pull one out, looking at the label. It's peeling up on the right corner.

Just like baking, I stopped making candles.

When I left this town, so young and pregnant, I left behind pieces of me. It was like I was trying to forget the parts of myself that reminded me of Thayer.

"Hey, is something wrong?" He approaches me, gently settling his hand on my lower back.

"No." I set the box down. "It's just some of my old candles."

"I wondered where those were. I bought them forever ago and Allie was holding onto them for me."

I whip around, almost smacking my head into his chin. He takes a step back, putting out a hand to steady me.

"You're the one who bought these?"

"Yeah."

"Why?" I blurt out, surprised.

His brows furrow in confusion. "You really have to ask why?"

I nod. "I want to know."

"Because, you left and I had nothing but our memories, that ring," he points to my finger where the ring sits that he got me so long ago, "and a few candles. When I burned all those up and the house didn't smell like you anymore, I came here and bought more."

"They're all peony. I smell like peonies?"

"You do. And they're your favorite flower. I guess it had a two-fold purpose."

"So, you what, just bought up all the peony candles?"

"No, I bought them all."

"Yeah," I point at the box, "all the peony ones."

"No." He shakes his head, gripping my hips. "No, Sunshine. I bought *all* of them. Every last candle you made, and I've slowly went through them over the years. This just happened to be what I was saving for last. I just never got it picked up. Your mom held onto all of them for me since it was a lot."

"You ... you got all of them? Thayer," I choke out a laugh, "there must have been at least two-hundred."

"At least," he agrees. "But I couldn't let anyone else have them."

"You ... I ..." I can't seem wrap my head around this.

He cups my cheek. "I lost you, for what I thought was forever. I wanted to hold onto you in any way that I could." He presses a gentle kiss to my lips. "Let's leave this for now. There's something I want to show you."

I'M SURPRISED WHEN WE PULL INTO THE DRIVEWAY OF THE house. "Why are we back home?"

Thayer puts his truck in park, shutting off the ignition. "Because what I want to show you is here."

I rack my brain, trying to think about what he could possibly be referring to but nothing comes to mind.

Undoing my seatbelt, I climb out of the truck and follow him. He doesn't go inside like I expect, instead I follow him out back.

He leads me around the fenced in pool, following the pathway that leads to the greenhouse. I haven't ventured out here yet. I'm not even sure why.

Opening the door, he waits, letting me go in first.

My jaw drops. Spinning in circles, I take in the beautiful pink flowers. They're everywhere. The entire greenhouse is filled with peonies.

"This is where you've been getting the bouquets?" I ask, but I already know the answer. My hands go to my mouth.

"Yes," he answers softly, watching me spin in circles.

I blow out a breath, trying to wrap my head around this.

My favorite flower.

Thayer Holmes has lovingly grown my favorite flower in his greenhouse all this time just because it reminds him of me.

"I don't know what to say."

"You don't have to say anything."

"There's so many of them." The greenhouse isn't massive, but it is a decent size, and he's utilized every available inch to grow my favorite flower.

"What do you do with all them?" I touch the stem of one, inhaling the scent.

"Before you came back?"

"Mhmm."

Surely, he sells them or uses them in his landscaping business in some way.

"Nothing."

"Nothing?" I gasp, startled. "You just grow them? That's it?"

"Yeah." He says it so innocently. "The first time I ever cut one was for your first bouquet. Technically I cut them before that, but only when they died."

"You are ... You ... I ... I don't know what to say."

"You don't have to say anything."

I brush an errant tear off my cheek. Thayer Holmes loves me. He loves me more than I think anyone has ever loved another person before. And all this time, he stayed in the shadows, letting my life go on because he knew I was married. He did all this never thinking he'd get another chance with me.

I wrap my arms around his neck, his own arms go around my body. He holds me tight against his solid, warm chest.

"I love you," I whisper into the skin of his neck.

His lips press a soft kiss to the top of my head. "I love you, too, Sunshine. Thank you for loving me back."

That's one thing he doesn't need to thank me for.

Loving Thayer isn't a choice. It just *is*. Loving him is natural, automatic, just like my body's need to breathe air.

FORTY-THREE

Salem

"Dad! I'm here!" Seda runs into the house, dropping her bag on the floor.

I've been meeting Caleb halfway for pickups and drop-offs so one of us doesn't have to go the whole way and I've finally gotten him to agree that it makes the most sense for Seda to live with me, which means I need to get her enrolled in the local elementary school as soon as possible.

"Hey, bunny." He comes around the corner just in time for her to launch herself at him. "Whoa. Someone missed me."

"I missed you guys."

"We missed you, too," I say, picking up her bag and carrying it to the steps.

"What's for dinner? I'm hungry."

"I'm making homemade pizza. You want to help?" Thayer asks her.

"Oh, yes!" She jumps up and down. "I love helping."

The two of them disappear into the kitchen so I carry her bag all the way up to her room. I unpack and put away her things, hanging the duffel bag on the closet door. I go ahead and set out a pair of her pajamas in the bathroom since it'll be time for bed soon. I know more than likely she won't like the pair I picked and will choose another, but oh well.

Downstairs, I smile when I find my two favorite people at the kitchen island. Seda sits on the counter, placing pepperonis onto one of the pizzas. There are three total, one for each of us.

Winnie paces on the floor, hoping to snag a bite of cheese or anything edible.

"What kind of pizza are you making?" I ask Seda, smacking a kiss on top of her head.

She giggles playfully trying to push me away. "Ew, mom. No kisses when I'm cooking." She holds up the stack of pepperonis she's holding. "I'm making a pepperoni pizza."

"And what kind are you having?" I poke Thayer's side, scooting behind him.

"Meat and veggies. Put whatever you want on yours and I'll pop these in the oven."

"All right."

I spoon some sauce onto the dough, add my cheese, and then top it with onions, green peppers, and olives.

"Those look gross, Mommy." Seda points at the olives. "They look like eyeballs."

"They're not eyeballs. They're olives," I explain. "I promise they taste good."

Seda crooks her finger at Thayer, urging him to bend lower to her level. When he does she cups her hands around her mouth like she's going to whisper, only at a normal level of volume she says, "I think she's lying. They must taste disgusting."

Thayer chuckles. "I don't like them."

Shaking my head, I cluck my tongue. "You two are ganging up on me."

Thayer puts a hand to his chest. "It's not my fault you like those things."

He sets all the pizzas in the oven, then turns to Seda. "Let me put you down."

"No, piggyback ride!"

"Seda," I warn.

"Please?" she adds.

Thayer turns around. "Hop on."

She does just that, giggling when he takes off running with her on his back. Winnie runs after them barking at his heels.

"Be careful you two," I plead.

They're going to be the end of me, I swear it. But I love it, love *them*, and the bond they've been able to form so quickly. I worried that even though Seda knew she had another dad that she'd struggle to connect with Thayer. But my worries were for nothing.

When our pizzas are finished baking, we sit on the back deck to eat our dinner.

"This is so yummy." Seda chews on a slice of her pizza. "Can we make this again?"

"Sure." Thayer smiles, pleased she likes it.

"I like this way more than delivery, Mommy."

"I guess we'll start making all our pizzas at home," I joke, tapping her nose.

She giggles, touching the spot my finger was at. "Did you get sauce on my nose?"

"Maybe."

"Ugh, Mom." She grabs a napkin, wiping frantically at her nose. "You made me dirty." Thayer watches us, amusement in his eyes. I can see how happy he is and it makes my heart soar. Setting her napkin back down, she asks, "After dinner can we watch a movie?"

"How about after you have a bath?"

She huffs. "Fine."

"HER FAVORITE MOVIE IS *HOCUS POCUS* TOO?" THAYER whispers in my ear.

Seda is fast asleep on the opposite side of the sectional couch with Winnie and Binx curled up beside her. She didn't even make it fifteen minutes into the movie.

"What can I say? I watched it a billion times while I was pregnant with her and when she was a baby. It must have rubbed off on her."

"She's not scared of the zombie dude?"

"Billy?"

"Yeah, that guy."

"No." I shake my head. "He's actually her favorite."

He shakes his head, tsking softly. "My girls are so weird."

I love the sound of that—not the weird part, but that we're his girls.

"You're one to talk, Mr. Lord-of-the-Rings."

"Those movies are amazing." He takes a handful of popcorn from the bowl. "The books too."

"You read the books?"

He looks at me like I'm insane. "Yes, I read the books."

"Aren't they like massive?"

"Not really. Did you think I couldn't read?"

"Of course, I didn't think that," I laugh softly. We're still whispering because of Seda. The last thing I want to do is wake her up when I know she needs her sleep.

"I guess I just didn't picture you sitting around and reading. I mean, you're already so busy and you have other hobbies and—" He shuts me up with a kiss. "What was that for?"

"Because you're adorable when you ramble."

"Oh."

He stares at me intensely and I wonder what he's thinking. Right about now I wish I had the power to read minds.

He leans forward, swiping a marker off the coffee table from when Seda was coloring.

I narrow my eyes, wondering what he's doing.

"You haven't let me sign your cast yet," he says in response to my questioning gaze.

"I didn't know you wanted to."

I hold my casted arm out to him. There's a lone bare spot left in the upper part of the cast near my elbow. He tugs my arm closer, lowering his head so I can't see what he's writing. It seems like he's writing out more than his name.

When he sits back up, he meets my gaze and holds it. Lowering my eyes, I look down at my cast.

My breath catches in my throat.

Marry me?

My eyes dart back up to his. "What?"

He shoves the blanket off his lap, kneeling on the rug in front of me. He takes my hands in his eyes.

"I wasn't going to do ask you like this, but sitting here with you, with her," he glances over at Seda's sleeping form, "I thought what am I waiting for? You already know how I feel about you and I know you love me. We want to keep building our family and our life together and so why not do that as husband and wife?"

There's nothing else for me to say but, *"Yes."*

He smiles, taking my cheeks in his hands he kisses me deeply. "Wait here." He gets up from his kneeling position on the floor, and heads upstairs. He comes back a minute or so later and opens a ring box. I can't help but gasp. The ring is emerald cut, with a thick silver band, and a pale pink diamond. It's unique and yet simple—the most beautiful ring I've ever seen. He slips it onto my ring finger and it's a perfect fit. "I saw this ring a few weeks ago and I had to buy it. I knew it was perfect for you."

"I love it. I love *you*."

He kisses me again, and Seda chooses that moment to wake up. "Why are you guys kissing? We're supposed to be watching the movie."

Thayer chuckles and I shake my head, beyond amused that she's oblivious to the fact that she's been sleeping.

"I asked your mom to marry me. Is that okay with you?"

She lights up, sitting up fully. Winnie gives a little whine at the change in position. "Does that mean I get to be a flower girl?"

Thayer and I exchange a look, both trying to hide our amusement. "Yes," we say in unison.

"Then it's definitely okay with me."

FORTY-FOUR

Salem

My toiletry bag sits half-packed on the edge of the bathroom sink. I stare at the handful of tampons sitting in the bottom of it from the last time I took a trip. I start counting up the days, realizing I'm almost a week late.

I'm supposed to be leaving for Las Vegas in only a few hours, but now...

"Thayer?" I call out from the bathroom. He's in the bedroom, getting ready for work, so he pokes his head in right away.

"Yeah?"

"I'm late."

He looks at his watch. "What? No, you're not. Your flight is still hours away."

"No, babe. My period. It's late."

"Oh fuck." His eyes widen. "You ... you're pregnant?"

I bite my lip, my hands unconsciously going to my stomach. "I think I could be. I'm going to run to the store and get a test."

"No, you stay and finish packing. I'll go buy it. I'll be back as fast I can." He finishes tugging his shirt on, the one with the Holmes Landscaping logo over the left side of the chest, and a bigger version of it on the back.

I pace the bathroom and bedroom while he's gone, haphazardly throwing my things into my overnight bag. I'm only going to be in Vegas for two nights, so I'm definitely over packing which isn't like me, but my head is all over the place.

I knew this would eventually be the outcome when I tossed my birth control, so it's not a surprise that I'm probably pregnant, but I know I'll feel unsure until I take the test.

I stand in front of the mirror, lifting my tank top to reveal my bare stomach. Obviously, there's no bump there, but I place my hand beneath my belly button, rubbing in small circles.

Is there a baby in there?

My feelings are vastly different than when I missed my period with Seda. Then, I was a terrified nineteen-year-old, panicked at the idea of an unplanned pregnancy and being a single mom.

This time around, I feel nothing but excitement at the idea of becoming a mom again.

It's crazy to think a few months ago I wasn't sure I'd ever have more kids. Deep down I knew I wouldn't want to have kids with anyone who wasn't Thayer.

I hear the front door open and nearly burst with nervous energy when Thayer strolls into the bedroom. He passes me the pharmacy bag and I remove the box. He splurged and got one that leaves absolutely no confusion that says either PREGNANT or NOT PREGNANT.

Hurrying into the bathroom, I close myself into the little room with the toilet while Thayer waits on the other side.

"It says it takes five minutes for results to appear," he says through the doorway.

I finish my business and pull up my shorts. Opening the door,

Thayer moves out of my way. I cap the stick and lay it on the counter, washing my hands.

"How do you feel?" He wraps his arms around me, hugging me tight to his chest.

I bite my lip, leaning my head back to peer up at him. "Nervous. Excited. Happy. You?"

"Happy," he repeats with a grin, rubbing his thumbs over my cheeks. "So fucking happy."

"It might be negative," I remind him, though I'm convinced it won't be.

My period is never late, so the only logical conclusion is that I am pregnant. But there's always that small chance that I'm not, so I pace the length of the bathroom waiting for the five minutes to be up. Thayer watches me from the corner of the bathroom, his lips quirked in amusement. He doesn't say anything, just lets me get out my nervous energy.

"How long has it been?"

He looks down at his watch. "Another minute."

"Ugh!" I groan in frustration.

After the longest minute of my life, I pick up the pregnancy test. I stare at it in surprise. Thayer comes up behind me, looking over my shoulder.

NOT PREGNANT.

"Oh," I say softly, gently laying the stick back on the sink. "Oh," I say a bit louder this time. "I thought for sure I was pregnant. I..."

Devastation fills me.

I burst into uncontrollable sobs. It's stupid, I know, but I feel like I've failed at something. I know we haven't been trying long, and these things take time, but I guess I naively thought since I got pregnant with Seda while taking my birth control religiously that when I actually stopped it would just happen immediately.

So stupid of me.

On top it are the confusing emotions of grief for my mom that makes me extra emotional with everything these days.

"Hey," Thayer reaches for me, "it's okay."

"It's late, my period is late," I defend. "But I'm not..." I trail off, still in disbelief.

"Fuck, baby." He rests his chin on top of my head. "I'm sorry."

He's apologizing? Why? It's not his fault. It's not mine either, I know that, but I'm just sad. After so much devastation lately, I felt excited at the prospect of being pregnant.

"It's okay," I sniffle, pulling out of his hold. I grab a piece of toilet paper, using it to dry my blotchy face. "I'm just dealing with a lot right now." I fan my suddenly hot face with my hands. "It's no big deal."

I don't know whether I'm trying to convince him or myself.

"You're allowed to be upset."

"I-I know that." I hastily put the last few things in my toiletry bag and zip it up. "I need to go. I can't miss my flight."

"Salem—" He reaches for me, but I scoot out of his hold.

I add the small bag into my suitcase and zip it up. "I'm going to call an Uber." I look around for my phone, not able to remember where I last set it.

"Salem," he says my name again, sterner this time. "Maybe you shouldn't go."

I snort. "Not go? It's Lauren's bachelorette, I have to go. She's my best friend."

I'm not going to let this overshadow her weekend. That would be selfish.

"Please, just talk to me." He grips my arms, forcing me to stop pacing around the room. "I'll drive you to the airport." I open my mouth to argue that he'll be late for work, but he beats me to it. "I'm the boss, I can be late if I want. I just want to know how you're feeling. I don't want you to keep this bottled inside. You do too much of that as it is."

I shake my head back and forth, biting my lip. "I don't want to talk about it."

"You need to," he insists.

But I don't want to voice my thoughts aloud. I know I'll sound selfish and whiny and that's not at all how I want to be as a person.

"Salem," he insists. "Please, talk to me. There's nothing you could say that would bother me."

"I don't want to complain."

"How is me *asking* you to talk about it, you complaining?"

I sit down on the edge of the bed. "Sometimes I think I'm being punished," I whisper the bad thought out loud. "That I'm not allowed to be happy."

His face falls. "Why would you think that?"

"My dad." I barely utter those two words. They taste like tar on my tongue. I don't like talking about him. Thayer kneels in front of me, his hands on my knees. "Maybe," I go on, "because of what he did to me, I'm supposed to suffer." This is a thought I've only ever shared with my therapist. It's one that hasn't haunted me in a long time, but when my mom's cancer came back terminal this time, that thought reared its ugly head again. I also had it when I had to leave Thayer. "It's like I can't catch a break. My mom got cancer, Forrest died, I lost you, the cancer came back, my mom died, and I just..." I let my head fall. "It's like every time I start to feel happy something happens to ruin it and maybe it's the universe saying I don't deserve that."

"Hey." I can hear the tears in his voice. He takes my cheeks in his hands, forcing me to look at him. "Don't think like that. It's not true. I don't believe it for a minute. What he did—that's on *him*. You did nothing wrong. Do you hear me, Salem? You. Did. Nothing. Wrong. You didn't ask for that to happen. He was an evil, disgusting man, and those choices are on him. He has to pay for them, not you. But sometimes," his cheeks are wet with tears, and it breaks my heart more, "things just happen. Life isn't perfect. It's not smooth sailing. There are good days and bad. Things happen that we don't understand, and we just have to keep going. I'll never understand why my son had to leave this earth before me, but I know I have to keep living for him even if he's not here to see it. Your mom getting cancer is a tragedy and it's awful, but it was just life and how things go. It wasn't to punish you. Please, don't think that. And neither is this," he tosses his thumb over his shoulder at the bathroom, "it's *one* negative test, and if it worries you, I'll pay whatever the fuck I have to for every test we both need to ease your mind. But I fucking hate that you, even for a second, think any of these things are your fault."

I swallow past the lump in my throat. I don't deserve this man, but I'm so thankful he's mine.

I wipe the tears from his cheeks. "I love you."

He kisses me softly, tenderly, and I still manage to feel it all the way to my toes. "I love you, too, Sunshine."

Taking a moment in the bathroom to splash my face with water and try to get myself looking like ... well, like I didn't just spend the last I don't know how many minutes crying which requires actually applying some makeup which I normally never bother wearing. When I come out of the bathroom, Thayer's sitting on the bed and my bag is gone. He holds a single peony in his hands.

He doesn't say a word. He merely stands up, hands me the flower, and leads me outside.

That's Thayer.

He doesn't need words to remind me he's got my back.

FORTY-FIVE

Thayer

I pull up to the airport drop off and park my truck. Salem seems to be feeling better, but the negative pregnancy test rattled her.

Hopping out, I grab her suitcase from behind my seat and wheel it around stopping in front of her where she waits for me on the curb.

"Have fun," I tell her. "I mean it. Don't dwell on things. Just have a good time with the girls."

She smiles but I can tell it's a little forced. "I will." She stands on her tiptoes, pressing a quick kiss to my lips. Grabbing the handle of her suitcase, she tries to escape from me quickly.

"Wait." She stops, looking at me over her shoulder. "Call me if you need me. If you get upset, or need to vent, or just want to talk. Whatever it is, whenever, just call and I'll answer."

She tries to hide her tiny smile. "Even in the middle of the night?"

"Especially in the middle of the night."

There's only a few feet separating us and I close it in practically one stride. I give her a deeper, longer kiss, before I let her go. I stand by my truck, watching her disappear into the airport. I ache watching her leave me, especially like this. I'm worried about her.

When I can no longer see her, I hop back in the truck and drive toward the first work site of the day that I need to check on.

Immediately the guys sense I'm distracted. No one says anything, but I feel the way they watch me.

By the time I make it to the second site, I'm a flustered mess.

"What's wrong, boss?" Aaron, one of my guys, asks.

He's been the first one brave enough to pose the question. "Nothing," I grumble.

"Ah, come on, Thayer—we're not blind. We can see something's up with you."

"It's my girl," I bite out. "She's upset."

"What'd you do?"

"I didn't do anything," I snap, leaning against the back of my truck. "There's just some shit going on that's upsetting her and I don't know how to make her feel better."

I'm not about to tell my employees the intimate details of our personal life, that we're trying to have a baby.

"When my girlfriend is mad at me I give her chocolate," Jake, another one of my guys, pipes in. "Chicks love chocolate."

"I don't think chocolate is going to make this better."

"Just go home, man," Aaron says, shooing his hand at me. "You're no good to any of us in your foul mood. Go talk to her and whatever."

"She's not home."

"Then go wherever she is. Is she working? Take her out to lunch."

I ponder his words. *Go to wherever she is.* The last thing I'm going to do is crash Lauren's bachelorette and ruin their girl trip, but I *could* go to Vegas and be nearby in case she needs me. It would make me feel better to be in close proximity to her. I don't like that she got the bad news this morning and had to leave.

"You know what," I snap my fingers at Aaron, "I think you're on to something."

He chuckles, backing away with a shovel in hand. "That's why you're going to give me a raise, right boss?"

I toss the gloves from the back of my truck at him.

He barely dodges them, laughing as he goes. I scoop the gloves back up, finish what I need to at the work site, and go home. It doesn't take me long to book a flight, pack my shit, and head to the airport.

IT'S EVENING BY THE TIME I LAND IN VEGAS AND MAKE MY way to the hotel. I managed to get a room at the same hotel Salem's at and I'm just praying I'm not on the same floor. I don't want to run into her and for her to think I'm stalking her.

I plan on taking a shower and ordering dinner in my room.

Salem and her friends are here tonight and tomorrow night, leaving in the afternoon on Sunday, so I booked a morning flight back on Sunday.

Hopefully Salem will be fine this weekend and not need me, but for my peace of mind, I'm glad I'm here.

The hotel bathroom is fancy, with a walk-in steam shower. I wash away today's worries and throw on a pair of sweatpants when I get out.

The hotel's room service menu is beside the bed. I pick it up, looking it over. The prices are ridiculous, but I'm hungry and not in the mood to go hunt down food. I put in an order for a burger and fries, just about the cheapest thing on the menu at thirty bucks.

Turning the TV on I log in to Netflix, putting on a random movie I come upon for background noise. I put in a quick call to Thelma to check in on Winnie and Binx. I asked Thelma and Cynthia if they'd be willing to watch the two animals and they were all too eager to help.

It takes my food nearly an hour to arrive and by the time it does I'm ready to eat my arm.

The guy that brings it looks at me expectantly for a tip. I nearly shut the door in his face because I just want to eat my food, but I remind myself that it's more than likely not his fault my food took so long, plus it's a big hotel. I hand him some cash and finally I'm left with the peace of my hotel room and my dinner.

Settling at the table, I unbox my burger and shove some fries into my mouth.

My phone lights up on the table beside me. It's a text from Salem.

Salem: Is everything okay there?

Me: Quiet. Just about to eat dinner.

See? I'm not lying.

Me: How are you feeling?

Salem: Lauren's keeping me distracted. She's freaking out over the ring. She's happy for us. We're getting ready to go to a show. I'll check in throughout the night even though you'll probably be asleep.

I smile at her paragraph long text.

Me: Just have fun.

I've only managed to scarf down about half of my burger when I get a FaceTime call from Caleb—well, not Caleb, but Seda.

Originally, we'd talked about Seda staying with me this weekend so we could have a chance to bond just the two of us. It ended up not working out, mostly because Salem and I noticed how uncomfortable it made Caleb and since I don't want to step on the guy's toes too much I backed off.

"Hey." I smile at my little girl's face. "Are you getting ready to go to bed?"

"Mhmm." She points at her pajamas with smiley faces on them. "Just had my bath too." This time she points at her wet head. "Daddy brushed my hair for me. I hate doing it. It gets all tangled and it hurts. But he uses this stuff, what's it called, Daddy?"

"Detangler," I hear Caleb say off screen.

"Detangler," Seda repeats. "That stuff helps."

I chuckle, amused by her rambling. "Are you going to read a book before bed?"

"Yes, I already picked it out. It's about a duck that lives in a purse?"

"Is that so?"

"Well," her nose scrunches, reminding me of Salem, "I think so, but I can't remember. Where are you?" she asks, inspecting what she can view of the hotel behind me. I spot Caleb leaning into the camera, checking it out too, so I scoot the phone closer to me.

"I'm out," I answer vaguely.

"Oh, you went out to dinner. It's kind of late, Dad."

"You're right, it is kind of late. We better say goodnight so you can get some rest."

"Night, Dad. I love you."

"I love you, too, pumpkin."

She runs off, but the call doesn't end. Caleb picks up the phone.

"Where are you?" he asks in a bossy, demanding tone. His eyes are narrowed. "It looked like you were in a hotel room. I swear to fucking God if Salem is in Vegas and you're cheating on her I will personally hunt you down and slit your throat."

"That's very specific." I try not show my amusement.

"Salem and I aren't together anymore, but I'll always care about her, and that means I don't want to see her hurt."

"I am in a hotel," I tell him, and he looks like he's going to jump through the phone and strangle me. "Settle down. I'm in Vegas. Don't say anything to Salem. She was … it was a rough morning, okay?" I'm not giving him the intimate details of our life and I doubt he'd like it very much to know we're trying to have a kid when Salem didn't want to have a baby with him. "I decided to book a room in case she needs someone."

"Lauren's there."

"So? It's Lauren's bachelorette weekend, I think we both know Salem won't want to rain on her parade."

He sighs, running his fingers through the blond strands of his hair. "You're right."

"Don't say anything to Salem that I'm here. I only wanted to be close if she needs me."

"Fine. All right. I won't say anything." He looks like he's smelled something sour, so it surprises me when he says, "You really love her, don't you?"

"More than you can possibly comprehend."

I don't mean it as a slight at him, it's just the fucking truth. Sometimes I'm even shocked that it's possible to feel this much for another person.

"I won't tell her."

He ends the call and I exhale a sigh of relief.

I hope wherever Salem is she's having a good time.

FORTY-SIX

Salem

Our first night in Vegas isn't so bad. We go to a Cirque Du Soleil performance and it's phenomenal, followed by a dinner out, with drinking and dancing at a club. Well, Lauren and her friends drink and dance, I mostly just sit there and cheer them on because it's not my kind of thing.

But the next night, I'm not feeling it. Not when I go into the bathroom and find the signs that my period has started.

Since my period still hadn't started, I'd held on to hope that maybe I had taken a test too soon. But that's clearly not the case. I'm not pregnant, just late, which might be from coming off my birth control and it effecting my cycle.

I send a text to Lauren, asking if she has any tampons with her since I idiotically didn't think to pack any after I unpacked the old ones from my bag. She texts right back that she'll be in my room in a few with some.

I clean up and wash my hands—which is awkward with the cast. I still haven't gotten used to showering and washing up. There's a knock on my door within a minute since her room is right across from mine.

"You didn't pack tampons?" She pushes her way inside, setting them on the counter. "It's not like you to forget something."

There's accusation in her tone. Lauren isn't stupid, she's probably figured something is going on.

"I took a pregnancy test before my flight."

She gasps in surprise. "You're not miscarrying, are you?"

I shake my head. "Just late."

"Wait." She shakes her hands back and forth in front of her face. "Are you glad your period started? Like was this an accidental scare or are you trying to get pregnant?"

I smile bashfully. "Trying."

"Salem!" She swats at my arm. "How could you not tell me this?"

I shrug. "It didn't seem like a big deal."

"You and Thayer have only been back together a few months and you're already talking about having a baby? That's a huge deal to share with your best friend. And engaged too." She reaches for my hand, looking at my pink engagement ring. "Listen, I'm not trying to be a bitch, just your friend, so please don't bite my head off, but do you think you're rushing things?"

I understand where she's coming from. If things were reversed, I have no doubt I'd be asking her the same question.

"Sure," I agree, "technically things are moving quickly, but you have to remember I loved him in secret for almost an entire year, and then I spent six years without him. In many ways, it's been too long and we're not rushing at all."

"When you put it like that, I understand." She looks down at the tampons on the counter. "I'm sorry."

"Thanks. You look amazing by the way."

She's dressed in a pale pink sequined mini dress that makes her already golden skin glow even more. Her dark brown hair is slicked back in a sleek low bun at the nape of her neck.

"Thank you." She strikes a pose, adjusting the sash around her body that says BRIDE across it. "I'll leave you to your business. Let me know when you're done. I'm ready to get my dance on."

I'VE HAD A FEW DRINKS AND FIND MYSELF OUT ON THE dancefloor with all the other girls tonight. It feels nice to let go after feeling so heartbroken. Lauren takes my hands, spinning us in a circle. She's definitely drunk but having a blast. A couple of guys have been bold enough to hit on her despite her bride sash, maybe thinking she wants one last hook up before the big day, but she was quick to send them on their way.

I'm still not sure why she wanted to come to Vegas other than maybe the shows and dancing, but we could've done basically the same thing in Manhattan. Sometimes it gives me a headache trying to get inside her brain.

The music changes and I'm not feeling the song, so I head back to the bar, careful to let the girls know where I'm going first. Stranger danger is a real thing no matter how old you are—at least if you're female. I don't think men really have to worry about that kind of thing. At least not the way we do.

I order my drink and wait, leaning against the bar.

"Hey," a deep voice says to my right.

I turn, making eye contact with a hot guy. He's probably a few years younger than me, maybe twenty-two, with closely cropped brown hair and striking green eyes. With sharp cheekbones he looks like he could be a model.

"Hi," I say, practically yelling to be heard above the music.

"I'm Dylan," he says.

"Salem."

"Salem," he repeats, licking his lips. He looks me over, standing there in my silky orange dress. It covers more than probably anyone else's dress in this club, only showing a hint of cleavage and ending right at my knees. But the way he's looking at me makes me think I'm very much naked in his eyes. "Like the Salem Witch Trials?"

"The very one." I slide some cash to the bartender, taking my drink.

"I was going to pay for your drink," Dylan says with a pout.

"That's okay. I'm taken." I hold up my ring finger.

His smile grows, and he looks a tad high on something. I probably don't want to know what.

"I don't care. We can still have fun. Your man doesn't have to know."

"That's okay."

"Oh, come on," he grabs my wrist, "don't leave so soon."

"I'm okay, really." I try to move away but his hold tightens. "Let go."

"Fuck you." He releases me, moving on to another woman to annoy.

Rolling my eyes, I carry my drink back to the section where a few of the girls are sitting. Lauren is still out on the dancefloor along with Kelsey.

Sabrina eyes my drink. "Ooh, what's that? It looks yummy."

"I honestly don't know," I admit, stirring my drink up. "I just picked something random."

She stands, tugging down her dress. "I'm going to go get another. Be right back."

I sip happily at my drink, but my mood is soured when Sabrina returns with Dylan.

"This is Dylan," she introduces him to us. "We're going to dance. Do you mind holding this for me?" She doesn't wait for a response, just shoves the drink at me. I don't complain, because I plan on staying right here anyway.

Dylan winks at me before she pulls him into the crowd. I flash my engagement ring again. I can't believe this dude actually thinks I care.

Checking my phone, I frown when I see nothing from Thayer.

I shouldn't text him, besides it's probably like … I try to do the math in my head of what time it is back home. I can't seem to figure it out, so I text anyway.

Me: I miff zoo

Me: Huh

Me: Mizz too

Me: I MISS YOU

Me: R u tripping?

Me: Stripping?

Me: Zipping?

Me: Sleeping?

My phone rings in my hand and I jump like I've been scalded. Thayer's name lights up in the glow of the screen like a beacon.

"Hi," I answer.

"Are you drunk?" He doesn't sound accusatory, only amused.

"Yes," I hiccup. "I started my period tonight, so I'm definitely not pregnant. I didn't drink at all yesterday, just in case." My lower lip trembles with the threat of tears. "I had to tell Lauren we're trying. I didn't have tampons, so I had to borrow some and I—"

"Sunshine," he says tenderly, and just with that one word I feel like I've been enveloped in a blanket of warmth. "Where are you?"

"Vegas."

He chuckles in amusement. "I know. But what club?"

"Uh ... hang on." I look at my texts from Lauren, scrolling back to where she mentioned what club we were going to tonight. I take a screenshot and send it to Thayer. "That one."

"I'm coming to get you. Stay put."

"How? You're in Massahootest. No, that's not right," I mumble to myself. "Damn, these drinks are strong."

"Just promise you'll stay there."

"I don't know. I really have to pee."

"You can go pee, Salem," he sounds like he's trying not to laugh. "I only meant don't leave the club."

"Oh. I got it. I won't leave, promise."

The call ends and I stare down at the screen. But wait, how is he supposed to get me if he's not even here?

I shake my head and go to find Lauren or at least one of the girls and let them know I'm going to pee. Elizabeth is quick to join me.

The bathrooms are packed, and we have to wait in line to finally make it to a stall. Thankfully I remembered to put some tampons in my clutch. I need to run by a drug store and get more before we go back to the hotel.

When I leave the restroom I run face first into a wall—well not a *wall*, but a person. For a moment I panic, thinking it's Dylan or another creep, but then the familiar scent of wood and pine and all things manly invades my senses.

I look up, up, up into Thayer's face. I drunkenly touch the heavy scruff on his cheeks.

"My lumberjack." His lips quirk. "I must be dreaming. What a weird dream, though." I look around at the club.

"You're not dreaming, Sunshine."

"You're really here? In Vegas?"

"I am."

"Why?" I ask, stunned.

"I thought you might need me." My jaw slackens. This man got on a plane and came to Vegas this weekend just in case I needed him? He must think because I'm silent that I'm mad, so he hastens to add, "I wasn't going to just show up and crash your weekend. If you were fine, I was going to be back in Massachusetts before you even left tomorrow, but I—"

Standing on my tiptoes I grab the back of his head and pull his mouth down to mine. He doesn't seem to care that I taste like alcohol. He kisses me back, his hands on my hips, pulling me impossibly closer.

"I love you," I murmur.

I say it because I mean it, I say it because I *can*. Our love is no secret anymore. It's the most beautiful thing and deserves to be celebrated.

When I finally stop kissing him, my cheeks redden in embarrassment when I find that Elizabeth has joined us from the restrooms. "Who's this?" she asks in amusement.

"Oh, um, Elizabeth this is my Thayer. My boyfriend. My fiancé. Yeah, that one. Thayer, this is Elizabeth. She's Anthony's sister."

He knows all about Anthony now and has been looking forward to meeting him at the wedding.

"It's nice to meet you." Thayer holds out his hand to Elizabeth.

"Likewise." She gives me a look that says she thinks I picked a good one. I can't help but laugh. Thayer's oblivious to the effect he has on women. He turns us all to mush.

We make our way through the club, finding the other girls, and I let them know I'm going back to the hotel with Thayer.

Lauren sends a smirk my way like she knows exactly what's about to go down. I roll my eyes. I'm on my period, in case she hasn't forgotten. I've never had sex on my period, and I doubt tonight will be any different

"If I had known our guys were invited, I would've told Anthony to tag along," she jokes, sipping on a pink-hued beverage.

"Ugh, no, I don't care if you're marrying him, my brother would rain on my parade."

"Yeah, sorry about this," Thayer says sheepishly. "I just—"

"Go on." She waves us away. "Have a good night. I'm going to call it quits soon anyway. I can't party like I used to. I like my sleep too much."

I give her a quick hug goodbye and let Thayer guide me through the throng of people to the exit.

We step out onto the street, and I eagerly breathe in the night air. Only, it's far from clean and filled with cigarette smoke and God knows what else.

"Do you want to walk?"

I shake my head. The hotel isn't far from here, but I don't feel like walking in my heels.

He quickly gets us a taxi, but the ride back takes forever thanks to traffic on The Strip. Walking might've been quicker but at least my feet aren't hurting.

The taxi finally reaches the hotel and Thayer pays for the ride. As we head inside, my stomach decides to grumble, reminding me I didn't eat much of my dinner, which is a shame because it was expensive.

"I'm hungry." Thayer glances down at me, his brows furrowed. "Stop frowning at me like that. You're going to get a wrinkle there." I reach up and smooth down said wrinkle.

"I'll order room service."

"Are you taking me back to your room then, Mr. Holmes?"

"Yep." He pushes the button to the elevator, trying not to show his amusement.

"Remember that concert? You were so mad you had to share a bed with me." I giggle at the memory.

"I remember." He says it in a way that makes me think he's thought about that night a lot.

"That's still one of the best nights of my life."

"That's only because you think the lead singer dude looked right at you."

I scoff, stepping onto the elevator. "Think? He very much did look at me. And don't act like you don't know his name."

"Mathias," he sighs. "I also remember you telling me that night after he looked at you that you were going to marry him."

"What can I say? I was overcome with lust." My heart gives a soft lurch, realizing that I was making that statement to my actual future husband. Wow. "Marry me," I blurt out, his eyes widening in surprise, "right now. We're in Vegas. That's what people do, right?"

"It might be, but we're not." He leans against the elevator, crossing his arms over the wall of his chest.

"Why not?" I pout, the doors sliding open on his floor. I follow him out and down the hall.

"Because, you're drunk right now and that's the only reason I need."

"I'm tipsy, not drunk."

"Salem," he looks at me over his shoulder, "do I need to pull up the string of unintelligible texts you sent me?"

"Okay, okay. Point taken. But I already agreed to marry you and I was perfectly sober then, so obviously I do want to marry you."

He sighs, coming to a stop in front of a room. He unlocks the door and holds it open for me. "You're not going to be able to convince me."

"I can be very persuasive."

"Sure." He shuts the door behind us. "What do you want to eat?"

"Something greasy."

He shakes his head, reaching for the room's phone to dial for room service.

"I'm going to shower." I start wiggling out of my dress.

His eyes watch me hungrily as the dress shimmies past my hips and lands on the floor. I'm not wearing a bra, and even though I don't have a lot going on when it comes to the size of my breasts, you wouldn't be able to tell that the way he's looking at me.

With a smirk, I close the bathroom door and lock it.

He really thinks I'm too drunk to know if I want to marry him or not?

I'm pretty sure I would've married him at eighteen. At almost twenty-six is no different, if anything the feeling is stronger. I want the world to know that man belongs to me.

I shower, washing away the sweat that has stuck to my body from the night of dancing.

I use the hotel's shampoo and conditioner to wash my hair. It feels gross and sticky from being in the club. I stay beneath the warm spray longer than necessary, but it feels so nice I don't want to get out.

When my fingers start to prune, I decide enough is enough. My casted arm aches too from holding it out of the shower. Stepping out, I wrap my body in a fluffy towel. I run my fingers through my hair since I don't have a hairbrush. It's the best I can do if I don't want it to tangle.

There's a robe hanging on the back of the door. Dropping my towel, I slip it on and step into the room. Thayer lays stretched out on the bed; his feet crossed.

He looks over at me, eyes zeroed in on my robe.

"I set a shirt out for you." He points at a white cotton shirt on the bed.

"Actually, it was nice meeting you and all, and thanks for letting me use your shower, but I'm going to head back to my room. I have pajamas there."

Those intense brown eyes narrow on me. "Nice joke, Sunshine. Get in the bed."

"Okay, but I don't need your shirt."

I let the robe drop, his jaw dropping along with it. I love that every time he sees me naked, he looks at me like it's the first time.

I slip beneath the covers, pulling them up to my chin.

"I don't think so," he growls, yanking the covers down to reveal my breasts. He hums in approval, reaching to cup them.

"No funny business. I started my period."

"I don't care." He lowers his head, flicking his tongue over first one nipple then the other.

It's on the tip of my tongue to say that I do care, but when he does that it's impossible to speak.

My eyes close and I moan when he sucks on my breasts, my body arching up to meet his mouth. "Thayer," I pant his name. I don't know how it's possible, but I feel more turned on than ever before.

Unfortunately for me, we're interrupted when there's a knock on the door from room service. Thayer groans, his mouth leaving my breast. It's wet with his saliva and with the AC on it sends a shiver down my spine. He tosses the sheet over my body even though you can't see the bed from the door. He gets up, not at all bothered by his obvious erection and grabs the food.

I sit up, eager for my meal despite also being desperate for his touch.

He sets the tray of food down on the bed and swipes a bottle of water from the fridge, handing it to me.

"Eat up," he says lowly, "you're going to need it."

FORTY-SEVEN

Salem

I wake the next morning, smiling at the sleeping man at my side. He's on his stomach, his arms curled around the pillow beneath his head. The sheet barely covers his body and I take him in hungrily.

He starts to stir, feeling me staring at him.

He slowly blinks his eyes open. "What time is it?" he asks, stifling a yawn.

I sit up, looking at the clock on his side of the bed. "Seven."

We've only been asleep around two hours. I know that's going to suck later.

"Fuck." He rolls over onto his back. "I need to get to the airport."

"Or we could change our flights and go back together?"

571

"You want to change flights?" He yawns again.

"Duh."

He chuckles, reaching for his phone. "Let me see if I can make this work." It takes him a couple of minutes, but soon he declares, "Done. We fly out at eleven."

"Good." I roll over, laying my chin on his chest. "That means you can marry me today."

HE LOOKS AT ME IN CONFUSION. "YOU SERIOUSLY WANT TO get married in Vegas? What about Seda and—"

I cover his mouth with my hand. "I want to marry you today. I don't want to go another day without calling you my husband. We can have a ceremony later, but Thayer, I've waited a long time to marry you and I just don't want to wait anymore even if that means marrying you in a drive-thru chapel."

"Are you sure this is what you want?"

"Completely."

I DON'T TELL LAUREN WHAT WE'RE UP TO. THIS WAS HER weekend, and I don't want to make it about me. I'm sure she'll want to strangle me later on when she finds out I didn't tell her, but for now, what she doesn't know won't hurt her.

After getting some clothes from my room, Thayer and I go shopping since neither of us has something wedding appropriate and I don't want to marry him in my usual shorts and tank top combo.

The white dress I find is a simple sundress with a corseted top and open in the back. It's not a wedding dress, but I wasn't looking for one anyway, just something a little nicer. I pay for the dress and change in a nearby restroom while Thayer does the same, changing into whatever he found.

When I walk out of the stall, I try to do something with my hair, but give up and leave it hanging down in its usual loose waves.

Walking out of the bathroom I'm met with Thayer leaning against the opposite wall in a pair of khaki-colored pants and a crisp blue button down. My eyes eat him up.

I get to love this man every day for the rest of my life.

If I could go back in time and tell my eighteen-year-old self that, I wonder what she'd think? She'd probably be cheering me on, to be honest.

Thayer looks me over in the white sundress. His tongue slides out, wetting his lips.

"You look..." He can't find the words.

"Back at you."

We already picked our wedding spot and called ahead for an appointment time. We head straight there since as soon as it's over—which shouldn't take long—we have to grab our stuff and head straight to the airport.

The venue is cheaply decorated with gaudy, stereotypical décor, but I don't care. As we stand in front of the officiant all that matters is the man at my side.

Thayer Holmes.

My asshole neighbor.

My boss.

My lover.

My child's father.

My *someone.*

And with the echoes of our vows, and the rings on our fingers, he finally becomes...

My husband.

FORTY-EIGHT

Thayer

The entire flight home I hold the hand of my *wife*. Did I think when I went to Vegas this weekend, I'd be marrying Salem? Absolutely not. Do I regret it? No.

I've waited a long time to marry this woman.

When the plane touches down, I can't wait to get home and just continue to live life with her.

It's fucking crazy, but with her, existing is enough. With her, I crave the little things—watching TV together, staying up late talking, even doing the dishes, which is just baffling.

But Salem Holmes is my best friend.

Salem Holmes. I love the sound of that so fucking much. Having her wear my last name is such a turn on. I would've been more than fine if she wanted to keep her maiden name, but she wanted my last name.

"Did you drive to the airport or take a taxi?"

"I parked my truck. It's this way." I wheel her suitcase behind me, my bag slung over my shoulder. It leaves one of my hands free to hold my wife's.

My wife—I grin to myself. I can't stop thinking about those two words.

"What are you smiling about?" she asks.

"You."

"Me?" She scoffs. "Oh no!" She starts to panic. "Do I have donut on my face?" She rubs at her mouth with the back of her free hand.

"No, your face is perfect."

"Then why do you have that goofy look?"

"This goofy look?" I let go of her suitcase long enough to point at my face. "That's called love, Sunshine, and it's all for you."

"Oh." Her cheeks turn the softest shade of pink.

We reach my truck in the parking garage and I load our stuff into the backseat.

The weekend away was unplanned, but nice, just like our spontaneous decision to get married, but I'm going to be happy to get home.

"Oh my God." Salem looks at me with panic just as I start the engine.

"What?" I look around, thinking I did something wrong or forgot something or maybe something is wrong with the truck.

"Winnie and Binx! You didn't leave them alone, did you?"

"Of course not," I scoff. "They're in the very capable hands of Thelma and Cynthia."

"Oh no," she says softly.

"What?"

"There's no telling what Thelma has done to them."

She probably has a point.

I KNOCK ON THE DOOR OF THE HOUSE ACROSS THE STREET, eager to get my pets back. It takes a moment for one of them to reach the door. It's Cynthia. She opens it with a smile.

"Come in, come in. Thelma is out back with Winnie. I think she wants one of them short squatty dogs now."

"A corgi?" I ask when Binx comes running out from some hidden corner, rubbing his body against my legs.

"If that's what they're called then, sure, that."

She opens the back door and yells for Thelma that I'm here. I scoop up Binx before I lose him again. He nuzzles his soft head into my neck. The cat and I have really taken to each other. I look him over and I—

"Is that nail polish on his nails?" I eye the hot pink glitter coating his nails. It definitely is, but I need to hear confirmation to believe my own two eyes.

"We had a spa night, boy," Thelma responds through the screened door, coming up the porch stairs. "And on spa night we pamper ourselves."

"And so you painted the cat's nails?"

Thelma shrugs. "He picked the color."

It takes me another fifteen minutes to get Winnie and Binx's things packed up, finish up talking to Thelma and Cynthia, before I finally can head back home.

Inside, there's a commotion coming from the kitchen. I set Binx down and take Winnie off her leash, both animals sprinting for the kitchen.

I follow along, more slowly, coming to a stop when I find Salem humming along to music, her hips swaying, as she stirs something in a bowl.

"Are you baking?" I try to hide the astonishment from my voice.

She whirls around, gracing me with a smile. She looks happy, and fuck if that doesn't make my chest puff up with pride because I know I'm part of the reason she feels that way.

"Yeah." A bit of pink flushes her cheeks. "I felt like it."

"I know you don't really bake anymore..." I trail off, eyeing the ingredients. "Cookie dough cupcakes?"

"I miss it," she admits with a shrug. "I stopped because..."

"Because, why?" I prompt, needing to hear the answer.

She sets the bowl down, picking up cupcake liners and lining them up in a cupcake pan. "It reminded me of you too much. My candles too. But I have you again and now those things don't feel so painful anymore. I want to give it a try again. It was nice too, before my mom died, we made cupcakes a few times. She's pretty insistent when she wants—" She winces. "She *was* pretty insistent when she wanted something. I can't help thinking she wanted me to find my passion again."

"Your mom probably knew deep down you missed it."

"Probably." She smiles sadly and I know her thoughts are now with her mom.

"I'll leave you to it, then." I head out back to my greenhouse. I want to cut a bouquet for my wife.

My wife. I can't help the stupid grin that overcomes me just thinking about it.

It doesn't take me long to trim enough flowers for a bouquet. When I come back inside from the back deck, Salem is sliding the cupcakes into the oven and she's spread the ingredients out for the icing.

"Caleb called. He's on his way to drop off Seda."

"All the way here?" I ask, since one or both of us usually meets him halfway. Besides, it's late.

"That's what he said. I assume he's going to spend the night at his parents or something. I didn't ask. I try not to pry into his business. I need to take Seda back-to-school shopping tomorrow and we need groceries." She starts naming off all the things she needs to do.

"All right. Let me know what I can help with." I grab a vase, adding some water into it and then her flowers. "These are for you."

She smiles. "They're beautiful." She turns her attention back to the frosting, her nose wrinkling in a way that I know she's thinking about something.

"What is it? You know you can talk to me about whatever is on your mind."

She sighs, powdered sugar smeared across her cheek. "It's just that, for so long I haven't known what I want to do with my life, what makes me happy. I didn't go to college, I didn't want to, and I've worked a few odd jobs just to bring in some income." She stares into the container of powdered sugar like maybe it holds the answer to everything she's searching for. "I want to find something that's just *mine*. Does that make sense?"

"It makes perfect sense. I want you to do whatever it is that makes you happy. I don't care. I'll support you no matter what."

"Thank you," she whispers almost shyly. "I want to keep my mom's store." I've suspected as much. She's far more attached to it than her mother's house, which we're hoping to put up for sale in a few weeks. "I'm just trying to figure out how. I can't keep it and not use it, you know."

"I'm sure you'll figure something out. I mean, you could always do this." I point at the spread of items for the cupcakes.

"Do what?" She sounds stunned. "Open a bakery? Thayer, I'm no professional."

"Lots of home bakers open their own business. You could do it too, Salem. I know you could."

Her nose crinkles as she thinks it over. "Hmm, maybe."

"What were you considering before?"

She shrugs. "Nothing I was crazy about, but cupcakes," she muses. "You might be on to something and I know it sounds crazy but I think my mom would be proud to know that I was making cupcakes in her shop."

"I think she would too."

"And maybe I could start making candles again—make ones in cupcake scents and sell them too." She's starting to glow now, getting excited over this idea.

She continues to ramble about what colors she'd paint the walls, what kind of décor she'd want, she might not realize it, but I do.

She's just found her passion.

IT'S FULLY DARK WHEN CALEB PULLS INTO OUR DRIVEWAY. Seda hops out from the back, running over to hug her mom and then me.

Caleb gets out, grabbing her bag and slowly approaches us on the porch.

"Seda, why don't you run inside and grab a cupcake?" Salem asks her.

"Really?" Her eyes light up. "You never let me have sweets before bed."

"Tonight is an exception."

"Yay!" Seda runs inside, the door slamming closed behind her.

When she's gone, Salem asks him, "You're not going all the way back to Boston tonight, are you?"

He shakes his head. "No, I was actually wondering ... well, I wanted to talk to you guys about something."

"Oh?" She arches a brow.

"Why don't we sit down?" He suggests, looking slightly uncomfortable.

Salem and I end up on the swing while Caleb pulls up one of the other chairs on the porch.

"Is everything okay?" Salem asks, genuine concern in her voice for her ex.

"Yeah, nothing's wrong." He runs his fingers through his hair.

"So, what is it?"

I narrow my eyes on the man across from me, watching him curiously.

With an inhale of breath, he says, "You're selling your mom's house, right?"

Salem's brows furrow. "Yeah." She crooks her head to the side. "Why?"

"And you're planning on living here? You won't be moving?"

Salem looks at me, a question in her eyes.

Do we tell him?

I nod. I'm not going to stop her from letting him know and he's so involved in our lives he deserves to know.

"Thayer and I got married this weekend."

Caleb's eyes widen. "Oh, wow. Uh. Congratulations."

"Thanks." Salem tucks a piece of hair behind her ear. "To answer your question, yes, we plan on staying here. Thayer's updated this house and I love it. It feels right to stay."

"Good, good." He rubs his hands over the legs of his pants. "I want to buy your mom's house."

"What?" Salem blurts, stunned.

I narrow my eyes on the man across from me, wondering what his thought process is behind this.

"I want to buy it. Seda's going to be with you the majority of the time and I know that makes the most sense with school and every-thing and I like the idea of her growing up in my childhood home-town." Salem told me once that Caleb is descended from our town's founding family. "If I buy your mom's house that means I get to see her more often. I'm close, but I have my own space. I can fix it up and make it my own. I'd keep my place in Boston and I'd be there most of the time, but I could come here on the weekends. It might do me some good to get away from work and the city." He exhales heavily. "I want to be close to my little girl. I don't want our relationship to change. I promise you guys will hardly see me. I'll keep to myself. Whatever you and Georgia plan on selling the house for, I'll pay it."

Do I love the idea of Salem's ex living right next door?

Fuck no.

But at the same time, I understand his motivation and commend him. Not many men would go out of their way for a child that is biologically someone else's. I have my issues with Caleb—and if I'm honest with myself they all stem from jealousy—but he's a good man. He deserves to find his own happiness in this world, and I hope one day he does.

Salem and I exchange a look, a million words passing unsaid between us. It's a beautiful thing when you can talk to someone without even opening your mouth.

"All right," Salem says. "It's yours."

Caleb lets out a sigh of relief. "I thought you'd say no."

Salem shakes her head. "Honestly, I think it's a great idea for Seda. Perfect, really. But are *you* going to be okay with it?"

Caleb looks between us, his shoulders falling. "I am. A part of me will always love you, Salem. You were my first love, but seeing what you two have ... we never had that." He rubs a hand over his jaw.

"I've been seeing someone. I don't know where it's going to go. We've only been on a few dates, but I thought you should know that."

Salem nods in thanks. Even though it isn't something she talks about with me, I know she worries about Caleb. He was her best friend, her first love too, and she wants him to be happy.

"The house is yours then."

FORTY-NINE

Thayer

We clear out the rest of Allison's house, Georgia and Salem both keeping only a minimal amount of their mom's stuff. I can tell it's hard for her, accepting that her mom is truly gone, but she's handling it better than I could've imagined.

"The relator is going to start the process this weekend while we're gone." She stuffs some socks in her bag. We're headed to the Hamptons for Lauren's wedding.

Despite us being a couple now, a married one at that, I didn't expect to get an invite to the wedding. I know Lauren's not my biggest fan, and I've accepted that. I appreciate it, even, because Salem is lucky to have a friend who cares so much.

My phone rings and I'm not surprised to see that it's my brother. I hold up my phone, letting Salem know I'm taking the call and step outside our bedroom. She's already added her touch, switching out my gray comforter for a white one, and changing the lamps beside the bed.

"Hello?"

"Hey, loser, how are you?"

I roll my eyes at my brother's greeting. "Fine. What's up?"

"Nothing much. Mom and Dad are bugging me about going to visit you."

"Why?" I ask curiously, leaning against the wall in the hallway.

"Well, I'm guessing because you're married now with a kid that was a secret for years. They want to meet them both and they're old so need me to fly to them and drive them up there."

It's the middle of September now, the end of summer. The past few years I went to them for the holidays—Thanksgiving and Christmas—but maybe this year we should go back to our old tradition, and I'll have them here.

"What if I had Thanksgiving at my place again this year?"

Laith's quiet. "You would want that?"

I haven't hosted the holiday since Forrest passed. It felt too lonely, that's why going to see my parents was easier.

"Sure, why not. It's a few months away still, but I think it would be nice, all of us together. And it would probably be easier for Seda and Salem to meet them here where they're comfortable. Seda's young, I don't want to take her away from her home to meet strange people for the first time."

"I'm telling Mom and Dad you called them strange."

"You know what I meant," I grumble.

"No, I get it. It makes sense and that way I won't have to take too much extra time off work."

"I'll talk to them about it, and we can make plans."

"Cool. Talk to you later." He ends the call and I slide my phone back in my pocket.

When I come back from my phone call, Salem stands outside the closet, double checking her bridesmaid's dress.

"What's wrong?"

My stuff is already packed and by the front door along with a tux since apparently this wedding is black tie. Lauren knows a guy, so I was able to get one custom fitted. It cost a pretty penny, but I wasn't about to not do what the bride asked.

"It's just this stupid cast is going to stick out like a sore thumb." She pouts, holding up her arm.

"I'm sorry, babe. But it's on for a few more weeks. There's nothing we can do about it."

She sighs. "I know, and Lauren says it's no big deal, but I know it's going to stick out in photos."

"I think Lauren would rather you be alive and in a cast, than worry about how it's going to look in photos."

"You're right," she agrees. "It's probably me that it bothers the most anyway. Showers are awkward and it itches."

"It'll be off before you know it. Do you have everything you need?"

She does one last check of her bag and nods. "Let's go."

THE TRAIN RIDE IS EASY ENOUGH, AND WHEN WE GET OFF Lauren is waiting to pick us up. She hugs Salem, dissolving into a spiel about wedding details that sounds like gibberish to me.

She lets Salem go and surprises me when she opens her arms to me. "Come on, neither of us is going to melt from a hug. Besides, Salem is like my sister, which means you're practically like my brother-in-law." I accept her hug, not at all surprised when she whispers, "The threat still stands."

"Yeah, yeah, I know. You'll slit my throat. Pretty bloody if you ask me."

She lets me go, and turns back to Salem, launching back into wedding talk like she didn't just threaten to kill me.

Women are hostile—at least Lauren is. I wouldn't want to cross her. I have a feeling she knows how to hide a body and get away with it.

She leads us out to the parking lot and to a waiting SUV. We all climb in the back since there's a driver.

"Anthony insisted," Lauren explains of the driver. "He was worried about my road rage if I drove."

Salem laughs, her eyes shining in amusement. "The man just knows you suck at driving."

"Do not." She sticks her tongue out. "I'm an excellent driver."

"Tell that to your twenty plus speeding tickets."

"It's not that many. You're exaggerating."

The girls talk the entire way from the train station to her fiancé's parent's place. That's where we'll be staying since supposedly the place is huge.

We pull up to a gate that slowly opens to reveal...

Fuck, she wasn't lying. This place isn't just huge, it's a whole fucking compound.

We're let out at the front of the house, with the driver grabbing our bags.

"The guest house is this way," Lauren says, motioning with her hand for us to follow.

Salem shoots me a look, thinking the same thing I am, that there's a whole separate house for guests?

"This is where you all will be staying." Lauren lets us into a cottage-like building on the property. "Rehearsal dinner is at six o' clock out back. Don't be late. I'll leave you two to it for now." She waves over her shoulder, taking a pathway toward the main house.

"This place is insane." Salem spins around in a circle, taking it all in. "I can't believe people live like this. This isn't even their house. It's for *guests*," she hisses the last part under her breath like she's afraid someone is going to pop out from behind the potted plant in the corner.

I take our bags into the bedroom, Salem trailing behind me.

We get ready for the dinner, and I dress up in a pair of gray slacks and a white button down. I'm rolling up my sleeves when Salem steps out of the bathroom. She takes my breath away in a blue dress, her hair curled and cascading down her back. Her eyes rake over me, and I look down at myself.

"This is all right, isn't it? I know Lauren is particular. I have another shirt—"

"My husband is *hot*."

I grin. "You think so?"

"Oh, yeah."

"Stop looking at me like that or we'll never make it to the dinner."

"I wouldn't mind ... but Lauren would."

She straightens my collar, smoothing her hand down my chest to rub out any wrinkles—at least I think that's what she's doing.

She takes a step back, her eyes zeroing in on the simple black band around my finger. "I wish my mom was still here. I think she'd be happy for us."

"She would be." I cup Salem's cheek in one hand. She leans into my touch with a sigh. "She knew how much you meant to me."

"She wanted this, didn't she? Us together?"

"I think she wanted whatever would make you happy."

Salem steps back, fanning her face. "I can't cry. I don't want to ruin my makeup."

"By the way," I say, leaning against the wall, "I was thinking my parents could come up to our place for Thanksgiving."

She smiles, swiping a tissue to dab at the remaining moisture in her eyes. "I think that's a great idea. I'd love to finally be able to meet them in person."

Salem and Seda have been getting to know my parents through FaceTime calls for the past few months. It works fine, but it's not the same as getting to know someone in person.

"They can be a bit much," I warn, resting my hands on her hips. "I know they're going to want to spoil Seda silly and probably tell you way too many embarrassing stories about me."

"Family is important," she reminds me. "Not everyone has a great one. My father was trash. They're good people, I want them to come. Stop worrying over nothing." She smooths out my brow with her thumb.

I smile. "I'll try."

"Good." She takes a step back. "Let's go to dinner. I'm starving."

I haven't seen Salem in hours. She left early in the morning to get ready with Lauren and the other bridesmaids. I take my seat, waiting for the ceremony to get underway and more than eager to see my wife.

While I've been waiting, I called my parents this morning and cemented the plans for them to come for Thanksgiving. I could tell they weren't happy about the wait but understood where I was coming from when I laid it all out. We can't take Seda out of school right now for a long trip, and besides I think it would be a bit much for her since she doesn't really know them yet.

I also texted Laith to let him know everything was a go and all he did was reply with a one-word text of: **Good.**

Little dipshit. We're adults and he's still driving me crazy.

The wedding planner points me in the direction of my seat, and I head over there, giving a head nod to the group of people I'm seated with but don't know. Most of these people seem familiar with one another, while I'm the odd man out. But that doesn't bother me.

The music changes, signaling the bridal party is going to begin coming out.

I hold my breath, waiting for Salem to appear. When she finally does, she takes my breath away, and it makes me glad we decided to have a ceremony one day, because fuck I want to see her walk down the aisle to me.

Her eyes search the aisles, stopping when they land on me. A smile takes over her face and she winks.

I don't want to take my eyes off her.

I had resolved myself to a lonely fate, one where I lived out my days alone, and I didn't get the girl. It's what I thought I deserved. I was the villain of my own story in my eyes. When Forrest died, I thought I didn't deserve to live either, and I'm sure if it wasn't for my brother and therapist I probably wouldn't be alive today.

Salem told me once, that she wanted to have the confidence of wildflowers. She wanted to grow and thrive no matter what life tossed her way. And she's done just that.

But if she had the confidence of wildflowers, then I was the resurrection of wildflowers. My soul withered with the death of my son. I was lost and that version of myself was gone forever. But I came back —I came back and now I'll grow and thrive alongside her.

When Lauren comes out, on the arm of her father, I get choked up because I realize one day I'll be walking Seda down the aisle to whomever she chooses to give her heart to. And while I won't get to experience the same for Forrest, I know he's always with me, because the love in my heart for my son has never dwindled. If anything, it has grown stronger.

As I watch Lauren start down the aisle, I swear I can feel Forrest's small hand in mine. Like he's reminding that my beliefs aren't crazy, that he's right here.

Our loved ones never really leave us—not as long as we remember. Even when it hurts, even when the pain is unbearable, we have to remember.

FIFTY

Salem

The last of summer comes to an end, the final days of warm weather bleeding into the crisp cold weather of October. Caleb moves into my mom's house, spending most weekends there and his weekdays in Boston. It's an adjustment at first, having him right next door, but it turns out to be the right thing all the way around for us and for Seda.

The door to my mom's shop opens—*my* shop now, I remind myself. I set down the paint roller, smiling when Thayer walks in with our daughter. She sets her rainbow backpack down and runs over to me, giving me a hug.

"I got an A on my spelling test, Mommy. Mrs. Lowell says she thinks I should be in the spelling bee."

"Wow, that's amazing." I tap her nose. "Do you have homework?"

She pouts, muttering, "Yes."

"Go get started on it while your dad and I paint. If you need help just yell for us."

"Fine." She grabs her backpack, running into the back where a commercial kitchen is almost finished being put in. It feels far too fancy for me, and I question whether I'll even be able to make a go of all this, but the only true failure is in not trying.

"Here, I got you something."

I narrow my eyes curiously on my husband. "And what is it?"

From behind his back, he holds out a Diet Coke. "For you."

I put a hand to my chest, then take the soda. "My hero." I stand on my tiptoes, kissing his scruffy cheek.

"I like this color." Thayer picks up another roller, dipping it in the pan.

"You do?" I'm a tad surprised he likes the burnt orange color. That's only the base color, and then I'm having someone come in to paint a mural of retro style flowers. It seems like a lot of bakeries go the pastel route, and there's nothing wrong with that, but I wanted to do something different. A little quirky. Something that was ... *me*.

"I do. With the flowers it's going to look great."

I take a sip of the Diet Coke, looking around at the transformed space. Jen has already been by to congratulate me. It'll be a while before we open, but what matters is that I'm doing this, and I think my mom would be proud of me. I think she'd be happy knowing that this space will continue to exist with a new life. I even kept some of the vintage pieces for wall décor and there's a green colored couch from the 70s that will sit beneath the big window in the front.

Thayer and I work together, mostly in silence since we can get more done that way, and manage to finish the second coat on one whole wall. It's progress, so I'm not going to complain.

"Are you done with your homework?" I ask Seda, poking my head in the back.

"Yeah. Mostly."

"What does mostly mean?"

"I need some help with a few questions when we get home. You were busy so I didn't want to ask."

590

"Sweetie, I told you if you needed help, we would."

"I know." She shoulders her backpack. "But I wanted you to paint so you can open this place and I can have cupcakes anytime I want."

I sigh in amusement. "Sound logic."

"You have paint on your nose," she tells me, brushing by me into the main shop space.

That's my kid, always keeping me humble.

Thayer's truck is parked outside, and I make sure Seda's secure in her seat, then get in myself.

"There's somewhere I want to take you ladies before we go home."

"And where's that?" I ask as he pull away from the curb.

"You'll see."

A few minutes later we're parked outside the cemetery. I send him a questioning glance, but he only motions with his hand for me to follow him out of the truck.

"Are we visiting Grandma and brother?"

"Yeah," Thayer takes her hand, "we are."

"But we didn't bring flowers." She frowns, seeming highly distraught by this fact. "Wait." She pulls her hand from Thayer's and takes off running for the field beside the cemetery. She plucks a handful of wildflowers, smiling at her bouquet. The flowers are dry and brittle, practically dead since the weather has been getting cold, but she smiles at them like they're the most beautiful thing she has ever seen.

She runs back over to us, taking each of our hands and somehow managing to keep ahold of the flowers too. Thayer looks down at her, then up to me, and I wonder if he feels it too. How despite the tragedies we've both had to face in our lifetimes, that our lives are still beautiful, still filled with love, and though some might think we're extremely unlucky, I'd argue the opposite. We've come out on the other side scarred, but beautiful. Life has tested us in some of the cruelest ways, but we're both still standing here. We're smiling. We're thriving. That's the true test of a person—the beauty they're able to find in the simple things.

In the wildflowers that bloom and blossom freely.

In the bees that pollinate our earth.

In the sound of the wind rustling the leaves.

Those are the things that matter.

This. Us.

Thayer leads us through and around. He has the path memorized. My mom isn't beside Forrest, but they are near, so as we approach, I notice something new, something different.

"What's that?" I ask.

"It's a bench, Mom," Seda says like she can't believe I don't know what one looks like.

She lets go of our hands, running ahead and to her brother's grave first.

"Did the cemetery put a bench in or something?" I search his brown eyes for an answer.

He shakes his head, tugging a beanie down over his ears more. "No."

"Then why? I ... I don't understand."

We get closer and I start to take in the detail of it. It has my mom's name carved into it. Forrest's too. My hand flies to my mouth, tears stinging my eyes. Damn him for making me cry.

"I made it," he says softly. "We're here often enough and I spoke with the caretaker. I was able to buy an empty plot almost exactly between them, so that way we can sit here and we'll be close to both of them."

I gape at him. "You bought a whole grave plot just to put a bench on it?"

"Yes."

One word. So simple. But it speaks volumes about the kind of man Thayer is.

He put a whole gym in his basement and now he bought an entire grave just to put a bench on it so we can be with our family.

"You ... you're amazing." I throw my hands around his neck, my feet lifting off the ground with his height. His arms wrap around me, his face burrowing into the crook of my neck.

"I'm really not."

"And that's even more of a reason why you are." I take his face in my hands. "You do these things from the goodness of your heart.

592

Because you want to. You're not asking for credit, but you deserve it anyway."

This man deserves *everything*, and I hope I'm the one who can give it to him.

I take a seat on the bench, and he joins me.

Closing my eyes, I lay my head on his shoulder.

I feel at peace. Despite the chaos of our lives, the turmoil, the ups and downs, and everything it took to get us to this point, I feel thankful in a strange way. Thankful that we're here, together, and didn't let the bad things break us.

We sit there, together, as the sun sets, watching Seda speak to her grandma and brother, leaving her flowers trailing behind her, our hands clasped together.

I get a flash of what Thayer spoke about one time, of sitting on the front porch swing one day, watching our grandchildren run around the yard.

And I smile.

FIFTY-ONE

Salem

I t's a strange thing, hosting Thayer's family for the Thanksgiving holiday. Of course I know Laith, not well but enough, but I don't know his parents at all. Not really, in my opinion. We've been FaceTiming with them weekly since Thayer first broke the news to them of our relationship, past, and Seda, but it's been awkward getting to know them that way, and I fear they won't like me. After all, I kept their grandchild a secret for six years. I could understand if there was animosity. But when the car shows up, Laith driving since he flew all the way to their house in Florida just to drive them here, Thayer's mom is all too eager to get out of the car and hug me.

She smells of freesia and her hug feels like home.

"Elaine," I hug her tighter, "it's so nice to meet you."

She pulls away slightly, taking me in. "It's nice to meet you too, sweetheart. My Thayer is different, he's happy again. *You* made him smile again—his real smile. I can never thank you enough for that."

Her words touch my heart. Over her shoulder, Thayer meets my eyes with a small, almost shy smile. He's been nervous about this, I think because he knew I was feeling that way. Meeting the parents is always an awkward affair.

Seda is next door at Caleb's house. The three of us decided it would be best for her to meet her grandparents and uncle tomorrow. Seda is smart, kind, and understanding but this is overwhelming for a girl her age so while we explained they were coming to her, and how they're related, we figured we'd let everyone get settled tonight and introduce her tomorrow.

It's been surprisingly easy, adjusting to parenting with three of us, and it's actually been nice, and good for Seda, having Caleb next door most weekends.

I thought things might get weird, but they haven't, and while things haven't worked out with the one woman Caleb was seeing, he's been dating and is happy. That's all I want for him.

"Come inside," I tell Elaine. "I'm sure you guys want to rest, and dinner is almost ready."

"That would be nice. Laith drives like a maniac. He shaved five years off whatever is left of my life."

"Mom!" Laith yells, having heard her. "Don't say that. I did no such thing."

She purses her lips, shaking her head. "He did. Too much time with that motorcycle of his and now he doesn't know how to drive a proper car."

"A proper car?" He argues, coming up the porch stairs. "That is a minivan, tell me why you and Dad need a minivan."

"Well, son," their dad says, walking up to join us, "there's more room in the back if you catch what I'm saying."

Behind him, Thayer shakes his head, trying not to laugh. Laith's eyes widen in horror and he gags.

"Fuck, Dad, don't say that shit around me. Gross."

Ignoring Laith, their dad, Douglas, comes up to me, opening his arms for a hug. "Hi, Salem. It's so nice to meet you."

"It's nice to meet you as well."

We lead everybody inside and let them get settled in the guest bedrooms. While they're resting up, Thayer and I finish dinner. We decided to make lasagna since that was simple enough and put it in the oven earlier. He turns the oven light on, checking on the progress.

"It should be ready in about thirty minutes."

"Perfect." I put the finishing touches on the homemade garlic bread we'll pop in the oven just before the lasagna is finished cooking.

Thayer pushes a button, turning on the music speaker. A Taylor Swift song comes on from my playlist.

"What are you doing?" I ask, fighting a smile as he closes the distance between us.

"I want to dance with my wife. Can't I do that?"

I don't answer him, not with words anyway. I let him take me into his arms, slowly twirling me through the kitchen. As a little girl, I used to wonder if true love existed between a man and woman. My parents certainly weren't a good example. My father craved power, control. He didn't love my mom, or care about her. To him, she and by extension my sister and me, were a part of an image he wanted to cultivate in the public of being a family man.

It was all a lie.

Behind closed doors he was a monster in more ways than one.

To this day, I'm glad he's gone.

I've never shed a single tear for him, but I *have* shed tears for the little girl I was, who should've had a dad who loved and cared for her. Who protected her and showed her how a man treats a woman. Sometimes, that little girl doesn't even feel like me. To survive what I did, I had to separate myself mentally from my past. I don't know if that's how it is for everyone, but that was my coping mechanism.

I feel blessed, that as a teenager, I met Caleb. He was kind, caring —my best friend. He treated me the way every guy should treat a girl. Then I met Thayer too.

I've had two good men in my life to prove to me that they're not all like my father.

I know not everyone's story plays out like mine.

Thayer continues to sway us to the song, and I lay my head against his chest, listening to the steady pounding of his heart against my ear.

I love this man.

And I'm thankful every day the universe sent him my way.

He turns us again and I find his parents standing in the entry way to the kitchen, watching us. Each has a wistful expression. I'm sure after Thayer's divorce, and Forrest's passing, their worry for their son was beyond what I can imagine.

Sometimes, when you're in the midst of tragedy—of heartbreak—it can be impossible to see the other side. It's like you're drowning beneath the weight of your emotions, memories, your very thoughts, but if you just keep going, keep swimming, then eventually you make it to shore. You're tired, but stronger, and look at yourself in a new light. I think it's our tendency to doubt ourselves, to think we're weaker than what we are, but there's more in all of us than we realize.

I rest my chin on Thayer's chest, looking up at him with all the love I used to think I would never be capable of. Closing my eyes, I rest my head on his chest once more.

I made it.

"My son," Elaine begins, whispering quietly so Thayer won't hear, "he's different with you. It's beautiful to see."

"He is?" I ask, taking the macaroni and cheese out of the oven.

She nods, smiling over at him. He stands with Caleb, his brother, Dad, and Seda. His hands are on her shoulders, and she's looking up admiring him. It stirs something in me, seeing Seda look at him like that. Their bond has grown naturally, and I know Seda loves him as much as she does Caleb and me.

Thelma and Cynthia sit at the table, watching everything with keen eyes. The two little gossips. We wanted to invite them over, though, because they've sort of turned into extended family.

"You make him happy." She sets out the green bean casserole.

We're lining everything up on the counter buffet style so people can plate themselves and sit in the dining room.

"He makes me happy."

"I've only ever wanted my boys to be happy. When ... well, when Forrest died, I worried I'd lose Thayer. A parent's grief has to be unimaginable, and I worried he might take his own life. I'm thankful that he's still here, that he's doing as well as he is, that he's found love. Seda too, she's such a blessing. An amazing girl. You've done well."

"You don't ... you don't hate me for keeping her a secret?"

Elaine gives me a soft, motherly smile. "Us mothers will do whatever it takes to protect our babies, so I understand you were only doing what you thought was right. But the past is the past. Let's not dwell on it. Not when we have such a beautiful life to live."

We finish setting out all the dishes and call everyone over. Winnie and Binx toddle over as well, hoping to snag some scraps from the floor. Once everyone has their plates we sit down to eat.

Caleb ends up on my left with Thayer on my right. Seda opts to sit by Laith who I think has quickly become her new favorite person, probably due to the fact that he's basically an adult man child and has no problem playing with her.

Thayer clears his throat. "I ... uh ... I wanted to say some things before we start eating." Everyone quiets, and Laith sets down his fork, trying to pretend that he doesn't have a mouthful of turkey at the moment. "I'm really glad that we're all here together. It means a lot to be sitting down with all of you. I'm thankful to Salem," he squeezes my hand beneath the table, "for giving me a second chance and for becoming my wife. I'm thankful to you, Caleb, for ... well, for a lot, actually, which probably sounds so strange to you, but ... yeah." He trails off, clearing his throat. "Mom and Dad, you two have always been a strong presence in my life, showing me how to be a strong, kind-hearted person. Laith ... you suck. Thelma and Cynthia, thank you for joining us for dinner and always being willing to lend a helping a hand. And Seda, I'm so proud to be your father. You're the brightest little girl I know. I'm so lucky." He looks around at all of us. "So lucky."

"Since I suck and all, I'm going to be the one to say it, you've turned into a sappy fuck."

"No cussing in front of my kid," Thayer growls at his brother.

Seda just giggles, not at all fazed by it.

Thayer shakes his head, his eyes meeting mine.

I look from him, to all the people gathered around us. Our family might be unconventional to some, but for us, it's perfect.

FIFTY-
TWO

Salem

The New Year comes and passes. In a blink it's March and the opening of my bakery. To say I'm nervous is an understatement. But as I stand outside looking at the building that was once my mother's antique shop, I can't help but feel a little proud. I think she would be proud of me too. She worked hard to make this place her own, and I've done the same to make it mine.

"There's one last thing it needs," Thayer says from beside me.

We're due to open at noon, and more than a few townspeople have already stopped by to wish me luck and give me flowers.

"What is it?"

"Hold on," he says, jogging over to his truck.

He returns with a metal sign. It's carved with the name of my shop. In an elegant script font, it says: Sunshine Cupcakes.

I gasp. "It's beautiful. Did you make this?"

He sets it down, going back to grab a ladder. He's thought of everything.

"I did, with help from one of my guys. He does welding on the side as a hobby so I asked him to help me out with this."

He grabs the rest of his tools and gets to work securing the sign where my mom's once was. The spot was bare since I hadn't found a sign I liked yet. Leave it to Thayer to fix that problem.

When the sign is secure, he climbs back down and we stand on the sidewalk, taking it in.

"You did it, Sunshine." The pride shines in his eyes. "You found your calling."

I did. I guess, ironically, I found it a long time ago and I didn't want to see it.

Maybe all along, my mom knew what I was meant to do. Perhaps that's why she kept asking me to bake with her. In those final weeks, I would have given her anything that she wanted, even if it meant setting foot in the kitchen and baking cupcakes again. Mothers have a way of always knowing what we need before we do. I suppose in a way this was her final gift to me. And maybe she hoped too that I would keep the shop.

I hope wherever she is, she's happy. I hope she's looking down on us, smiling at me right now. More than anything, I hope she's proud. I miss her so much every day. Even after I moved away, we talked on the phone multiple times a day. I always knew that no matter what, my mom had my back. She was strong even when she thought she was weak. And I know she didn't think that she was worth admiring, but I always looked up to her.

"You did this," Thayer says, wrapping an arm around my shoulders. He rubs up and down over my jacket, trying to stave off the chill. But with the ice and snow, there's no way to stay warm out here. It's March, but in Hawthorne Mills that just means winter isn't done with us yet.

"It wasn't just me."

Thayer stops beside me, looking up as well. "Hmm," he hums. "They do look brighter." A soft smile touches his lips.

"How do you feel?" I ask.

His gaze lowers to mine, immediately knowing I'm asking since it's Forrest's birthday. "It's always a bittersweet day."

"I'm sorry."

"I'll see him again one day. I feel it. Somehow, someway, I will. I have to believe that."

We stand in the cold for a minute longer, taking in the night sky before we get in the truck and drive home.

Home.

The house I used to sneak over to, is my home now, but that's also just a shell. It's framework and drywall, while the man at my side is my real home.

As long as I have him, I'll have a place I belong.

The house is dark and quiet since Seda is with Caleb. Winnie and Binx watch us from the couch with annoyed expressions for disturbing their beauty sleep.

"We should eat something," Thayer says as I follow him into the kitchen.

"We probably should," I agree, biting my lip, "but..."

"But?" He turns around, looking me up and down.

"I want you."

He doesn't hesitate. His mouth is on mine in an instant. I melt beneath his touch. He lifts me up, legs going around his waist. He carries me up the stairs and straight back to our room.

My back hits the mattress and he undresses me slowly, kissing every part of my skin as he exposes it. I try to reach for his shirt, but he steps away from me. "Not yet."

"Not yet?" I whine.

He shakes his head, his eyes dark with desire. He loops his arms around my legs, pulling me to the edge of the mattress. Dropping to his knees, he wastes no time. He licks my pussy like he's been waiting all day to taste me.

"Thayer," I pant his name.

He licks and sucks, drawing out every moan and curse word he can from me.

He brings me right to the edge and stops. "Thayer!" I cry out his name in a pleading tone. "I need—"

"I know what you need," he says in a voice that tells me not to argue with him. "The delayed gratification will be worth it. You'll see."

He hooks his thumbs in the back of his shirt, yanking it off and letting it drop to the floor. My core pulses with need and desire as I watch him undress the rest of the way.

He palms his cock, his eyes heated. He looks at me lying on the bed, naked and wanting for him.

"You're mine, Sunshine," he growls in a way that is somehow both possessive and needy all at once.

"Yours."

I belonged to Thayer Holmes the summer of my eighteenth year. Neither of us knew it, but when he moved in next door, it was about to change both of our lives.

He pushes his way inside me, and we both moan from the pleasure of it.

"Do you feel that?" he asks, his voice huskier than normal. "Do you feel the way your pussy grips my cock? Your pussy was made for me and only me."

He fucks me hard and fast, like he can't get enough of me.

"Fuck, I love you," he growls into the skin of my neck. I push him over, and he obliges, lying on his back so I can ride him. I roll my hips, my head falling back.

My hands lay flat on his chest for balance. He looks up at me like I'm a fucking goddess and dammit if I don't feel powerful.

His thumb finds my clit and I gasp. "That, right there, don't stop," I beg, desperate for an orgasm after he denied me my first one.

He listens, though, and he was right, because when the orgasm overtakes me, I feel it through my entire body. I've never felt anything so powerful and intense.

My legs shake, threatening to give out and he switches our positions easily. His fingers dig into my hair, pulling at the strands.

I cry out again, another orgasm ripping through my body. "Thayer, oh God. Don't stop."

He fucks me so hard I know I'm going to feel it in my entire body tomorrow. But I don't care. I love the reminder that I'm his.

He pulls my body up, until we're sitting, rocking against each other. He's looking right into my eyes. It's intense, romantic, sexy. I wrap my arms around his neck, his chest hair tickling my bare skin. I kiss him, our tongues meeting just like our bodies.

"I think ... I think ... *oh my God.*" It feels impossible that my body can hit that peak a third time, and so close together, but it does.

Then he's coming too, shouting my name.

We collapse onto the bed, our skin damp with sweat. He wraps his big arm around my torso, tucking me against him.

We both lay there, marveling in the intensity of our love.

I don't care that this man is more than a decade older than me. It used to worry me, falling for someone so much older than me, what people might think. But fuck them, they don't know us, they don't know our love, our life, how hard we've fought to get here. I wouldn't take back loving this man. Not for a thing.

FIFTY-THREE

Thayer

"**B**abe." I knock on the door for what feels like the hundredth time. "Let me in."

"No. I have the stomach flu and I don't want you to get it." I hear her heave over the toilet. "Has Caleb gotten in from Boston yet?"

"No, not yet."

I hear her throw up again. "I'm going to take Seda and run to the store. You need some Gatorade to keep your electrolytes up."

She gags when I say Gatorade. "No Gatorade. Please."

"Well, I'm getting something. There's water in here on the night-stand. Try to drink it while I'm gone."

I hate leaving her when she's sick, but if she's this bad off, then I need to get some things.

Downstairs, Seda sits at the kitchen table with her coloring book. "Hey." I ruffle her hair and she looks up at me with a beaming smile. "We need to run to the store to get your mom a few things."

"Okay. Can I get ice cream?"

This kid. She always knows how to sucker me. "Sure."

She closes her coloring book, putting her crayons away. We drive into town to the pharmacy. I grab a bottle of Gatorade despite Salem's protests, and some Pedialyte. Sure, it's for kids, but what could it hurt? Seda trails along with me as I go down the next aisle, searching for some medicine that might help her kick this flu.

That's when I stop dead in my tracks in the family planning aisle.

"Ow." Seda rubs her forehead from where she bumped into the side of me. "Dad, why did you stop?"

Salem hasn't bothered to take a pregnancy test for at least three months since it was constantly negative.

But it's possible what she thinks is the stomach flu is ... more.

A baby.

I swipe a pregnancy test and add it to the basket.

"What's that?" Seda asks me.

"Well, you know how your mommy and me have been trying to have a baby?"

"Yeah." She nods vigorously. "I want a sister."

I chuckle. "We don't have any choice in whether the baby is a boy or girl, but we'll love them no matter what, right?"

"Mhmm," she hums, running her finger along the goods that are lined up as I continue through the store. I'm still going to grab some flu medicine while I'm here, just in case I'm wrong. "But I still want a sister."

My shoulders shake with barely contained laughter.

Once I've gotten the medicine, I check out and drop by the local ice cream shop before heading back home. Seda licks happily at her vanilla ice cream the whole way.

Caleb isn't in yet—Salem had me call him to see if he'd come up so Seda could stay with him and not catch the flu.

The flu.

I chuckle to myself.

I don't think what Salem has is contagious. But it's cute of her to think so.

Putting a movie on for Seda, Winnie and Binx jump up on the couch to join her. "I'm going to check on Mommy."

"Okay," she replies, completely unbothered.

Grabbing the bag of goods, I jog upstairs and into the bedroom. Salem's not in the bedroom, so I try the bathroom. The door is locked.

Giving a knock, I say, "Salem, let me in."

There's a groan on the other side of the door. "I can't give you medicine if you don't unlock the door."

"I'm contagious," she whines. "I don't want you to get sick."

"Sunshine," I say through the door, "my tongue has been inside your pussy. Your sick germs are the least of my concern."

She squeaks from the other side, the door finally opening. "That was unnecessary," she mutters, her hair mussed around her face.

"It got you to open the door, didn't it?"

She rolls her eyes, holding her bathrobe tighter around her. She watches me with narrowed eyes as I set everything out on the counter. The pregnancy test is the last thing I put there. She snorts when she sees it.

"I'm not pregnant," she scoffs.

"Are you sure?"

"Are you seriously asking me if I'm sure?"

I hand her the test. "Humor me."

"I don't have to pee. Besides, you're supposed to do it in the morning."

"That's never stopped you before."

She huffs out a breath, snagging the box from my hands. "Fine. But I can't wait to say I told you so."

She closes herself off in the separate space with the toilet. While I wait, I clean up the bathroom as best I can in just a few minutes.

The door opens and she sets the test down, washing her hands. Her nose wrinkles at the Gatorade on the counter. "I told you I didn't want that."

"And I didn't listen."

"This isn't morning sickness. In case you didn't realize, I've been sick all day long for two days now."

I clear my throat, hesitant to bring up my ex. "When Krista was pregnant with Forrest, she was sick all day the first trimester. She lost a lot of weight because of it. It was bad."

Salem exhales unsteadily. "I'm not pregnant."

I know why she's so insistent. After so many negative tests in the past I don't know how many months, she's scared to get her hopes up. I know she's been devastated time and again. I don't want to be wrong this time, for her sake, and I don't think I am. But we need that confirmation.

Salem turns a light shade of green and lunges back for the toilet.

"Sunshine," I murmur, pulling her hair back. Her body lurches.

"Go away. You shouldn't see me like this." She tries to shove me back, but her attempt is weak.

I massage the back of her neck. "In sickness, and in health, right?"

She dry heaves, gagging. "Fuck off."

I grin to myself. I love it when she gets feisty with me.

When she settles, no longer heaving, I ask, "Can I go look now?"

She slumps against the floor, shooing me away with her hand. "Knock yourself out."

I walk over to where she left the stick. My heart jolts, speeding up at the positive test.

"Salem?" I only get a groan in reply. "You're pregnant."

Her eyes widen. "No, I'm not. Don't lie." She starts to cry. "Don't lie. Not about this."

I crouch down in front of her, cupping her cheek in my hand. "I'm not lying, Sunshine. We're going to have another baby."

She sobs, and I sit down on the floor beside her, gathering her into my arms and just holding her, because that's what she needs

"RIGHT THERE," THE DOCTOR POINTS TO THE SCREEN AT A tiny little blip that doesn't even look like anything yet. "That's your baby."

Salem's hand hovers over her mouth, her eyes glued to the black and white image displayed on the screen.

I pick up her other hand, kissing her knuckles.

"That's our baby, Sunshine. Look at them."

I think to myself that this is how things should've happened with Seda, but life had other plans for us. We needed to be apart to grow into the people we've become. Our love is stronger for the trials we've endured, and both of us knows how precious life is, how important it is to cherish every moment. At the end of the day, it isn't the expensive things, or the big things you remember. It's the people you love and the simple moments—dancing in the kitchen together, sitting down and having a meal together, just *existing*.

Life is not an infinite source—it's finite, and the best thing we could all learn, is to treat it as such, because each breath in our lungs is a precious gift we shouldn't waste.

FIFTY-
FOUR

Salem

I t's beneath the treehouse, the entire structure covered in the peonies Thayer has lovingly grown for me, and a bouquet of them in my hands, just two months after finding out we're having our second baby, that we're having our official wedding ceremony in front of our loved ones.

Ironically, it was this same day a year ago that I returned to Hawthorne Mills, and now I never plan to leave this small town. We didn't plan for it to work out that way. Thayer just wanted to finally have a real ceremony, and to make good on our promise to Seda that she could be the flower girl.

The backyard is covered in peonies and white twinkle lights. It looks like something out of a dream.

I walk down our makeshift aisle on my own.

I don't need someone to give me away. I'm not an object to be given to another. I'm my own person and I chose to be Thayer's partner, his equal, a long time ago.

My bare feet brush over the grass mixed with the petals Seda scattered. She stands at Thayer's side, smiling like a sweet little fool. Her blonde hair is curled in ringlets, hanging down her back, with a floral headband sitting like a crown on top of her head.

She's so beautiful and so grown up.

I haven't even made it to Thayer and I'm already going to cry.

The people we have here with us are an eclectic mix. Thayer's parents and brother, my sister and her family, Caleb, Cynthia and Thelma, Lauren and her husband Anthony, Hannah and Susanne from my cupcake shop, and even Jen that owns the shop in town and who has become a good friend. At the end with Thayer and Seda sits Binx and Winnie. Binx looks dapper with a bowtie and Winnie is sporting a tutu, both made by Thayer.

I finally reach the end, stopping beside my husband.

There's no officiant since our marriage is already official, this is just the icing on the cake, I guess.

Thayer's eyes crinkle at the corners. There's more gray at his temples now than a year ago, but I love it. I love *him*.

We're going to be exchanging our own vows today, new rings as well, since before we just got whatever we could in Vegas and it was nothing special or meaningful.

Thayer looks down, at the small swell of my belly pushing against the white satin of my slip dress. You can barely tell I'm pregnant yet, but soon enough my belly will pop. We've decided not to find out the gender. We thought it would be more special to wait until the birth. The anticipation might kill me, but I know it'll be worth it.

Thayer clears his throat. "I'll go first." He takes each of my hands in his. "When you came into my life almost eight years ago, I should've known from the get go that you were going to shake up my life. With your blonde hair, long legs, and beautiful smile you were the most gorgeous thing I'd ever seen but also the most confounding. It drove me crazy when I realized you were running so early in the mornings and the way you'd sit on your roof nearly gave me a heart attack." I laugh, shaking my head. I think I worried everybody but myself with my love of sitting on the roof. "I fell for you slowly, accidentally, and suddenly you became my whole world. Our journey to this moment wasn't a straight line. We've had a lot of ups and downs, but they've made us who we are, and I love you, I love us, and I love the life we've built together despite everything stacked between us."

I pull one of my hands from his, wiping beneath my eyes. "You made me cry."

Chuckles sound around us and Thayer smiles down at me.

I give myself a moment to catch my breath before I start.

"Thayer, Thayer, Thayer," I cluck my tongue. "Do you remember the first thing you ever said to me?" He smiles, knowing where I'm going with this. He certainly didn't smile at me that day. Oh, no, all this man did for the longest time was glare and grunt at me like some prehistoric caveman. "You said, and I quote, 'You're trespassing.'" I make my voice deeper when I say it, ringing out laughs from everyone. "And *now* you're marrying that trespasser in the exact spot you were that day. How about that?" His smile grows bigger. "You said it best when you said our path wasn't linear. There's been a lot of trials and tribulations thrown our way, but somehow, we've come out stronger in the end. Thank you for letting me love you. Thank you for choosing me. I love you. Today. Tomorrow. All my days."

I sound like such a sap, but I'm pregnant so I'm allowed to be.

Cupping my cheeks, he leans forward and brushes his nose against mine, our lips a breath apart. "I love you, too, Sunshine."

His lips meet mine, kissing me with a promise.

When we break apart, Lauren passes me his new ring and Laith hands Thayer mine.

I slip the thick black band onto his finger. The inside is gold, so he'll always have the sun close to his heart.

He takes my left hand, smiling as he slips the ring in place. It's gold with suns carved into it all the way around. It's perfect and I love that we had similar thoughts with our choices.

He kisses me again, his hand on my stomach.

A year ago, I was still angry at him.

A year ago, I was terrified to face him.

A year ago, I never could've imagined us standing in this spot.

But a lot can happen in twelve months. That's three-hundred and sixty-five days of change.

Each one leading you a step closer to your destination, whatever that might be.

I thought our story was over when I left town seven years ago, but sometimes what you think is the end, is only the beginning.

EPILOGUE

Salem

Thayer's head presses against mine, tears coating his cheeks. Our baby isn't even here yet and he's already having trouble keeping it together.

"You can do it, Sunshine. You're almost there. We're going to meet our baby."

I feel like I've waited forever to meet this little one and grow our family.

Seda's going to be a big sister and Forrest is going to be a big brother again.

"One more big push, Salem," my doctor coaches.

I squeeze Thayer's hand, giving it my all. I'm so tired, but I just want to see my baby. To hold him or her and shower them in kisses.

And then, with a cry, our second baby comes into the world.

The doctor holds the baby up for Thayer to see—we told her ahead of time that we wanted him to tell me the gender.

Crying, he kisses me and murmurs, "We have another little girl."

I cry with him as they lay her onto my chest. I count her tiny toes and fingers. There's a light dusting of sandy brown hair on her head. Thayer's hair color.

"Hi, little baby." She curls her finger around mine. "I'm your mommy."

Thayer kisses the top of my head, then hers, then back again. "My girls." He places his hand on her back. "My little sun." He touches her cheek. "Welcome to the world, Soleil."

She cries out like she approves of the name. At least, I hope that's what she's saying.

"She's perfect." I hold her tight to my chest, not wanting to let go, but know they'll soon take her from me to do their checks.

"So are you," Thayer murmurs. "I have the three most perfect girls a man could ask for."

"You're definitely outnumbered now."

"No such thing." I know he means it too.

They take her from me then, getting her weight, height, and everything else they need.

Hours later, when things have calmed and Soleil has taken to breastfeeding, I finally get to watch Thayer have his moment with her. He sits in the chair, his shirt off, with her tiny little body resting in his arms against his chest for skin to skin. She looks so tiny in his arms, the little wrinkles in the back of her neck the cutest thing I've seen in a long time.

He starts to sing to her, and tears spring to my eyes.

"You are my sunshine. My only sunshine."

We struggled to come up with a name for a long time, knowing we wanted to go with something that was special to us and could be gender neutral.

I don't even know when or where we heard Soleil, but we knew instantly it was perfect, because when the sun doesn't shine, we have our own little sun now.

ALSO BY MICALEA SMELTZER

Outsider Series

Outsider

Insider

Fighter

Avenger

Second Chances Standalone Series

Unraveling

Undeniable

Trace + Olivia Series

Finding Olivia

Chasing Olivia

Tempting Rowan

Saving Tatum

Willow Creek Series

Last To Know

Never Too Late

In Your Heart

Take A Chance

Always Too Late Short Story

Willow Creek Bonus Content

Home For Christmas

Light in the Dark Series

Rae of Sunshine

When Stars Collide

Dark Hearts

When Constellations Form

Broken Hearts

Stars & Constellations Bundle

The Us Series

The Road That Leads To Us

The Lies That Define Us

The Game That Break Us

Wild Collision

The Wild Series

Wild Collision

Wild Flame

The Boys Series

Bad Boys Break Hearts

Nice Guys Don't Win

Real Players Never Lose

Good Guys Don't Lie

Standalones

Beauty in the Ashes

Bring Me Back

Temptation

A Love Like Ours

The Other Side of Tomorrow

Jump (A 90s novella)

<u>Desperately Seeking Roommate</u>

<u>Desperately Seeking Landlord</u>

<u>Whatever Happens</u>

<u>Sweet Dandelion</u>

<u>Say When</u>

ACKNOWLEDGMENTS

This duet has been one of my greatest joys and greatest challenges to write. Salem and Thayer go through a lot, but their love is beautiful, and I hope you love their happy ending as much as I do.

A huge thank you to Emily Wittig for creating the two most stunning covers I've ever seen. But mostly for being the best friend I could ever ask for. You are the most supportive, kindest person I've ever met and I'm so lucky to have you on my side. I believe fate made sure our paths crossed.

Kellen—thank you for being my constant cheerleader. You came into my life at a very challenging time for me and your friendship has meant everything. Let's go get cheesecake now.

Cheyenne and KatieGwen, I can't thank you both enough for taking a chance on my books (and my crazy self) and ordering my books for your Barnes and Noble. You guys are so great and your passion for books (the spicier the better) is unparalleled. Please keep entertaining all of us with the best reels and tiktoks.

Thank you to Melanie for being so patient and fitting me in last minute for edits on this. You're the real MVP and I appreciate it so much. Truly.

To all the bookstagrammers, bloggers, tiktokers, and readers who have spoken so passionately about this duet. Thank you. From the bottom of my heart, thank you. Your love for Salem and Thayer has been a beautiful thing to see. Thank you for loving them like I do.